The Fanatic

James Robertson

FOURTH ESTATE • *London*

This paperback edition first published in 2001
First published in Great Britain in 2000 by
Fourth Estate
A Division of HarperCollins*Publishers*
77–85 Fulham Palace Road,
London W6 8JB
www.4thestate.co.uk

5 7 9 10 8 6

A catalogue record for this book is available from the
British Library.

ISBN 1-84115-189-0

Typeset by Avon DataSet Ltd, Bidford on Avon,
Warwickshire B50 4JH

Printed in Great Britain by Clays Ltd, St Ives plc,
Bungay, Suffolk

The Fanatic

James Robertson is the author of two collections of short stories, *Close* and *The Ragged Man's Complaint*, two collections of poetry, *Sound-Shadow* and *I Dream of Alfred Hitchcock*, and a book of *Scottish Ghost Stories*. *The Fanatic* is his first novel. He lives in Fife.

for Ange

In that same year 1670 was that monster of men and reproach of mankind (for otherwayes I cannot stile him), Major Weir, for most horrible witchcraft, Incest, Bestiality, and other enorme crymes, at first confest by himselfe (his conscience being awakned by the terrors of the Almightie), but afterwards faintly denied by him, brunt. So sad a spectacle he was of humane frailty that I think no history can parallell the like. We saw him the fornoon before he died, but he could be drawen to no sense of a mercifull God, so horribly was he lost to himselfe. The thing that aggravated his guilt most was the pretext and show of godlinesse wt which he had even to that tyme deceived the world. His sister also was but a very lamentable object . . . She was hanged.

—*Journals of Sir John Lauder, Lord Fountainhall, with his observations on public affairs and other memoranda 1665–1676*

This is the world's old age; it is declining; albeit it seems a fine and beautiful thing in the eyes of them that know no better, and unto those who are of yesterday and know nothing it looks as if it had been created yesterday, yet the truth is, and a believer knows, it is near the grave.

—*From a sermon by Hugh Binning (1627–53), minister of Govan*

The wild heads of the tyme do dream,
There's a world in the moon,
O, to deceive if I were ther,
For heir will trust me none.

—*Lines from a satirical poem on Archbishop James Sharp,
c.1667, Analecta Scotica*

Prologue
(Bass Rock, March 1677)

James Mitchel was dreaming. The kind of dream that mocks, constantly slipping in doubts: this is real, this is not real.

In the dream he was awake and lying in bed. The room was heavy and warm with the smell of woman. A great sadness was welling up in him. He lay there in the growing light and felt the sadness rise from the pit of his belly, a physical thing, spreading through his chest and to his throat till he thought he would have to cry out. But he didn't; he didn't want to wake her. Elizabeth. Aye, it was her right enough, he could hear her regular breathing. He heard his own breath, the air passing against the hair of his nostrils, a sound that was of him and yet not of him. Like the sound of your voice when you put your fingers in your lugs. Like the sound of the sea in a shell.

The dawn squeezed into the room. He reached out for Lizzie, and felt cold stone. Suddenly he felt fully, really awake. He turned his head and she wasn't there. He knew then that they would never touch again. *My beloved put in his hand by the hole of the door, and my bowels were moved for him*. He wanted to scream or just to greet quietly but the constriction in his throat prevented it, would only allow a whimper.

He was lying in a tiny, damp cell that smelt of salt and urine. Daylight inched its dwaiblie way in and gave up. His bed was a wooden shelf hard up against the stone. He was alone. His right leg oozed pain.

He fell away again. Now he dreamt a face staring at him, evil, a bishop's face sneering and cold beneath its black skull-cap. Mitchel stared back, refusing to flinch. But then there was another figure, darker and larger, wearing a hood with holes cut for the eyes. The figure reached for him, almost tenderly; lifted his right leg at the ankle, and laid it out straight as if streeking a corpse. Mitchel clamped his teeth together. He was seated in a chair, his arms bound behind him, his leg boxed like a planted sapling. The hooded man turned away, then back again. He was holding an iron-headed mallet in one hand, and a wooden wedge in the other.

The leg convulsed and Mitchel woke again. He sat upright. Through the wall he could hear a man reading from the Psalms: *O my God, my soul is cast down within me; therefore will I remember thee from the land of Jordan. Deep calleth unto deep at the noise of thy waterspouts: all thy waves and thy billows are gone over me. Yet the Lord will command his loving kindness in the daytime, and in the night his song shall be with me, and my prayer unto the God of my life . . .*

Mitchel minded where he was.

He was Maister James Mitchel, MA, preacher, tutor, soldier and sword of Christ, prisoner of the King. His enemies called him by a different set of names: fanatic, enthusiastical villain, disaffected rebel, assassin. He had been tortured to extract a confession for a crime he did not consider a crime, an act committed in the service of Christ. His wife Elizabeth was fifteen miles away in Edinburgh. He was incarcerated in the stinking prison of the Bass Rock off the east coast of Scotland, and he did not expect ever to be free again.

He shared the Rock with half a dozen others, also of the godly party, but they would hardly speak to him. Some thought him foolish, wrong-headed, ignorant; and some among them blamed him for having enraged the government and brought its wrath upon their heads. He had been in the Bass nearly two months and if he did not remain till he died it would only be because he had been fetched back to Edinburgh for execution.

His leg was a thrawn limb, in more ways than one. Under the torture of the 'boots' it had been so mangled and crushed that it was now not much more than an encumbrance. Even more than a year later he could put little weight upon it. The external injuries had healed, after a fashion, but it remained mere pulp within. It might as well have been missing altogether for all the use it was, and yet it refused to let him be. The pulsing and throbbing might start at any time in the day or night, and cease just as suddenly. It was like having a dog gripped onto him, a sleeping dog that woke hungry from time to time and gnawed at him as if meat and marrow were all he was.

Nine strokes of the mallet he had suffered. The number was hammered into his brain like iron studs in an oak door. He would wake sweating in the night from a dream of himself crushed into a coffin, unable to move, while some demonic servitor, having transported him thus like a living dead man, chapped nine dirling blows at the gates of Hell. Even though Mitchel knew that he was destined not for that place but for Heaven, the memory drove spikes of fire through his ruined leg.

It was ironic that the man who had caused his suffering, the man in the black skull-cap, had not even been present at the torture. James Sharp, Archbishop of St Andrews, had been in London at the time, but Mitchel did not absolve him on that score. Nobody was loathed by an entire people as Sharp was. The minister of Crail who had been so strong, apparently, in defence of Scotland's Covenant with God; who had been sent by the Kirk to negotiate with King Charles in the year of his Restoration to the throne, and ensure the maintenance of Presbyterianism; who had gone to London to put down bishops and come back an archbishop ... Judas Sharp, traitor of traitors. At Mitchel's torture, some of those on the committee of counsellors and judges appointed to interrogate him had hidden their faces from him when he was brought before them in the vaulted room below the Parliament house in Edinburgh. They feared reprisals if his sympathisers got word of who they were, or they were conscious of their own guilt, or both. To Mitchel, Sharp was no more absent from the laich chamber than those other men were made invisible by covering their eyes. It might just as well have been St Andrews himself, and not the public executioner, hammering the wedges home.

Sharp should have been dead and Mitchel free. Mitchel had had his chance to kill him nine years before, but something had taken it from him, either his own hesitation or God's finger spoiling his aim. And part of the rage that Mitchel felt was that he still did not know which.

Through the wall of the cell the voice read on from the

next Psalm: *Judge me, O God, and plead my cause against an ungodly nation: O deliver me from the deceitful and unjust man.* Mitchel would have said Amen loudly to that but it was the minister James Fraser of Brea reading in his distinctive northern accent, and Fraser, though they had been brought together under the same guard from Edinburgh, had remained cool and disdainful of Mitchel because he thought his grasp of Holy Scripture suspect. Fraser was gentry, the son of a bankrupt Highland laird. A pox on him, Mitchel thought.

He concentrated on his leg instead, seizing the knee with both hands and pressing as hard as he could with his long, bony fingers. Sometimes he could drive the hurt downwards in this manner. He did not understand why this worked, since the damage was concentrated at the knee and below, nor could he recall how he had learnt it as a method of controlling the leg's contumacy. He had tried everything, though, and by trial and error his hands had refined their haphazard skills. Sometimes he spoke aloud, mockingly, like a preacher excommunicating a malignant royalist: *Thou art a girning apostate dog of a leg.* He had a fantasy in which he imagined his leg being cast into eternal hellfire come the day of Christ's judgment, while he ascended, hopping, to Heaven. A less than perfect saint among the saints.

He thought it was not blasphemous to contemplate this scenario in an effort to stem the floods of pain that the leg brought upon him. In fact, the idea of being unique in Heaven appealed to him. They would honour him there for his suffering. Christ Jesus knew him to be true: Jesus knew that he believed his Word, that legless or not he would be remade whole and glorious in the everlasting kingdom.

All Christ's good bairns go to heaven with a broken brow, and with a crooked leg. He minded that. It was a line from a book he had once possessed, the letters of Samuel Rutherford, a book that had been loathed by the government and burnt by the hangman for its righteousness and truth. Mitchel's copy was long since lost, but he had loved and treasured it, and still had whole passages by heart. Rutherford was like a second Bible to him. He took dry comfort from that sentence. The crooked leg he had already, and the brow would be broken soon enough.

4

He clutched his arms around himself and tried to squeeze out the cold. It felt like the sea itself had got into his bones. Outside he could hear the solan geese screaming. The Bass was home to thousands of the birds. They had arrived from wherever they spent the winter – Africa, some said – about the same time as Mitchel. The air was filled with their wheeling and pitching and screaming as they built their nests and pierced the sea for fish. He minded the approach to the Rock by boat, seeing the great streaks of shit down its hulk, its cliffs smoored white and green with the droppings of centuries. The swell of the sea sucked and belched against the foot of it, where steps had been cut leading up to the prison buildings. He had come there from Edinburgh a year after the torture, having lain in chains for most of that time in the city Tolbooth. Twelve horse and thirty foot soldiers had brought him, together with James Fraser, on a bitter day at the end of January. Soldiers had helped him from the boat and oxtered him up the steps and dumped him in this icy chamber, wrapped in a blanket, feverish and shuddering.

In the first week of his being there his fellow-prisoners had tried to mend his leg and restore his physical strength, but the best they could offer was their prayers. They were ragged, slate-faced men, scrunted and thin, and bent, like the handful of wizened cherry trees that grew at the top of the Bass, by the constant buffeting of the wind. Then these men withdrew from him by degrees, because they could not reconcile themselves to the vehemence of his will. Mitchel knew that they thought him embittered, even deranged. But he saw through their weakness: he had only carried the principles that they all upheld – the right of God's people to resist unholy rule, the *duty* of God's Scotland to defend the Covenant against prelatic blasphemy – to their logical conclusion. What they shied away from was their own fear: they were *afraid* to strike the righteous blow, to be the sword of the Lord and of Gideon.

Because of his leg, he had spent nearly all of the two months lying helpless in his cell. There was no possibility of escape from the Bass, which was sheer and devoid of landing-places on three sides and heavily fortified at the one spot on the fourth where a boat, in calm weather and with a favouring tide, could come in; and so the prisoners were allowed, one or two at a time, to walk everywhere upon it. But this was no advantage to him, crippled as he was. In any case, he was subject to special, more restrictive orders.

Some of the others, in fine weather, or even in wet, cold-blasting storms, spent more time out stravaiging among the solans than in the company of each other. Alexander Peden, the prophet of Galloway, had been there nearly four years, and Alexander Forrester and William Bell, arrested for field-preaching in Fife and in the Pentland Hills, almost as long; James Fraser had arrived on the same boat with Mitchel, and shortly after had come another minister from the north, Thomas Hog of Kiltearn, and a man called George Scot, com-mitted for harbouring fugitive ministers; and there was one Robert Dick, a merchant, who had organised and attended the Pentland conventicle at which William Bell had preached. Together or alone, standing among the pecking solans that moved like a crop of bleached barley in the stiff wind, these men could look across the narrow, impossible sea and dream of re-crossing it. The soldiers of the garrison used to joke that the ministers took lessons from the birds in whining and preaching, so that if they ever got back to Scotland they could deave the whole country with their piousness.

The solans' screaming never ceased. It sometimes sounded to Mitchel, who could only get to his door and back again, as though the cell must be the only place in the world not filled with birds. A madman would think the constant racket was inside his head. Several times a day Mitchel made a conscious effort to separate the white bird noise from his thoughts; to reclaim his mind from it.

For in his dreams, behind the skull-capped bishop and the hooded torturer, there lurked a third figure, an old man, also a prisoner. Mitchel laboured at his prayers and his Bible because when his mind grew slack this old man approached. He had long white hair damp with seaspray and the skin of his face looked like it had been eaten away by years of salt. More years than Mitchel could bear to think of. He feared the old man; the doubt and self-loathing in his milky eyes. He knew who it was, and it was not himself; but he feared becoming him.

6

Sometimes in rough weather supplies of food could not be got across from North Berwick for a week or more. In February the prisoners – and the soldiers who guarded them – had been reduced to mixing snow with oatmeal, and chewing on dried fish. The soldiers would sometimes catch fish from the sea, nail them to wooden boards and then float the boards on ropes under the cliffs. A diving solan, spotting the herring, would impale the wood with its beak and be hauled in to be roasted, but these adult birds, some of them twenty years old or more, were tough and oily meat. It was better to eat the fish.

In late summer, men would come to catch the solan chicks, when they were fat and tender but not yet able to fly. Hundreds were taken every year, and sent to London as a delicacy, and yet the colony showed no signs of decreasing in numbers. When the catchers were at work with their nets on the upper part of the Rock, or descending on ropes to knock the flightless chicks on the heads and fling them into the sea, where other men waited to pick them up from a boat, it was like watching Satan's helpers harvesting souls.

The captain of the garrison administered this business on behalf of the governor, in return for an annual salary and a percentage of the profits. The governor was the Secretary of State for Scotland, John Maitland, Duke of Lauderdale. The solan crop was worth around eighty pounds annually. But, this aside, neither he nor anybody else cared much how the captain exercised his power. If he chose, the captain could shut the prisoners in their cells and deny them access to the meagre criss-cross of paths that usually they could share with the birds and the two dozen scabby sheep that grazed the upper slopes of the Rock. He could put a stop to mutual prayers, or prevent visits from friends or family, some of whom travelled for days to reach North Berwick. There was no set of rules, no higher arbitrator to whom the prisoners could apply: the Bass fortress lay off Scotland as impregnable and cold to human comfort as a castle in the moon.

Edinburgh, April 1997

Hugh Hardie needed a ghost: one that would appear down a half-lit close at ten o'clock at night, and have people jumping out of their skins. He also needed a drink. He was seated at a table in Dawson's, while Jackie Halkit was up at the bar getting it for him. The drink, he thought, might be business or it might be pleasure. He hoped both.

Dawson's was a large overbright bar in Edinburgh's Southside, that lurched between douceness and debauchery depending on the time of day. At four o'clock on a Monday afternoon in early spring it was quiet. Office workers were still at their desks; students from the university, with few exceptions, were attending lectures or dozing in the library. The juke-box was silent: the most noise in the place came from three old men settled in one corner, supping halfs-and-halfs and murmuring smug discontents at one another. One student, barely rebellious, was reading the *Sun*, and nursing his pint like a hospice patient, till all life had gone out of it. A woman, possibly a tourist, since she had a small rucksack beside her, was writing postcards at another table. She was drinking mineral water and to Hugh Hardie looked like she had been disapprovingly sober since the day she was born. The old men, he decided, were at that moment the liveliest patrons Dawson's had. Himself and Jackie excepted, of course.

They were in Dawson's because it was handy for them both. Hugh's flat was a few streets away in Newington, and Jackie's workplace, a small publishing house, was not far in the other direction, off the Canongate. Hugh had an idea for a book that he thought Jackie might be interested in publishing. Jackie was pretty certain already that she wouldn't be but she hadn't seen him for a while and she seemed to recall that she'd found his eager boyishness irritatingly attractive. Plus it gave her a good excuse to leave work early: the office was too cluttered and cramped to

8

receive potential authors in any privacy. When she had suggested meeting in a pub on the phone, Hugh had named Dawson's. Now she was returning from the bar with a pint for him and a gin and tonic for herself. She had insisted, in her role as interested publisher, on buying the first round.

'Bit early for this,' she said. 'What the hell. *Slàinte*.'

He raised his glass, souked an inch or more out of it. '*Slàinte*.' It was only recently that he'd learnt that this was Gaelic for 'health'. For years he'd said 'slange' thinking it was an obsure Scots term signifying 'slam your drink down your throat and let's get another in'. It was watching *Machair* the Gaelic soap opera that had enlightened him.

'Well, good to see you,' he said.

'Yeah, you too. I can't remember when I last saw you,' she lied.

'That Chamber of Commerce day conference on tourism and small businesses,' he said with precision. 'Last autumn, remember?'

'Oh aye,' she said. 'That was a long time ago. And now it's spring, and the tourists are almost upon us again.'

Simultaneously they said, 'And how *is* your small business?', and laughed. It sounded like a line from a *Carry On* film.

Carry on Kidding Yourself, Jackie thought. Not for the first time, she found herself entering a conversation that somehow, for her, wasn't . . . well, it wasn't *authentic*. It had been the same at the conference. So-called experts and consultants delivered talks on resource management strategy, maximising customer/product interface potential, tactical merchandise-redeployment awareness – it all meant nothing and had her nodding off almost immediately.

Later she and Hugh shared a joke or two at the consultants' expense, but it was apparent that he had taken in about ten times more of what they had said. And yet he derided them, agreed with her when she dismissed them as bullshitters. She wasn't naive: he was two-faced in a perfectly harmless way; but then, so was she; and all night maybe he was trying to get up her skirt, but she didn't mind that. It showed initiative.

He was transparently shallow but she wasn't sure she wanted profundity in a man. She wasn't sure she wanted a man. She was, however, interested in the idea that Hugh might be interested.

'Well,' she said, 'you tell us about your book and then I'll tell you about my small business. Cause that's the order they're going to have to come in.'

'Oh,' he said. 'Is that how it is?'

'Aye. That's exactly how.'

'Okay.' He didn't protest, didn't even hesitate. 'Well, you know about my ghost tours, don't you?'

'Of course. How are they going?'

'Put it this way, we're through the winter. That's always kind of tough. The problem is, quite a lot of locals want to come on the tours but – and I can't say I blame them – they're not keen to wander round the Cowgate in the dark in a freezing January wind. We do a limited programme, depending on the weather and the demand. But it gets better from now on in. In July and August we could run tours every other hour if the Council would wear it. So, to answer your question, things are going all right. A healthy little number, but seasonally dependent.

'That's where this idea of mine comes in. I need to spread the potential income across the year. So I've been thinking, you know, spin-offs. The mugs and T-shirts option isn't really an option, don't you agree? But a book is a different proposition.'

'The book of the tour?' said Jackie doubtfully.

'Exactly. Well, not exactly, no. I mean, you could just make a kind of pamphlet out of the tour script, but it wouldn't be very long and it would need a lot of rewriting for it to work on the page. You know, you can't have a rat running across someone's feet every time they turn over page thirteen.'

'You've got a rat that runs over people's feet? Did you train it or something?'

'Not a real one. A rubber rat on a string. You'll have to come and get the full rat experience one night. It's very atmospheric.' He paused, and Jackie wondered if he was going to offer her a free pass, but he only drew breath before breenging on with the sales-pitch.

'Anyway, I had in mind something a bit more substantial than just a twenty-page pamphlet. A proper paperback stuffed full of Edinburgh's haunted and macabre past. There's tons of stuff, Jackie, as I'm sure you know, and a big market of people who want to learn about it. Or get scared silly, in an unthreatening kind of way. It's not as if I'm the only person operating ghost tours after all.'

'You certainly are not. You can't move around St Giles in the summer for folk like you trying to flog their wares to the tourists: what with all the ghoulies and ghosties and body-snatchers and stranglers, you'd think Edinburgh history was one long overflowing bloodbath.'

Hugh shrugged. 'I can't help history. Give the people what they want, that's my motto. I don't see many of them signing up for the Edinburgh Social and Economic History Peram-bulating Lecture, do you?'

'All right, point taken. What about the book?'

'The blurb would relate it to the tour, so that hopefully people who picked up the book somewhere would come along to do the real thing, and vice versa. But it would stand on its own too, and sell as a good read to visitors and locals alike. Now, I don't have time myself to mug up all the stories that would be in it, but we could commission someone to do the research and write it all up. Then all we need is a spooky, eye-catching cover design and a snappy title. I had in mind *Major Weir's Weird Tales of Old Edinburgh* for that, by the way.'

'Wait a minute,' said Jackie. 'Commission someone to write it? Who's going to do that, you? And who's Major Weir when he's at home?'

'A very good question. He's one of the characters on the tour. I thought he could maybe do an intro to the book – from beyond the grave kind of thing. We don't want it too po-faced after all. Which reminds me, you wouldn't happen to know of anybody who might want a bit of casual evening work, would you?'

'Don't dodge out of it, Mr Hardie. If you're not going to write this book, I hope you're not expecting us to pay someone else to.'

'You're a publisher, Jackie. Surely that's your job. No gain without pain. And let's face it, you'd get the bulk of the profits. I mean, I'd only be looking for a fifteen or twenty per cent royalty depending on the print-run and the cover-price.'

'Hugh, in a moment you're going to get up and buy us another drink, but before you do, listen to me a second. One, I – the company – wouldn't pay a fee up front for a book that hasn't been written. All we can afford to take on are finished manuscripts that we think are going to sell, and publish on the basis of the author getting paid a royalty. Two, in the unlikely event that we did pay a writing fee, we certainly wouldn't be paying a royalty on top of that. Three, the absolute maximum royalty you can expect is ten per cent – if *you* write the book. You know all the publishing jargon, Hugh, but you're short on the realities.'

'But don't you think it's a great idea for a book? We're talking about three or four different overlapping markets: local history, ghosts, tourists – '

'Sure. If you had a finished or even a half-finished manuscript, I'd read it. I'd consider it. But I couldn't commit to anything on the basis of what you've told me. To be honest, Hugh, you should think about publishing it yourself.'

'I wouldn't know where to begin.'

'Well, go back to the pocket guide to publishing you've obviously been reading and look in there. It's really not that difficult these days. All you need is a computer and a DTP package. The technology's sitting waiting for you, and once you've paid the printers, so is all the profit.'

Hugh gave an incredulous laugh. 'Listen to you, you're talking yourself out of business.'

She laughed back. 'Publishing isn't like any other business. Scottish publishing isn't like any other publishing.'

'Bullshit.'

'It's true. It may not be how it should be but it is. Scottish publishing is about avoiding anything that might drag you into a swamp of debt and drown you in it.'

'No wonder it's the country cousin of London then.'

'Quite. Now get us another drink.'

Hardie went up to the bar and ordered in his loud, boolie voice. It wasn't offensive to Jackie, it went with his friendly, disarming smile, but she saw the old men glower at him suspiciously. Dawson's was used to students but not to entrepreneurs. Jackie could still make out the Edinburgh merchant's school accent underlying the mid-Atlantic drawl, but only because she knew it was there. The auld yins probably thought he was English.

Waiting at the bar, Hardie thought about his chances with Jackie. She might have knocked him back on the book proposal, but she'd asked for another drink. She was nice enough looking – but not so she could afford to be choosy. She had thick dark hair and brown eyes, and cheeks that must have been podgy ten years before and would be again in another ten. The same went for her figure – short and tending to dumpiness. But warm and inviting for all that. He imagined her in a white fluffy bathrobe, pink from the bath. It was a heart-stirring thought.

He also thought about his ghost. The old ghost had quit on him that morning, complaining of poor wages and conditions. He'd handed over the cape, staff, wig and rat, demanded the twenty pounds lie wage held back against the return of these ghostly accoutrements, and walked off, never to be seen again. You'd have thought he might have treated the twenty pounds as a kind of bonus, but no. His last words had been to the effect that Hardie was a miserable tight-arsed capitalist bastard and he hoped his trade would drop off. Hardie wasn't unduly upset. The guy hadn't done a convincing haunt for months.

'This is probably a stupid question,' said Jackie, when he told her his problem, 'but why do you have to have a ghost anyway? Surely you can do the tour without one.'

'Sure I can, Jackie, but a ghost tour without a ghost . . . ? Come *on*. Look, in the main season we do three tours a day. The one in the afternoon doesn't need a ghost, it's broad daylight and it tends to be more, how can I put it, historical. Mary Queen of Scots, John Knox, Bonnie Prince Charlie, that kind of stuff. The six o'clock tour doesn't need a ghost either: it's still daylight, and it caters for the fat Yanks who are about to hurry back to their hotels for the usual haggis and bagpipes tartan extravaganza that's laid on for them there. The tour is just an hors d'oeuvre. BPC features heavily again. But the nine o' clock tour – that's different. That's the cream of ghost tours. It starts' – his voice dropped and assumed an exaggerated tremor – 'as the night draws in, and ends in darkness. The people who come on this tour expect a ghost.

Some of them have been drinking all evening. They're in high spirits. They're Swedish inter-railers and rowdy English students and gobsmacked Australian backpackers. I charge extra for this tour. There are little tricks and hidden delights in store for the people who come on it. One of them is a ghost. I must have a ghost.'

'You must have a ghost,' Jackie repeated. She was looking past his shoulder towards the door. 'How about him over there, then?'

Hugh half-turned to look. A tall, slightly stooping man had just come in. He reached the bar in three long strides that seemed almost liquid in their execution, or as if he were treading through shallow water and the splashes of each step were left for a moment in the space where his foot had just been. He was over six feet, skinny and gaunt, his face so white you'd think he'd just walked through a storm of flour. He was almost bald apart from a few wild bursts of hair above the ears. He ordered a pint and while it was being poured stared grimly into space, seeming to aim his gaze along the length of his nose. Hugh Hardie was transfixed.

'He's perfect. My God, he's perfect. You're absolutely right, Jackie.'

'He's not the ghost to solve your problems. He's out of *my* past.'

'You mean to say you actually know this person?'

'Sure. Haven't seen him for years, right enough. We were at the uni together.'

'This is uncanny. Quick, call him over.'

'Now just hold on a minute. Like I said, I've not seen him for ages. I'm not sure that I want to renew the acquaintance.'

'Don't be sulky, Jackie. Get him over and we'll toast your alma mater. Why ever not?'

'Well, to be honest, he's a bit weird. He was a postgraduate when I was doing final year Honours. He sat in on a course I was doing – First World War or something. The guy running the course was supervising his PhD. But he dropped out – never finished it as far as I know.'

'Shame,' said Hugh. 'Get him over, won't you?'

'Wait, I said. He was weird. Gave me the creeps.'

'As far as I'm concerned, you're just writing him a great CV. He has got something, hasn't he? To look at, I mean. That woman over there can't stop checking him out. He's *disturbing* her. Don't you see?'

'It doesn't surprise me,' said Jackie. 'All the women in the class felt the same. You tried to avoid his eye. Not that he actually ever did anything, you understand.'

'Some people have that, don't they? That amazing ability to upset other people just by being themselves. They don't have to *do* anything.'

The old men, who had glanced at the man when he came in, had not paid him any attention since. Hugh, who made his living by exploiting how different people reacted to what they saw, noticed this and liked it. The old men were never going to be his customers. Jackie and the tourist were the ones who mattered, and they had the right responses. The barman, who probably saw the guy regularly, wasn't bothered by him. The student seemed to have fallen asleep.

'What's his name?' Hugh asked.

Jackie shook her head.

'It's all right, I won't shout it out or anything. I won't embarrass you.'

'Carlin,' she said. 'Alan, I think. No, Andrew. Andrew Carlin.'

'Andrew!' shouted Hugh. The others in the bar stared at him, and the student woke with a jerk. 'Andrew Carlin! Over here!'

'You bastard,' said Jackie.

'Sorry,' said Hugh. 'No gain without pain.'

Carlin sat with a quarter-pint in front of him, and said nothing. Hardie had jumped up to buy him a drink as soon as the one he had was less than half full. 'Less than half full, rather than more than half empty, that's the kind of guy I am,' said Hardie jovially and without a trace of irony. 'What is that, eighty shilling?' Carlin looked at him without expression, and nodded once. When Hardie went to the bar, there was an awkward silence between the other two. Jackie had been badgered earlier by Hugh into reminiscing about the class she and Carlin had both attended. The responses from

Carlin had been monosyllabic. Now she tried a different tack.

'So what have you been up to since I saw you last? It must be, what, six years? I mind you gave up on the PhD. Can't say I blame you, I was scunnered of History after one degree. Well, maybe not scunnered, just tired.'

'Aye,' said Carlin. He gazed at her. She wasn't sure if he was merely acknowledging what she'd said or agreeing with it. She was aware again of the piercing stare that had been so oppressive in the class, and lowered her eyes. Even as she did so she felt she'd conceded a small victory to him. She made herself look back up, and found him off guard, and saw something she hadn't expected. A woundedness? Damage? Fear? She couldn't tell.

'Six years, I'd say,' said Carlin. 'Mair or less. Whit I've been up tae: this and that.'

Jackie thought, Christ, is he on something? She wished Hugh would hurry up.

'Are you working?' she asked.

'In whit sense?'

'You know, in a working sense. In a job sense.' She felt herself growing angry at him. She wasn't a wee undergraduate any more, she ought not to be intimidated by his weirdness.

'Na,' he said, 'no in that sense.'

Hardie returned. 'There you go, mate, get that down you,' he said chummily. Jackie cringed. Carlin shifted the new pint behind the unfinished one but otherwise said nothing.

'Have you got a job at the moment, Andrew?' Hardie asked.

'She jist asked me that.'

'Oh, has she been filling you in then?'

'Has she been filling me in? I don't think so.'

'I've got a job for someone who needs a bit of extra cash,' said Hardie. 'The pay's not great but the work's steady and there's not much to it. I think it would really suit you.'

More than you might bargain for, Jackie thought, you'll end up with corpses all over the Old Town.

'I run these ghost tours, okay? Three a day, seven days a week. The last one of the day, that's a bit special. I charge the punters more for it and it always sells out. Well, it does in the summer anyway. It's a bit of fun, but a bit scary too, right?

16

Plus we do some special effects in the half-light. That's where you come in. If you're interested.'

Carlin inclined his head. He might have been encouraging Hugh Hardie to continue or he might have been falling asleep.

'I need someone to play the part of a ghost. As soon as you came through that door, before Jackie even said she knew you, isn't that right Jackie, I said you were perfect. You see, you look like someone. A guy called Major Weir, the Wizard of the West Bow. Have you heard of him?'

Carlin shook his head. When he spoke his voice was slow and toneless. 'Is he like, real? A real person?'

'Oh, definitely. *Was* real, yeah, for sure. Basically he and his sister Grizel, well, they were kind of Puritans, you know, the tall black hat brigade, Bible-thumping Calvinists.'

'I ken whit Puritans are,' said Carlin.

'Good. Great. Well, anyway, one day they got found out. They were complete hypocrites. Satanists, I guess. They used to meet up with the Devil and stuff. And they were shagging each other. Grizel – isn't that a brilliant name? – was kind of out of it, she was just a crazy old woman, but Major Weir, he was a *baad* guy. Not only did he shag his sister, he shagged cows and anything else that moved.' Hardie broke off. 'Of course, I'm paraphrasing. We don't put it quite like this on the tour.'

'I should think not,' said Jackie. 'Is this the man you want Andrew to impersonate? I take it he doesn't have to be too realistic.' She didn't understand herself: one minute she was disturbed by Carlin, the next she felt he needed protecting. She noticed how he sat: hunched, or coiled. When Hugh's expansive gestures got too close, he seemed to shrink back. And yet this was less like a timid reaction than like, say, the natural movement of a reed in the wind.

'No,' Hugh said, 'for the purposes of the tour, our ghost just does a bit of straightforward spookery. Appears suddenly at the ends of closes, that kind of thing. The Major got burnt for witchcraft and for years after that people were supposed to see him in the Old Town, round where Victoria Street now is and down the Cowgate, so that's what we've got him doing – revisiting his old haunts, ha ha! I supply all the props – cloak, staff and wig. Oh, and a rat, but I'll tell you about that later. If you're interested I'll walk you through the part. On location, as it were. So, waddya think?'

'Every night?' said Carlin.

'Yeah, but if you can't manage the occasional night that's okay, as long as I know in advance. It's only an hour and a half. How about it?'

'Whit's the pay?'

'Fiver a night. I know it's not much, but for an hour or so, hey, that's not a bad rate these days. Well above the minimum wage, if there was one. Oh, and nothing to come off it either. Cash in hand, thirty-five quid every week, no questions asked. Are you on benefit? Forget I said that. Waddya think?'

Carlin finally drained his first pint and started on the second. 'It's a commitment,' he said after a while. 'Every night, like.'

'Well, as I said, if you can't make it sometimes, we can negotiate. Get a stand-in. But I need someone to start straight away, and believe me, you'd be great for the part. Look, I'll tell you what. Here's an incentive: if you do it seven nights a week without missing one, I'll round the cash up to forty quid. If you miss a night, you only get paid for the nights you work. That's pretty fair, isn't it?'

Jackie snorted and Hugh Hardie gave her what she assumed was supposed to be a withering glance. Some long and complicated process seemed to be going on in Carlin's brain. Eventually he said, 'I'm no sure.'

'What aren't you sure about? Talk to me, Andrew.'

'The haill idea. It's no the money. It's the idea.'

Hardie made a shrugging gesture. 'I don't understand what you're talking about.'

'Well, that's whit I'm no sure aboot. This guy Major Weir. You jist packaged him up in ten seconds and haundit him ower. Life's no like that. I mean, d'ye ken whit ye're daein wi him?'

'He's just a character, that's all.'

'You said he was real.'

'Well, yeah, but he's been dead three hundred years. Now he's just a character. A "real character", you might say.' Hardie laughed a little nervously. 'Anyway, we take the people round the places he lived in, tell them about the past. Not just him,

Burke and Hare, Deacon Brodie, all that stuff. I'll take you on the route and you can see for yourself what we *do* with him, as you put it.'

'That'd be guid,' said Carlin. 'I would need tae know, ken.'

'Look,' said Hugh, 'I haven't got time to show you the ropes if you're not going to take the job. I need you to start this week. Tonight if possible. Tomorrow definitely. So, come on, how about it? Meet at the Heart of Midlothian at, say, eleven tomorrow morning and take it from there, eh?'

Carlin drank more of his pint. 'And I'm like him, am I?' he said.

'The spitting image,' said Hugh Hardie.

'Show me the ropes then,' Carlin said. 'When I'm sure, I might no dae it. But I'll dae it while I'm no sure aboot it.'

Although this was delivered in the same flat monotone, Hardie interpreted it as a joke of some sort and laughed loudly. Maybe it was relief. 'Brilliant!' he said, raising his glass. '*Slàinte.*'

Carlin didn't respond. Jackie Halkit, raising her own drink instinctively, noticed that his glass, which only a couple of minutes ago had been almost full, was now down to the dregs. She hadn't been aware of him drinking in the interim.

'So what about the book, Jackie?' Hardie turned and asked. 'Is it a project?'

'If you make it one,' she said. She was aware of Carlin swivelling on his stool, standing up. Maybe he's going to buy a round, she thought, and laughed into herself. She dragged her mind back to answering Hugh's question. 'As far as I'm concerned, at this point in space and time, no, it isn't,' she said.

'Great,' said Hardie. 'It's inspiring to work with you too.' For a moment she thought he was angry at her, but then he gave her that winning smile. She had a sudden image of herself, seated in a pub late one afternoon, her consciousness being worked over by two men, both of whom intrigued her though she found them, for different reasons, slightly repellent. She felt she needed to get out in the sunlight.

'Hey,' Hugh said, 'maybe I could get *him* to write it. Being a historian and everything.'

She brought herself back. 'Where is he?' she asked Hugh. Carlin had disappeared.

'Gone for a slash, I assume,' said Hugh. But at the end of five minutes, and after Hugh had been on a scouting expedition to the toilet, it became clear that Carlin had left the pub.

'Fucking marvellous!' said Hugh. 'I mean, what's that all about? Is he going to do it? Did we make arrangements? I don't even know where the guy lives. Maybe this isn't such a good idea, Jackie.'

'Perfect for the part, I think you said. Don't expect any sympathy from me, you rat. I did try to warn you.'

'But he *is* perfect. I really want him scaring the shit out of my tourists. Do you not know where he lives?'

'No. And I don't want to either. But you did make arrangements, even if they didn't seem very definite to you. That's one of the things I mind about him, you only needed to say something once and it lodged, it stuck there in his head and he never forgot it.

'One time when I was a student, someone sort of half-suggested we all go for a drink after the last class before we went home for Christmas, in Sandy Bell's it was supposed to be, but it never came to anything, people just sloped off in different directions muttering cheerios. But then a couple of the girls caught up with me and said, Come on, let's get pissed, so we did, just the three of us, we hit the Royal Mile and had a right laugh.

'We all stayed in different flats over in Marchmont, so we were heading that way at the end of the evening and one of them says, Right, in here quick, one for the road before we get raped across the Meadows, and it was Sandy Bell's, and would you believe it, the bastard was in there, cool as you like, propping up the bar listening to the folkies, and he turns to us and says, Well, I thought yous were never going to show. And we had a round but the fun had gone out of us like balloons, we just all stood around in a circle watching each other drink, him with his eyes on us all the time, and then he walked with us home across the Meadows cause he stayed up in Bruntsfield somewhere. I tell you, we were all that freaked we had to lie we all stayed in the same street cause none of us wanted to be the last one alone with him.'

'Now that's scary,' said Hugh Hardie. 'Creeps that hang

around all night on the basis of a throwaway suggestion. I hate that kind of no-hoper stuff. But you can't get away from it, he's an ideal match for Major Weir. They might have been made for each other. So, Heart of Midlothian at eleven, was that what we agreed? Do you think he'll show?'

'Unless he's changed in six years,' said Jackie. 'Which I don't think. Seems to me he just got weirder than he was already. You turn up there on time, I'll bet he's waiting on you.'

Their glasses were empty. 'I'd better go,' she said. 'I've got stuff to do tonight.'

'What stuff?'

'Lassies' stuff. You know, cleaning the bath, reducing the ironing pile, that kind of everyday homely stuff.'

'God. Glad I'm not a lassie. Sure you don't want another?'

'No thanks, Hugh. But – and I know this is going to sound pathetically girlie too – what I would appreciate is if you'd just get me down the street a wee bit. I've got this feeling about Andrew Carlin. I don't want him following me home or anything.'

'Come *on*,' said Hardie, looking at his watch. 'Six o' clock. It's kind of early for stalking.' Then he saw that she wasn't joking. 'Yeah, sure, no problem. Where do you stay again?'

'New Town,' she said. 'Just chum me a block or two, if you don't mind.'

'I'd chum you all the way,' he said, 'but I'm going to have to do some haunting tonight, I guess, so I'd better go home too, get myself organised. The traffic'll have died down a bit by now, though, I'll flag you a taxi.'

'I'll walk,' she said. 'I'll be fine. It's just – seeing him again.'

Out on the street they had to negotiate past a drunk man coming towards them. He lurched at Hugh, who put a hand out defensively to prevent him falling into his arms. The raincoat slid greasily under his palm.

'Dae I no ken ye fae somewhere?' said the drunk man. He looked old; his jaw bristled with sharp white hairs and was shiny wet with slavers.

'I don't think so,' said Hardie, easing him back. He side-stepped to the left but the drunk man miraculously matched his footwork with a neat shuffle and blocked his path again.

'Let me pit it anither wey. Dae you no ken me fae somewhere?'

Jackie burst out laughing.

'Whit's she findin sae bluidy funny?'

'Nothing,' said Hugh. 'Look, I definitely don't know you.' The man looked intently up into his face. 'Why do you think I would know you?'

'Christ, I don't know,' said the drunk man. 'Thought I'd seen ye before. Thing is, I was kinna hopin ye'd ken me. Cause I don't have a fuckin clue whae I am.'

This time he moved first, gliding around Hardie's static figure like a winger of the old school of Scottish football, a wee ugly knot of accidental perfection. He hauled off into the gathering evening, swearing profusely.

Jackie was still smiling when they reached Nicolson Street. 'It's okay,' she told Hugh, 'I don't know what got into me. I'll be fine from here. But thanks anyway.'

'Right,' he said. 'Well, see you around. Come on the tour some time.'

'I'll do that,' she said. 'I'll call you.' Then she was away, across at the lights, still wondering if he'd expect her to pay for a ticket.

Andrew Carlin was the kind of man that might slip between worlds, if such a thing were possible. He inhabited his days like a man in a dream, or like a man in other people's dreams.

There were three mirrors in Carlin's place: one in the bathroom, one on the door of an old wardrobe that stood against the wall of the lobby, and one over the fireplace in the front room, which doubled as his bedroom. This was an old, ornately gilt-framed mirror, mottled at the edges, and with a buckle in it that produced a slightly distorting wave in the glass. It was like a mirror that hadn't had the courage to go the whole bit and join a travelling show, where it could turn those who looked in it into fully-fledged grotesques.

This was the mirror Carlin talked with, mostly. It had once been his mother's. It was flanked by two heavy brass candlesticks, which he had also inherited from her. In his parents' house the mirror and the candlesticks had been crammed onto a shelf among the bric-a-brac and debris that his mother couldn't stop snapping up in charity shops. She would come home laden with bargains and they'd have to eat beans for the rest of the week. When his father died it got worse. From the age of fourteen Carlin missed the dogged, watchful presence that had balanced the magpie frenzy of his mother. The only time he benefited from her obsession was when he first got the flat in Edinburgh, a tiny conversion on the top floor of a tenement in a street that was too near the canal to be really Bruntsfield. It was cheap enough to rent on his own, but came with a minimum of furnishings. She sorted out a few items for him – dishes and jugs and ornamental vases, most of which he sold on to junk shops or returned to charity. His mother never came to see him, so would never miss what he got rid of.

The mirror was one of the things he liked and held onto. When she died some years later and he cleared the house, he put most of what remained to the cowp. The candlesticks, however, he brought back with him and set on either side of the mirror. The three objects seemed to feed off each other, acquiring a new dignity of their own. Now Carlin felt that where they were was where they had always belonged.

He lit the gas fire, warmed his legs against it for a few minutes, then turned the fire down and faced the mirror. He thought of Hardie saying he was like this Major Weir. How the fuck did he know that? He looked and looked to see Weir in the mirror, but he didn't know what he expected to see. And he thought of Jackie Halkit.

Edinburgh was a village, if you walked around it you saw the same faces all the time. He'd seen her once or twice in the last year, and each time it had been by chance. He'd recognised her, but he'd never made an attempt to speak to her. You didn't do that. You didn't go up to folk. If something was going to happen, they would come to you. That was how it worked.

That was how it had worked till now. He'd broken in on her. He tried to imagine her with himself live in her head again. What would she be thinking? But he couldn't touch how she might be, just couldn't feel it.

He saw himself standing outside Dawson's in the late afternoon. It had been light outside and lighter still in there, because the place was full of bright electric bulbs at the bar and over the tables. Carlin preferred the gloom. He liked candlelight and shadows. Between the street and the inside of the pub there hadn't been much to choose.

Then suddenly, as he stood there, he had been invaded by a sensation so strong that he had had to put out his hand and steady himself with the tips of his fingers on the varnished wooden beading of the pub door. Just a touch to get his balance back. It was as if he had been right on the edge of something. It was like the other feeling he sometimes got, an overwhelming sense of being elsewhere, or that he could reach out and touch things that were long gone.

The past. He could stretch his fingers and feel it, the shape of it. It was like having second sight in reverse. It was like holding an invisible object, both fascinating and disturbing. Or like feeling your way in the dark.

He'd read that seers didn't like their gift of seeing the future because there was nothing they could do about it. They had visions of horrible accidents, injuries, deaths, and they couldn't stop them. There was a guy up north, the Black Isle or somewhere, who took the money from people who came to see him and then was rude and abrupt with them. He had no wish to see their future trials and losses, their rotten endings and stupid tragedies. But he could not turn them away. People came to his door every day, desperate to be warned of things that could not be avoided.

The past was like that for Carlin: a hole at the back of his mind through which anything might come.

'I've a bit o work if I want it,' he said to the mirror.

'Guid. Aboot fuckin time. Get ye aff yer fuckin erse.'

'Dinna start.'

'Dinna talk tae me then. Think I care aboot yer fuckin work?'

'It's no a job but. It's jist play-actin. Part-time.'

'Aw ye're bluidy fit for. Gaun tae tell us aboot it?'

Carlin stared until the mirror had the gen. Sometimes that was enough.

'Thing is,' he said, 'I want tae check this guy oot.'

'Who, Hardie? Forget it. A right wanker.'

'No, Weir. Somethin aboot him. Mebbe he had a bad press.'

24

'Aye. On ye go, son. Bleed yer sapsy liberal hert dry, why don't ye. Listen, if ye find oot he was a nice Christian buddy eftir aw, keep yer geggie shut or ye'll be oot o work again.'

'I'm no sayin he wasna an evil bastart. But it seems everybody has him marked doon as a hypocrite. Jist because ye lead a double life disna make ye a hypocrite.'

'Well, you would ken, wouldn't ye? Sounds tae me like ye might be buildin yer argument on shiftin sand though, friend. I mean, pillar o society by day, shagger o sheep by night – how much mair hypofuckincritical can ye get?'

'Aye, aye. I jist don't like pigeon-holin folk. Ken, an early version o Jekyll and Hyde, earlier than Deacon Brodie even – it's too pat.'

'Well, jist brush him under the carpet then. Lea him alane. The last thing we need's anither split fuckin personality. We've got mair than enough o them. Fuckin Scottish history and Scottish fuckin literature, that's all there fuckin is, split fuckin personalities. We don't need mair doubles, oor haill fuckin culture's littered wi them. If it's no guid versus evil it's kirk elders versus longhairs, heid versus hert, Hieland and Lowland, Glasgow and Edinburgh, drunk men and auld wifies, Protestants and Catholics, engineers and cavaliers, hard men and panto dames, Holy Willies and holy terrors, you name it Scotland's fuckin had it. I mean how long is this gaun tae go on, for God's sake? Are we never gaun tae fuckin sort oorsels oot? I am talkin tae you, by the way.'

'I ken. Hardie would say that's fine. He would say it's guid for business. Gies us somethin tae sell tae the tourists.'

'Don't come the bag wi that fuckin shite. Since when was that pricktugger a fuckin culture expert? And onywey, whit kinna basis is that for an economy? Whit gets sellt tae the tourists is an unreal picture o an unreal country that's never gaun tae get tae fuckin grips wi itsel until it runs its ain affairs.'

'Independence? The likes o Hardie would run a mile. We'd be like Switzerland. Dead borin, only withoot the money.'

'Noo I *ken* ye're playin the Devil's advocate. Don't fuckin mock the Swiss. You've been there. It's a clean country, everybody's got jobs, everybody uses the trains and they don't fuckin go tae war wi onybody. The Swiss fuckin ken where it's at, if ye ask me.'

Carlin turned the backs of his legs to the fire again. 'Your language,' he said. 'Away and wash yer mooth oot wi soap.'

Carlin twitched the nylon fishing-line to make sure that the rat was free to run. He knew it would be but he couldn't stop himself. He felt the weight of the rat shift slightly at the far end of the line, just a fraction of an inch, and let his fingers go slack again. Then he waited for the people to come.

He was huckered against a wall halfway down a steep close between Victoria Street and the Cowgatehead. There was a dog-leg at this point, so that anyone descending could not see him until they turned the corner, and could not see the second half of the close until they turned again at the place where he was standing.

He was wearing a long black cloak, fastened at the neck, over his ordinary clothes. When he walked the cloak billowed and swirled around him, but now, as he stood still, it hung limp and heavy like a shroud. Leaning next to him against the wall was a black wooden staff, as tall as himself, and surmounted by a misshapen knucklebone head. A straggly wig of wispy auld man's grey hair fell about his neck, framing the ghastly whiteness of his face. The previous ghost, Hugh Hardie had said on the run-through that morning, had used clown make-up, but he didn't think Carlin needed it.

The close was little frequented by locals. It was not on an obvious route to a pub or other destination, and its length and dinginess gave it an unhealthy reputation. It was used by drunks and destitutes as a urinal more than as a throughway. Tourists were seen in it only if they had got lost. Or were on a ghost tour.

The nylon line ran from his hand along the ground to a hole in the wall a few yards up the close, just before the dog-leg was reached. When the tour party reached this spot, the guide would bring everybody to a halt, and describe the living conditions of this part of Edinburgh in the seventeenth century. Hardie had rehearsed this with Carlin earlier. The guide would talk about the lack of sanitation and ask his listeners to step carefully. 'This close was once called the

Stinking Close,' he'd say, 'and it still in some respects is deserving of the name.' 'That,' said Hardie, 'is your cue, your amber light.'

Carlin's first task was to pull the large rubber rat, which was secured to the fishing-line through a hole in its mouth, across the ground and round the corner, causing alarms and excursions among the tourists as it skited over their feet.

As soon as he'd reeled in the rat, he had to move on. The guide would usher the people on round the dog-leg. They were supposed to get a glimpse of swirling cloak and a shadowy figure carrying a long staff disappearing down the lower part of the close. 'At the entrance onto the Cowgatehead,' Hardie stressed, 'stop and wait for a few seconds. You'll be silhouetted in the archway. Turn and glare back up at them. It'll look brilliant.'

Meanwhile the guide would tell them the tale of Major Weir, pointing out that he had lodged just off this very close with his sister Grizel. He would describe how he had confessed his terrible crimes before a shocked assemblage of fellow Puritans; how he had been tried and convicted of incest, bestiality and witchcraft, and burnt at the stake on the road to Leith; and how poor, mad Grizel had tried to take off all her clothes on the Grassmarket scaffold before she was hanged, just a few yards from where they were now standing. Ever after, the Major and she would be collected at night in a black coach drawn by six flame-eyed black horses, and driven out of the town to Dalkeith, there to meet with their master the Devil. At other times the Major's stick, with the satyr-heads carved on it which seemed to change shape and expression, would float through the dark wynds and closes, going like a servant before him and rapping on the doors of the terrified inhabitants.

'As you have seen,' the guide would say, 'Major Weir lives on. Perhaps, as we journey through these old dark corners of Edinburgh, you may catch another glimpse of him . . .'

And so they would. They'd turn into the Cowgate and see a tall, cloaked man moving silently along the wall ahead of them. They would follow him as the guide told more stories of ghosts and murders and other half-hidden horrors. They would be brought, by and by, back towards the High Street, where their tour had started, by a series of narrow stairs and closes. And at the last turn, those at the front of the party would find themselves staring up at the looming, gash-faced Major Weir, glowering disdainfully down his nose at them – just for a second or two, and then he'd be gone, and the adventure would be over. 'Tell your friends,' the guide would conclude, 'but – don't tell them everything. Leave them to be *un*pleasantly surprised.'

Hardie had handed Carlin the props – the wig, the cloak, the staff and the rat. 'You hang onto them in the meantime,' he'd said. 'But don't lose them. The other guy used to carry a plastic bag with him, to put the stuff in when he'd finished. He said he felt a bit of a prat walking home otherwise. But there's not much you can do about the stick. Still, should stand you in good stead if anybody gives you any hassle, eh? Now, the tour kicks off at nine o'clock. It usually gets here at about half-past, but you'll need to be in position ten minutes before that. And sometimes there's a bit of rubbish lying about, you know, some broken glass or a few old cans. If you can kick anything like that to one side I'd appreciate it. I'm all for realism but we don't want people stepping in anything too nasty.'

Now Carlin waited. This was playing at history. He should chuck it. But it had kind of happened upon him, the whole thing. Because that was the way of it, he'd let it go on. In any case, he wanted to find out why he was like Major Weir. If he was like him.

Linlithgow, September 1645

The moor was a place of refuge. The boy saw that. In its endless browns and greens you could become nothing, be hidden from the eyes that sought you. You could coorie under a peat bank, in the oxter of a rock, or beneath the grass overhang of a burn. In winter, when the ground was a bog and the mist clung to it like a dripping blanket, men on horses could not follow you among the black pools and moss hags. You could be yards away and they'd never ken you were there. You'd be invisible. The only one you could never hide from, even out here in the worst of weather, was God.

But this was September. The ground was as dry as it would ever be. The boy, hunkered in the sun on a grassy hummock pockmarked with burrows, picked up yellow-brown pellets from the dirt and cut open a couple with his thumbnail. 'Tabacca's low,' his uncle had said. 'Awa up on the hill, James, and fetch us mair rabbit purls. Mind that they're no full dried oot, but crotlie – like this, see.' He handed him a twist of brown leaf, breaking it up with his fingers. 'On yer wey then. Whit the sodgers dinna ken'll no hurt them.'

The boy fished the sample out of his pouch and compared it with the compacted shite in his palm. Slivers of grass, like colourless veins, were pressed into the tiny balls. He tore off some tobacco and stuck it in his mouth, began chewing on it. After a minute, when the first bitter shock had diminished and his mouth was filling with juice, he selected a rabbit pellet and pushed it in too, crushing it with his teeth. He couldn't taste it under the flow of tobacco.

He began to gather the purls, dozens of them, into the pouch. The town was a mile or two away, out of sight, a thin straggle of houses stretched beside a loch, dominated by the old royal palace which had lain empty and unused for years and was beginning to fall into disrepair. The army was encamped in and around the town, and under the walls of the palace. The boy was only eight, and might have been fearful alone on the moor, but he was not. He was used to being alone. Nothing much made him anxious.

His uncle had come to Linlithgow because of the army, and when the army moved on so would he. He might take James with him but more likely he would return him to his mother in Falkirk. He sold goods to the soldiers: wee eating-irons, needles, cured and salted meat, eggs (if he could get them), anything not too bulky which a soldier might need or in his boredom might believe he wanted. But his main sales were of tobacco. The war had involved the movement of great numbers of troops throughout the country – not least when the Covenant had sent an army into England against the King the previous year – and demand for the weed had exploded. Some people in distant parts had never even seen tobacco, but they were quick to acquire a taste or a craving for it. Very few had much idea about the quality of what they were buying.

A whaup flew overhead making its plaintive cry and the boy looked up at the long thin curve of its beak. He stood with his pouch of shite and walked to the top of the hummock, to see where it landed.

On the other side, not twenty feet away, a man lay sleeping. The boy dropped onto his front and all the juice in his mouth burst out onto the grass with what seemed to him a horribly loud gurgle. For a minute he did not dare raise his head to take another look. When he did the man had not moved.

The boy saw the chest rise and fall. A dark-faced man, in ragged, filthy clothing; his hair and beard thick, black and matted. The boy breathed in, deep but silent, and caught a stench like that of a fox. The man's hands lay half-clenched at his sides. The boy could not see a weapon of any kind lying nearby.

He was looking at an Irish. He had never seen one before but he kent that was what it was. One of the terrible Irishes from Montrose's army, who had burned and murdered their way from Aberdeen to Dundee to Kilsyth. They ate bairns. If they couldn't get enough Scots bairns to eat they boiled their own up in big pots and ate them. But the days of their terror were over. The Covenant had destroyed them a week past

30

near a town called Selkirk, fifty miles away. Scotland was safe again and Montrose had fled back to the mountains of the north. Most of his men had been slaughtered in the battle; others had been caught and killed on the high ground between the border country and the Forth, the ground that stretched away south under the boy's gaze.

He thought of the rabble of women and boys, the camp followers, wives and sons of the Irishes, who had been captured and brought to Linlithgow. They had spent the night huddled up against the old walls of the great palace, seventy or eighty of them, staring glumly at their guards and the curious townsfolk, or breaking into the strange mutterings of their incomprehensible language. Their clothes were rags, their bodies were smoored in dirt, reddened with cuts and sores. Most of them had no shoes. The boy had watched them for a long while. Some of the lads looked about the same age as himself. In the shadow of the crumbling palace, the light cast by the fires they were permitted seemed to make them more like small demons than real people.

That morning his uncle had warned him to keep away from the army camp and from the Irish prisoners. He was told he was too young to be among soldiers and see the things that they were sometimes obliged to do. Then he was packed off to the moor. But something special was happening in the camp, he could tell. The Irishes were being moved from the palace to the west port of the town, towards the river, where they were hidden from sight. The boy was desperate to go to the river but his uncle would have had him cutting and mixing wads of tobacco and rabbit shite all afternoon. Not now though. Not now that he had discovered the stray Irish.

He kent what he had to do. He slid back down the slope on his belly, then got to his feet and crept away. Only when he was well out of earshot did he start to run.

The Irish was a stranger in a strange land. He was weak, hungry and weaponless. He did not stand a chance.

They brought him in to the town around noon, his wrists tied by a rope to the saddle of a trooper's horse, like a stirk that had wandered. His eyes were wide and panicky, dangerous too; he looked as though he would break and run

31

if he got the chance. Somebody asked the soldiers why they had bothered to bring him back. Why had they not struck him down on the moor as they had any others they'd found in the last week? One of the soldiers laughed and said they were taking him to be with his own kind.

The boy ran beside them as they rode along the thick brown streak that was the town's thoroughfare. The prisoner stumbled and the boy's heart leapt. The Irish was his. His uncle would be proud of him.

Folk from the town were hurrying back from whatever had been going on at the river. Some were laughing and shouting; others looked grim and tight-faced, shocked, even. They seemed hardly to notice the group of riders and their prisoner.

The little procession went straight through the town, through the west port, towards the high bridge over the river. There were more people on the road, and many soldiers, armed with long pikes and swords. And here was a minister too, black among the buff leather and steel, holding out his hand to stop them. If anything made the boy anxious it was ministers. He knew they could be fierce as well as kindly; they were eloquent and decisive and when they spoke people listened. And he saw that they had something which other men, even if they carried swords and guns, did not necessarily have. They had power.

'Where did ye find this ane?' the minister asked.

'Twa mile yonder, abune the toun,' said one of the soldiers. 'He was asleep when we took him.'

'I fund him,' said the boy. He could not bear to think that his part in it might not be mentioned.

The minister bent towards him. He had a grey beard and grey hair which fell to his shoulders from beneath a tight black cap. 'Did ye?' he said. 'And how did ye come tae be there?'

The boy hesitated. He still clutched the pouch with its dubious contents. Some of the soldiers might be his uncle's next customers.

The minister crooked a finger. 'Come here, lad. Ye needna be feart frae me. Whit is yer name?'

'James. James Mitchel.'

'Are ye feart frae me, James Mitchel?'

'Na, sir. Only . . . I am feart frae God, and he is wi ye.'

Somebody among the riders laughed, but the laugh was cut short by the minister's swift glare. Even the horses stood quietly, heads bowed, in his presence.

'The laddie's richt,' he said. 'He is richt tae be feart frae God. See how God punishes them that resists him. Blessed is everyone that feareth the Lord. Tell me, James, were ye feart frae the Irish when ye fund him?'

'Na, sir. I kent God wasna wi him. I ran, but I ran for help, no for I was feart.'

'This is an uncommon bairn,' said the minister. 'Whase bairn is he?'

'His faither's deid,' somebody said. 'His uncle is Mitchel the packman.'

'Mitchel the pauchler,' said another. There was laughter, and the boy's face burned with shame. He wanted to change the subject.

'Whit will happen tae him?' he said, pointing at the Irish, who was watching the exchange with a blank and bewildered face.

'He will be punished,' the minister said. 'Gie me yer hand, James.' They stepped out of the road, and the minister waved the soldiers on. The prisoner was jerked forward on the rope. As he went he turned his head and fixed his eyes on the boy until the horses behind him obscured his view.

The minister clapped James's head. 'He thinks you are the cause o his punishment. But ye're no. You are only God's instrument, delivering his enemies up tae him. Noo, let's see if we canna find yer uncle.'

James pulled away from him, in the direction the soldiers had taken. 'I want tae see whit happens,' he cried.

'It's no for your een. Come awa noo.'

But the boy struggled harder, echoing back the minister's own words. 'I delivered him up tae God. Let me see where they're takin him.'

The minister seized him by both shoulders and lowered himself to his level. The blue eyes above the grey hairs on his cheeks seemed like pools of ice in deep caverns. The boy saw himself reflected in them.

'Ye want tae witness God's fury? Very weill then. But mind you are jist a bairn. Ye dinna ken yet whit God has in store for ye. He micht hae Heaven or Hell laid up for ye. Ye're ower young tae ken. Sae think hard on whit ye see, James. I think ye are a guid laddie, a Christian laddie, but only God can look intae yer hert and ken the truth o it.'

Then they were striding after the soldiers, towards yet more folk coming in the other direction. There was a silence on these ones like a heavy load. A man was staring at the ground as he walked, shaking his head.

The minister began to call out as they went through them. *'If it had not been the Lord who was on our side,'* he shouted, *'if it had not been the Lord who was on our side, saith Israel, when men rose up against us, then they had swallowed us up quick, when their wrath was kindled against us.'*

A woman was weeping. 'They were bairns,' she said. It seemed that she was ashamed even to speak such a thought before him. 'They were jist bairns like oor ain, even if they were savages.'

'Then the waters had overwhelmed us,' the minister thundered back, *'then the proud waters had gone over our soul. Blessed be the Lord, who hath not given us as a prey to their teeth.'*

His strides were now so long that the boy James had to trot to stop himself being dragged. His hand was gripped in the iron hand of the minister. They were approaching the high bridge over the river. The soldiers had dismounted and left their horses tethered at one end. As the minister and the boy drew close they saw that the Irish was up on the parapet, his knees bent as he tried to maintain his balance. Swords were jagging against the backs of his thighs. They saw him stumble in the air, half-turn, heard his scream as he fell into the gorge below.

By the time the pair reached the middle of the bridge, the soldiers were leaving. One of them, wiping sweat from his brow, nodded a greeting to the minister. 'Warm work the day, sir.'

The minister hoisted James up above the parapet so that he could see into the slow-moving river below. The Irish was face down, his body spinning like a graceful dancer in the current.

'Is he deid?' the boy asked.

'Aye,' said the minister. 'I doot the faw has killt him.'

The boy raised his head and looked further downstream. There was a bend in the river there, and a rocky bank where a number of men were standing. Some were dragging things like swollen sacks from the water. Others had pikes fifteen feet long, and were using them to impale the floating sacks and bring them into the bank. The Irishes. There were piles of them lying wet and motionless in the sun. The river churned in little eddies as it swept round the bend, bringing the bodies in to where the men waited for them. If any of the Irishes still moved, if they tried to swim past or clamber out, men with pikes and clubs swarmed over them, and when they dispersed again the Irishes were still. The boy saw wee bundles the size of himself spread out among the skirts and plaids of the dead women. They were like dolls.

'This river flows tae Hell,' said the minister. 'All God's enemies sail on her.' His voice had become gentle again. 'James, we are a chosen people. We must dae God's work. Dae ye ken yer Bible?'

'Aye, sir. I read it tae ma mither when I'm wi her.'

'And when ye're wi yer uncle?'

James shook his head. 'He disna hae a Bible.'

'Ye shall hae a Bible o yer ain. And perhaps, if ye study hard at it, ye could learn mair than readin. Ye could be a college lad, wi the richt assistance. Would ye like that?'

He lowered James from the parapet. The boy's last sight was of the body of the Irish he had found asleep on the moor, still spinning slowly as it approached the crowded bend of the river that flowed to Hell.

Edinburgh, April 1997

'Would ye say I was weird?'

'Fuck aye, I would certainly say ye was weird.'

'Whit wey am I weird?'

'Whit *wey*?'

'Awright. In what *ways* would ye say I was weird?'

'Well, there's this talkin tae yersel for a start. That isna normal.'

'Who says it isna? Whit dae you ken?'

'It isna *considered* normal. It's *considered* a sign o insanity.'

'Baws tae that. Ye'll need tae define normality first, and then insanity. Name anither instance o ma supposed weirdness.'

'Ye seem very defensive. Truth gettin tae ye?'

'Answer the question.'

'It wasna a question.'

'Answer!'

'Shut up. I'm thinkin.'

After a long pause the mirror said, 'Whit aboot the wey ye talk tae ither people?'

'Whit dae you ken aboot that? Ye've niver seen me.'

'I hae an informer.'

'Aye, I ken whae that is. Weill, onywey, whit aboot it?'

'That's weird tae. Aw that monosyllabic stuff, starin intae space, repeatin back whit folk say tae ye. Dinna kid on ye're no aware o it yersel. Dinna pretend ye huvna noticed.'

'That's how I am.'

'It's no how ye are *here*. Listen, we're haein a normal conversation, awmaist.'

'*Listen?*'

'Ye ken whit I mean. You answer *ma* question. Whit aboot that, how ye talk tae people?'

'That's how I am, *oot there*.'

'Ah. An interestin qualification. Whit are ye, some kinna agoraphobic?'

'You ken I'm no.'

'I only ken whit ye tell me.'

'I ayewis lie tae ye.'

'That sounds like the start o wan o thae undergraduate pub philosophy discussions. Ken, a statement that contains its ain internal contradiction.'

'Right. An organism that contains the seed o its ain destruction. So can ye no deal wi that, eh? Whit's up? Am I makin ye feel uncomfortable?'

'If I could,' said the mirror, 'I would turn ma face tae the wa.'

Wednesday. Carlin stood patiently in the Scottish department in the basement of the Central Library on George IV Bridge, while an old guy in a mouldy raincoat produced a dozen books from an enormous briefcase and asked if he could renew them all again.

'All of them?' asked the librarian.

'Yes please. I'm doing research. I need them all.'

'Well, so long as nobody else has requested them. Could I have your card, please?' She began to bring up the different titles on screen, checking them in and checking them back out again. The old fellow wiped his brow with his raincoat sleeve.

'You could save yourself carrying them back and forth if you phoned us,' the librarian said while she worked. 'We can renew them over the phone.'

'I'm not on the phone,' he said.

She reached the last book. 'This one's been requested, I'm afraid. I can't let you have this one again.'

'But I need that one. That's the most important. In fact, it's essential.'

'I'm sorry. You could request it back again, for when the reader who's requested it returns it, but you can't have it just now.'

'Don't you have any other copies? I mean, who else is wanting to look at that particular book?'

The librarian checked on the computer. 'No, that's the only

copy. I'm sorry, but it has definitely been requested.'

The old man tutted. 'Well, who is it that wants it? It's very obscure. Nobody else would be interested.'

'Somebody obviously is,' said the librarian.

'Give me a name then,' said the auld yin.

'I can't do that.'

'The other ones are no use without that one. If I can't have that one I don't want any of them.'

'But I've just renewed them all for you.'

'I didn't know you weren't going to let me keep that one. If I'd known that I wouldn't have bothered asking for these ones.' He turned and stumped out through the door.

The librarian sighed and began to cancel all the entries she had just made. A queue had formed. There was a cough from behind Carlin and a man's voice asked quietly who was next.

'I am,' said Carlin.

'How can I help you?'

He had very thick-lensed black-framed glasses and what was left of his reddish hair was stretched across his freckled pate like an abandoned cat's-cradle. Something about his appearance appealed to Carlin; he looked like he might lead the same kind of isolated life. Together, they took a few steps away from the desk, a move that seemed to be spontaneous, shared by both of them.

'I'm lookin for as much information as ye have aboot someone called Major Weir. D'ye ken him?'

The man smiled. Carlin noted from a badge on his lapel that he was addressing Mr MacDonald.

'You've come to the right place. The infamous Major. Yes, I think we've a few bits and pieces on him.'

For the next ten minutes MacDonald darted among the stacks, producing books of varying size and antiquity. He got Carlin to fill in some request slips for the more obscure ones. Most of the material was incorporated in secondary sources, and much of it had clearly been recycled from one book to another over the years. There was a good chunk in Robert Chambers' *Traditions of Edinburgh*. Weir was mentioned delicately in Hugo Arnot's *Celebrated Criminal Trials*. The supernatural elements of his tale were detailed in George Sinclair's *Satan's Invisible World Discovered*, and in a strange document called 'A Collection of Providential Passages Antient and Modern Forreign and Domestick' written by James Fraser, who claimed to have known the Major. There was a modern collection of *Scottish Ghost Stories* which had conflated the most salacious details from these and other sources. There was a book of *Justiciary Proceedings* containing the seventeenth-century equivalent of transcripts of the Weirs' trial. Their names cropped up in most books on Edinburgh's past, usually with the true nature of their crimes glossed over or summarised as 'too horrible to dwell upon'.

By careful cross-reading, Carlin began to deconstruct Hardie's potted account: Weir's sister was called Jean, not Grizel (the latter name, that of a former landlady of the Major's, having somehow attached itself to her at some stage). Jean, not her brother, was accused of witchcraft, and she was found not guilty of it, but was convicted of incest. Weir was accused of fornication, adultery, bestiality and incest, and convicted on the latter two charges. The lurid tales of witchcraft and satanism, it seemed, had been spread like a coverlet over the truth. But if reality was hidden, there was barely disguised glee in many of the accounts that a man so grimly good on the surface should have been found so exotically bad underneath: a witness enthusiastically reported that Major Weir and his staff, which was burnt at the stake with him, 'gave rare turnings' in the fire at the Gallowlee.

MacDonald seemed to have an extraordinary knowledge of where to locate even passing mentions of the case. He sat Carlin at a desk with a pile of books and periodically appeared at his side with another old clothbound volume. 'This is interesting,' he'd say. 'There's a record of the court pro-ceedings in this one.' Or his finger would point at a column of dense print: 'Just here. Another devilish trick our dear Major was supposed to have performed.' Carlin nodded his thanks and read on.

MacDonald came back after a while with a small cardboard box in his hand. 'Have you used a microfilm projector before?' he asked. They went over to the big-screened machine and MacDonald took a roll of film out of the box and fed it onto the spools. He flicked a switch and the machine whirred into life.

'You turn this spool to go forward, this one to go back,' he explained. 'This is your focus control. Sit down, please. Now wind it forward.'

A grainy image of antique-looking print appeared.

'This is a copy of a pamphlet called *Ravillac Redivivus*,' said MacDonald. 'It was written in 1678 by an Englishman called George Hickes, chaplain to the then Scottish Secretary of State, the Duke of Lauderdale. Francois Ravaillac was a French Catholic who in 1610 stabbed King Henri IV to death for supposedly betraying the faith. The pamphlet goes into some detail about this crime.'

'Whit's it got tae dae wi Weir?'

'Well, Hickes was a propagandist. The pamphlet's title was supposed to show that Ravaillac's fanatical spirit was alive and, ah, kicking in Scotland, but at the opposite end of the religious spectrum, in the person of one James Mitchel. Mitchel was a Covenanter who'd tried to assassinate the Archbishop of St Andrews. Hickes's pamphlet is a hatchet job, basically, linking Mitchel to the bestial Major Weir. That's your connection. The two of them had once shared lodgings in the Cowgate, at the house of Grizel Whitford, and Royalists like Hickes were keen to rake up as much muck as possible about poor old Mitchel. Being associated with Weir would be like getting a reference for a teaching post from the Marquis de Sade.'

Carlin said, 'It says Mitchel got a degree fae Edinburgh University. Like masel. Canna hae been aw bad then, eh?'

'Well,' said MacDonald, 'it might not have meant quite the same thing in those days.'

Carlin went back to the shelves to try to find out more about the period. He felt ignorant and cheated because he had only a sketchy idea of what had happened in Scotland in the reign of Charles II. Or any of the Stewarts for that matter. He had gone through a four-year history degree at university without once having had to open a book about the history of his own country. He had studied American, Russian, British (meaning English, a gorgeous tapestry with a few Celtic fringes tacked on to stop it fraying), medieval and modern European, but Scottish history had not been considered a necessary ingredient to a well-rounded higher education. And

40

then, when he unexpectedly got good results in his finals and the possibility of staying on as a postgraduate arose, he found he needed some distance, physical distance, from what he had been doing. And from Edinburgh too. He got out.

Years later, thought became important again. His mother had died after more than a decade fading away among her ever-growing collection of curios, and he was astonished to find that, in spite of her habit of accumulation, she had not spent all his father's savings. The money that came to him meant that he had some freedom. He applied to go back to the university to do research. It seemed natural to go into more depth in one of the areas he had studied for Honours. He ended up with a vague proposal to study military strategy in the German spring offensive of 1918. After seven months he admitted defeat: history, which he had hoped would welcome him back, was tired of him and spat him out.

In retrospect he was glad, or at least not disappointed, that he had not finished his PhD. It would have taken him back into the past again, and that was not what he needed. The trouble was, between the present and himself there was virtually no rapport. He rolled around in it like a discarded coke bottle on the top deck of a bus. History had kicked him out, maybe for his own good, but it had left him stranded. And now he felt it pulling at him again, like a needy, wilful parent.

By the end of the afternoon Carlin had worked his way through all the sources supplied by Mr MacDonald, and a few others that these had led onto. He felt like a door had been opened for him. He certainly knew a lot more about Major Weir and the society he lived in than Hugh fucking Hardie did. In fact he reckoned he now knew as much about Weir as anyone, with the possible exception of MacDonald. Maybe he could compete on the last ever series of *Mastermind*, with The Life, Times and Sexual Deviations of Major Weir as a specialist subject. Carlin took the pile of books back to the desk.

MacDonald approached him from the lending stacks.

'How did you get on, Mr Carlin?'

'Awright. Ony chance I could keep a couple o these aside till tomorrow?'

'Of course. You can keep them on reserve for up to six days. After that, if you've not been in, they just get reshelved.'

'Thanks,' said Carlin.

'I was thinking about your request a little while ago. I'm sure there's another reference to the Weirs somewhere – quite a detailed thing – but I can't recall it. If I think of it before you're in again I'll put it aside as well.'

'Ye've a guid memory,' said Carlin. 'It'll come back tae ye.'

'Yes, it will,' said MacDonald. 'I've been here forty years. You get a pretty good knowledge of the stock over that length of time. Especially the older items, the stuff that's been here since before you arrived. It becomes like your own furniture.'

Carlin said nothing. He thought MacDonald had finished. He was turning to leave when the librarian rushed on unexpectedly.

'Furniture's to be used, that's what I think. If not, chop it up for firewood – why not? Something like this happens – you coming in here – it starts a ball rolling, doesn't it? A mechanism – cogs turn, balances shift. I'm always interested that other people are interested.'

'Interested?' Carlin said. 'Whit in?'

'That's the thing – anything, anything at all. You never know what significance will be found in the utterly trivial. Otherwise' – he made a sweeping gesture that seemed to incorporate not just the Scottish department but the entire library on all its floors – 'what would be the point of all this? What would be the point?'

Carlin smiled. It was as if the man was justifying his existence.

'I'll be in again the morn,' said Carlin.

'Good,' said MacDonald. 'Ask for me if you need anything, won't you?'

He had to go back to his flat in off-Bruntsfield to collect the wig and cloak for that evening's performance. He left the library and walked along George IV Bridge, passing the bronze statue of Greyfriars' Bobby beside which, even this early in the year, a couple of tourists were photographing each other. But the past – Carlin's past – was there with them too; he could never go by that dog without seeing it coated in yellow paint – some unsentimental person had once cowped a tin of the stuff over the statue and now he always saw it like that.

There had been a jeweller's shop right beside it called Abbotts of Greyfriars, then it became a fruit-machine arcade, now it was a grocer's. The arcade owners had economically removed the A and two Ts from the old fascia and rearranged the remaining letters to read BOBS OF GREYFRIARS: every time Carlin saw the shop-front now, with its fruit and veg stacked out onto the pavement from the windows, he glanced up and remembered that earlier transformation, and saw the flashing lights that had beckoned folk in to chance the coins in their pockets.

To his left, down Chambers Street, was the Museum, where, if he looked, he would catch the echo of someone he had once seen, a tiny lost lassie in a blue coat crouched on the steps. He kept going. Further along, in Forrest Road, was Sandy Bell's pub, where he had once watched an old man share his pint with his dog and then order the beast outside when it failed to buy the next one: there was a thin, skeerie-looking mongrel hotching anxiously outside the door now as he passed.

On Middle Meadow Walk he observed to his left the backs of some of the few original buildings of George Square, including one once lived in by a young Walter Scott. The university had destroyed most of three sides of the square in the sixties and seventies and replaced the Georgian houses with concrete-slabbed office-blocks. Later, when he was a student, it was widely circulated that these buildings were themselves threatened with demolition owing to a fault in the concrete. 'A result of material weakness in a false construction placed on the original premises,' Carlin had once said to himself. And now that laboured witticism looped round in his head again: he couldn't erase it. He would never get free of those wee lumps and craters of time.

Crossing the Meadows now was like watching a film of himself crossing the Meadows. He was nearly forty years old. It was twenty years since he'd first walked there. The light wind blew pink cherry blossom from the trees lining the path, as though a corridor of wedding guests were throwing confetti at him. He laughed out loud at the thought. He was aware of himself, saw the steps he took between the trees, shoes scuffing at the bits of browned blossom that had been crushed on the tarmac. He saw himself pass through the whale bones that arched at the end of the path and gave it its name, Jawbone Walk. He minded the time somebody had spray-painted the L on the sign into an N.

Sometimes he crossed the road anywhere, angling a gap in the traffic. Sometimes, like now, he deferred to the walking-man at the lights. He was alone. He pressed the button and waited for the lights to turn through amber to red and to hear the bleeping of the signal and to watch himself cross.

Edinburgh, September 1656

James Mitchel, recently graduated from the Toun's College, stood on the High Street of Edinburgh and contemplated the skull mounted high up on the north face of the Tolbooth. Years of wind, rain and the attentions of gulls had removed the flesh and hair from it, and the stripped bone looked now more like a part of the stonework, a defective gargoyle, than something human.

The street was narrow at the point where he stood, between the jutting Tolbooth and the tall lands behind him. It was evening, and chilly, and the light was almost gone. Not many folk were about, but those that did hurry past had to step around him, giving him dark looks. *Whit's the daft laddie daein goavin up at the jail there? Dis he ken some puir body locked up inside? Or is he – aye, he's lookin at the skull.—Weill, that isna worth a spit. Nae need tae look up there eftir sax year.—Awbody kens whae that was, though he isna sae bonnie noo as yince he was.—Daft loon. Get oot o folk's road, would ye.*

A shadow fell across Mitchel's gaze. A hand lighted like a trained bird on his shoulder. His nose twitched at the familiar smell of cheap, stale tobacco.

The tall man beside him said, 'That is the empty head of a vain and prideful villain.'

Mitchel turned. 'I ken,' he said. Then he added, 'But he yince held Scotland in his hand.'

'For a few months only,' the tall man said. 'A moment – less than a moment – in God's scale of time.'

Major Weir was no stranger to Mitchel: they were neighbours in their Cowgate lodgings, and Weir had often spoken to him, coolly but not unkindly, in his deliberate, Englished tones. Still, Mitchel found it hard not to be in awe of the older man, who was recognised and deferred to everywhere he went, either as a preacher or as an officer of the City Guard.

Although he ought not to have been surprised at Weir's appearance, since the Major's duties took him all over the town, day and night, sometimes he wondered at the frequency with which they met away from Mistress Whitford's house. It was ridiculous to imagine that Weir followed him; and yet Weir's eye always seemed to be taking note of his appearance or behaviour. There was something both flattering and unnerving in this assessment.

'Why do you look upon that head?' Weir asked. 'Not with regret, nor in adulation, I can see that. What does the dead mouth of James Graham tell you?'

'Naethin,' Mitchel said. 'It is silent. I never saw him in life, but when I was a bairn he had Scotland chitterin on its knees, and folk fleggin ye wi tales o his army. But when I look noo I'm no feart. And he disna say ocht.'

Weir tapped the ground with his staff. 'Or ye dinna hear ocht,' he said. He shifted his hand from Mitchel's shoulder to his elbow, turned him with the slightest pressure.

'Walk with me, James,' he said, once more in his clipped, careful voice. 'I was at the Netherbow Port, inspecting the guard, and now I am on my way to a prayer-meeting. I would be obliged if ye'd convoy me to the Grassmarket.'

They began to walk up the street, past the hulk of St Giles, Weir's left hand cleiking Mitchel's arm, while his right leaned heavily on the staff. His grip was tight, but he seemed to be labouring on the hill, like a man well beyond his mid-fifties. When he stumbled, Mitchel asked hesitantly if he felt unwell.

'I am fine, I am fine,' he said. 'Just weary. It's a hard path that we have trod since Graham was dealt with. Scotland was delivered out of his hands, it seems, only to be given over to Cromwell and his vile English army. And now they say when Cromwell and the English go, we'll hae a Stewart back again. All this suffering, all this long dark nicht, and for what? You say you heard nothing, but when I look up at Graham's head, I sometimes fancy I hear him laughing at us.'

He stopped as they reached the top of the West Bow, and they stood looking down the long street, across which a few well-wrapped figures were flitting. Weir coughed and spat on the ground.

'I had him in my charge the night before he was executed,

46

did ye know that? In that very prison which his head now adorns. He laughed at us then, the savage. Combing his locks and preening himself, and brushing out his finery as if God would care a docken what he looked like when He cast him into the furnace. And he spurned the services of the ministers sent to attend him by the General Assembly – good men, strong in the Covenant that he himself had signed and then betrayed, Davie Dickson and James Durham and James Guthrie and Robert Traill. He said he, *the Marquis of Montrose*, would make his own peace with God. Doubtless he'd have corrected God if God didna address him by that false title. He was a proud and foolish man, James. There was a huge scaffold biggit for him, thirty feet high, and the street was tight with folk come to see him die. But when I took him out there in the forenoon, he still would not show remorse for his crimes. He climbed that thirty feet as if he were going to his bed.'

He broke off and drew himself up to his full height, and rapped the staff hard on the stones. 'But we are stronger,' he said sharply. 'We are stronger because we have God with us. The godly *will* prevail.'

'I believe that,' said Mitchel, as they started to walk again. 'It is oor destiny. Principal Leighton at the college, afore oor laureation, tendered tae us the Covenant, and I subscribed tae it. Ye canna tak some and no the haill o that document. It is signing away your life tae Christ.'

'The life of the haill nation, James, but you see how many who have signed it have fallen away from its principles. Beware of Robert Leighton even. His tongue speaks the right words, but he is ower tolerant. The land is full of holy wobblers like him, and they are a great danger. At least a man like Montrose, you could mark him for an enemy.'

At the foot of the Bow, where their ways parted, Weir stopped again, but did not release his grip.

'Will you not come to the meeting, Maister Mitchel? You a graduate and a man of the right party. Why do we not see you at our meetings? Do you not like my company, or the sound of my voice?'

'Na, na, I hae often heard ye preach,' said Mitchel. 'And admired ye, tae.'

'You should hear me pray,' said Weir. 'A sermon is a text with a wind at its back. But prayer, prayer is wind and fire together. Why do you not come?'

Mitchel shook his head, and looked away to the bottom of the Grassmarket, behind which the last of the light was now a deepening red in the sky. 'I am uncertain,' he said, then added in an embarrassed mumble, 'if I hae grace.'

He felt Weir shift his position, heard him sigh heavily.

'You are very young, James. Ye needna be ashamed. You have grace. Look at me when I tell ye this. You have grace. You are of the elect. I can feel it.'

'I must be sure, though,' Mitchel said. He looked at the blaze in the older man's eyes, and longed for such conviction.

'There's no harm in prayer, even if you are in a state of doubt,' Weir told him. 'Prayer can lead to assurance. You should come.'

But Mitchel stepped back. 'I am indebted tae ye, sir. And I will come. But no this nicht. This nicht I must pray alane.'

Weir nodded. 'Very well. But this will not last. The Lord will find you work, James, and you will receive assurance. Believe me, it will happen.'

Edinburgh, April 1997

Jackie Halkit left a message on Hugh Hardie's answer-machine: 'Thought I might go on your tour tonight. Maybe see you there?' He didn't return the call, but she decided to go anyway. It didn't matter about paying three or four pounds or whatever the fee was. She was more interested in seeing Carlin playing the ghost. Since the meeting at Dawson's it was as if he had set up camp in her mind.

It was still early spring, and cold at night. Only seven other people turned up: three Japanese visitors – two men and a woman – and a slightly drunk office party – three women and a man. The man kept going 'Whooooh!' and running his fingers over his companions' necks. It was amazing to Jackie that they seemed to get almost as much of a kick out of this as he did. When the guide started to talk the man settled down, and tried instead to impress the women with the seriousness with which he paid attention. 'That's very interesting. God, I never knew that, did you know that?' he would say periodically, and chuckle knowingly at the guide's jokes. The Japanese said nothing, but smiled politely when the others laughed.

Jackie had to admit, the tour was quite well done. The script was informative and not too patronising, though it spared little in the way of gore and the macabre. The guide was dressed in black, and introduced himself, removing a hood with rough-cut eyeholes, as a former public executioner who had made it his life's work to gather all the sins of the city together. He started with a dramatic gob on the heart-shaped setts in Parliament Square which marked the site of the entrance to the old Tolbooth: it was an act, he explained, originally performed by prisoners when they were released from the jail, but since these unfortunates were all long dead he felt an obligation, as the man who had despatched so many of their fellows on the scaffold, to uphold the tradition on their behalf. 'Oh,' said the office party man, 'I thought you were a Hibs fan.' The guide shook his head. 'I make it a rule never to discuss football, there's been too much blood in these streets already,' he said. The office man was delighted to get such a lad-conscious response. The guide led his party up the High Street to the Lawnmarket, telling stories all the way, then, via the surviving upper section of the West Bow, down some steps onto Victoria Street, towards the site of his former work in the Grassmarket, thus retracing the old route of those condemned to die.

At the top of Anderson's Close he paused, raising his arm ominously.

'Ladies and gentlemen, I must warn you before we enter the next stage of our journey, that you are about to learn of one of the wickedest and foulest personages who ever stalked the streets of Auld Reikie. And I must warn you too, that some say he still roams the wynds and closes hereabouts. I refer to the so-called Wizard of the West Bow, the notorious Major Thomas Weir.'

He brought the party down into the narrow close, and invited them to gather in around him. There wasn't much room. The man from the office party took the opportunity to put his arms around the shoulders of two of his colleagues. Jackie moved away from them down the slope, just behind the guide.

'In the late 1600s,' the guide said, 'this part of Edinburgh was packed with dwellings. Some of the buildings here were the skyscrapers of their day, rising ten, eleven or even more storeys. Sanitation was at a minimum and disease was rife. Beware! If you hear the cry *Gardy-loo!*, it means somebody is about to throw the contents of a chamberpot or bucket out of a window. Mind where you step – this close was once called the Stinking Close and it still has a certain *je ne sais quoi* about it. None of you are afraid of rats, I hope? You won't be too upset if we disturb any as we continue on our way?'

There was a scuffling sound at the foot of the wall next to Jackie, and something shot across the close and hit her shoe. She let out a short scream and jumped. The thing skeltered on and collided with the unattached office-girl, who also screamed and threw herself into her friends. The Japanese visitors yelped and grabbed at one another. The rat careered off the wall, flipped over and then disappeared on its back round the corner.

The guide gave them only a few seconds to recover. Everybody was suddenly laughing and gasping with relief as he ushered them on round the dog-leg. 'Was it us?' he was saying breathlessly. 'Was it us or something else that disturbed it?' Jackie found herself being pushed forward. Ahead of her she saw him, Major Weir, filling the close like a wind, moving silently and smoothly away. At the Cowgatehead end he turned, and for a moment was illuminated from behind, white-faced, with a long staff swaying beside him. Then he was gone.

The office man was speechless. Everybody else was gibbering away in their own language. The guide let them get the excitement out of their systems before filling them in on whose ghost it was they had just seen.

It was very effective, Jackie conceded that. She only half-took in what the guide was saying, but realised that, in terms of the tour experience, his words were not too important anyway. They were history babble. The *effect* was everything. And Carlin had played his part well. He had looked threatening, ghostly, ancient, yes, all these things. But something else . . . she couldn't figure it.

'If you go down Leith Walk,' the guide concluded, 'very nice down at the waterfront these days – nice wine-bars, bistros et cetera – well, if you go down Leith Walk you pass the spot where Major Weir was burnt to death. It's no longer there, of course, but it was just beside where the Lothian Transport bus depot now is. So we can conclude that the place of public execution has become the place of public transportation.'

The office man laughed. 'Well, there you go,' he said. 'I never knew that.'

The group made its way along the Cowgate. Jackie kept looking for the cloaked figure. She knew from Hugh Hardie that Carlin was supposed to appear again. A few people, in twos and threes, were strolling in each direction. None of them was like a ghost.

*

'Would ye say I was depressed?'

'Dae ye want ma opinion?'

'Aye. Ye were that guid on weirdness. Would ye say I'm showin any o the symptoms o depression?'

'Don't get fuckin smart wi me, son. How would I ken? You're the one that was gaun tae be a doctor.'

'No that kinna doctor. Look, I'm no lookin for a cure. I jist would like yer views on the subject.'

'Tell us yer symptoms then.'

'It's like there's a fire in the small o ma back. I start sweatin aw ower ma body. I canna work up enthusiasm for onythin. I've got a shitey wee job and I canna even finish the shift. I feel physically run doon aw the time. Seik. Knackert.'

'There's a lot of flu aboot.'

'And I keep gaun intae dwams. Real stuff disna feel real and the dwammy stuff does. Does that sound like the behaviour of an emotionally balanced person?'

'Na, but we ken ye're no that. We ken ye're a fucked up, awol, fairychummin moonlowper. In yer ain terms yer behaviour is entirely normal. Dodgy terms of coorse, but we'll jouk an let that jaw gang by. Mebbe there's nuthin much wrang wi ye. Ye jist canna face the tedium o everyday life. Ye're bored by it because everythin seems pointless and cruel. So yer mind switches aff and yer body follows. How am I daein?'

'No bad. But it's no so much like ma mind switches aff, mair like it switches on. It's like the past isna past, it's right there happenin in front o me. Tae me.'

'The past? Yer ain past?'

'Ither folk's past. Frae way back, fuckin yonks. I'm supposed tae be playin Weir's ghost but it feels mair solid than that. Real.'

'Let's talk aboot yer ain past.'

'Na, let's no. This is mair important.'

'That's a matter o opinion.'

'It's important that I'm seein aw these auld images. But they're no mine.'

'Ye're tellin me ye're dreamin stuff frae somebody else's life?'

'No dreamin exactly. I could unnerstaun that. I've been

52

daein aw this readin so it wouldna surprise me if that was comin intae ma heid, when I was asleep ken. But this is different. It's like I've got a front row seat at the pictures.'

'So, if it's botherin ye that much, ye ken whit tae dae. Naebody's forcin ye tae stey. Staun up an walk oot the bluidy picture-hoose.'

'Aye.'

'Weill?'

'I canna.'

Mr MacDonald beamed at him. 'I have something for you,' he said.

'Guid,' said Carlin. 'Cause I feel like I need somethin. A way in. It's like I'm no close enough.'

'Do you really want to get *close* to Major Weir?' said MacDonald.

'It's no a question o wantin. You ken whit I mean. Aw these ministers were gaun intae him in prison, tryin tae get him tae repent, but they werena gettin close at all. Was there naebody else? Was he totally friendless? Somebody must have gone tae see him.'

MacDonald was holding a manilla folder. They moved out of the way of the other readers and librarians.

'You would think so,' said MacDonald. 'It's not often you get the chance to view the incarnation of pure evil. But maybe that was the trouble. He was too dangerous. His former Covenanting comrades couldn't put enough distance between him and them, once his crimes were made known. And the nature of the crimes – he was dangerous in a much deeper sense than just political. His sister was accused of witchcraft but claimed that the real sorcerer was him, not her. People took that very seriously in 1670 – they believed in the immortality of the soul, that life on earth was just a prelude, an overture to eternity. Major Weir was up to his oxters in stuff that would send you straight to Hell.

'The only folk that wanted to visit him in prison were his enemies – Royalists going to gloat at the fallen Presbyterian, or Presbyterian ministers going to look on the face of Satan. And then, he was convicted on a Saturday and executed on the Monday. He was probably in the Tolbooth for less than a week before the trial, while they prepared the evidence against him, so there wasn't a lot of time for sympathetic visitors.'

'How do you ken aw this?' Carlin said. 'Is this a pet subject of yours or somethin?'

'Your interest revived mine,' said MacDonald. 'I had the opportunity to turn over a few pages this morning. As I said before, when you've been here as long as I have, everything becomes familiar. The Weirs have a certain morbid appeal, but you have to see them in the context of the times. Religious terrorism, political repression, economic uncertainty . . . it's not surprising some individuals went off the rails, is it?'

'I was thinkin aboot this guy Mitchel,' said Carlin. 'The man that tried to shoot the archbishop. Him and Weir used tae ken each ither. Where was he when Weir was in trouble?'

'In Holland probably,' said MacDonald. 'Although now that you mention it we don't really know where he was in 1670. Wandering about trying not to get arrested, doubtless. No, I don't see how he could have got near Weir. But I have somebody here for you who did.'

He handed Carlin the folder. 'Sir John Lauder,' he said. The folder was about an inch thick between stiff cardboard covers. It had a label on the front bearing a catalogue number, and down the spine another label which read ANE SECRET BOOK. It felt ponderous and dense.

'He became Lord Fountainhall, a judge in the Court of Session,' MacDonald explained. 'When he wrote this – *if* he wrote it – he was just plain Maister John Lauder, an advocate. I told you yesterday that I thought there was more on Major Weir somewhere. I knew it was in an unusual source but I couldn't remember where until I was up in the Edinburgh Room this morning and I overheard someone checking their council ward. They gave their address as Fountainhall Road and it suddenly clicked.'

Carlin flipped open the front cover. There was a typescript, a blue carbon copy on foolscap sheets:

Ane Secret Book of John Lauder
later Lord Fountainhall
being his account of sundry matters of public interest
many not revealed in his Historical Observes and Historical Notices

transcribed and preserved by D. Crosbie and presented to
Edinburgh Public Library 1912

'Lauder kept records about everything,' said MacDonald. 'He kept journals and notes about both his private affairs and public life from the time he was admitted to the Faculty of Advocates – just a few weeks before Mitchel tried to kill Archbishop Sharp – right through to the Union and beyond. He didn't approve of the Union. A lot of what he wrote was published in the nineteenth century by historical societies like the Bannatyne Club. He's regarded as an important source for the whole period.

'Now he mentions in one of the published journals that he did visit Weir in prison on the day he died, but he doesn't say much about him – except that he was a monster of depravity and deserved all he got. Standard sort of response which wouldn't really help you much, but the document you have in your hands, that's another story. You see, many of Lauder's manuscripts were lost. There's a story that most of what was preserved was discovered in a tobacconist's by a lawyer named Crosbie in the later eighteenth century. You'll note the name D. Crosbie appears on the title-page of that document. One is tempted to presume it was a descendant. The earlier Crosbie is supposed to have been half the model for Sir Walter Scott's lawyer Mr Pleydell in *Guy Mannering* by the way – I'm sorry, this is hardly relevant, is it?'

Carlin shook his head. 'No, but it's awright,' he said. 'Tell me aboot this thing I'm haudin.'

'To be honest,' said MacDonald, 'I'm a wee bit embarrassed by it. I mean, it has no historical credentials, there is no proof of its authenticity at all. There's a note at the front which says it was typed from a handwritten copy, made by this D. Crosbie person's grandfather, of an original manuscript. The original was crumbling to dust and the copy was virtually illegible, so it's claimed. But we have no idea who D. Crosbie was – no address, no autobiographical details – nothing. The library has no record of where the document came from, or why it was accepted. There's no corresponding copy in the National Library, or anywhere else that I know of, although there must have been a top copy. Nor is there any guarantee that John Lauder even wrote it, although the internal evidence is reasonably strong: the characteristically erratic spellings, the references to individuals Lauder knew and so on. On the other hand, it's not altogether in his style. Not as *lawyerish* as you'd expect. I don't think professional historians have ever taken it seriously – most of them probably don't know it exists. Possibly it's a great missing chunk of our history, but – and this is why I suggest you should be cautious and regard it with the utmost suspicion – it's more likely to be an elaborate fake.

'However, there's no obvious reason why anyone would perpetrate such a hoax, unless the library paid money for the thing, but that would be unlikely and certainly then I'd expect much better documentation. The title-page text would suggest it was a donation. So why go to all the bother of inventing all this? If, by some chance, it is by Lauder – and I don't see how we'll ever know that now – it certainly fills a gap. Among the manuscripts of his that went missing were twenty years' worth of his *Historical Observes*, which would have included all of the 1670s.'

MacDonald looked flustered, as if his statement had taken a lot out of him. 'I don't know what to say,' he finished. 'Have a look at it, by all means, but . . . well, I'd be interested to know what you think.'

There were little beads of sweat on his brow, under the latticework of thin red hair. He took off his glasses and wiped his head with a large faded blue handkerchief. 'I must go now,' he said. 'Must get on. That really belongs upstairs, but as you're consulting books from this department too, it'll be all right to look at it here.'

He turned away and seemed almost to dart back behind the counter, which was unoccupied. Still mopping his head, he pushed through a door beyond which Carlin could see stacks of leatherbound books. He watched MacDonald's round-shouldered figure until it turned left and disappeared among the shelves. He found a vacant desk and sat down at it with the typescript. He opened it, read the note by D. Crosbie that MacDonald had mentioned, and turned to the next page.

10th day of Januar 1678 – I am just now returned from the tryal of James Mitchel at the Criminall Court. He was pannelled for attempting the life of the Archbischop of St Androis. This tryal is the sum and end of many bad things, that I have sein and heard thir last ten years, whilk I maun putt doune tho I fear to doe it. Unsemely and stinking are the wayes emploied to sicker this man's doom, but soe is al thats gane befoir. I am sweert to write anent this afair in my other journal. This is ane new and secret book.

It is ane yeir since Mitchel was putt to the Bass, and but nine month since I socht leave to see him there from my father in law Lord Abbotshall . . .

Edinburgh, April 1677

Sir Andrew Ramsay, Lord Abbotshall, till lately Lord Provost of Edinburgh, considered leaving his long, luxurious wig on the stand where he had placed it earlier, while looking over his accounts. It was a very fine wig, thick and lavishly curled, but it made his head hot and got in the way when he was trying to read. Still, he did not really like to be seen without it; he was approaching sixty, and the wig gave his large face a dignity it otherwise lacked. Without his expensive clothes and headpiece he might have been taken for a publican or a shopkeeper. Not that Sir Andrew had anything against publicans and shopkeepers; on the contrary, he was their prince. Or, at least, he once had been.

He was expecting his son-in-law and although John Lauder was family, Sir Andrew still liked to impress his formidable personality upon the younger man. He stood up, took the wig and, in front of a mirror, carefully lowered it onto his head. He laid the ends of it over his ample shoulders and briefly admired himself, large, sedate and solemn in the glass. That was his style in these times of wild ranters and gaunt rebels. Some might think him fat and graceless, but he saw himself as a dancing-master; nobody could jouk and birl like Sir Andrew Ramsay when it came to politics. He was the great survivor. 'Andra, ye're a richt *continuum*,' a friend had recently told him. And there was no better evidence of his political brilliance than the fact that, over three decades of war, religious upheaval and governments of utterly different complexions, he had become progressively and irresistibly more and more rich.

He cleared his throat with a grumble of self-approval, and sat back down to his books, his dreams of political intrigue, and his decanter of brandy. He was a merchant, the godfather of the city's trade, and a laird with extensive properties in Fife and Haddingtonshire. He had served as provost under two regimes, first during the Commonwealth and then after the Restoration, when it suited the new government to install someone with a proven record, rather than trust to the vagaries of council elections. Once he had consolidated a power base on the council, elections were reintroduced and proceeded without alarm. Sir Andrew managed to remain Lord Provost year after year as if, like some portly extension of the royal prerogative, he had been restored to a throne of his own.

Being a man with his own interests at heart he was as amenable to receiving bribes as he was adept at making them. He'd had a knighthood from King Charles, which discreetly obscured the one he'd received from the usurper Oliver Cromwell. Other honours accrued like interest. He was a Member of Parliament, Privy Counsellor and Commissioner of Exchequer. In 1671 he had achieved a further triumph: he was made a judge, an appointment for which he had no merit and only one qualification. His patron Lauderdale, the Secretary of State for Scotland, had raised him to the bench as Lord Abbotshall, although they both despised the law's proclaimed adherence to that kittle principle, justice. That was the qualification.

It was not a bad record of worldly achievement but there was no doubt about it: what Sir Andrew called management and his enemies called corruption was an exhausting business, and he was no longer young. For years he'd stayed one step ahead of the pack, cajoling here, wheedling there, showing a palm of gold one minute and a fist of iron the next. Sometimes he could be charm itself in the council chambers; other times he would blow in like a gale, driving all opposition before him. Once he'd even had to organise a riot in the street outside the council windows to emphasise his opinion. After twelve successful elections to the provostship, Sir Andrew had had just about enough of Edinburgh.

And then, too, there had been the strained relationship with the Duke of Lauderdale, who'd been breathing down his neck on account of complaints about the competence, even the legality, of some of his decisions in the Court of Session. Finally, three years ago, Lauderdale had suggested that it was time to pull his finger from the fat pie of provostry, that his short stay on the bench must also come to an end, and that he should spend more time with his family at Kirkcaldy. The provost demurred. Lauderdale insisted, and Sir Andrew reluctantly resigned.

But as his glory days were fading, he liked nothing better than to recount them, to anybody who would listen. His son-in-law, John Lauder, who owed him much in terms of placement and preferment, usually had no option but to lend an ear. It was a source of satisfaction to Sir Andrew to have a lawyer on the receiving end of his reminiscences: as a judge he had been deaved with lawyers' arguments long enough in court, and their contempt for his ignorance was only matched by his hatred of their souple-tongued smugness.

Not that John was by any means the worst. That prize would have to go to his cousins the John Eleises, father and son. The father was in his sixties now, and not so active, but the son was even more offensive, a subversive do-gooder who seemed to show no fear of his betters in arguing against them in favour of outed ministers, rebels and witches. It was Eleis who, with his mentor Sir George Lockhart, had been a ringleader of the advocates in 1674, when forty-nine of them had been debarred from practising because they dared to insist that they could appeal to parliament against decisions made by the Lords of Session, in spite of a royal edict forbidding it. Sir Andrew, though he had by then resigned from the bench, had been outraged by the presumption of these meddling pleaders.

He could not abide the younger Eleis, who had even dragged John Lauder into the advocates' dispute. John had foolishly stood on a principle as one of the forty-nine, and had been banished out of town to Haddington for more than a year until a compromise was reached: without sufficient advocates, the procedures of the courts ground almost to a halt, and the forty-nine were grudgingly readmitted.

It was a great misfortune that John Lauder was infatuated with Eleis's devotion to the principles and process of law: it had got him into trouble and would do so again. Nevertheless, Sir Andrew was fond of his daughter's husband. He and Janet had been married nine years and provided him with five grandchildren to date. Lauder was only thirty, an open-minded, modest man who could yet be moulded.

The Lauders stayed in the Lawnmarket, a stone's throw from the courts. Sir Andrew's residence in town was also at the upper end of the hill, but it was not the power-house it had once been. He still made huge amounts of money from various bits of business, and his accounts showed that the Toun itself owed him nearly two thousand pounds in rents and other debts, but he was no longer the driving-force of municipal commerce and enterprise, and folk no longer queued for an audience with him. More and more, he was taking Lauderdale's advice and spending time at Abbotshall, across the Firth and away from the scenes of his past triumphs. A visit from his son-in-law, then, was not unwelcome, although it was fairly unusual. Their relationship was easy enough but there would always lie between them the shoogling-bog of their differences regarding the law. It was something they stepped around as a rule, to avoid an embarrassing slip on either side; especially on Sir Andrew's, since he had been so very bad at law and John was very good.

Today however it was John who was on the uncertain ground. He had come with a set of questions anent the Bass Rock and the black dogs that lay in it. He had been down in East Lothian often, sometimes visiting the Ramsay policies at Wauchton, and of course all the while he was in exile at Haddington the coast had been just a short ride away. He had seen the Bass stark in the great grey sea, but had not ventured across to it. The tide or the winds had always conspired against him. Now he was wondering about a trip to view the prison: 'Would my lord Lauderdale object tae my gaein ower, dae ye think? I wouldna want tae gie offence by speirin if it was only tae be refusit.'

'Whit for are ye wantin tae gang tae the Bass, John?' said Sir Andrew. 'The place is a midden o zealots. Ye're no seekin business frae ony o *them*, are ye?'

'Their business wi the coorts is by wi, I think,' said Lauder. 'But I would like tae see the place. It's a curiosity.'

'It certainly is. But ye micht no be wise tae disembark there, John. There's a touch o the rebel aboot ye, as I mind. Yince they had ye in the Bass, they micht no want tae let ye back hame again.'

It was a kind of joke, but he neither laughed nor smiled as he made it. He noted that his son-in-law was at least sensible enough to show some humility in response.

'I hae learned a lesson frae the advocates' affair, my lord. I canna pretend that we dinna differ on that maitter, but I am mair inclined tae compromise these days. I'd hae thocht that would be enough tae distinguish me frae the recusants and guarantee my return tae North Berwick.'

It was an even drier joke than Sir Andrew's. The older man grumphed.

'Weill, ye're probably richt. But it's a grievous dull place, John. There's naethin there but solans and sneevillers.' He reached for the decanter of brandy, refilled his own glass and poured one for Lauder.

'I'm tellt the birds are in such numbers that they're a marvel o nature, my lord. I would like tae see that, tae step amang them.' He cleared his throat. 'And mebbe, if I was there, I would tak anither keek at this fellow Mitchel, that's been the cause o such grief tae the Privy Cooncil. He's the only yin that still has a chairge hingin ower his heid, I think. Aw the rest has been convictit.'

'Mitchel,' said Sir Andrew, his brow lowering. 'A vile and dangerous fanatic if iver there was yin.'

'Aye,' said Lauder. 'That's whit I would like tae see – the worst kind o fanatic. There was hardly onybody got tae see him aw the years he lay in the Tolbooth, as ye ken. But I would like tae see him noo, him and Prophet Peden and the ithers. They hae a kind of philosophic interest tae me.'

'Ye philosophise ower much for yer ain guid, John. Ye may gang tae study Mitchel, but be assured he will study you harder. He will mark yer face in his een and yer words in his lugs and if ye dinna come up tae his impossible mark – which ye'll no, no bein a Gallowa Whig or an Ayrshire rebel – and he should iver win free o that place – which he'll no, if guid coonsels prevail, unless it's tae mak a journey tae the end o a short tow – he'll seek ye oot wi his pistols jist as sune as he's fired a better shot at his grace the Archbishop. Stay awa frae him, and ye'll no run that danger. Ye can dae nae guid there, and he can dae ye hairm.'

'His leg is destroyed by the boots, my lord, and his brain is hauf gane as weill, by whit I hear. He's no fit tae hairm onybody but himsel.'

'A wild beast is maist dangerous when it's caged,' said Sir Andrew. He had picked up his glass, and now, staring hard at Lauder, he brought it to his lips. He took a long, slow mouthful of brandy, the stare never shifting as the stem of the glass rose. With his round drink-bludgeoned face it might have been the blank look of a soft-brained bully, but the eyes were cold and hard like a bird's, and the large hooked nose was a bird's beak. He looked as though he had spotted something shiny in the dirt.

'Speakin o beasts,' he said, after swallowing noisily, 'wasna Mitchel an associate o that auld hypocrite Thomas Weir? Perhaps it would be interestin, eftir aw, tae see if he shared ony o his, eh, recreational tastes.'

'I imagine that connection's been explored,' Lauder said, 'by His Majesty's law officers. Onywey, Weir's been deid seiven year noo. There'll be naethin tae discover there, I doot.'

Sir Andrew regarded his son-in-law gravely. 'Ye had a terrible affection for Weir's sister, gin I mind richt. That's whit vexes me aboot ye whiles, John. Ye will get ower close tae bad company. Fanatics, witches . . .'

'I was hardly close tae Jean Weir,' Lauder said, his face reddening. 'I didna ken her at aw. I felt sorry for her. It was a bad business awthegither.'

'Major Weir the yaudswyver,' Sir Andrew mused. 'Dae ye mind we visited him in the Tolbooth? No a bonnie sicht . . . Even you wi yer odd sympathies, John, I think would find it no possible tae imagine hoo onybody could get pleisure oot o carnal relations wi a horse.'

'We're gettin waunert, my lord,' Lauder said.

But Sir Andrew was enjoying himself. 'In fact,' he said, 'hoo exactly dae ye manage it wi a muckle craitur like a horse? Ye could mebbe ask Mitchel if he kens. Dae ye get it tae lie doon, or whit? And when it's doon, hoo dae ye persuade it no tae get up again when it sees ye approachin wi yer dreid weapon furth o its scawbart? Or mebbe ye let the beast staun, and approach it wi a ladder. It's a mystery, is it no, John?'

Lauder smiled, to show that he was not too strait-laced to appreciate his father-in-law's humour. 'Aboot the Bass . . .'

'The Bass is nae langer mine tae say ye can or ye canna gang ower,' said Sir Andrew. 'That's Lauderdale's domain noo. Ma advice tae ye's this: bide in Edinburgh. Leavin it's nae guid for ye unless there's plague.'

'I thocht,' said John Lauder, 'that wi yer auld interest in the Bass ye micht hae speired o his lordship for me.'

'He's the Secretary o State, laddie. He's mair important maitters tae occupy him than issuin warrands tae would-be philosophers. Onywey, we're no sae chief as yince we were.'

'That may be true, my lord,' Lauder said, 'but surely it was by yer ain guid offices that the Bass fell intae his hauns? Athoot yersel, he wouldna hae it noo as a prison for the rebels.'

Sir Andrew sat back, wiping his mouth. 'Ye dinna want tae hear that auld tale again, surely?' But Lauder sat back too, nodding, while Sir Andrew, who could never resist reliving one of his greatest coups, stroked the tresses of his wig and got into his stride.

'Lauderdale owed me a favour. It's peyed noo, that's the difficulty. The Bass Rock was yin hauf o the bargain atween us, and the tither . . . weill, the tither was the port o Leith.

'Ye would only hae been nine or ten, John, so ye'll no mind this, but when Cromwell occupied us in the fifties, he fullt the port o Leith wi English and had a muckle fortress biggit there, a citadel they cried it, the object being baith tae hae English sodgers watchin ower us and tae set the place up as a tradin rival tae oor ain guid burgh.'

'Ye can still see bits o the stanework doon there,' Lauder said encouragingly.

'Aye, but they're scant, for it was maistly made o turf. Onywey, the English settlers wantit the port freed frae Edinburgh's grup, a thing that would hae had the maist grievous repercussions on oor finances. I hadna been a twalmonth in ma first term as provost, but I could see the only wey tae retain oor superiority ower Leith was tae invest in it. Cromwell's commander in Scotland was General Monk. I had the Cooncil gie five thoosan pund tae the construction o the citadel, and that satisfied Monk – I think he could see

Cromwell wasna lang for the warld, and that mebbe it would be silly tae lose aw favour wi us for the sake o a wheen English brewers and glessblawers. Sae naethin changed, and of coorse as sune as the young King wan hame at the Restoration the citadel was ordered tae be dismolished.

'But noo comes Lauderdale, His Majesty's new Secretary o State, upon the scene. He'd managed tae get the site o the citadel gien intae his chairge. He was fain o the auld plan and got a charter o regality tae raise Leith intae a burgh. It was a ludicrous notion – hoo could sic a clarty boorach be a burgh? – but Lauderdale had set his mind on it, sae it behooved me tae find a wey roon his plans, jist as I had afore wi Monk, or he would hae broke the trade o Edinburgh. Aw the duties on wines and ale that the Toun levied frae Leith my lord would hae acquired for himsel, and in my capacity as a public servant I couldna let him deprive us o oor richtfu taxes.

'Sae I says tae him, where's the sense in fallin oot ower a puckle bawbees? Ye want tae mak a profit oot o Leith – I'll spare ye the bother o administerin the levies, suppressin corruption amang yer officials and the like. I'll *buy* the citadel back frae ye for Edinburgh. And tae compensate ye for the loss o income, I'll gie ye a lump sum in lieu o the wine imposition. Ye'll walk awa wi yer pooches fou, my lord, I said, and Edinburgh will keep control o her ain destiny. There's no mony men that can speak sae free wi Lauderdale nooadays.'

John Lauder acknowledged this with a half-smile. 'How much was it again,' he asked, 'that Lauderdale wanted for being deprived o his livelihood?'

Sir Andrew laughed. 'Ay, he's *such* a puir man! Him wi a hoose in Lunnon and the estate at Thirlestane and land aw ower Scotland. He drave a reasonable bargain, John. Rich men can aye be civil wi each ither. I offered him sax thoosan pund for the citadel, and five thoosan pund for the levies, which was a generous sum, but worth it tae keep my lord sweet – sae he got eleiven thoosan pund aw tellt, no a bad income for nae labour.'

'The Toun wouldna been happy at peyin oot sic an amount?'

'The Toun didna hae ony choice,' said Sir Andrew. 'I *was* the Toun in thae days, John. Onywey, haudin the duties in oor grup was my priority. Wi the citizens' drouth and capacity for liquor, it didna tak lang for the Cooncil tae realise I'd made them a guid niffer.

'That was awa back in 1662, when the King was newly hame and there were debts and favours fleein aboot the country like a flock o stirlins. Aye, an plenty o scores tae be settled tae, eftir twenty years fechtin an sufferin under the kirk elders. I kept ma heid abune it aw when I couldna keep it ablow the dyke, John, an I advise ye tae dae the same in these troubled days – especially since ye hae Janet an the bairns tae think on tae, an no jist yersel wi yer high notions o the sanctity o law.

'I held ontae that favour eicht years, and there were times, I confess, when Lauderdale's position at coort wobbled a wee, when I thocht I michtna get the chance tae redeem it. But then the miscreant tendency began tae stir themsels again, and the government was lookin aboot for a siccar place tae lodge the rebel ministers and keep them awa frae the lugs o the ignorant. That's when the idea o the Bass insinuated itsel intae ma heid, and I went tae Lauderdale and offered him it. There it was, a muckle lump in the middle o the sea, wi an auld fort upon it – needin some repairs, of coorse – inaccessible but handy enough for Edinburgh, and wha should happen tae be in possession o it? Why, Sir Andrew Ramsay, Lord Provost o Edinburgh, that had gotten it as pairt o the lands o Wauchton frae a puir laird fawn on hard times. I niver would hae thocht the brichtest jewel o that inheritance would be an auld tooth stickin oot in the Firth, but there ye are.

'I reckoned ma income frae the Rock was nae mair than fifty pund per annum, and that was frae sendin lads ower tae lift the solans' chicks, but I tellt Lauderdale it could be doubled if there was a permanent garrison pit there, the birds managed on a proper basis, and sundry charges levied on whaiver micht be pit tae live in the place. Hoo muckle would ye want for it, says my lord? Oh, says I, no as muckle as I peyed ye for Leith, it's only a Rock eftir aw. But, I says, it's mebbe gotten a hidden value if it keeps the kingdom free o rebels. Oot o Scotland, oot o mind, as it were. Weill, Lauderdale took the hint. I'd been votin his wey in Parliament aw thae eicht years, and takkin maist o the ither burghs wi me forby. Weill, he says, suppose ye live tae be an auld man o ninety, that's nigh on forty years' income ye'd be losin. At a hunner pund a year, by your accoont? I'll ask the King tae gie ye fower thoosan pund for it. And he did, John, he did. Fower thoosan pund,' he finished hoarsely, pouring himself a fresh brandy, 'for a lump o rock, a flock o geese and a rickle o stanes that ye wouldna keep pigs in. At that price I didna even fetch back ma sheep – it would hae been ower pernickety, d'ye no think?'

John Lauder could not help admiring his father-in-law's grotesque self-confidence. He himself was always questioning – his own nature and motives, the accepted norms of daily life, the habits of individuals and of society. But Sir Andrew was like the Bass, a solid relentless rock in a swirling sea of change. He was beholden to him in many ways, certainly he could not afford to offend him, but there were times when he wanted to wring his fat neck. Just now though, he wanted his influence to clear him a passage to the Bass. And there was no motive that Sir Andrew needed to know of, other than the one he had given out loud: he wanted to see James Mitchel, the fanatic to beat all fanatics. He wanted to see what made him what he was.

'Will ye speak wi the Secretary o State then?' he asked. 'He kens me. He kens ma loyalty to the King. I would like to see the prison and cast an objective eye ower prejudice.'

It was a nice touch. Sir Andrew shrugged. 'John, ye're a guid lad, though ye whiles keep company I dinna care for. Yer cousin Eleis hasna pit ye up tae this, has he?'

'This is my concern alane, my lord,' said John Lauder. 'John Eleis has naethin tae dae wi it. It's mair than a week since I last spak wi him.'

'Then I'll hae a word,' said Sir Andrew. Then he seemed to change his mind. 'In truth, I hardly think it necessary tae fash Lauderdale wi sic a triviality. I can arrange it masel. They are ower lax wi the rebels and permit them parcels o food, letters and visits frae freens and faimly when the boat is sailin. There'll be nae restrictions, I would think, on an honest leal fellow like yersel.'

Lauder had not told his father-in-law the whole truth. It was correct that he had not seen his cousin John for a week: Eleis had been through in the west, where there was an ongoing outbreak of witchcraft, which had already led to a trial and some executions, and would probably be the excuse for more; he had gone to try to establish who or what was fanning the fire of accusation. But Lauder and he had discussed Mitchel in the past, and they had already arranged to meet later that day. Eleis was due back from Glasgow in the evening, and would meet Lauder at Painton's shop for some food and drink.

Painton's shop was half-full, but there was a table in a back-room where they could talk undisturbed over their ale. In fact, Lauder noted with some relief, there was enough noise in the place that they would not be overheard, if their conversation should turn on anything requiring discretion. With his cousin that was always a possibility.

Eleis was full of the witch alarm, which had been dragging on since before the winter. In October Sir George Maxwell of Nether Pollok, a noted anti-government man who had been fined and imprisoned several times for promoting conventicles, had fallen ill, complaining of pains in his side and shoulder, and suffering from terrible night-sweats. Around that time a lassie of thirteen or so, named Jonet Douglas, recently arrived in the area from the north, began to linger around the big house at Pollok. She was deaf and dumb, but managed to attract the attention of Sir George's three daughters, and told them by means of signs and drawing pictures that she knew what was causing his illness. She persuaded them to send two men with her to a nearby cottage. This was the home of a woman called Jean Mathie, whose son had been locked up some time before for stealing fruit from the Pollok orchard. They entered the cottage, and when the woman's back was turned, Jonet stuck her hand in at the lum and pulled out a little waxen image wrapped in a linen clout. She gave it to the men who carried it back to the laird's daughters. The wax figure had two pins stuck in the right side, and another down through the shoulder. They removed these, without saying a word to the patient, their father. That night he slept well again for the first time, without the sweating sickness, and the pains in his body slowly receded.

After a couple of days, when it seemed clear that his

recovery would be complete, his daughters told him what had happened. Jean Mathie was arrested and sent, protesting her innocence, to the Paisley tolbooth, where she was pricked for witchmarks, which were found in several places.

'I am scunnert o the haill affair,' said John Eleis. 'Sir George grew no weill again, as ye mebbe ken, at the start o the year, and you or I would hae pit it doon tae the rheumatics, or creepin age or some such thing. But this Jonet Douglas lass – who, mark this by the way, aw this while canna speak a word but seems tae ken Scots, English, French, Latin and a wheen ither leids when they're spoken tae her – discovers the auld wife's son John tae hae made a second doll oot o clay, and when they gang tae the cottage they find it where she tellt them tae look, ablow the bolster in his bed, wi three preens intil it. Noo they had kept the lass back at the door, sae she couldna be said tae hae laid the effigy there hersel, though it seems tae me she could easy hae been there in secret afore, she's that flittery and daunerin. Sae they cairry John and his wee sister Annabel tae Sir George's hoose, and tell him whit has occurred. And Sir George begins tae mend again.'

'Why the sister?' Lauder asked. 'Whit was her pairt in it?'

'Och, the usual thing, ye ken, when ye mix young lassies wi witchcraft. She's jist aboot ages wi Jonet Douglas, and had a fit o the hysterics, sae they thocht she was possessed. And eftir they had worked on her for a while, of coorse, they discovered that she *was* possessed.'

'By Satan?'

'By a muckle black man wi cloven feet cried Maister Jewel, if ye please. Satan by anither name. Her mither made her lie wi him for the promise o a new coat. And this Maister Jewel had been comin intae see John at nicht tae, throu the windae, wi a rabble o witches at his back, and John kent the witches for his mither and three neibour wifes. He confessed under examination and then aw the weemun were taen and examined and *they* confessed. Weill, except Jean Mathie, she said she was innocent tae the last. They were aw burnt at Paisley, John and the fower weemun, but the assize spared Annabel, in their mercy and wisdom.'

'Is it finished then?' Lauder asked. 'Or is there mair tae come?'

'Mair,' said Eleis. 'I'll no deave ye wi the details, but if there's a witch in aw the west country, it's the lassie Jonet Douglas. Sir George is seik again, and she's castin aboot for anither effigy tae find, and I doot she'll be successfu, for there's a tide amang the folk that's cawin her on. Oh, and here's a thing: she has her voice back. Suddenly she's able tae speak, and awbody's bumbazed. She disna ken how she gets the information aboot aw thae witches, she says it jist comes intae her. But no frae the Deil, mind – *she* has nae correspondence frae *him*. I wish the doctors would examine her insteid o the folk she accuses – the limmer's a richt wee miracle o intuition.'

'She's a gift tae the folk that want tae hunt witchcraft tae extinction,' said Lauder. 'That's the trouble wi it – ye canna cry the dugs aff yince their bluid's up.'

'Oor freen John Prestoun is slaverin at the bit tae be involved,' said Eleis. 'If it comes tae a commission, which I doot it must, Prestoun will be hankerin for a place on it.'

'He aye hankers,' said Lauder dryly. 'There's no an advocate like him for pleadin for himsel. He fell in fast enough wi the royal edict against appeals, and he has the same enthusiasm for findin lanely auld weemun and licht-heidit lassies tae be witches.'

'I hate these trials,' said Eleis. 'I wish I could keep awa frae them. But if I didna plead for the puir craiturs, there's gey few ithers would – no wi ony conviction, leastweys, for ye canna get a less popular panel than a witch – and the likes o Prestoun would hae a clear road tae drive them tae slauchter. There's an unpleasant mochness in the air this spring, cousin. That thick feelin afore the thunder breaks. I fear there may be a storm o witchery aboot tae burst upon us.'

'It may be a fierce summer then,' said Lauder. 'Ye'll ken better than I, but I hear the west is awash wi fanatics forby witches, that they haud their conventicles weekly on the moors, wi thoosans in attendance. Lauderdale's patience must be near whummelt. He claps the recusant ministers in the jyle, but there aye seems tae be mair tae rise and tak their places.'

'Like hoodie-craws amang the corn,' said Eleis. 'It's the Archbishop that's forcin that issue, though. Lauderdale, in himsel, disna care a docken where folk gaither tae worship, if they dinna threaten the stability o the land – that's ma opinion, though of coorse he could niver say as muckle. But St Andrews sees the field-preachins as a slight tae his ain authority, and has pushed and pushed Lauderdale tae act agin them. Sae the conventiclers cairry weapons tae their prayers noo, and there's some o them jist ettlin for a chance tae defend their cause frae the dragoons. Noo that's whit Lauderdale canna thole, for it threatens him, and sae ye're richt, John, skailt bluid will follow.'

'Lauderdale's no entirely innocent, surely,' Lauder said. 'Ye ken whit he's said in the past aboot drivin the people intae rebellion. That he wished they *would* rebel, so he could bring ower an army o Irish papists tae slit aw their throats.'

'Aye, aye,' said Eleis impatiently. 'And if the tortoise would only pit oot its heid, he would cut it aff. Rhetoric, man, pure rhetoric. Lauderdale innocent? – of coorse he isna. But St Andrews is the chief pot-stirrer, I assure ye.'

'I grant that the Archbishop detests the rebels – they remind him that he signed the Covenant himsel when he was plain Maister Sharp,' Lauder said. 'But sae did Lauderdale afore he was a duke. I dinna see that they're sae different.'

'Sharp disna unnerstaun the subtleties o keepin power – he simply feels if he's tae be primate o aw Scotland then aw Scotland must be thirlt tae prelacy and made tae honour and obey the bishops if they canna love them. Then he's surprised that madmen prefer tae shoot at them.

'Lauderdale, on the tither haun, has aye been a politician. He would shoot the odd bishop himsel if it would strenthen his grup on the country. I mind when the Act cam in for renouncin the Covenant, Lauderdale's enemies believed he wouldna be able tae stomach such a change o hert and would be forced oot. That was the wishin o bairns. They baith swure, him and Sharp, but it was Sharp that prevaricated, and Lauderdale that did it laughin, sayin he would sign a cartful o such oaths afore he would lose his place. Onywey, the point is this: if ye drive folk ontae the moors tae pray, ye mak them intae rebels as surely as the pricker's needle maks witches oot o auld hags.'

'Speakin o madmen and shootin at bishops,' said Lauder, 'I hae a mind tae visit the Bass. I was speirin ma guidfaither aboot it earlier. James Mitchel is the man I want tae see.'

Eleis raised his eyebrows. 'Caw cannie, man,' he said.

'Aye,' said Lauder. 'That's whit Sir Andrew said, mair or less. But Mitchel's politics isna ma interest. It's somethin else. Whit we were talkin aboot a minute ago.'

'Witchcraft?' said Eleis. 'Mitchel's clean o that at least. Folk o his persuasion are ten times harder on it than Sharp or ony Privy Cooncil commission, ye ken that. Hauf o them think Sharp himsel has Satan tae supper and hures and gambles the nichts awa wi him.'

'Aye, aye, and he can transport himsel atween St Andrews and Edinburgh through the air,' said Lauder.

'Weill, whit is yer interest in Mitchel, then?'

'John,' said Lauder, 'suppose I said tae ye that there was a controversy ragin in ma ain heid, that disna let me rest? Would ye say I was seik?'

'I'd say ye should tell me mair,' said Eleis with a smile.

'Look at us,' said Lauder. 'We share common views anent the law, and religion, and the state o the nation. We baith believe that the times will improve if oor ain ideas prosper – *we* are the progressive people o this age. But we canna aye *say* this, we must steik oor gabs tae be wise, and dae oor day's darg and no challenge the kirk, or the state, or some o the prejudices and enthusiasms powerfu men hae. Ye ken this is true – we canna change the wey folk think, but we can search oot a better wey o thinkin for the future.'

'Frae the man that's mairrit on Lord Abbotshall's dochter,' Eleis said, laughing, 'that must come frae the hert.'

'Bluid's thicker than law, in the case ye mention,' said Lauder wryly. 'He's a byordinar man. I canna deny I'm muckle obliged tae him, and that gars me bite ma tongue, but it wasna himsel I meant in particular.' He paused, trying to articulate what he felt. His cousin waited patiently.

'Dae ye mind when I was in France eftir I finished at the College? Twa years I was there, studyin the law, but the truth is, I learnt mair by bein in a foreign place than iver I learnt frae the lectures, whether in Poitiers or in Edinburgh. And it was life I learnt, no law. I gaed there as John Lauder, and I cam back as John Lauder, but it wasna the same fellow that wan hame.'

'Aye it was,' said Eleis. 'Ye were jist twa years aulder, and ye kent mair. Onywey, law *is* life. That's aw it is. And I was there in France afore ye, mind. Ye couldna live at Daillé's and come awa kennin less than ye kent when ye arrived.'

Both of them, when they had graduated, had gone abroad to continue their studies. They might have gone to the Low Countries or Germany, but instead they had been sent to France. Lauder had arrived in Poitlers with a letter of introduction from Eleis to a Monsieur Daillé, with whom he was to lodge. Daillé was a sad wee man, with a libertine for a wife. She was never home before him, and if he went away on business she'd hardly be home at all. She had a bairn of four or five that was supposedly a parting gift from another Scot, Will Douglas, who had been there at the same time as Eleis. Lauder had only to mention Douglas's name and Daillé would fall into a gloomy despondency, shaking his head and saying that, much though he liked the Scots, Mr Douglas was one that he could not think on with kindness. And yet he never admitted that the bairn was not his own.

Lauder laughed. 'Puir Monsieur Daillé, I had hauf forgot him. But ye keep divertin me, John. It's frae that time in France that I saw Scotland afresh. Ye gang awa and see yer ain land frae a distance, and ye see it better. Syne ye win hame and ye see the haill world in that new licht. But it's changin fast, cousin, changin even as we look at it. That's whit interests me. Mitchel, you, me, we're teeterin on the brink o time. I feel there are things that can be seen noo that mebbe in ten or twenty years folk winna be able tae see at aw. Oor minds are closin tae things because they're openin tae ither things, and I want tae see in baith directions.'

Eleis shook his head. 'I'm lost,' he said. 'Ye're speakin in riddles.'

Lauder said, 'A riddle is a means o disguisin a thing, syne when ye ken the answer ye see it in a different wey. That's jist whit I mean. There was a madman we heard tell o at Marseilles, that believed himsel tae be made o glass, and when folk cam ower close he would cry oot for fear they would break him. Sae his freens took a sand-glass and smashed it ower his heid when he was haein yin o his fits. He cried mair hideously than iver, that his heid was broken aw tae pieces. Syne when they had calmed him they showed him the sand-glass. The glass is broke, they tellt him, but ye arena broke. Ye canna be made o glass. And sae he had tae confess that that was the case.'

'Ye may break aw the glass ye like on Mitchel,' said Eleis, 'but ye'll no persuade him his leg wasna crushed in the boots. As for confessions . . .'

'He confessed tae shootin at Sharp,' said Lauder, 'when he was promised his life in exchange for the confession. Then he denied the confession in coort, because he didna believe they would keep the promise. But there's nae riddle there, that's a simple case o self-preservation. It's whit lies ahint that's harder tae fathom.' He seized the pitcher that stood on the table between them in both hands. 'You and I, we ken Scotland will go on wi or withoot Mitchel, wi or withoot Sharp. We're set tae inherit land frae oor faithers, we'll see oor faimlies settled on their estates and we'll prosper and grow auld because we dinna think the world's comin tae an end. But aw that is naethin tae a man like Mitchel. It's a delusion. This life and this world is naethin tae the glory he will inherit for keepin his covenant wi God and for bein yin o the elect. Noo, John, is he made o glass or are we?'

'Ask Mitchel if ye see him,' said Eleis, '– if he'll see you.' He looked serious. 'That's a dangerous question o faith, cousin. I ken ma ain answer. But you, you be careful who hears ye ask it.'

'I need tae see the things that are becomin invisible,' Lauder said. 'And Mitchel's the man I need tae show them tae me.'

'Why him?'

Lauder smiled. 'I need tae ask him aboot an auld acquaintance,' he said.

There was the world and there was a world that moved through it, beneath it: Lauder thought, walking home to the Lawnmarket, this is what we believe, now, at this moment. A day would come when human beings might forget the other world: or they might be taught to avert their eyes from it; to shield themselves from it. Then gradually people would unlearn fear, and believe only in the world they could touch and see, and they would assure themselves that this world was all they needed to know. But would they be right?

Lauder felt his intellect being torn asunder. One part of him yearned for a reality in which the only world was the one you woke to, the food you ate and the wine you drank, the objects you handled and the people you embraced. How much simpler life would be. Such a world would be a world of laws, not articles of faith; of reason rather than passions. Surely that was to be welcomed.

But another part of him feared what would be born of such an arrogant assertion of the knowledge of men. Just because you lost sight of ghosts did not mean they had gone. That was the argument of a John Prestoun, he realised, but there was more to it than that. Already he could see those who were most worldly in Scotland abusing power and despising law. They were happy to let the eyes of others go on seeing the visions and horrors of the other world. It served them well to have the populace believe what they themselves no longer believed. Witches were good fuel to keep the fires of ignorance burning. But this was not the rule of reason, it was the rule of subtlety and calculation. If these men were not deterred by the Covenant, a piece of law which bound the kingdom of Scotland and all that happened in it to the kingdom of God, why would they have any respect for mere human law?

And what if they, the worldly, had calculated too fast, too far? What if fanatics like Mitchel were right, and the Covenant could not be destroyed even if the paper it was printed on was? What if the Devil was still there, lurking in the shadows? Who then would be the wise and who the foolish? Who would be sane, and who made of glass?

Edinburgh, April 1997/October 1987

Carlin made his way north, across town. The traffic on Princes Street was quieter these days, since they'd banned cars and lorries from travelling east along it. But the pavement on the north side of the street was still as busy as ever: a massive battlement of shop-fronts, below which an army of shoppers and tourists were being constantly drilled by pipers stationed on every other corner. Some beggars and a larger number of *Big Issue* sellers had also taken up positions, and were tolerated or ignored like good Indians hanging around Fort Laramie.

Beyond Princes Street, in the New Town's Georgian grid, the atmosphere changed again. The brutal electronic beeping and printing of cash-registers and credit-card machines became more muted. The shops on George Street were more sedate, less desperate, more contemptuous of the public. If money talked on Princes Street, on George Street it gave a comfortable purr.

It was Friday. Carlin had been in the library again, reading another chunk of Lauder's *Secret Book*. He couldn't make up his mind about whether it was genuine, and MacDonald had not been around to offer his views. Carlin had had a look at some of Lauder's other writings, trying to pick out similarities and differences of style, spelling, attitude. The *Secret Book* contained plenty on Major Weir that seemed more considered, less certain, than the brief mention given in his *Journals*. That would suggest that they were not written by the same man. But then again, you'd expect a different emphasis, perhaps an opposite view, in something labelled 'secret'.

It was afternoon by the time he put the document back on reserve and walked down the Mound. He was heading for a refuge; an island of the Old Town which had somehow drifted north and settled itself off Charlotte Square. It was a pub, entered through a tiny front shop that was usually crammed with regulars, with a larger, drab room through the back which occasionally got half full in the evenings. Carlin would go there for a pint or two in the daytime, to sit alone in the back room and read, or just sit alone. He liked the fact that the barman never seemed to take offence at his lack of conversation, and that he always served a good pint. Although it was well out of his way these days, he also kept going back out of a weird sense of loyalty. The pub had done him a favour once.

There'd been a time when it had been much more than just a quiet place for him to sit in his own company. It had been a haven when he couldn't stay in the flat alone. He felt safe in the back room. He didn't have to do anything there, except decide whether to order another pint. By the end of the evening, he'd walk home up Lothian Road with a bellyful of beer, tired and drunk, and the worst thing he'd do to himself was fall into bed without drinking any water. He'd sleep off the bevvy and in the morning, or the afternoon, things wouldn't look quite so bad for a while. When they started to close in again he'd head back down the road.

There was a nagging question that he couldn't shift: what's the point? Such a small, loaded, insignificant, enormous question. He knew it was a cliché which people used to justify laziness, fear of change, inactiveness, suicide even. But it could also be a rhetorical put-down of all these. What's the point of wasting life, doing nothing with it, exiting it? The question ran round his mind, trapped like a metal ball in a pocket maze.

He'd worked in a bookshop for a couple of years. Every day he came down to the town centre and put in his shift. It was a time when bookshops were being revolutionised. In the seventies, when Carlin was first a student, Edinburgh's bookshops had closed on Saturday afternoons. Even when they stopped doing that they retained a slow, old-fashioned atmosphere. Then, in the eighties, the Waterstone's chain arrived from London and everything changed. Soon the bookshops were all opening on Sundays, and till ten at night through the week. Carlin didn't mind working the late shift: it wasn't so busy, and as for the anti-social hours, well, it was a long time since he'd been bothered by anything anti-social.

After work, or during his dinner hour, he'd sometimes nip round to the pub for a calming drink alone.

After a while he began to take his job personally. He liked experimenting with the stock he was buying for the Science Fiction and Horror sections he was put in charge of. He knew nothing about either but he was good at watching what moved fastest. He felt like he was playing with coloured bricks, building them up, rearranging them, stacking them in the best way to attract customers. It became a contest between him and the people that came into the shop, to see if he could outguess them as to what they wanted, make them buy things they probably didn't want at all.

The shop manager was impressed. He was also surprised, because Carlin hadn't exactly fitted the typical staff profile. He was non-communicative and morose with the other booksellers, and he looked all wrong – tall and ill-looking and unkempt, whereas the manager preferred his staff to be neat, healthy, smiley and female – but he was good at controlling his stock. The manager knew he was never going to promote Carlin. On the other hand, he could confidently leave him to get on with the job.

Which Carlin did. But somebody else began to interfere. At first Carlin didn't pay this person much attention. He would come in and wander through the shop three or four times a week, browsing, and eventually end up at the SciFi and Horror shelves. There were a few chairs scattered through the shop, and the guy would pull one over and sit down to dip into a selection of books in more detail. Carlin didn't have a problem with this. The guy looked down at heel and as though his days were long and empty; if he wanted to use the shop as a library that was fine. He never saw him buy anything but that was fine too. Sometimes Carlin would catch his eye as he went past, and the guy would look at him sadly with the expectation of one about to be moved on, as if Carlin was some kind of literary polis. Sometimes he'd ask the time, a feeble defensive mechanism. Carlin felt something for him: 'the guy'. He saw himself there, in another life.

But then he began to notice other things about him. He always carried a small rucksack. He seemed to have a constant cold which he kept sniffing back up into his head. His

78

vulnerable look, when Carlin saw it from a distance, and not directed at himself, became shifty and knowing. And now Carlin saw gaps on his shelves whenever the guy had been in. They were disguised sometimes – books were left facing out instead of spine-on, or laid flat on their backs – but there were definitely gaps.

The bastard was nicking the books.

Fuck it. They weren't Carlin's books. He quite admired the dexterity of it, and was surprised by his own naivety. People were always nicking books. Probably he should do something, tell the manager, tell the store detective when he saw her next. But Carlin hated the store detective, who was hired part-time from a security firm. She was vicious. She loved catching the obvious shoplifters. She caught a hippy once who had hidden a book about summer work abroad in his combat jacket: he couldn't afford it, but he needed it to find out about going to France for the grape-picking. He needed it to get himself a job, in other words. The hippy was a bear of a man, with a beard that half-covered his big placid face. He could have burst out of the place no bother, but he sat like a lamb in the store-room where they took shoplifters. Carlin was in there too – if the detective made an arrest she had to have a member of staff with her all the time as a witness – and at one point thought the hippy was going to start greeting. He got him a pencil and paper and told him to write down as much information about grape-picking as he could before the polis arrived. The man thanked him. When the polis came he thanked them too. The only person he didn't thank was the store detective.

If he told the manager, Carlin reasoned, he'd just tell the detective. So he'd leave it. It didn't matter. And yet Carlin found he couldn't ignore the situation. The job had got to him that much.

'I've got this dilemma. Should I shop a shoplifter?'

'How's that a dilemma? D'ye think folk should be allowed to break the law or no?'

'It's mair complicated than that. Folk arena perfect. Neither's the law. It's mair a question aboot masel.'

'How d'ye mean?'

'Ma sympathies lie wi the guy. I dinna ken him, or onythin aboot him. He disna cause ony bother in the shop, he jist nicks a few books wheniver he comes in. He looks like he's on somethin. Could be a junkie, needs tae pey for his habit, ken?'

'So let him get on wi it. If that's the wey ye're feelin.'

'Thing is, it's niver gaun tae stop if I dinna stop it. He'll jist keep comin in, I'll keep on re-orderin stock for him tae nick, it's pointless. It isna daein either o us a favour at the end o the day. He's beginnin tae bug me. I feel like I'm an accomplice.'

'Ye are. Ye ken aboot it but ye're daein nuthin.'

'Plus it's a pain in the arse. I canna keep the right stock in because o him. And I think he kens I ken, tae. It's like he's got me workin for him. It's like I'm his supplier.'

'And that's it, is it? Bleedin hert versus self-interest? Ye think that's a fuckin dilemma? Christ. How d'ye think ye'd cope in a real crisis? If this guy's a junkie, the fact that he's shopliftin isna even on his agenda. He's probably cleaned oot his granny's life savings and pawned his faither's gold watch by noo.'

'Aye, well, I've nae illusions that I'm tryin tae get him aff his habit or somethin.'

'Oh, thank the Lord in his infinite mercy for that. I'll tell ye whit ye have got illusions aboot though – reality. Same as the junkie, only he's got an excuse. Ye jist canna haunle it, can ye? Ye want tae get through life withoot engagin wi it. Ye're away wi the fairies, man. Don't come tae me wi this kinna crap. Bring me real issues, bring me the real world. Otherwise, forget it. I'm no interestit.'

Carlin turned his back and made a mock pout. That was him tellt.

Finally he realised who he had to speak to. Not the manager, not the store detective. He had to speak to the guy. The junkie. If he was a junkie. He found him in his usual place one evening when the rest of the shop was quiet.

'Got the time, mate?'

Carlin noticed the rucksack sitting beside his chair, its straps undone. He couldn't see inside it.

'Look,' said Carlin, 'I ken whit ye're up tae.'

The guy looked at him. 'Eh?'

'I'm jist warnin ye. Ye should quit while ye're ahead. Before ye get caught.'

'Whit ye talkin aboot?'

Carlin felt the skin on his shoulders coming out like hen's flesh. Surely the guy wasn't going to deny it.

'You know whit I mean,' he said.

'Na,' the guy said. 'I dinna. I'm jist sittin here mindin ma ain business – am I no allowed tae sit here or somethin?'

Carlin shook his head. 'Look,' he tried again, 'ye can sit there if ye want, but . . .'

'Aye?'

Carlin's head was filling with all the stuff they got told in training: you can't accuse somebody till they leave the shop with goods, you must be certain they've taken something and not paid for it, you must get another member of staff to witness you stopping the thief. If in doubt, leave it. What on earth had he been thinking of, to get into this? And how was he going to get out of it now he was being stonewalled?

The guy helped him out. 'I get it,' he said. 'Ye think I'm stealin the books, is that it? Is that whit this is?'

'I'm jist sayin, I ken whit ye're daein.'

'There's a lot o that in here, is there? The shopliftin?'

They stared at each other. The guy's eyes were a greyish blue. There was no depth to them, Carlin thought. It was like staring at an overcast sky reflected in two dubs in the road. He'd had a vague hope that if he could make some contact there the guy would have hung his head in shame, or something like it, and left.

'Well, is that it?' He was raising his voice now, trying to embarrass Carlin, trying to make him back down. 'Cause ye've got tae prove it before ye make that kinna accusation, pal, that's whit ye've got tae dae. So are ye accusin me of shopliftin?'

'I think you should leave,' said Carlin. 'That's aw I'm sayin.'

'Got tae have a reason,' said the guy. 'All I'm askin ye for's a reason. Is that so wrang?'

'I don't need tae give a reason,' said Carlin. He was cursing himself, wishing he could turn time back a few minutes.

'I don't think ye're being very nice,' said the guy. He stood up, and Carlin saw for the first time what a puny, insignificant, shilpit wee nyaff he really was. He was desperately thin and his hair looked like it would snap off in strands.

'I'm no gaun tae make trouble,' said the guy. 'But this isna right. I mean, are ye barrin me or whit?'

They began to walk towards the door together. Neither of them instigated this move, it just seemed to happen between them. They could have been two friends about to go for a pint. Carlin was thankful that the shop was almost deserted.

'Ye want tae check ma bag?' said the guy, shouldering it. It looked solid with whatever was inside it. 'Ye want tae see if I've got fuckin books in it?'

Carlin shook his head. They were almost at the door, he wasn't going to start another round.

'No,' he said, 'I dinna. I dinna want tae check it.'

'So how d'ye ken I'm stealin? If ye're no gaun tae check it?' But he made no effort to present the bag to Carlin. Carlin made no effort to look into it.

'I think ye're jist prejudiced,' said the guy, standing in the doorway. 'That's disappointin, a shop like this. I mean a fuckin bookshop. I thought anybody could come in here and read a book. But ye've got tae look the part, is that it? That's fuckin disappointin, pal, so it is.'

He held Carlin with his cloudy, shallow stare, then sniffed and hawked and landed a huge gob on the pavement in front of him. He got a few yards down the street, turned and shouted back, 'That's ma fuckin life, that!' He was slapping the rucksack with the palm of his hand, producing a heavy papery drumbeat. 'Ye've nae idea, have ye? Fuckin fascist bastart. This is ma fuckin life!'

Carlin waited till he was out of sight. He felt sick. He went back inside. The manager was approaching. 'Trouble?' he asked anxiously.

'No,' said Carlin. 'It's under control.' But he was shaking. And it wasn't.

For a week or so he thought he had made his life easier. The guy didn't come in the shop. The gaps stopped appearing on the shelves. The daily contest between Carlin and the rest of the public re-established itself. But then the space where the guy had been began to be as disturbing as his presence. Carlin was disconcerted by the empty chair beside the Science Fiction section. Nobody else seemed to sit in it now that he had gone. But that was absurd: the other customers didn't know about him; it wasn't his chair. And yet every time he came round the corner Carlin expected to see the hunched figure sitting there, with the rucksack on the floor and a pile of paperbacks beside it. The blank space constantly surprised him. Eventually he shifted the chair a few feet away, to break the pattern.

Then one evening the guy reappeared. Carlin was looking for a book for someone further up the shop, and his side-vision picked out the figure, bent over, reading on the chair, which was back in its customary position. Carlin shook his head and handed the book to the waiting customer, then looked again.

The guy hadn't seen Carlin, who slid back out of view so that he could watch him. It was late, just over an hour before the shop closed. As he watched, the guy checked up and down the aisle, flicked open his rucksack, lifted what appeared to be about half a dozen books off the floor and dumped them inside. Then he closed the rucksack and carried on reading.

Carlin was fired up, felt cheated. A flush of anger went through him. Right you bastard, he was thinking, try humiliating me on your way out the door this time. Try making me feel guilty on this one.

He had to get help. The deputy manager was on duty, but he was nowhere to be seen, had probably slipped out for a fly pint or something. There was a part-timer, a student called Alison, working at the back of the shop, in the children's department. Carlin had hardly spoken to her in the few weeks she'd been working. He went back there, watching the guy as far as he could.

'I need you for a witness,' he said. 'There's a guy aboot tae leave wi a bag full o books. Come on.'

She looked at him as if he were insane. 'What d'ye mean?'

'He hasna paid for them,' he explained. 'A shoplifter. He's been gettin away wi it for weeks, but I've clocked him this time.' Her eyes were wide with terror. 'It's awright, ye don't need tae do anything. Jist watch me. Jist be a witness.'

She followed him down the shop. Halfway there, Carlin realised he didn't want a witness. This was between him and the guy. He was about to tell her not to bother when he saw the guy hoisting his rucksack on one shoulder and standing up to leave.

Carlin caught up with him outside the door. He said, 'Right, pal, d'ye want tae come back in the shop till I see whit's in yer bag?'

He hadn't thought what he would do if the guy made a run for it, or lashed out at him. But he needn't have worried. The guy didn't look like he had the energy to do either. The rucksack slipped off his shoulder and Carlin caught it as it fell. He gestured to the door and the guy scuffed his way back in. Alison was right there. She pressed herself against the glass to let them by.

They went back to the store-room. Carlin indicated to the guy to sit down on one of the two plastic chairs. He opened the rucksack.

There were no Science Fiction or Horror books in it at all. Carlin felt sick, then, digging past a crumpled carrier bag, relieved. There *were* books. He pulled them out. Philosophy, religion, poetry, occult. All new. He must have gathered them from different parts of the shop. Thank God he was guilty. It didn't matter that the books were so different from the ones he'd expected.

'See this?' he said to Alison. She nodded, his witness. 'This is whit he's no paid for. Is that right?' he asked the guy, who looked on as if what was happening in the room had nothing to do with him.

'There's a phone number on the wall above the desk in the office for the polis station,' Carlin told Alison. 'Would ye gie them a call and ask them tae come doon for him?'

She nodded. Then she said, 'Can we no jist take the books off him and let him go?'

'No this guy,' said Carlin.

'Look at him.'

He smiled at her. 'Sorry. This guy's been pissin me aboot.'

'It's nearly nine,' she said. 'Will they not take ages?'

'I'll wait wi him,' said Carlin. 'They'll no be long.'

They were ages. Alison was needed on the shop-floor. The guy stared into space. Carlin pulled the other chair over and sat on it, reading the backs of the books.

The guy sniffed. Carlin glanced at him, anxious for a moment, but it was all right. His eyes were too dead-looking for tears to come from them.

'Gaunae let us go, pal?' the guy said. 'Otherwise, tell ye, I'm fucked, I'm finished. This is ma fuckin life.'

'Too late,' said Carlin. 'The polis are on their way.'

'That's me then. Finished.'

'Should hae thought aboot that before,' said Carlin. 'I warned you the other day, mind?'

The guy gave a sort of laugh. As if he could mind the other minute. Sniffed again. The sniffs were very loud in the store-room: they slapped around the breeze-blocks of its walls. It was hot in there too.

'Can I get a drink? Some water?'

Carlin needed a drink himself. He went to the door, called to Alison. 'Could ye get us some water?'

He held the door open till she returned from the staff-room with two paper cups of warmish tapwater. 'No sign o them yet?' he asked, taking the cups from her.

'No.' She wouldn't make eye-contact. Carlin knew she was offended by what he was doing.

He closed the door and handed one of the cups to the guy. Then he sat down and read the blurbs again, one after the other. Single copies of books that would have no resell value. No football, no Stephen King, no Terry Pratchett. Were the books for himself then?

The guy had knocked back half the contents of the paper cup. Now he put it on the floor and pulled a small packet from his pocket. Carlin saw foil. The guy began to tear at the foil, breaking out wee white tablets.

'Whit's that?' said Carlin.

'Mind yer ain fucking business,' the guy told him. He shoved a few of the tablets in his mouth, and carried on breaking more out.

'Whit are ye daein?' said Carlin.

'Whit d'ye fuckin think, ya wanker.' It wasn't a question.

He stuffed another handful of the pills in.

'Christ, whit are they?' Carlin demanded. 'That's no a guid idea, pal.'

'Na it's no, is it? Should hae fuckin thought aboot that before though, eh?' There was a thick slimy froth on his lips now. Carlin minded when he was a kid, lying submerged in the bath and speaking through the water. The guy's voice sounded like that.

The guy gulped down the rest of the water. 'Can I get some mair?' he said, holding the cup out.

'No, I don't think so,' said Carlin. 'I dinna think . . . ye shouldna be takin these, man.'

'Jist get us some fuckin water,' the guy shouted. Carlin jumped up. What was he supposed to do? Make the guy throw up? Phone an ambulance? Maybe the pills were nothing, it was just another con. To blackmail him into letting him go.

The guy said 'water' again. His mouth hung open. Carlin thought of when you take your breeks out of the wash and find you've left a wad of tissues in the pocket. He went for the water.

When he came back a minute later the guy was slipping down on the chair. He was having difficulty keeping his eyes open. Carlin wondered, whatever he's swallowed, can it take effect that quickly? He didn't have a clue. And then he thought, what else has he got in his system already? He touched his shoulder. No response. He shook him. 'Here's yer water, mate.' The guy rolled towards him, came awake. He took the cup in his hands and drank from it. 'Thanks, pal,' he said.

Long minutes passed. Carlin watched the guy falling, sitting up, falling. 'Come on for Christ's sake,' Carlin said. 'Come on.'

The door opened. It was Alison. Behind her stood two uniformed policemen. They walked in past her. One of them curled his lip at Carlin, then realised he wasn't the shoplifter.

'Aye,' he said, covering himself with a curt nod. 'This him then, is it?' He pointed at the guy, who was almost on the floor.

'Aye,' said Carlin. 'Look,' he said, 'he's taken something.

He asked for water and then he stuffed aw these pills in his mooth.'

'How long ago?' the polis asked.

'Five minutes, mebbe ten,' said Carlin. He reached over and took a strip of foil from the guy's fist. There was writing on it but it was hard to read. It was covered with stringy white slavers.

'Here, you want tae watch yersel,' said the polis. 'Dinna get that on yer fingers. These bastarts can be carryin every bloody disease.'

'Canna be too careful these days,' his mate said. 'Whit's his name?'

Carlin shrugged. 'Dinna ken. Never got that far.'

But he'd had time. There'd been time to ask questions, and all he'd done was read the backs of the books. Hadn't thought about a name for the guy.

The second polis got down on his hunkers and shook the slumped figure. 'Right, then,' he said loudly. 'Wake up, son. Can you hear us, John?'

There was a groan. That was about it.

The polis stood up, turned and got out his radio. 'Think this boy's gaun for a hurl,' he said. 'Get himsel pumped oot.' He spoke into the radio, requesting an ambulance.

The first polis shook his head at Carlin. 'Shouldna have let him take thae pills,' he said.

'Whit was I supposed tae dae?' Carlin said. 'Fight them affae him?'

'Aye, right enough,' said the second one. 'It's no your job is it?' He tried to rouse the guy again. 'Hih, John, gaun tae come oot o that?' But by now there was no response at all.

The first polis flicked through the wee pile of books. Nietzsche, Ouspensky, Crowley, Huxley, James Thomson. 'Is that whit he nicked?' he asked, looking contemptuously at Carlin.

Carlin knelt beside the figure on the chair. 'Come on,' he said. Don't die on us.' He picked up the guy's stick-like wrist, tried to find a pulse. 'Christ,' he said. 'D'ye think he's still there?'

'Dinna ken,' said the second polis. 'Hard tae tell.' They both began to pinch and shake the figure. 'Come on, John.

Wake up, John. Come on.' Carlin felt something swirling and draining away in the pit of himself. They weren't going to reach him. How would you pay attention if it wasn't your name being called? He rocked back on his heels. He said, 'If he'd jist be sick or somethin. Can we make him sick?'

The paramedics arrived. They checked him out, went back for a stretcher. 'Ye still wantin us tae charge him?' the first polis asked Carlin. 'I mean, we're gaun tae have tae go wi him tae the hospital, see if we can find oot who he is.' He touched the pile of books. 'We'll need tae take these as evidence, write oot a list tae say we've taken them, get a statement fae you and the lassie . . .'

One of the paramedics said sharply, 'Well, we're getting oot o here now, whitiver you decide, or he'll no be appearin in any court, gaun tae the jyle or gaun hame tae his mither.'

Carlin said to the policemen, 'Forget it. Leave the books. It's no worth it.' To the paramedic he said, 'Where are ye takin him?'

'The Royal. How, ye gaunae send him flooers?'

They carried him out. The polis took Carlin's name, then put away their notebooks and radios and picked up their hats. 'End of story, then,' said the first one.

The other one clapped Carlin on the shoulder as they left. 'Happens aw the time,' he said. 'But whit can ye dae, eh? We see it every day. Every day.'

The shop was empty, except for the few staff who were cashing up, locking the doors, tidying away bags of rubbish. The deputy manager walked in from the street, wiping his mouth on his sleeve. 'All right, folks?' he said cheerily.

Carlin felt the polis's handmark burning through his shirt. He took the guy's books and distributed them back to their correct places.

Alison passed him with her coat on, heading for the exit. 'Hope ye're proud o yersel,' she said. He didn't answer.

He headed round to the pub. A pint and a dram. A pint and a dram. A pint and a dram. As they went down the words were swirling in the tilt of the glasses. *Proud o yersel. Proud o yersel. Proud o yersel.*

When he stumbled back to the flat, hours later, and looked at himself, haggard, bubbly, wretched, the mirror was silent.

In the morning, he walked to the nearest phone-box and called the infirmary. He wanted to check on somebody admitted last night, he said. He gave the details: picked up by ambulance, about ten, the address. No, he wasn't a relative, he didn't know the man's name. He worked in the bookshop. He was just concerned.

'Hold on a minute,' the receptionist said.

He held the receiver under his chin and closed his eyes. He heard the breathing he made below the hiss in his lug. He felt himself slump against the news he knew was coming.

'Hello,' said the woman.

'Hello.'

'Did you say you were a relative?'

'No,' he said, 'I was workin in the shop where he was . . . where he was picked up. I was jist wonderin.'

'We don't know who he is yet,' she said. 'That's why I asked.'

'Oh,' he said. 'Then . . .'

'No,' she said. 'He didn't make it. Sorry.'

Carlin sat in the pub. Nine years gone and only the posters for Fringe shows were different. Nothing had changed. Everything had changed. How could it not have after that night? He'd brought an anonymous man to a small hot concrete cell and sat with him while he overdosed and died. He'd handed over the water to help the pills go down.

He still saw the guy. Sometimes he was lying in a shop entrance. Sometimes he was fucked out of his head in Princes Street Gardens, the Meadows, Calton Hill. Sometimes he was old, sometimes younger. He'd seen him just a week ago. This time he was a big fellow, tall and strong-looking, slumped against the railings of St John's Church at the West End. Two polis, a man and a woman, were standing beside him. A polis van was pulling up alongside. The two officers were snapping on plastic gloves.

Carlin had handed in his notice at the shop. He'd had holidays due. He went sick for a week. Never went back. He became a regular fixture in the pub. One day, on his way to or from it, he couldn't be sure which, he realised he hadn't called his mother. He did this once a week, an obligation, to check that she was all right. He stopped at the first phone box he came to.

The voice that answered sounded like his mother's, but it wasn't. It was her sister. 'Andra,' she said, as soon as he spoke. 'Ye'll need tae come hame. Yer ma's no lang for this world, son.'

He sobered up on the train, but he'd have been better taking a carry-out. By the time he reached Stirling he felt dreadful: sore head, bones, belly, everything. His aunt's husband met him on the platform. They had to take a taxi straight to the infirmary, he told him. She'd been dwining away all afternoon.

They got there ten minutes too late. His mother looked tiny and unreal in the bed. He put the back of his hand to her parchment cheek and was surprised at the feathery feel of it.

'Did she say anything?' he asked his aunt.

'Aye. She sat up and asked for yer faither. That was aboot three oors ago. Since then, naethin.'

'Whit did she say?'

'She said, is that Eddie? Quite loud, like that. Like she was in a panic, feart or something. Mebbe she seen him, I dinna ken. I calmed her doon, I says, dinna fret Mary, there's naebody here but us. She was quite placid eftir that. Lay back doon and niver said anither word.'

Of the two deaths, the one that left him most bereaved was the guy's, the junkie's. He started to think of him as John because he couldn't bear the anonymity. His mother was old and had been dying for years. He didn't know what age John had been. He guessed about twenty-five. Younger than himself, for sure. That was the thing. When you saw someone go out of the world before their time, it was like death tapping you a reminder – *This is ma fuckin life!*

For months the mirror gave him nothing. When finally it did, it mocked him. 'Don't fuckin kid me ye're grievin for Johnny lad. Who was he onywey? Jist a junkie. So yer mither'd been dyin for years, that cunt was dyin frae the day he was born. And awright, you gied him the water but ye didna gie him the pills or aw the ither shite he had jaupin aboot in his system.

'Forget him.'

Bass Rock, April 1677/Edinburgh, December 1666

James Mitchel was trying to persuade himself that he did not miss freedom. He had to keep telling himself that freedom was nothing, that even in a filthy prison on a barren rock you could be as free in the love of Christ as you could be anywhere. He remembered Samuel Rutherford again, writing from Aberdeen exile: *I have learnt not to mourn after or seek to suck the world's dry breasts. Nay, my Lord hath filled me with such dainties that I am like a full banqueter, who is not for common cheer.* He wished he had Rutherford's conviction. He wished he had Rutherford's poetry in his own heart. He wished he had the book of letters by him: it had been a great source of strength in the years of his own exile and wandering through the world. He could still mind other phrases: *The world is not my home, nor my Father's house; it is but his foot-stool – let bastards take it ... The greatest temptation out of hell is to live without temptations ... Faith is the better for the free air and the sharp winter-storm in its face ... Grace withereth without adversity ... Now I say to laughter, 'Thou art madness'.* When he turned these words over in his head they were like names on a map of his own life.

Rutherford had been a leading light of the General Assembly of 1638, the mighty Glasgow Assembly which threw out the bishops and re-established Presbyterianism. For two years before that he had been banished from the Lowlands to Aberdeen, forbidden to preach publicly because of his attacks on the Englishman Laud, him that had tried to force the prayer book down Scotland's thrapple. Rutherford had sent a stream of inspirational letters to his friends and supporters from the grey north. It was these that had been gathered into a book after his death.

Mitchel had met the man who had published it. His name was Robert MacWard and he had for a while been

Rutherford's secretary. After the Restoration settlement in 1661 which brought the bishops in again, MacWard had been imprisoned and then driven abroad. He had settled in Rotterdam, a refuge and a glowing forge for holiness. That was where Mitchel had met him, ten years ago. MacWard was as fierce a saint as any. He had been patronising, almost dismissive of Mitchel, and would doubtless have forgotten him entirely by now if God had not chosen him to be the instrument of his wrath. James Mitchel, the slow, the weak-minded, the stickit minister – raised from obscurity by the design of God. Mysterious and wonderful his ways! None of them would forget him now – not one of them.

His leg felt better today, but he was not allowed out to walk on the Rock like the others. He was still the subject of a stricter regime. Some days the soldiers let him sit outside, but on others – it seemed to depend on how vindictive the garrison captain was feeling – he would be left in his cell, deprived even of a few minutes' proper daylight, and this was very hard to thole.

Some of the private soldiers had become friendlier to him. He was not a minister, he was a man of action, and they admired that. They admired the fact of his torture too: it raised him in their eyes. They would offer him tobacco, and sometimes if the officers were not around they would sit in his cell and smoke with him. This was ironic. Before his imprisonment he and Elizabeth had run a stall selling spirits and tobacco in Edinburgh, and she still did. It was their only source of income, and if she had been allowed onto the Rock she could have kept him and the soldiers well supplied. But he had not seen Elizabeth for fifteen months: even when held in Edinburgh he had, by the orders of Sharp, been denied all visitors.

The soldiers wanted to hear about the assassination attempt, but Mitchel was careful to say little on that subject, and certainly did not admit his own part in it. For all their friendliness, it was possible they were being paid to extract information, so that later they could be used as witnesses against him. But he had no objection to talking about it in general terms. After all, he had never denied that he'd been in Edinburgh on the day, 9 July 1668. On the contrary, he told them, he had been one among the crowd who searched for the attacker.

The soldiers hated the Bass at least as much as did those they guarded. They did not care about the rights and wrongs of religion, and so had no reason to practise the patience of martyrs. The place was a hell-hole and anybody who said otherwise deserved to be rotting in it. They did not understand the ministers' relative calmness. Of course, even as prisoners the ministers had a better life than the soldiers. Some of them had servants with them; they were sent food and messages of comfort from Scotland; their families received support from loyal congregations. The soldiers, on the other hand, had nothing. Their boots leaked, they had rotten teeth and little money. They feared their captain, and were indifferent to their prisoners. All that was certain in their life was the constant cry and stench of the solan geese.

One of the soldiers, an old veteran called Tammas, had been a member of the Edinburgh Town Guard in the sixties. Mitchel had a vague feeling that he knew his face. At first this made him extremely wary, but as time went on he realised that if Tammas had ever seen him before he either did not remember or did not care.

Tammas was ugly beyond redemption: he had two lower teeth sticking up like fence palings at the front of his mouth, and one or two others still serviceable at the back. His nose had been broken so often that it seemed to have no bone left in it at all: a battered auld neep gone soft in the middle of his face. His cheeks had been badly marked by a pox of some kind. Between the pits and sores reddish hair grew in feeble patches.

'I kept watch ower the Archbishop's hoose when the rebels cam oot the west in the year '66,' Tammas told him. 'The rebels – or whitiver ye'd cry them – that mairched frae Dumfries tae the Pentlands, and wis bate by mad Tam Dalyell the Muscovite.' He pointed his pipe at Mitchel. 'Ye wouldna hae been mixed up in thon, would ye?'

Mitchel shook his head. The gesture was not quite a lie. It had been late November, grey, wet and miserable. He had ridden out from Edinburgh to join the tiny Covenanter force – you could not have called it an army – and had actually spent the night before the battle in the field with them. But in the morning, against all his protestations, he had been sent back to the town with sealed messages for certain parties. He never knew what was in those messages: by the time he had ridden round the government troops, and before he could deliver the letters, the news that Dalyell had routed the insurgents after a fierce engagement was racing through the streets at his heels. He burnt the letters and wondered what to do next.

'That auld bastart Andra Ramsay was feart that somebody would hae a crack at pistollin Sharp or cuttin his thrapple, and he would get the wyte for no lookin eftir him,' said Tammas. 'So ye michtna hae been the first tae try it, and ye'll no be the last,' he added, trying to catch Mitchel's eye. 'Onywey, we was ordered tae staun watch on the street ootside his hoose aw nicht, in case o an attack. In November, man! The only yins that was gaun tae be deid in the mornin was us, wi the cauld. Sae we kept oorsels warm by raisin an alarm ivery hauf an oor. It was "Staun tae!" and "Haud, or I fire!" aw nicht. The bishop was fair dementit atween want o sleep and fear o bein murdered in his bed. Eftir the first couple o nichts he gaed up tae the castle and lodged there insteid.'

Dalyell had brought the captured Covenanter remnant in from Rullion Green, and his troops had roamed through the town, hunting out sympathisers. Mitchel's name had somehow got on the wanted list. In growing horror he watched from the shadows as men known to him from Galloway and elsewhere were brought before the courts, found guilty of sedition and armed rebellion, and condemned to death. Through the first two weeks of December the town pulsed with a terrible excitement. On the seventh the first ten condemned men were hanged on a single, groaning cross-tree at the Mercat Cross in the High Street. The crowd was muted, sullen. They knew that many of the defeated Covenanters had been armed only with heuks and graips and whittles. The bodies were dismembered and the heads sent back to be stuck on the gates of their home towns in the west. Their ten right hands, which had been raised in solemn oath when the Covenant was renewed at Lanark, were sent to adorn the roof of the tolbooth there. On the fourteenth a second batch of prisoners was executed.

'Man, thon was fierce times,' Tammas continued. 'There was mair bluid in the syvers than ye'd see on a mercat day. They werena aw hingit, of coorse. There was some puir bastarts that set oot tae walk jist frae Dumfries tae Edinburgh that niver stopped till they reached Barbados. Ye'd hope they were the lucky yins but I mind thinkin ye couldna get closer tae hell than a passage in the kyte o a plantation ship. I hadna seen this place in thae days, richt enough. But it was worse for ithers. There was a young minister, a fell guid-lookin man, that aw the women were grievin ower, that wis pit tae the boots afore he was killt –' Tammas broke off in midflow and stared guiltily at Mitchel's leg. 'Christ save us, I'm sorry, sir.'

Mitchel excused Tammas with a wave of his hand: the profanity offended him more than the talk of torture. 'Hew McKail,' he said. 'The minister was cried Hew McKail. If iver there was a saint, it was him.'

Tammas nodded. 'The womenfolk doted on him, if that's a sign o haliness,' he said thoughtfully.

Not just the womenfolk. Mitchel had mingled in the crowd at the Mercat Cross to see him die. McKail was twenty-six, just a few years younger than himself, and a brilliant, enigmatic preacher. Ill health had kept him from being in the field at Pentland, but his reputation as a relentless critic of the government made him far more dangerous than any cottar with a heuk. He was arrested trying to return home to Lanarkshire, brought to the capital and tortured for information on other insurgents. Refusing to co-operate, he was sentenced to die on 22 December. A plea was lodged for clemency, but there would be no mercy for a man who, in a sermon preached at St Giles, had referred to the King as an Ahab on the throne, and to James Sharp as a Judas in the kirk.

Six men were to die that day. At their last meal in prison, McKail had encouraged their appetites: 'Eat to the full, and cherish your bodies, that we may be a fat Christmas pie to the prelates.' News got around Edinburgh fast at such times. When McKail appeared on the scaffold, white-faced and dragging his ruined leg behind him, half the people gathered there already knew the joke he had made the night before, when asked if he was in pain: 'Oh,' he had replied, 'the fear of my neck makes me forget my leg!' Now it seemed as though the entire world fell silent as it watched him struggle to keep upright. Here was a man going to his death and already like an angel. Women began to greet and there was a rumble of anger through the crowd, but McKail held up his hands and the people fell silent.

The crush in the street was oppressive; every window overlooking the scaffold was packed with faces. The Privy Council had placed McKail on the greatest stage he could have wished for. Mitchel felt he would faint like a woman at the passion and simplicity with which the condemned man addressed the crowd. He would speak no more with flesh and blood, he said, but begin his intercourse with God, which would never be broken off. He would bid farewell to his father and mother and to his friends, farewell to the light of the sun and the moon, and enter into eternal light, eternal life and everlasting love and glory. He pulled himself up the ladder with difficulty and then spoke again:

'This is sair work, friends, but every step on this ladder is a step closer tae Heaven.' His voice faded a little and some of his next words were lost in a new sound; a swelling, pro-longed groan, that Mitchel realised was coming from himself and from the people round him. 'Welcome sweet Jesus Christ,' McKail was saying, almost singing, 'welcome blessed Spirit of grace, and God of all consolation! Welcome glory! Welcome eternal life! Welcome death!' The crowd was now ecstatic in its anguish. Men and women alike were sobbing and holding up their hands to the figure on the scaffold. There were soldiers in solid ranks around the platform, and their officers looked terrified at the effect McKail was having. But McKail had finished. He gave a sort of wave and turned to the rope. A minute later he was swinging like a sack of straw from the gibbet. A man positioned below him jumped up and clung onto his legs. There was a dreadful choking sound, then silence, but the man held on for as long as he could, like one insect trying to mate with another. Mitchel recognised him as a cousin of McKail's. He would have paid the hangman to allow him in close, to speed young Hew on his way to Heaven.

Mitchel left the Grassmarket with tears streaming down his cheeks. He made no effort to hide his face, although he was probably safe enough – if the troops had tried to make any arrests there would have been a riot. He was transfixed by what he had seen. McKail had been noble, visionary. It was as if he had left his broken body even as he steered it up the ladder, and was flying like a dove into Paradise. Mitchel was in awe. Mitchel was in admiration. Mitchel was jealous.

He wanted what McKail had. He wanted that purity of vision, that transcendence. He wanted the adoration of the crowd. But you would get these things not by deception or manipulation. As with McKail, they would come through faith, devotion to the cause, and through clarity of purpose.

Mitchel was no preacher. In his heart he knew it. He had struggled for that gift but he could not unleash the rivers of prayer that had gushed from the lips of men like Rutherford or McKail. God must not mean to speak through him in that way. Then how? Through deeds, perhaps, not words.

And it came to him then as he walked away, outpacing others from the crowd, with the very certainty he had always lacked: not his tongue but his arm would speak for Christ. *O Lord, I know that the way of man is not in himself: it is not in man that walketh to direct his steps.* God had led him by his own mind's wanderings to the answer. God had brought him to the scaffold, to watch McKail's beautiful death. What for if not to show him the true path? What better purpose could there be than to be the instrument of God's vengeance? And who better to avenge than sweet Hew McKail?

He had been flitting between the houses of different sympathisers in the town, staying just for a night or two before moving on again. He had almost nothing in the world: a small amount of money, a change of clothes, his Bible and *Joshua Redivivus*, the title under which Samuel Rutherford's letters had been published two years earlier. He was aware that those who were giving him shelter were increasingly nervous of his presence. An act of council had been issued by the government, listing disaffected persons and concluding:

We command and charge our lieges and subjects, that none presume to reset, supply or intercommune with any of the foresaid our rebels, nor furnish them with meat, drink, house, harbour, or victuals; nor any other thing useful or comfortable to them; nor have any intelligence with them by word, writing, message, or otherwise, under the pain of being repute and esteemed art and part with them in the crime foresaid, and to be pursued therefore with all rigour.

Most of the men named as rebels by the government had left Edinburgh days or even weeks before. It was time for him to follow. He went back to his tiny room in the Potterrow to gather his possessions.

He sat on the narrow bed and took out Rutherford's letters. They had been printed at Rotterdam, a sanctuary for the righteous, and Mitchel at once resolved that that was where he would go. He let the book fall open and read from the first sentence he focused on: *Woe is me for the day of Scotland! Women of this land shall call the childless and miscarrying wombs blessed. The anger of the Lord is gone forth, and shall not return, till he perform the purpose of his heart against Scotland. Yet he shall make Scotland a new and sharp instrument having teeth to thresh the mountains, and fan the hills as chaff.*

A new and sharp instrument! Sharp. Mitchel believed in signs, and this was another. First Rotterdam, now Sharp.

He lifted the Bible. He did not have quite the confidence to let it fall open anywhere, and stopped to think what to do. If there was to be a further sign, how would God lead him to it? By a path he already knew, surely. He chose the Old Testament, and the Book of Psalms. He looked on the last page of Psalms. He looked at the second last Psalm. Yes, God had guided his memory there: *Let the saints be joyful in glory: let them sing aloud upon their beds.* And there he was – upon his bed! *Let the high praises of God be in their mouth, and a twoedged sword in their hand; to execute vengeance upon the heathen, and punishments upon the people; to bind their kings with chains, and their nobles with fetters of iron; to execute upon them the judgment written: this honour have all his saints.*

Tammas was shaking him. 'Maister Mitchel? Are ye richt, sir?'

He came back to where he was: in the Bass, with Tammas's

repulsive divoted face inches away from his own. The cell was full of tobacco smoke.

'Aye,' he said. 'I was in a dwam. I'm fine.' But his leg was pounding again.

Tammas was called away by another soldier. A boat was coming over from North Berwick, with several folk in it, and he was required to assist with the landing. He pulled to, but did not lock, the door behind him.

Left alone, Mitchel slipped back into the past again.

That year-end of 1666, he had left Edinburgh with a chastened but uplifted heart. The picture always before his eyes was that of Matthew McKail dropping to the cold earth as he slid from the corpse of his cousin Hew, once the last breath had left him. Matthew had gone to the hangman John Dunmore's house the night before, and paid him six dollars and a few drinks to let him take the corpse. He had lain motionless for a moment, as if he also were dead, then got to his feet and tilted his glistening face to heaven. His fists were clenched and raised and it was as if he had taken some of Hew's strength and been reborn with it. Mitchel imagined a caption under that picture, or a banner of words coming from Matthew's mouth like those he had seen printed in pamphlets: *The king of Babylon hath devoured me, he hath crushed me, he hath made me an empty vessel, he hath swallowed me up like a dragon; BUT THE VIOLENCE DONE TO ME AND TO MY FLESH BE UPON BABYLON, SHALL THE INHABITANT OF ZION SAY.*

Mitchel left the house in the Potterrow when the long night closed itself around the town, and walked in a little way, down Candlemaker Row to the Cowgate. From here, having checked that he was not being followed, he slipped into the warren of closes that lay in the elbow of the West Bow, passed into a tiny court, and mounted a set of steps to the house of Major Thomas Weir. He chapped gently but persistently on the door. The Major had helped him in the past. He must beg his assistance one further time.

The door was let open a crack.

'Is he in?'

Jean Weir, the Major's sister, held a lamp up to him, and he lifted his hat from his face so that she could see who he was. She stepped back.

'Is it you, James Mitchel? Aye, come in. He is here. We are baith here, lamentin that puir broken laddie.'

He followed her in. The house was warm against the bitter night. A fire blazed in the main chamber, and the Major had drawn a chair in close, and was contemplating the flames. His big nose and pale brow shone in the firelight but his eyes were dark.

Even seated and unprepared for a visitor, Thomas Weir was an impressive presence. He was a man of straight lines, from his long face, protruding nose, and the strands of fine grey hair that hung from his head, to the bony angularity of his body. His thin white fingers trailed over the ends of the chair's arms like roots. His legs, bent at the knees but sticking out towards the fire, were like pikestaffs snapped in the middle. And yet he was not ungainly. Mitchel had only ever once seen him stumble, and knew that if Weir stood up it would be, in spite of his advancing age, with a languid ease that much younger men did not possess. When he turned his head to see who had come in, the dark eyes flared briefly with a fierce and impressive energy.

Mitchel had been to many of the Weirs' prayer-meetings in the last ten years since their encounter on the High Street. Whatever doubts he had had about his own grace, he could not for long resist the Major's reputation. Folk of the godly party would travel in from miles around to hear him, and he was often invited to journey furth of Edinburgh to join in other religious meetings, especially in the west country, where he and his sister were from. His tall dark-clad figure leaning on the blackthorn staff, his sonorous tones rising to tremulous ecstasy, could drive his listeners, especially the women, into a sweaty fervour. McKail, Peden – and Weir: these were among the men that Mitchel had heard in the last decade, and all of them had the gift of prayer and praise. To his deep regret he had never even seen Rutherford, and he had heard Peden and McKail only a handful of times; Weir he had heard more often than any.

The Major seemed to like Mitchel. He encouraged him to attend and learn from him. But, as with the others, the lesson had been a hard one: he had become envious of Weir's ability to be both passionate and articulate, aware of his own failings in spite of his best efforts. It was only now, in the wake of McKail's death, that he understood that such power of delivery was only vested in these men by God, who had reserved an equal, more devastating power for himself.

Jean was a few years younger than her brother but time had treated her more harshly. She was in her late fifties, but her face was sorely lined and she had a hirpling kind of walk and an almost permanently skeerie expression as though she was expecting a hit at any moment. She was nervous of the world and who could blame her? She would have been destitute and alone had her brother not taken her in when he was widowed. Mitchel had not seen Jean for some time and thought she had aged greatly. In his experience, she only emerged from the protective shadow of her brother at the prayer-meetings, when she became animated and her face was lit with a sense of wonder that was childlike. Mitchel thought of her as one who perfectly represented the idea of the soul inhabiting the impure and frail clay of humanity.

'Maister Mitchel,' said Weir. 'I have been expecting ye, since I heard your name proclaimed at the Cross.' His voice was flat. He spoke, as he usually did in Mitchel's memory, and as some others of the most rigid persuasion also did, with a layer of English smoored over his Scots. That too was a hard discipline – like reading out the Bible into a riving wind – that Mitchel for one could never master. It made most Scotsmen sound like shadows of themselves, but Weir somehow carried it off.

His right hand rose to point at the chair opposite. Mitchel went to it and sat down. From its warmth he realised that he had taken Jean's seat. He was about to stand again but Weir pointed at him, as if warning a dog to stay. Jean removed herself to a stool across the room, out of the immediate range of the fire's heat. She smiled weakly at Mitchel, then bowed her head and picked up some unfinished needlework. Where she sat, he thought, she would hardly be able to see the needle, let alone the stitches.

'I am staring into Hell,' said Weir. His gaze was back on the flames. 'I am staring into Hell and thinking on them that have sinned against God this day, in the torture and slaying of his servant. I hear them crackling and a-spitting there.'

There was an exaggerated quake in his voice. He would have made a good dempster, reading to the condemned the sentence of the courts upon them. Thinking that thought, Mitchel said:

'Them that has judged, they shall be visited with judgment.'

'Aye, but how long? Why does God tarry so late in his vineyard?'

'I am the man that will be his battle-axe,' Mitchel said. It came from him spontaneously. As he heard himself utter the words he felt uneasy. Weir might turn and criticise him for his presumption. He went on quickly, 'I am the wind that will eat up the false pastors. This has been given to me today. But the time is not yet. I must leave Scotland, but you will hear the roar of his anger when I return.'

He was not certain of the phrases he used. Jeremiah, he thought, but some of them might have been his own. It didn't matter: to be obscure was often a virtue, since God would make all clear in time. Mitchel felt God speaking through him. And Major Weir did not sneer or question. He looked at him with his bright eyes and nodded.

'Aye, I believe you. I will hear that fierce wind, James Mitchel. But,' he went on, 'act not from the violence of your heart's grief. Vengeance is not thine, but the Lord's.'

'I ken that,' said Mitchel. 'But we are pit here for God's purpose. Even in the workin o his miracles, does he not uise us? For in dividin the Red Sea tae deliver Israel oot o Egypt, he commanded Moses tae stretch forth his hand. And Christ, when he opened the blin man's een, made uise o clay and spittle. Ma time isna yet, but it will come.'

Suddenly he had never felt so strong, so sure of himself. Verses from the Bible flooded his mind, and it was with difficulty that he stopped himself from spouting a string of justifications. How he could have impressed a prayer-meeting at that moment!

'I must beg siller frae ye, sir,' he said. 'I must awa tae the

Low Countries for a spell. It is in the cause of the Lord, but if ye will lend me enough for ma passage I will repay ye baith in siller and in deeds.'

Weir's face set like a stone. Mitchel knew that he was not a wealthy man, by the standards of some. On the other hand, he had no one to support but Jean. The Toun still paid him sporadically for work associated with the Guard and the collection of sundry duties: although his religious principles were obnoxious to the Ramsay regime, he was an experienced official. He was Mitchel's best hope. They both understood this.

The older man leant towards his sister. 'Jean,' he said sharply. 'Will ye gang oot for a minute?'

She instantly stood up and made as if to move ben, but he barked at her again. 'Na, na – oot, I said. Ootby, if ye please. Maister Mitchel and I hae a private matter to settle.'

'It's gey cauld oot,' Mitchel protested. 'There's nae need, surely.' But Weir cut him with a look, and waited till Jean had gathered a shawl about her and stepped, without a word or a look of reproach, into the night. Weir stood up in a single movement and secured the door after her.

'Ye must not think me harsh, James,' he said. 'My sister isna herself these days, I'm vexed to say.'

'She's dwaibly lookin,' Mitchel agreed.

'If it was but her body,' said Weir. 'But her heid's no richt. I fear for her if I am taken by God afore her.' He put the tips of his long fingers over his mouth for a moment. 'She is going mad, my friend, that is the truth. I sent her out because I must save her from herself. If I dinna keep secrets from her she'll ruin us. She would be out giving siller to every shoeless bairn in the street.'

'I am sorry for yer trouble,' said Mitchel.

'Ye're an honest man, James, and I trust ye not to cheat me. I'm not wanting your signature – a paper with your name on it would be a dangerous kind of surety just now, I'm thinking.'

Weir moved around the room, as if trying to make a choice of some kind. Finally he stopped at a large chest that stood in one corner of the room. He bent and shifted it a foot or two out from the wall. Mitchel saw him reach down to the floor.

There was the scrabbling sound of a board being moved and replaced, and then he pushed the chest back into its original position. He returned to the fireside carrying a small cloth poke, black with soot and grime.

'This will see ye to Holland,' he said, handing it over.

Mitchel unfolded the cloth. A mixture of coins clinked as he did so. He counted it at a glance, rewrapped it and put it away.

'I thank ye, sir,' he said. 'I hae been in yer debt afore, and I ken I hae been a disappointment tae ye, but ye niver disowned me. You forgave me ma weaknesses and ma sins. This will see me safe till I can win hame again. I'll repay it wheniver I can.'

'It is in the cause,' said Weir. 'As for the past, we have all sinned. God kens all things and measures us not by our sins but by our recognition of them. I'll take the siller when ye return.'

'I am in yer debt,' Mitchel repeated.

'When I am in need, I hope ye will do likewise by me.' Weir took a pen and paper and wrote a few words. 'This is for the guards at the Netherbow Port. They ken me of course, and this will let ye pass this night. There is a ship at Leith cried the *Marcus* that will sail with the next tide to Newcastle. Speir for it, and for a man cried John Forrester, from Ostend. This second note is for him. He is a discreet man that has carried our people before, and will get ye a passage for a fair price. From Newcastle the ship will gang down the English coast and syne across the sea to Flanders. Once there you are safe. Are ye for Amsterdam or Rotterdam?'

'Rotterdam. I hae a cousin there that's a merchant.'

'There's plenty honest Scots folk there,' said Weir, 'and the Dutch too are good Christians, which no doubt is why Charles Stewart sends his English warships against them.'

He paused, seemed to hesitate. 'I should say perhaps . . .'

'Aye?'

'There is one John Nevay of Newmilns at Rotterdam. A powerful saint, as I mind. Do ye ken him?'

'Na, I hae only heard o him.'

'Be wary of him. Some think him too rigid, too hard in judging of others. He has not a good opinion of me, for example, although I never did him a wrong. I wonder whiles if his judgment is not unbalanced. Should ye meet him, I would advise against telling him I am your friend. It might set him against ye, and cause ye mischief.'

'But why would he – ' Mitchel began, but Weir stood up and led him towards the door. 'Wheesht, wheesht, James, we'll no rake ower auld ashes when the fire's weill oot. If ye meet him dinna tell him I said this. And noo, James Mitchel, God gang with ye. I'll hear in time if ye are safe.'

He unsnecked the door and Mitchel was hit by the icy night. They looked around but the courtyard was silent and empty. 'She'll chap when she wants back in,' the Major said. He might have been referring to a cat at a window. Mitchel felt a twinge of unease. He had always thought of Weir as his sister's stern but protective guardian. There was an uncaring edge to his voice he had not picked up on before. Cruel, even. But there was nothing to be done about it. Folk were being hanged and dismembered for the sake of conscience. A woman going daft in her dotage was a small sadness by comparison.

Weir closed the door and Mitchel hurried down the steps. He turned into the close to go back to the Cowgate, and from there to the Netherbow and Leith Wynd. From the shadows a shawled figure emerged.

'Jean, Jean,' said Mitchel. 'Ye may gang hame noo. Hurry noo, afore ye freeze.'

'I'll no freeze,' she said. 'I'm weill happit. It's no me that'll freeze.'

He was about to pass her when she reached up a hand and touched his cheek.

'Are ye awricht, Jean?' he asked.

'*You're* frozen,' she said.

'Na,' he said, 'I hae jist been in at yer fire.'

'Ye're aw frozen,' she went on, as if she had not heard him. 'Ilk yin o yese. Ye hae grat for a broken Covenant and the saut is frozen on aw yer faces. But wha'll greet for me, eh? Wha'll greet for me?'

He was embarrassed. Weir was right, she was losing her mind. He clasped her hand between his for a minute. 'Awa hame, Jean. I'll pray for ye.'

'Pray for me?' She gave him a weird, silly smile. 'Oh, I thank ye.' If she had been capable of it, he would have said she was being ironic. He let go of her and headed for exile.

Edinburgh, April 1997

Hugh Hardie had arranged to meet Carlin by St Giles on the first Sunday after he started working, half an hour before the tour was due to start. By then he would have done five nights and they could iron out any problems that had arisen, anything Carlin or he thought wasn't right. 'A kind of staff assessment,' he'd joked.

'I'm on the staff then, am I?' Carlin had said.

Hugh had also left a message on Jackie Halkit's answermachine: 'Sorry I missed you on Wednesday. Hope you enjoyed the tour. Your man seems to be doing the biz – be interested to know what you thought of it, and him. Why don't we have another drink next week? Phone me.'

That had been on the Thursday. Jackie had yet to return the call. Since then Hugh had spoken to his tour guide. Things had not been going as smoothly as he'd hoped. He wasn't looking forward to raising the subject.

Carlin was there waiting when Hardie arrived. He was carrying a large plastic bag which contained his costume, and was leaning on the Major's stick. Nearby was an array of garishly painted wooden boards, each advertising a different walking tour and claiming a higher quota of ghosts, witches and murderers than the next. Hugh noticed that several groups of tourists were cosying around the boards and their grisly depictions, while Carlin had yards of clear space to himself.

'Well,' said Hugh breezily, 'here we are then. How are you doing?'

Carlin shrugged.

'It should be busy tonight. A party of twelve Americans phoned up and booked themselves on, and there's always a few more strays hanging about on a Sunday. So you'll need to give it your best shot, eh?'

'Aye, I'll need tae.'

'Any problems so far then?'

'I've nane.'

'Right. Good.' Hugh waited in case Carlin wanted to add a qualification. He didn't. 'You're okay with what we *do* with Major Weir?'

'I'm checkin him oot.'

'Oh?'

'There's a few inaccuracies.'

'Oh. Well, if you find anything major – ha! – let me know. We can work it into the script, maybe.'

'Aye, maybe.'

Hugh decided not to suggest the book project as something Carlin could be working on in his spare time. Not just yet.

'There's one thing I wanted to mention. Gerry, the guide, said there was, um, a misunderstanding or something. On Wednesday? What was that all about?'

'Whit did Gerry, um, misunderstand like?'

Hugh laughed. 'Well, no, it wasn't him, it was you. He said you didn't turn up at the end, you know, the last bit when you appear in the doorway.'

'Whit's he then, a gaffer or somethin? Reportin back tae ye?'

'No, but, you know, that's what we agreed. That's what Gerry's expecting even if the punters aren't. It throws him off his patter, you know.'

'Can he no improvise? Work somethin intae the script?'

'Well, obviously, that's what he did. I just want to impress on you, you know, how important it is that you do all the various bits. It's part of the experience for the punters. And it's part of the job for you. Part of your job, okay?'

'I didna feel right. I had tae stop. I wasna weill. By the time I got started again it was too late.'

Hugh was doubtful, but tried to feel relieved. 'Oh, well, that's not so bad. I mean, I'm sorry if you were ill, but I was more concerned that you'd just sloped off, kind of thing. So long as you're clear about what you're supposed to do. About staying right to the end.'

'Oh aye, I ken whit I'm supposed tae dae.'

'Great. Right, well, that's that then. I'd better be off, let you get into position. But you're happy, are you? I mean, it's working out all right for you?'

'Whit aboot ma pay?'

'Your pay? Oh, right, Sunday. Yeah, let's see. Well, it wasn't a full week, was it? Tuesday to Saturday – five nights. That's twenty-five quid. So I owe you a fiver then.'

'A fiver?'

'Yeah, once I've taken off the deposit for the gear.'

'Whit ye talkin aboot?'

'Did I not explain? The cloak and stick and wig. You get your twenty pounds back when you finish, when you hand the stuff back. And the rat of course. I thought I said that.'

Carlin held the bag and the staff out to him. 'There ye are then. Now gie's ma money.'

'No, I mean, when you finish the job. For good. It's just because it's expensive to replace.'

'Oh,' said Carlin. 'Well, supposin I don't finish. For guid. Supposin ye like me so much ye keep me on. Ye're never gaun tae pay me whit's mine then, are ye?'

'Everybody's got to finish some time.'

'Aye. Well, I'm finishin right now unless ye pay me whit I'm due.'

Hugh was in a dilemma for about two seconds. He couldn't afford to lose his ghost, not at this moment. It was worth the risk. Hell, it wasn't even much of a risk.

He took out his wallet and handed over twenty-five pounds. 'You win,' he said. 'Just don't run off with the stuff, okay?'

Carlin looked at him and then, dismissively, down at the bag. Then he turned to go. Hugh Hardie felt like saying something impulsive. At the same time he felt that it was being dragged out of him, as if Carlin was making him say it.

'By the way,' he called, 'I do want to keep you on. You're good. You're so damned – spectral!'

Carlin half-turned and leered over his shoulder. Hugh laughed. 'So long as we understand each other!' As soon as he said it he realised that the leer had not been a joke, and that he did not understand Carlin at all.

Arsehole. Carlin strode up the High Street, resisting the temptation to stuff the Weir gear into a litter bin. But he was more angry with himself than with Hardie. He needed the money but not that badly. He should chuck it. He would chuck it, right now, if it wasn't for Mitchel.

Mitchel. As soon as that thought occurred he was astonished at it. He had no obligation to Mitchel. Some deluded holy joe from three centuries ago. But it was true: it was Mitchel, not Weir, that had gripped him.

At the junction with George IV Bridge he paused. He was supposed to be taking up his position for the tour, but there was plenty of time. He looked south, past the library, towards the university and Greyfriars. Nothing that he could see had been there in Mitchel's day. Except Greyfriars. The old tombs. The place where the National Covenant had first been signed in 1638. Mitchel must have gone there, years later. He'd hardly have been born in 1638, one or two at most, a country bairn without a trace of himself in his head. And then, when he arrived in Edinburgh in his teens, to be a student, he'd have gone there, to Greyfriars, to see where the story he was caught up in had started.

Carlin thought of his own first time in Edinburgh. His father brought him when he was eight. It was a birthday treat – to show him the Castle and the Royal Mile, and take him to the Museum in Chambers Street. Early that morning they'd caught a bus from their village to Stirling and a train from there. The journey had seemed endless. When they came out of the station up the Waverley Steps, Carlin's mouth fell open and stayed that way until his father reached down and gently pushed up his jaw. The department stores on Princes Street sailed before his eyes like a line of Spanish galleons. Across the railway tracks the Old Town, all spires and crags and overlapping snakes and ladders of windows, tumbled up towards the Castle on its dark plinth. And right in front of where they stood was a monstrous black stone spaceship, ready for launching, with the tiny faces of people keeking out from its top.

'That's tae Sir Walter Scott,' said his father. 'He was a famous writer, like Rabbie Burns, only he wrote stories mair than poems. He was a toff but a Scotch yin at least. He could speak Scotch wi the best o them.'

They walked along Princes Street past the monument, then up the Mound to the Old Town. They had to go slowly because of his father's legs. He'd been blown up in the war in North Africa and there were still bits of shrapnel in him, burrowing slowly through his body. When he walked any distance his legs would start to jag with the tiny skelfs that were in them. 'They're tae remind me I'm still alive,' he used to joke. He had been a soldier, now he was a socialist and an atheist. Eventually the shrapnel would wear him away inside and kill him.

They toiled to the Castle esplanade and looked down on the city. The boy thought he would never see anything so immense again in his life. His father pointed out places: the Forth, the port of Leith, the Lomond Hills across in Fife. He pointed to the north and west. 'That's where we cam fae this mornin, Andra. Oot o sicht awa yonder.'

'We're fae nowhere then,' said the boy. Like this, he meant, nowhere at all like this.

'Naebody comes fae nowhere,' said his father, 'but there's nane o us that'll no gang back tae naethin.' Carlin always minded him saying that, because of the strange progression of negatives. It seemed to draw a line between him and the ground he stood on: only if he was from nowhere could he really be here. Later, on the train home, his father's sentence would rattle in his head as the fences and trees fled past. A boy could take those words to pieces and put them together again endlessly, like toy bricks, or a metal puzzle.

After the Castle there followed a jumbled succession of ascents and descents – stone steps, narrow passageways, steep cobbled streets – that brought them at last to Greyfriars. They'd stopped and looked at the wee Skye terrier and then at some of the grim old gravestones. The boy was impressed by one of the memorial tablets, on the wall of the kirk itself, which showed a skeleton dancing jubilantly on top of a skull, a scythe in one hand and an open Bible in the other. The weathering of centuries had made the image indistinct, but somehow it was more powerful for appearing so old and battered. Then his father made them sit on a bench for a while, to rest his leg. After the roar and hurry of the streets, the kirkyard seemed quieter, more isolated even than their village. They were alone apart from a solitary man in a filthy anorak some distance away. They watched him making his way unsteadily across the grass, using the stones as handrests until eventually he came to a space that was too big to be crossed unaided. The man stood, as if being battered by a strong wind although the day was calm, gripping the last stone with stained, scuffed fingers.

'Let's go,' his father said. And when they reached the gates, and the boy glanced back at the man still clinging there, his father added, 'You haud on tae me, Andra. We're no wantin ye lost.' Buses and cars thundered past. They seemed to be in a domain of ragged, unshaven men, and the boy wondered if his father was worried that they might steal him. His hand was hot and small in the rough security of his father's as they crossed the road.

'Where are we gaun noo?' he asked.

'Ye'll see,' his father said.

It was the Museum, a black, towering building so vast that they had to climb steps that were half the length of the street, and then push through a revolving door of such weight that it took the strength of both of them to move it, just to enter. But inside the blackness gave way to galleries of glass and light, and bubbling tiled pools in which fat orange fish glided. The boy's mouth came open again. They wandered among fraying stuffed elephants, and motionless snakes that could swallow you whole, and Komodo dragons that were like small dinosaurs and might hunt you down in packs, and more bones – real ones this time – the skeletons of whales suspended in the air. It seemed that every corner revealed some new and astounding object which would take its place in his already crowded imagination.

Eventually they went to the café and had tea and a cake. His father looked at his watch. 'Come on,' he said.

Out on the long steps of the Museum there was a commotion of some sort. A group of people were surrounding somebody who seemed to have fallen. They were all leaning, stretching down, and a clamour of questions rose from them. 'Whit's yer name, darling? Were ye in there? Were ye wi yer mammy?' As Carlin and his father approached, they saw a tiny figure in a dark blue coat, sitting hunched on the steps, her fists against her eyes, her shoulders shaking but no sound coming from her. The questions kept coming: 'Whit's yer name? When did ye last see her? Are ye cauld? D'ye ken where ye stay?' Carlin's father said, 'Puir wee thing. We dinna want that happenin tae you son, eh?' Carlin watched her over his shoulder as they walked away, back towards the station. 'How will she get hame?' he demanded. 'Och, they'll find oot who she is,' his father said. 'Dinna you fash.' But he couldn't help himself. If you were lost in a place this size, how would you ever be found again?

Edinburgh was a dreamscape for him from then on. When he did well at school and it was suggested he could go to university, Edinburgh was the one place he could think of. Coming back as a student it was only his second visit. His father was dead by then, four years cold, and his mother was ailing. The shape of the city renewed itself to him instantly, clear and precise. But now he took in its hills and hollows and saw it not as a city but as land with the city draped and poured over it. The buildings and streets were at once solid and ephemeral. He got up early the day after his arrival and climbed from the halls of residence to the top of Arthur's Seat, from where he could look down on the Castle where he had stood with his father ten years before. A few sheep eyed him warily. Where he was from was still invisible beyond the Ochils, but the field of his vision had grown to the south and east: the Pentlands with the white scar of the dry ski slope on their flank, the Lammermuirs, the Berwick Law, the Bass Rock. Between him and the land now there was nothing, nothing but walking. Edinburgh was there but it was no barrier. He skited and stauchered back down the steep side of the hill and every step connected him with the land. When he reached the road he could still feel the beat of it pumping up through the soles of his feet.

It was there yet. The electricity of time. Even now, when he put on the ridiculous outfit. He made his way to the close for that evening's performance. The tap-tapping of Major Weir's stick on the pavement reverberated up into his head.

Rotterdam, January 1667

There were more clerics than lay folk in the congregation of the Scots kirk at Rotterdam, or so it appeared to Mitchel the first time he attended service in the cramped chapel of Saint Sebastian's in Lombard Street. The presiding minister was John Hog, who had formerly had the charge of South Leith. He preached with a vehemence that was somehow un-convincing, which puzzled Mitchel for a while until he looked around at the stern faces in the pews, and realised that Hog was having to push himself to the limit of his capabilities to avoid the criticism of his peers. John Carstairs of Cathcart, John Nevay of Newmilns, John Livingstone of Ancrum, John Brown of Wamphray – were your chances of being banished from Scotland higher if your first name was John? – were always keen to take a turn in the pulpit. Rotterdam was a thriving ministry. If Hog ceased to come up to the mark, or when in the fullness of time he was gathered to God, the competition to succeed him would be intense.

Mitchel had been fortunate since leaving Edinburgh. The journey had been largely without alarm. The most disturbing event had come half an hour after taking his leave of Jean Weir, on the deserted road to Leith. Halfway between city and port he had paused for a moment in front of a bizarre spectacle at the Gallowlee. A cage-like iron frame suspended from a wooden beam had acquired a layer of frost and icicles, which reflected the moonlight and gave the structure the appearance of a giant lantern. Within the frame the skeleton of some long-dead criminal, also frosted and gleaming, was displayed like an old twisted wick. As Mitchel looked, an enormous gull, which had been perched in shadow at the dead man's feet, rose out of the cage and flew off towards the sea. Startled, Mitchel turned away. He felt that he was being watched. Seized with a sudden panic, he broke into a run and regained the road. Then, thinking that if there were any soldiers out braving the cold a man running through the night to Leith would be sure to attract their attention, he slowed himself to a walk.

The *Marcus* had been preparing for departure as Major Weir had said. Forrester had transported him safely as far south as Hull and then to Ostend through a grey, sluggish, unviolent sea. A combination of walking and begged cart rides had brought him to Rotterdam. His cousin John, who travelled widely through Germany and the Low Countries as a merchant, had been there when he arrived, and was able to find him lodgings and lend him some money. He also offered him work, supervising the despatch and delivery of goods to various destinations. It was hardly the kind of employment Mitchel now believed himself to be made for, but he was not in a position to refuse. He did ask, however, for a week or two to rest and order his thoughts.

He spent time in the company of the old minister of Greyfriars, Robert Traill, who had befriended him when he was a student at the Toun's College. He had once recommended Mitchel to a tutor's post in Galloway, in the house of one of those who had subsequently turned out at Pentland. At the Restoration Traill had signed a petition to Charles II which, having congratulated him on his return, went on to remind him of his obligations to uphold the Covenant. For this he was imprisoned, then ejected from the country. Some of his fellow-petitioners were also now in Holland. Traill was anxious for news of his son, also named Robert, who had been at Pentland. Mitchel was unable to offer any comfort, having heard nothing of him.

Traill was a devout but dull man of sixty-three. Mitchel was warmed by his attentions but not flattered by them. But one day Traill said something which excited his interest:

'Robert MacWard is due in Rotterdam this week, James. I'm wondering if ye would care to meet him.'

Care to meet him! The man who had been Samuel Rutherford's secretary, who had edited his beloved letters! It would be an honour, Mitchel said.

'Maister MacWard bides in Utrecht these days,' Traill went on. 'He finds it' – he coughed – 'a pool less choked with the persecuted brethren than here. He's a muckle fish and needs mair space to swim in. Although I believe he would be back in a glisk were Mr Hog's place to become vacant.'

'He is reckoned a great orator,' said Mitchel. 'Rotterdam would be lucky tae hae him.'

'He certainly has a very oratorious style at preaching. Somebody once told him as much, a man frae Kilmarnock if I mind richt: "God forgive ye, brother, that darkens the gospel of Christ with your oratory." But ye shouldna be intimidated by him, James. A young man of promise such as yourself will, I'm sure, be of interest to Maister MacWard. And there will be others keen to hear frae ye, since ye have so lately been in Scotland.'

When Mitchel arrived the ministers were sitting around a long table on benches, drinking modest amounts of ale. They were pushing a small pamphlet around the table, giggling gruffly at it. He was introduced and took a seat at the end of one bench. The pamphlet was laid aside and the conversation shifted to a general discussion of the latest bad news from home. Questions were put to him, many of which he was unable to answer.

When the debate became overly theological he felt a panic coming on, but did his best to keep up. He was overawed by their combined intellectual muscle: an assemblage of the most educated, influential and respected men ever to have fled out of Scotland. Most of them were growing old. From their accents they might have arrived off the *Marcus* with him: it was easier, perhaps, to hold onto your Scots voice in Holland than, say, in England.

MacWard, who had not yet spoken directly to Mitchel, finally turned to him. 'Maister Traill tells me ye were oot wi Colonel Wallace and the rest?'

Mitchel shook his head. 'I wasna at Rullion Green itsel. I was sent back tae Edinburgh in the mornin, afore the fechtin started.'

'Dootless it was urgent business that engaged ye?' This was Mr John Nevay, the man Weir had warned him against. He was about sixty, a Christian so unbending that he opposed all forms of set prayer including even that suggested by Christ. He had made a translation of the Song of Solomon into Latin verse, which seemed to Mitchel a marvellous feat of scholarship;

and he had, during the war against Montrose all those years ago, so relentlessly urged the despatch of the captured Irishes that even the soldiers carrying out the executions objected, asking if he had not yet had his fill of blood. They had not his zeal and fortitude, and Mitchel, recalling the minister at Linlithgow, who had shown similar resolve and put him on the path of righteousness, could not help but admire him.

'Ye are correct, sir,' he replied. 'I cairrit urgent messages tae the Toun.'

'Sayin whit?' said Nevay. 'That the day was winnable if the Edinburgh folk could be fashed to get oot their beds? Or that it was lost and they'd be better keepin tae them?'

The sudden ferocity in his tone threw Mitchel into confusion. He had no idea what the letters had said; he had destroyed them. 'It wasna for me tae ken,' he mumbled. 'I was obeyin an order. Forby, the day wasna lost till the forenicht.'

Now MacWard came back at him. 'Ye werena *at* the fecht, and ye werena gaun *tae* the fecht, and ye kenna whit for ye were gaun *frae* the fecht, only that it was a maitter o urgency. I think we hae the measure o ye, sir.'

Mitchel reddened but said nothing.

Mr John Carstairs came to his rescue. The former minister of Cathcart and of Glasgow was said to be able to move whole congregations to tears with his prayers. Other ministers said of him that though they came close in preaching, in prayer he went quite out of their reach. Now he said to MacWard, in a gentle voice, 'Your insinuation is unwarranted, Maister Robert. Ye canna wyte a man for no bein martyred.'

'I only observe,' said MacWard, 'that it seems a great inconvenience, gien the smallness o his pairt, that he had tae come awa frae Scotland at all. But ye'll ken better than me aboot such social niceties, eh John?'

This was a dig at Carstairs's pretensions to be a gentleman. He prided himself on being able to hold polite conversation with lords and ladies, and could write a mannered letter when required. After the Restoration, when these same men now in exile first faced the prospect of being debarred from their pulpits, they had been gathered together one day, pretty cheerful in spite of things, and began to ask one another what they would do to make a living once they could no longer be ministers. One said one thing, one said another, and then John Carstairs had said, very gravely and dreamily, 'I think I could be a laird.'

'Come noo, Robert,' said Mr John Brown. 'We are all of us inconvenienced. And it isna worthy o ye tae cast up ae man's pairt in Christ against anither's. We aw dae whit we dae.' Brown was a close friend of MacWard. There was no doubting his reputation both as theologian and stalwart in the cause. He had recently published *An Apologeticall Relation of the Particular Sufferings of the Faithfull Ministers and Professours of the Church of Scotland,* and, among numerous other learned tracts, was working on a study of *Quakerisme The Path-Way to Paganisme.*

MacWard nodded, acknowledging that he had perhaps been over-harsh.

'Oor friend here is a stymie,' added Carstairs, indicating Mitchel. 'He sees but he disna see weill.'

'I ken, John, I ken.' MacWard gave Mitchel a smile, which vanished almost as it appeared. 'I am testin ye, sir, no mockin ye. There are ower mony time-servin folk in Scotland, that are aye at the edge o sufferin and never at the hert o it. Of coorse we can only be where God places us, but Scotland lacks not its Jonahs in these times, that are sent to cry against the wickedness of Nineveh, and rise and flee from the Lord unto Tarshish. Why are ye come here, Maister Mitchel?'

'Because I am declared a rebel, like yersels. Like Maister Traill here, and his son that's no been seen since Pentland.'

'We are all cried rebels by them that has rebelled against the Lord,' Traill lamented.

'And if I had been taen by Dalyell's men,' Mitchel went on, 'I would hae been hingit, and I canna be hingit till I hae wrocht God's purpose. Which, sirs, isna yet for ye or me tae ken.'

MacWard laughed. 'He's a wit, Maister Traill. I can see why ye thocht he would mak a guid tutor tae bairns.'

Mitchel smiled back – it seemed MacWard was severe rather than malevolent – then wondered again if he was not being made a fool of. Traill touched his sleeve to reassure him.

MacWard folded his arms across his chest and addressed Mitchel.

'When first I came here, driven frae the wrath of Charles Stewart, I was ashamed tae call my lot a sufferin lot. Ithers had been brocht tae the slauchter, but I was spared. Why was this? Why had God rather hied me frae the storm than exposed me tae its force? Noo I realise that I was sheltered for a reason, tae sing the Lord's song in a strange land, tae shine ceaselessly for his cause here, and no burn up in a brief and sudden blaze of glory. But you, Maister Mitchel, I do not believe you will be here long. You are still young, a footsoldier of Christ. You must return, I think, intae that darkness that is Scotland.'

Mitchel felt somewhat reassured. 'That is ma intention,' he said.

'James will do great things in the Lord. I am certain of it,' Traill added.

Mr John Livingstone was the former minister of Ancrum in Roxburghshire. Aged sixty-three, he had the longest record of nonconformity, having been deposed from his first ministry in Killinchy, County Down, away back in 1632. Like Nevay, he was against all set prayers such as the Lord's Prayer: a man so sure of his own salvation that he had once said, 'I am persuaded that if it were possible that I could gang tae Hell, yet Christ would come tae it tae seek me, and rake the coals o it tae get me oot.' Now, picking up on Traill's remark, he said:

'Hae ye onythin in particular in mind, Maister Mitchel?'

Mitchel hesitated. He did not have a plan, only an object of hatred. 'I hae a mind tae be a *sharp* instrument,' he said eventually, 'and deliver a *sharp* blow.'

There was general laughter. Livingstone lifted the pamphlet they had been looking at earlier and wagged it at Mitchel.

'Are ye such a wit as penned these verses, sir? Anent . . .' – he turned up a page and searched for a phrase – 'that *Judas Scoto-Britannus* of whom ye spak jist noo?'

'I dinna ken, sir,' said Mitchel. There was more laughter. Once again he was plunged into confusion.

'Ye dinna ken if ye wrote them?' said Livingstone. 'It's jist fresh ower the sea, man, arrivin aboot the time ye did yersel. Is this no familiar tae ye?' He read from the pamphlet.

My friends I basely did reproach,
Their cause I did betray
By lying and by flatterie
I for myself made way.

At length great Primat I was made,
I king and pastours mockt,
And of my benefactors all
The ruine I have socht.

Dae ye no recognise the target, James?'

'Sir,' Mitchel said, 'I didna scrieve thae verses. But I'm sure I ken the target.'

The ministers were loving this. Carstairs, who was one down from him, leant round and dunted Mitchel appreciatively in the shoulders. 'Let's hae mair, John.'

Livingstone shrugged. 'Since it's no Maister Mitchel's, I feel I can say athoot fear o offence, it's sinfu bad verse, but it has its virtues. Ach weill –

Most viper like, I in the birth
My mother's bowels rent,
And did cast out these zealous men,
Whose money I had spent.

Who from the dunghill raised me,
These stars in Christ's right hand,
The giants on whose shoulders strong
I poor pigmee did stand.'

'That's no sae bad, John,' said Nevay. 'That has truth in it.'

'Is that richt, John?' said Livingstone. 'Dae ye see yersel amang the giants and stars?'

Mitchel saw smiles and frowns flash around the assembled men. He was astonished to find such petty rivalry among the saints. Livingstone went on:

'But hear this, this is baith false verse and true:

I have made havok of the Church,
The Godly I abhor,

All who mak conscience of their way
To me are ane eye sore.

How many hundredth shyning lights
Are put out by my hand,
Of which might any one have been
A glory to a land.

Of all the blood that hath been shed,
The author I have been,
Of all oppression of the Saints
And ills which they have seen.

All men me hate, none truly love,
I can no man beguile,
My treacherie and my perjury
So notour is and vile.'

As he read, the laughter, uproarious at the first clashing rhyme, died away, and the last two stanzas were heard in silence. Livingstone closed the book and put it away. There was an embarrassed silence. Then John Brown spoke.

'How cam ye here, Maister Mitchel? Dae ye want siller? We hae a fund for those in distress.'

'Ma cousin John,' said Mitchel, 'that's a deacon in the kirk here, has me provided for. For ma passage I borrowed siller frae Major Thomas Weir which I hope tae repay in time.'

The name was out before he could stop himself. There were more significant glances around the table. Most of them would have known Weir from his time in the Edinburgh Toun Guard, when he had had charge of Montrose before his execution. Traill, for example, had visited Montrose – or James Graham, as the godly insisted on calling him, since they did not recognise his title – in the Tolbooth, trying to extract contrition from him for his crimes – but to no avail. But what, Mitchel wondered, was Nevay's connection?

'How is oor auld acquaintance?' asked Carstairs.

'He grieves for the sinfu state of Scotland,' said Mitchel. 'He is burdened wi his sister. She is wrang in the heid.'

'The sinfu state of Scotland,' said Nevay thoughtfully. 'Aye.

122

And did he mention masel? He kens I am here. Did he ask ye tae communicate ony message tae me?'

'No, sir,' said Mitchel, grateful that the last question enabled him to answer truthfully. 'He said naethin anent thon.'

'Anent *whit*?' Nevay demanded sharply.

'I mean, sir, he said naethin. He had nae communication for ye that I ken.'

The subject was not pursued. Shortly after this, Traill signalled to Mitchel that he should leave. Business had to be addressed that he could not be privy to. MacWard produced a sheaf of papers, and the ministers fluttered in around them like moths. Mitchel bowed and made his exit.

Only when he had left the room did he realise that he had not had a chance to talk with MacWard about Samuel Rutherford. But there was something about MacWard that he did not like. He realised that he did not want to be connected to Rutherford by such a man.

He knew that he had been assessed – weighed in the balances – but had he been found wanting? What had Nevay been angling for? And did MacWard think him stupid? Certainly they seemed to understand his insinuations about Sharp. But that would be his act alone, not theirs.

Traill's son was delivered safely from Scotland a week later. He had slipped across the Forth after the defeat at Pentland, and waited out his time in the fishing villages of Fife where his family had many friends, before deciding to join his father abroad. The old man was on his knees for most of a day and a night giving thanks.

Young Robert and Mitchel had met before. Traill was a year or two the younger, but was already a rising star at conventicles. Like his father, he was open and friendly to Mitchel. They exchanged stories about the rising. Traill was particularly keen to hear the details of McKail's execution.

'Did they save the corp frae the gallows?' he asked.

Mitchel was not sure. He'd heard that a group of men had carried it away for burial before it could be quartered by the soldiers. 'I think so,' he said.

Traill breathed out heavily. 'It's a terrible thing, tae see a man murdered. But tae butcher the flesh eftir the spirit has departed frae it, is baith senseless and barbaric.'

'James Graham's heid was prickit on the Tolbooth eleven years, and a cross-prick pit in it so his freens couldna steal it awa. That wasna senseless – it was an example and a constant mindin tae the people.'

'But think whase heid replaced it when it was taen doon – oor ain gracious Marquis, Argyle's. We canna aye be skewerin flesh, James – we must leave some work for Judgment Day. But that said, I'll no argue but that it maks for strenth o a kind. Ye'll hae strenth in yersel for haein witnessed Hew's end.'

'Aye, I hae that.'

'Ma faither's freen James Guthrie, that suffered at the Restoration, I saw him killt. It niver leaves ye. When I falter, I think on it and it gars me gang on.'

Guthrie had been minister at Stirling in the fifties. His had been a life of signs and signing. On his way to take the Covenant in 1638 he met the public hangman. This unsettled James Guthrie somewhat, and he went aside and walked up and down a little before going on, to think what this meeting might mean. Ah well, he judged it would mean he would pay for his act with his life, but could not think of a better cause to die for, so he signed.

At the Restoration he'd signed the same petition to Charles that had had the elder Traill banished. Guthrie's case was worse, however. Back in 1651 the General Assembly had passed an act of excommunication against General John Middleton, a man who had been second-in-command of the Covenanter army that defeated Montrose at Selkirk, but who had subsequently switched sides and raised a Royalist army in the north, Highland papists and malignants every one. The rising came to nothing, but the excommunication went ahead anyway, and it fell to Guthrie to deliver the sentence from the pulpit. Middleton never forgave him. When, at the Restoration, he became king's commissioner to the Scottish Parliament, one of his first acts was to have Guthrie arrested, tried and hanged.

On the last Sabbath before his arrest, Guthrie chose as his text the verses from Hebrews, chapter 11: *And what more shall I say? For time would fail me to tell of the prophets who through*

124

faith subdued kingdoms and stopped the mouths of lions; and others were tortured, not accepting deliverance; that they might obtain a better resurrection; they were stoned, they were sawn asunder, they were tempted, were slain with the sword; they wandered in deserts, and in mountains, and in dens and caves of the earth. He read out these verses in full, and as soon as he stopped his nose began to bleed, so violently that he was obliged to step down and let another preach for him. It was a terrible portent of what was to follow.

Mitchel had been in Galloway then. The way young Traill told it, the Guthrie execution had been as dramatic as McKail's. Then afterwards the body was taken down and dismembered. Guthrie's head and hands were cut off and stuck up on the Netherbow port, with the hands on either side of the dead face as if in prayer. Some weeks after the execution, when the remnants had long dried out, Middleton's coach was passing through the gate. As it did, a gush of blood fell from Guthrie's neck onto the coach. When Middleton's lackeys tried to wash it off, they found it had stained the leather irreversibly. Nothing would remove it. Physicians and scientists were called in to ascertain why the blood should have started to flow so long after death, and at that particular moment. They could give no natural cause. In the end Middleton had to get a complete new set of covers for his coach.

Mitchel knew this story well. It was recounted as a great and fearful marvel among the godly. The weird thing was, he could never quite rid himself of a sneaking sympathy for John Middleton. The man had come from a background as proletarian as his own. He'd been a pikeman in Sir John Hepburn's Scots Brigade in France before joining the Covenanters in the 1640s. He was brutal and unsophisticated, but he had risen to the highest rank and office. He'd fallen from favour because he did not have the aristocratic blood or political connections of his rival Lauderdale, and had been packed off to govern Tangier. Mitchel imagined him dreaming of wet Scotland, a tall, frustrated man baking in the African sun, drinking himself to death. He was fascinated by the story of the blood Middleton had called down upon himself.

*

During his time in exile, Mitchel went with his cousin John to Hamburg, Amsterdam, Antwerp, Leyden and Ostend. He made some of these journeys on his own also, accompanying or receiving consignments of cloth, wine and other goods. It was petty, tedious work for which he had no enthusiasm. Months passed. At night he dreamt of Edinburgh, and a gate that dripped blood whenever he approached it.

He knew it was time to be moving. He had saved money from his work – enough to repay Major Weir and have some left over. If he could work his way back to Scotland he might have more. But John was trading entirely within the continent. He got him to write him a letter of recommendation and went looking for a cargo that needed a native Scotsman to supervise its passage.

One night he dreamt of the gate again. It was like the Netherbow but not it. He expected the blood but when he reached the gate it swung open. Jean Weir was beyond it. She beckoned him on, giving him a silly, doited smile as he passed her. Then he was in a darkened room. It was the Major's house but it was not. It was a prison. A man was sitting under a tiny window, trying to read from a book. The room was full of smoke. Another man was standing by the door, puffing away at a pipe. The first man was coughing from the smoke. The smoker laughed. Mitchel saw his big-nosed profile. It was Weir. There was the sound of a gun going off.

Edinburgh, April 1997/July 1668

It was happening again. Carlin felt the fire and the sweat coming over him as he strode along the Cowgate ahead of the tour party. It was a mild night, the cloak was heavy and warm. Maybe it was the baldy wig, not allowing his scalp to breathe. He pulled it off and stuffed it into the plastic bag under the cloak. The black staff felt soft and hot in his hand. He had to get past the bridge, where he'd succumbed to the oppressive feeling last time. He pressed on.

He felt like someone else. A voice was going away at him, inside, saying something. He thought it might be MacDonald, who seemed to know just what he, Carlin, was looking for, even though he himself didn't. He wondered if it was Lauder and his *Secret Book*. It had to be Lauder's voice, surely, he was hearing? There was one passage he could remember quite clearly.

> *What is madnes? In France a man tauld us this story, that some gentlemen ware at Paris who on visiting the bedlam there the governour & physicians ware occupiet wt other matters, so they gave them into the hands of a fool to shew them the place. Thus this man pertinentlie gydes them throw the chambers saying heres one that is mad for love, here on other thats mad wt too much study, here a third mad wt drink, one a hypocondriack &c. The gentlemen being much impresst wt the luciditie and sense of their gyde, they come at last to one who, he informs them, thinks him selfe the Apostle Sanct John. But the gyde knew this was not so as he, being Sanct Petir, had nevir opened the door of heaven to him yet. The doctors after tauld them he was once a professor in the college of Sorbonne, but too much learning had reduced him to his present state.*

Aye, maybe that was it: Lauder's voice. Another world coming through those old pages, invading him. But if that was what was happening, how could he tell which voice in his head was his? The mirror was one thing, but this . . . He'd be no better than the man who thought he was Peter. Carlin got paid for what he was doing and he wore a kind of fancy-dress but otherwise what was the difference between them? And if he was mad, how would he recognise his madness?

He turned up Stevenlaw's Close, which, at its foot, was more a narrow road or vennel than a close. The tour route went up the hill a few yards and turned left before the close narrowed, went along another vennel, and emerged into Tron Square at the back of the tenements of the High Street. Gerry would lead his party across the square towards Assembly Close, which opened onto the street, but then shepherd them ahead of him to the right, along a narrow passage that gave onto Covenant and Burnet's Closes. It was out of one of these that Carlin was supposed to make his final appearance. When Hardie had shown him the set-up the first time he had queried the location.

'There's folk stey in these hooses. Dae they no get fed up wi aw the racket?'

'Never had a complaint yet,' Hardie had said. 'I guess that's just something you accept if you live in the heart of the Old Town. I mean, if you can't handle us going by, how are you going to cope with the pubs emptying, or all the people hanging around during the Festival? If you don't like it, don't live here, that's what I say.'

Just short of Tron Square there was a patch of broken concrete, dotted with weeds, set deep in shadow in the angle of a brick wall. As Carlin went past it something moved out from the weeds, touched his foot. He jumped back with a cry.

'Jesus fuckin Christ!'

Something was curled up in there under a blanket. Somebody. It was a leg that had slid out.

'Sorry,' said a muffled voice. A moment later it added, 'Fuckin hell, look at ye. I'm the one that should be gettin the fright.' It sounded like just a young boy.

'I'm the one that should be apologisin,' said Carlin. 'Did I wake ye?'

'Ay, kinda. I was jist settlin in. Didna think there'd be anybody much comin by here at this time.'

'Oh.' Carlin hunkered down. 'Well, I'm sorry tae disappoint

ye, but ye're right in the road o aboot twenty tourists that are headin up here in the next five minutes.'

'Fuckin hell. This is a guid spot tae. Oot the wey. Nae hassle. Or so I thought.' The body began wearily to gather itself, as if to move on.

Carlin peered a little closer. 'Hang on,' he said. 'I'm no bein nosy but . . . are you a lassie?'

'Mebbe. Could be. How? Whit's it tae you?'

'Christ,' said Carlin. A deep memory and fear welled in him. A lost girl surrounded by strangers. He said stupidly, 'Some folk dinna think aboot lassies sleepin oot in the street.'

'Oh, right, I get it. This is when ye feel that sorry for me, ye tell me I can kip at your place, then ye get me hame and there's only the wan bed. Well, sorry, mister. Been there, done that, as they say.'

'Na, na, that's no whit I meant. It's jist, you lyin oot here like this, and this crowd comin – that's no on. That's nae use at aw.'

'It's awright, I'm on ma wey. Nae bother, right?'

'Na, you stay put. Jist stay exactly where ye are. Canna hae aw thae folk trampin through a lassie's bedroom. Specially when ye're tryin tae kip.'

'Whit ye gaun dae aboot it?'

'Go back tae sleep. They can go anither wey the night.'

'Eh?'

'Whit's yer name?'

'Karen.'

'It's awright, Karen. I'll take care o it.'

'How?'

'It's ma job.'

He didn't have long. He ran on through the square, out onto the High Street, then doubled back down New Assembly Close. This came to what seemed a dead end, but it wasn't quite, he knew that. You went down some steps, along the back of the houses, and you came to a wooden door in the wall, with a snib on the inside. You couldn't open it from the other side without a Yale key. He put the snib off and went through. He was back at the top of Stevenlaw's Close, the steep narrow section. He belted down to the corner of the vennel near the foot and waited for the tour party. He could hear them coming up from the Cowgate, the guide giving them stuff about Sir Walter Scott's birthplace across the way.

When the first of them, led by Gerry, turned into the vennel, Carlin did the wildest fucking haunt he could muster. In fact he'd never really put any effort into it before that time. The result was spectacular. Pandemonium broke out. The tourists at the front screamed and tried to fight their way back against the press of those behind. Carlin steeled himself for contact, grabbed Gerry by the wrist and indicated with his staff that they should go back and carry on up the close. Gerry stammered a bit, then found his voice.

'Well, folks, I did warn you to expect the unexpected. It seems that Major Weir in person has arrived to escort us on the final leg of this walk.' They got ahead of the crowd as Carlin led him up the slope. Under his breath Gerry said, 'What the hell's going on?'

Carlin said nothing but glowered at him and kept the haunt going. Total silence, total staring absence of expression, that was the thing. The party were tripping along behind him like weans after a piper. 'Explain later,' he said to Gerry, and came to a sudden halt. He let go his arm, swirled his cloak and pointed the staff menacingly, then spun around and flew into the narrow entry ahead. He put on a burst of speed, slipped in through the wooden door, quietly closed and snibbed it. He heard voices expressing astonishment at his disappearance. Then he made his way silently back down past where the girl was, and away.

He didn't give a fuck about explaining later. Gerry could talk his way out of it. It would make the tourists' night. He wondered about Karen, if she'd be there the next night, and what he would do if she was. He passed under George IV Bridge and thought of the weight of the library with its rows and rows of books pressing down through the layers of the city. When he reflected on it, the blue carbon-copied pages of the Lauder manuscript seemed unconvincing. Anybody could have put that stuff together, Carlin thought: D. Crosbie, whoever he was; MacDonald himself even, although why he would do such a thing was beyond imagining. And yet . . . and yet, before, the *Secret Book* had read so true; had pulled Carlin in and got him thinking Lauder's thoughts, walking in his doubt-ridden, anxious footsteps. How could that happen?

His mind flicked through Lauder and alighted on a little passage and he laughed out loud.

> *Ther ware 4 French peasants in a village ance, that fell to talk about the King. They sayd it was a braw thing to be a King. Says the first if I ware King I would lie at ease all the day on that hy stack wt my belly to the sun. The second says, I would sup every day at bacon swimming in its juces. If I ware King (says the 3d) I would feid my swine from upoun ane horse. The 4t, alas, ye have left me nothing to choose; ye have chosen all the best things.*

Maybe he was the victim of a complex practical joke. Hugh Hardie, D. Crosbie and MacDonald could all be in it together, Jackie Halkit the lure on which they had reeled him in. The unwitting lure? Or maybe she was in as thick as the rest of them. Conspirators of history.

He found his way back to Anderson's Close, the Stinking Close of Weir's time. He was still in the Weir gear: it was strange, you could wander around this part of town in this rig-out and people hardly paid you any attention. A couple of times he'd met another ghost on the street, going to or from his work. Deacon Brodie, or a monk or something. 'Aye,' the monk nodded as he passed. 'Aye,' said Major Weir. They were from different centuries but they never even blinked.

Carlin emerged at the Cowgatehead and walked the few yards to the Grassmarket. He stood there watching people entering and leaving the pubs; noticed lights coming on and going off in the hostels for derelicts, and in the flats above the shops on the Castle side of the street. Some of those flats were council-owned, others were private, expensively refurbished – this part of town retained that mix of social classes and types that had characterised it for centuries. And yet, Carlin thought, there were not so many people here as there once were. There were more people in Edinburgh, sure, but not here in its heart, where once all the world crammed and jostled together. In the 1660s, thirty thousand souls maybe, and multiplying fast, once the plague no longer thinned them. A paltry figure these days, of course, at the height of summer, during the Festival; and at other times like the big council-promoted Hogmanay celebrations, when thousands spilled up from Princes Street. But these were exceptions and the crowds were not real crowds; not real people who lived in a real place, but people passing through a moment, for whom the Old Town was the decor for a party, a pasted-up backdrop.

Carlin in the shadows looked further, deeper in. He saw sheep in pens, tethered cows, snapping dogs and flaffing hens, a gridlock of carts and horses. He saw the crowds of filthy ragged people, the barefoot bairns, the hawkers and chapmen, soldiers, fleshers with their packs of dogs to guard the cattle, traders, ministers, merchants' daughters douce to look at but with tongues that would clip clouts, wifies at the well, women selling and buying food, wool, milk, cloth; he smelt the sweat of their common crushed struggling humanity, the mixture of glaur and blood and rubbish and shite trampled underfoot. He heard the din of bleating, bellowing animals and shouting herds, saw the battlements looming high above on the north side, the inns and drinking shops clustered along the base of the rock, the gaunt scaffold rising above the crowd at the head of the street. On one side, behind him, the mouth of the Cowgate; on the other, the foot of the zig-zagging West Bow down which the condemned would be drummed . . .

Carlin saw it all. It pressed in upon him like heat from a furnace.

Weir and Mitchel; Mitchel and Weir. Mitchel the vehement, the insecure, the enthusiast, the unconfident, grasping at knowledge with his ignorant fists. Weir, thirty years his senior, a man of reputation – devout, militant, sure in his commitment to the letter and blood of the Covenant. Weir has connections. Mitchel has none. It is 1658 and he is a penniless graduate. He needs a job.

One of those of the kirk party appointed to judge James Graham was Sir George, eighteenth laird of Dundas. As Montrose's jailer, Weir had come into contact with him. Now he hears that Dundas is looking for a chaplain and tutor for his bairns. Through an intermediary, he secures Mitchel an introduction.

Sir George is impressed by Mitchel's youth, and by his poverty. He gives him the job, and Mitchel flits from the Cowgate to Dundas's castle out by Kirkliston. It is a strange, difficult situation. Though he is adequate at prayer, he is woefully bad at teaching. As Dundas is too busy with political affairs to notice, and his children too spoilt to care, this might not be disastrous; but Mitchel is an outsider. The other servants dislike him. They think him too sanctimonious for his own good, and it does not take them long before they believe they have found out his weakness. There is an auld taigelt gardener with a bored young wife, and it is obvious that the new tutor is susceptible to her charms. Rumour is spread like dung on rosebeds: Maister Mitchel is lustful; Maister Mitchel covets his neighbour's wife; Maister Mitchel commits adultery in his heart. Best of all, Maister Mitchel, aloof and totally unaware of the slanders circulating about him, is riding for a fall.

His accommodation is simple but secluded, a kind of summerhouse built onto the garden wall. One moon-bright night the gardener's wife is seen slipping across the lawns. The servants follow, note that the key is on the outside of the summerhouse door, and, when the hapless couple are at their coupling, they gently lock them in and run to fetch the laird. Some minutes later, a dog begins to bark. The woman tries to leave, becomes distracted: if her husband should discover her . . . Her master, watching the proceedings from a balcony of the castle, already has, and sees Mitchel help her through the window, and begin to lower her, dangling on one end of his shirt, to the ground. But the shirt is not long enough, she is afraid to jump the last few feet. Mitchel has to lean out further and further, clinging with one hand to the window frame, stretched like a lizard naked on the wall, till at last the shirt tears and she falls into some bushes. Oh, the sight of their pale limbs straining in the moonlight. Oh, the dishevelled skirts of the woman fleeing across the grass. Oh, the shame, next morning, of the tutor summoned before Dundas and dishonourably discharged. *O James Mitchel, ever learning and never able to come to the knowledge of the truth, thou shalt be cast out from thy mistress and from the garden of the laird.*

He returns to the Cowgate, disgraced but not humbled. He knows that great sin often comes before a calling. Even Samuel Rutherford fell in fornication and lost his first teaching post at Edinburgh just before beginning his pure ministry at Anworth. Mitchel waits in anticipation.

But times are changing for the godly party. Charles II, who can lie with a dozen gardeners' wives and neither think shame nor be expelled for it, is restored to the throne. He has no intention of going on his travels again. A parliament and independence are restored to Scotland, Scotland is restored to the rule of bishops and royalist incendiaries. All the acts and laws of the previous twenty-three years are annulled by an Act Rescissory. Presbyterianism is in retreat, riven by splits and factions.

Meanwhile the wife of Mitchel's old mentor Major Weir has died and he has moved a short distance from Mistress Whitford's to a house just off the West Bow, where he bides with his sister Jean. The Bow is a refuge of the saints in Edinburgh: a hotbed of holiness. Mitchel visits the Major, seeking his help again. If Weir no longer cuts the figure he once did in Edinburgh, he still has some influence among the disaffected, the many who are now obliged to toil under the yoke of episcopacy, waiting their chance to restore God's nation to God. Through Weir's intercession, Mitchel is found another place as chaplain, this time in the devout family of a niece of Sir Archibald Johnston of Wariston.

Johnston – a symbol of all that has gone hideously wrong. Once a pillar of the Covenant, he sold himself to Cromwell in London, then fled abroad at the Restoration, but was tracked down and extradited from France. Brought to Edinburgh and tried on his knees before parliament, he was reduced to a babbling, begging wreck, unable even to remember the words of his Bible. Johnston, the scourge of kings and princes, wound up hanged and his head spiked on the Netherbow Port, next to the fading skull of his former friend James Guthrie. Thus are the saints made martyrs; and thus the martyrs made a mockery.

Mitchel performs his new duties dully, without enthusiasm. This is not what he was put on earth for. Then in 1666 unrest among the godly explodes into rebellion in the west. An army of a few hundred – a thousand at most – marches through the middle shires towards Edinburgh. Mitchel abandons his job and rushes to join them. But this is not yet his time. He is sent back on an errand to the city, and while he's away the miserable force is met in the Pentland Hills and destroyed by the Muscovite beast General Tam Dalyell, whose beard, uncut since the execution of King Charles I, reaches to his waist, whose boots belch the smoke of hellfire and can walk at night on their own, and whose life can only be taken by a bullet made of silver. The rising of the saints is a complete failure. Mitchel is one of those specifically excluded from a pardon for his involvement in it and flees abroad to Rotterdam. A year later, though, he is back in Edinburgh, and now at last his time is at hand.

He lives like a spectre in the capital under the name of James Small, moving from one lodging to another, sometimes staying out of sight in one of the safe houses of the godly party's sympathisers. He steeps himself in Scripture. The voice of Elijah in the cave of Horeb is dirling in his head: *I have been very jealous for the Lord God of hosts: because the children of Israel have forsaken thy covenant, thrown down thine altars, and slain thy prophets with the sword; and I, even I only, am left; and they seek my life, to take it away.* And he reads of Jehu who was called by the prophet Elisha, and who came out of Ramoth-gilead to destroy Jezebel and all the house of Ahab, and how when the watchman on the tower of Jezreel saw the furious dust of Jehu's chariot approaching, they sent a messenger to him from the king saying, Is it peace? And Jehu answered, What hast thou to do with peace?

Then James Mitchel thinks of the false prophets, that come in sheep's clothing, but inwardly they are ravening wolves. And chief among these is the apostate and reprobate James Sharp.

These are the days of God's anger, the days of the nation's darkness, the perilous times of which Paul wrote to Timothy, when men shall be traitors, heady, highminded, lovers of pleasures more than lovers of God; having a form of godliness, but laden with diverse lusts. A pamphlet *Naphtali* has lately been circulating, so precise and threatening that the government has hunted and harried it, ordered it burnt and threatened any found in possession of it with a fine of ten thousand pounds. 'A damned book come hither from beyond the sea,' says the government; 'it hath all the traitors' speeches on the scaffold, and speaks with a tongue set on fire in Hell.'

'Take notice,' says *Naphtali*, 'of the many Sufferings and Sufferers hereafter mentioned, whose Heads and Hands standing betwixt Heaven and Earth, doth not only cry for Vengeance, but night and day bear open Witness against this Adulterous Generation.' Andrew Honyman, bishop of Orkney, like Sharp another Covenanter turned prelate, pens a reply, *A Survey of the Insolent and Infamous Libel, Entitled Naphtali*. 'Scotland, Ah Scotland!' says *Naphtali*, 'hath changed her glory for that which doth not profit. Be astonished, O ye heavens, and be horribly afraid. If God doth not heal his People we shall become such a proverb amongst the Nations, that the generation to come of our Children, and the stranger that cometh from a far Land, when they see the plagues of this Land, shall wonder and ask, Wherefore hath the Lord done this unto this Land? What meaneth the heat of this great anger?'

This is the word storm that crashes and roars through Mitchel's head in the spring months of 1668. He feels himself besieged by words, by threats, entreaties, instructions, warnings, challenges. He is looking for something he can do, something that will put these things in some semblance of order. He steels himself to act, to perform.

He goes down into the street one day, to the shop of Alexander Logan, dagmaker, in Leith Wynd, outwith the Netherbow Port. He knows that Logan turns a blind eye to some of his best customers, for by law he must not sell arms to anyone who has not subscribed to keep the peace, not fire-arms, sword, dirk, whinger or any such weapon. Mitchel has walked past the door many times, sometimes pausing, sometimes hardly daring to look, sometimes with his coat empty, sometimes carrying the money saved from his cousin John. On this day, like a shy man entering a whorehouse, he darts inside, and puts the money on the counter. 'Whit can ye gie me for this?' he asks.

Logan sells him a pair of long pistols, each with a bore like a musket, and shows him how to prime and load them. Mitchel carries them away in a box to his lonely room, and there he practises presenting them at the hearts of imagined men. Or one man, imagined over and over. A little paper has come into his hand, one of the squibs that fly from secret presses into the street, and he marvels at its ingenious wit and tries to memorise it:

Mercenarie, medling madcap,
Absurd, abjured, angry ape,
Sancts' SHARP scourge, Scotland's Satanik spot,
Trafecting, treacherous turncot,
Envy's exemplar eminent,
Rebell, relent, return, repent.

Infamous juglar, insolent
Ambitious and arrogant
Mischief's midwyfe, monstrous madman,
Erroneous, Erastian
Saucie, selfish Simoniak.

Servile Soulseller stigmatick,
Hell's hound, hideous hierarchist,
Abominable archatheist,
Railling ruffian, runagat,
Perfidious, perjur'd Prelat.

He pins the paper to the wall; turns, pulls the pistols from his coat, aims, turns again, aims. And he scours his Bible for a certainty of God's approval for what he intends to do.

When doubt enters his mind, he beats it back with the words of *Naphtali*: 'What shall be given to thee, O Sharp! Or what shall be done to Thee, O false Tongue? Sharp arrows of the Mighty and Coals of Juniper.' He thinks of Major Weir: 'The Lord will find you work, James.' And he thinks of John Knox, a century before, calling on the people and every member of the people to revenge the injury done against God's glory by his enemies, 'according to the vocation of every man and according to the possibility and occasion which God doth minister . . . Who dare be so impudent as to deny that this be most reasonable and just?'

On a Saturday early in July, about four in the afternoon, James Mitchel loads his pistols – three balls apiece – and arms himself with the best text of all, the verse from Deuteronomy that he carries in his heart: *And that prophet, or that dreamer of dreams, shall be put to death; because he hath spoken to turn you away from the Lord your God, which brought you out of the land of Egypt, and redeemed you out of the house of bondage, to thrust thee out of the way which the Lord thy God commanded thee to walk in. So shalt thou put the evil away from the midst of thee.* He leaves his room and enters onto the street, and makes his way to the top of Blackfriars Wynd. He hovers there, standing back from the folk that pass up and down the causey, watching the coach that sits outside the bishop's lodgings a few yards away. His palms are sweating and he dichts them on his coat, feeling beneath it the bulges of his ready weapons. He is about to take the life of another man and send him to perdition. *God strengthen my arm and my resolve.* Into himself he mutters the words of Deuteronomy, the words of Moses, the Word of God: *Thou shalt not consent unto him, nor hearken unto him; neither shall thine eye pity him, neither shalt thou spare, neither shalt thou conceal him; but thou shalt surely kill him; thine hand shall be first upon him to put him to death, and afterwards the hand of all the people.*

A servant emerges from the doorway, opens the coach door and stands to one side. His master follows and steps into the coach. Now is Mitchel's time, now he is *in* history. He draws the first pistol from within his coat, advances on the coach. There is a group of folk by it, poor bairns and beggars seeking alms, so his approach goes unnoticed. Nobody stands between him and the object of God's wrath.

But then, history betrays him. As he reaches the open door and levels the gun, he realises that another man has followed Sharp out of the house – a man in clerical dress – and is about to mount the step of the coach. Mitchel glances to see if he is mistaken, if this second man is in fact the Archbishop. It is not. He looks back and sees Sharp frozen in shock, staring right into his eyes. He aims again just as the arm of the second man, putting his hand up to steady himself, moves into his vision. Mitchel fires the pistol. In that moment he knows that he has hit, but missed Sharp.

The second man's hand and arm seem momentarily to separate; there is a spattering sound on the coach's upholstery. Blood and smoke everywhere. Mitchel understands that he does not have time to draw the other gun. He can feel men advancing on him. He ducks away and strides rapidly across the wynd.

His hand is grasping the butt of the second pistol. He pulls it out, trying to work out if he can return to kill Sharp with his remaining shot. But he knows it is too late. Everything that was clear in his vision a few moments before is now clouded. Noise and commotion are rippling out from the stationary coach. At the head of Niddrie's Wynd a well-dressed, broad-faced man blocks his way. Mitchel presents the pistol at him. The man backs off and lets him by. Mitchel hides his weapons again, forces himself not to run, not to attract attention. He reaches the Cowgate, turns up Stevenlaw's Close, checks behind him to see if he is followed, and chaps at a door. It is opened at once, he slips inside, is ushered up some stairs. The house of William Fergusson, a sympathiser.

Fergusson says, 'Man, there's powder marks on yer face and bluid on yer sleeve. Hae ye been huntin?'

'Aye, but the beast's no deid. Can ye fetch me new claes?'

Ten minutes later, re-wigged and new-washed, the pistols hidden by Fergusson, he is out on the streets again, in pursuit of himself, but keeping away from the soldiery. The citizens' chase is half-hearted at best. When the cry went up, 'A man is killt,' it was followed by another, 'It's only a bishop,' and loud laughter.

Mitchel walks as if in a dream. Could God have misguided his aim? If so, for what purpose? This *was* his purpose. A new verse from Jeremiah bombards him now: *Cursed be he that doeth the work of the Lord deceitfully, and cursed be he that keepeth back his sword from blood*. What is his purpose now? To avoid discovery, surely. God is testing him. Will there be another opportunity?

Sir Andrew Ramsay turns out the Guard. The bishops' servants were so stunned by the brazenness of the assault that the man who fired got clean away from them. Someone says he made for the West Port, where an accomplice waited for him with a horse ready saddled – they rode for Corstorphine. Lord Provost Ramsay sends men in pursuit, but orders the whole town searched in case they are still lurking there. He writes a feverish letter to Lauderdale – this kind of outrage is the last thing Edinburgh needs – bad for trade, bad for law and order, bad for Ramsay: *My lord, the fellow is none that belongs to this place, nor can this place be looked on with any worse eye because of this.*

A reward is posted. The Archbishop is shaken by the foul, bloody and cowardly attempt on his life. In a rare outburst of spiritual passion he is heard praying, 'My times are wholly in thy hands, O my God of my life!' But he is unharmed. His companion in the coach was Honyman, the bishop of Orkney. He is grievously hurt, the bones in his wrist all shattered.

Mitchel goes to ground. By whispered word he hears of, and from a window-chink in a shuttered room he sees, the chase spreading through the town. Soldiers are everywhere, searching any house where Whigs stay or where a Whig terrorist might be harboured. More than once he has to move. People are arrested and interrogated, and all who favour Presbyterianism are cast under a cloud of suspicion. There is even a rumour that the bishops themselves planned the attack: for the sake of a wounded hand all Lauderdale's plans to relax some of the prohibitions against non-indulged ministers are shelved.

Women as well as men are bullied, threatened with banishment to the plantations, and incarcerated because they will not speak. Mistress Janet Crawford, Mistress Margaret Kello and Mistress Anna Duncan – worthy, kenspeckle women of a Whig persuasion, known to have hosted conventicles in the past – are all brought before the Privy Council, a sign that Sharp will not rest until he has the name of the man who tried to kill him. The Chancellor, the Earl of Rothes follows in his wake, angry but also half-amused – he dislikes Sharp and is only outraged that a man should dare to shoot at a Privy Councillor. Mitchel hears how Mistress Duncan is put in fear of her life by these great men of state. When she will not admit to any knowledge of the assassination attempt, nor to any communication with 'rebels', they bring the public executioner into her, carrying the torture apparatus of the boots: 'Ye hae until five o the clock tae mind whit ye hae forgotten.' In the end, Lord Rothes saves her legs with a jest: 'My lords, this isna guid politics. Forby, it isna proper for a gentlewoman tae wear boots.' She is sent instead to the

Tolbooth and not released for more than five months.

And for more than five years Mitchel evades capture. Somebody, somewhere, has talked, and the name of James Mitchel, the Pentland rebel, is attached to the crime. Where does he go in these years? To Holland, some say. Others say, to Ireland, England, France. God has laid him by and does not call upon him. But still he is thirled to James Sharp by that frozen moment in the coach. Neither can forget it. Each believes that they will meet again, and that one will be the executioner of the other. Through all the affairs of kirk and state, the Archbishop nurses a cold place in his heart for the fanatic who would have killed him. In all his secret wanderings, Mitchel still dreams of levelling the pistol one more time at Sharp.

Then, one day early in 1674, Mitchel's gaunt figure is seen at the funeral of the old minister of Pencaitland, Robert Douglas. Word reaches Sharp that his enemy is back in Edinburgh. Spies are given a close description of him. Before long, one of them comes to the Archbishop with news that such a man now keeps a stall with his wife, in Blackfriars Wynd no less, selling brandy and tobacco. Sharp, not without trepidation, and flanked by servants, finds some pretext to pass by this stall. He lingers, tries a sidelong keek at the tall man's face, turns away abruptly when he thinks he is about to catch his eye. Five and a half years have gone by. He thought the image of those seconds in the coach was fixed forever. Is this him? He cannot be sure. He risks another glance, and this time, by coincidence, the stallkeeper raises his head at the same time. Sharp, heart pounding, makes himself stare, holding the narrowing stare of the other man, until he is as certain as he ever will be. Yes! He minds the sickening pause before the explosion of the pistol. Yes, this is the man.

He calls on his brother, Sir William Sharp, who organises a party of armed men and descends on Blackfriars Wynd before the fanatic can make his escape. But Mitchel, strangely, has not shifted. It's as if he believes himself immune from all but the Archbishop. He is seized on 7 February, removed to the Tolbooth, and at last, so long after the event, is brought before a committee of the Council for examination.

'Time itself,' says *Naphtali*, 'a great searcher and discoverer of secrets.' Down all these years a secret world has turned. And now, James Mitchel, is the moment when you step into the glaring light.

Carlin was shivering. His tee-shirt and jumper were soaked through, the sweat like a layer of ice on his skin. He could hear his mother's voice: 'Ye'll catch yer death.' He happed the Major's cloak tight around him, gripped the staff in his wet hand. He didn't recognise where he was. Some unlit close, not where he had been. What, had he been sleepwalking?

It would not have been the first time. When he was twelve or thirteen, his father had been dying quietly in his parents' bedroom. His mother, to give him peace, slept on a couch downstairs. Carlin minded waking up standing in total darkness in a room that might have been his own or any room in the house. The first time he stood still and called for help. His mother had turned on the light and he was only a couple of feet from his bed. She didn't seem to understand his confusion. She told him he had to be quiet and not disturb his father. He was a big laddie now. After that he didn't call for her. He'd wake on the landing, in the kitchen, on the stairs, and wait for what seemed an eternity until his eyes began to make out dim objects around him. Then he'd move gingerly, hands out in front until he found the wall, and feel his way back to his room. He'd get into bed and lie there wondering what was happening to him.

He felt like calling out now, but nobody would come. He took a single step and nearly lost his balance. He was on a slope. He began to walk down it, waving his stick like a blind man. He had to believe that if he kept going forward he would eventually get to a place he recognised.

Edinburgh, February 1670

'*Jean, Jean!*' Someone was calling her. A woman's voice. Not *him*, then. He'd gone out, she was alone in the house, and the door was bolted. She had learnt to be canny about voices, though. A man could have a woman's voice, a woman could be not just a woman. Like herself. She was not just a woman. She was all kinds of wonders.

'*Jean, Jean!*' There it was again. Like the start of a bairn's rhyme. *Jean, Jean, fairy queen!* But that could not be right either. There was only one fairy queen and it wasn't herself.

Herself? Maybe it was her own voice? It wouldn't be the first time. He'd catch her talking to herself once in a while, and he didn't like it. It was all right if she just haivered, but sometimes she'd slip in other things among the haivers, and a terrible anger would break on his face. Terrible, and yet feart too. She noticed that, and stored it away.

'*Jean, Jean!*' There was work to be done. She'd ignore the insistent calling. If she'd a mirror she could stand in front of it and when the voice came see if her lips moved. Then she'd know whether to be feart. But *he* didn't allow mirrors. Sinful vanities. Keek in a glass and all ye see is clay, *he* said. Keek in yer soul and ye'll mebbe see grace.

She moved around the room, a cloth in one hand, a stick in the other. Not *his* stick, with the nasty thrawn face. That was away out with him. *Her* stick was a dry old branch, peeling bark, fit only for the fire. She wiped surfaces with the cloth as she went, the table, a shelf, the arm of his chair. They were thick with stour. Bessie the servant had left and was never coming back. She couldn't blame her. She should have gone with her herself.

The house was in a state right enough, falling apart, and there was next to no food in it. She wasn't hungry any more. She couldn't eat for the thought of *him* coming back.

As she shauchled round, she sang a few notes to herself.

Maybe it was a psalm, maybe it was a pagan song. She didn't care. And with her stick she chapped the walls; the stonework around the lum, the wooden skifting at floor-level, the floorboards themselves. *Chap!* 'There a mystery,' she said. *Chap!* 'There anither.' *Chap!* 'There a secret, Thomas Weir.' *Chap!* 'There a wee thing tae keep tae yersel.'

When she'd been right round the room she threw her stick in the fire. A poor, sulky thing the fire was, the wind must be in the wrong airt. She turned about suddenly, as if she had heard someone at the door, but there was no one. Then she sat down, in *his* chair, and watched as the fire, slowly at first, then greedily and with a pleasing cracking sound, consumed the branch.

Over her shoulder, over the back of the chair, came the voice again. '*Jean, Jean!*' And now she knew it wasn't her own, for the voice was quite clearly coming from behind her. She gripped the arms of the chair and pretended not to hear it. If she sat there long enough, it might go away.

When you'd no mirror you learnt to see yourself else-where. She'd always been good at seeing pictures in the flames. She knew she looked like the crooked stick now, because when she put her hand to her face she felt the wrinkles, the hard knots of bone beneath the broken skin. When she got into bed at night, although she never undressed completely, not now, for it was too painful to see her nakedness, she saw enough of it to know that she was crumbling and brittle.

Had she ever been different? It was hard to think on now, but she believed she had. Not bonnie perhaps, but young and strong. Oh aye, she'd been those. At Wicketshaw, the house of her youth. In those days, she had gone naked. That had been a joy. To strip in the woods at Carluke, to lie in the long grass in meadows, to feel the good earth and the sharp blades of twigs and leaves pricking and tickling your soft flesh. It was a joy, not a sin. Even now she was sure of it. It was *he* who had made it a sin, he who had made their love impure after promising her it was purity itself. As pure as God. As free from censure as God.

The byre, the bedrooms, the hidden corners of the house. She minded these places and the times he had forced himself

144

on her and she hated them all now. But the times they had had out of doors, they were special. She minded Thomas like a white hind in the trees, coming towards her. His thing like a mushroom on a huge stalk, straining towards her. Later she realised how like some witch rite it had been, those frantic, joyous couplings under the green canopy of birdsong. Like how a witch's coven was supposed to be. A man with the head of a beast. A woman dancing wildly. At the time, though, it had been nothing to do with witches. It had been to do with saints.

'Jean, Jean, come awa noo!' The voice was soft, but mocking. It mocked her memories. To do with saints! What was she thinking of? She frowned. In the fire the last of the branch twisted and kinked. She unfrowned, and the branch broke and was lost among the rest of the embers.

She often wondered about things like that. Did she really have power? Did the branch obey her frown? She'd heard so many stories of women who could make spells, who could talk to the invisible world. And she knew which herbs to pick from the forest to make a cure for a child's sickness, her mother had taught her. But were these things power, and if so what kind of power?

Sometimes when she was alone in the woods she'd think of the naked days of her youth again, and she'd seem to picture more than just herself. Other women – witches – dancing in a clearing, and a muckle black man. If she could think these things, if she had that kind of knowledge, and if she had done what she had done with her brother, ah well then, maybe she could be a witch.

After they came from Carluke to Edinburgh and she kept the school at Dalkeith, had she maybe been a witch by then? She lived alone and that was enough in some folk's eyes. They tried to trick her. They sent a wee wifie, who pretended she came from the fairy world. *'Touch yer heid and taes, Jean, gie him awthin inbetween; hae whit iver thing ye list, iver mair ye shall be his!'* She saw what their game was. She sent the wifie packing. The Dalkeith folk were jealous of her. Her neat wee schoolhouse. Her skill at spinning. Her fine, upstanding brother, the Major, that could speak so English like and was so favoured by the kirk, the army and the city. Now that was a different kind of power, was it not?

But the wifie came again, and each time she came Jean's spirit weakened. For she knew her brother false by then, long before anybody else suspected. Before he suspected himself, even. Because he had turned away from her. She could tell that she repulsed him. Yet he would still come to her, when he could not get what he desired elsewhere.

'Whit is it ye want?' she said suddenly, out loud. Her voice was shrill in the empty house. It was proof that she had not spoken before. But now the spell was broken. As soon as she spoke the other voice vanished. If it had ever been there.

Thomas would be home soon. The day was darkening and he would be expecting food. Work to be done and she hadn't even started. There *were* some scraps of food: a bit of an old sheepshank, some carrots and kail. She could boil it all up with some barley for a broth. He would hate it, greasy and grey with the carrots floating like corpses. If he wanted to eat he'd not have any choice.

It might make him raise his hand to her. He had done it in the past and hurt her. He had had many ways to hurt her but this was the last and weakest. She liked to see him try it these days because now when the arm came up it always fell away again. Feeble, dwindling in strength. She understood why this was. He was drowning in doubt, and the doubt was becoming certainty.

She went to the window and looked out onto the roofs and walls. Their recesses and angles were fading into the gathering dark. She rubbed at the pane and saw herself distorted in its whorl, an old stick being souked down into blackness.

Into blackness, and never come back. She wished that of him. Never come back, Thomas Weir. May ye drap deid in the street. God strike ye doon. Oh she wished it, she wished it. She'd go to Hell for wishing it, if it would just give her a few months, a few weeks even, to be here alone, shut in from the world.

If she had a charm against him she would use it. But she'd none. For a witch she was fushionless. She could not keep him from coming home. But she had seen the fear in his eyes. Doubting Thomas. He was crumbling too. She had all his secrets numbered in her heart and he could not deny them. That was power of a sort.

'Jean, Jean!' She held her breath, listened. But now when she wanted the woman's voice, wanted whatever unknown promises the wee wifie might have for her, her hopes sank. For it was a man's voice. He was coming up the stair. There was the sound of his heavy tread outside the door, and the dull thump of his staff against it, demanding entry.

Edinburgh, April 1997

Jackie Halkit had a huge room in an enormous flat in Great King Street, in the New Town. It was the kind of place which she could never afford to own, but just to live in it was a pleasure. She shared it with two other women and a man, splitting the exorbitant rent and the astonishingly large heating bills four ways to make the costs just about bearable. Sharing itself was not much of a burden: the flat was too big to feel crowded or oppressive. If she ever got bored of her own room (about twelve feet by ten of bedroom tastefully melting into the same amount of sitting-room, complete with open fireplace) there was the vast and comforting kitchen, the bathroom with its acres of stripped floorboards between bath, sink and toilet, and the long elegant hallway to enjoy. There was a serenity about the flat that normally never failed to relax her.

But tonight was different. She lay on her bed and the room seemed too big and empty. She was thinking of Andrew Carlin. She'd been bothered all week by thoughts of him and it was driving her mad with frustration. He kept creeping up on her . . . No, that wasn't it, that was what she *expected* him to do, whereas what happened was he just kept being there. In her head. She'd be working on a manuscript and find she'd drifted away from the text in front of her and was seeing him instead. She'd be walking home and he'd be beside her. She'd wake up in the morning and he was there, in her mind.

It wasn't sinister or scary. It was like – well, the only thing she could think of made her even more angry with herself – it was like when she'd had a crush on a boy at school. That constant turning over of chance meetings and imaginary conversations. And yet this wasn't a crush. He wasn't attractive to her. If she fancied anyone lately it was Hugh Hardie, an uncomplicated lightweight with a bit of money and no hang-ups. Maybe, just maybe, she fancied Hardie. But Carlin, no, definitely not.

She tried yet again to remember when she'd last seen him, before he walked into Dawson's. There'd been that time in Sandy Bell's, six or seven years ago, when he'd walked her and the other girls from the class across the Meadows. He'd left them and headed off westwards. They'd all sighed and giggled relief and gone for a coffee in one of the others' flats. Then, the next term, had he come back? He must have dropped out around then, she decided.

She didn't fancy him, she wasn't afraid of him, not any more. On the tour, she'd been impressed by his performance. It wasn't like he was acting well, he seemed disdainful of the act. More that he couldn't help himself. Or he became himself.

He'd dodged out of the end of the tour. She knew that's what he must have done. No reason why he should have. He must know the route inside out.

He's lost, Jackie thought. That's it. That's what's on his face. It looks spooky to people because they're on this tour through all these wynds and closes and they see this figure that's supposed to scare them and it does scare them because it looks like he's been wandering around there for centuries trying to find a way out. A dead man in a labyrinth without a skein of thread.

Carlin is lost. Or he's afraid of being lost.

She sat up on the bed. She thought, I'm going to have to phone Hugh. I'm going to have to do his bloody tour again. I'm going to have to find out where Carlin goes when he gets lost.

Bass Rock, April 1677/Kippen, November 1673

Tammas's bulk filled the doorway of the cell, blocking out what little light might have got in.

'Ye hae a visitor,' he whispered. 'I'm shuttin yese in till jist afore the boat leaves. They think she's ower wi a servant o Maister Fraser's.'

Mitchel sat up, confused. He thought Tammas was talking about the boat. But a smaller figure came in past the soldier, who shut and locked the door. The figure moved through the mirk towards him. There was a familiarity about its shape.

'Ah, James, James,' it said, 'whit sair place is this tae find ye in.'

'Sweet Jesus Christ,' he said. 'Elizabeth.'

She came into his arms. He breathed in the smell of her, so fresh when all he had breathed for months was salt and smoke and the staleness of his body. Their faces were wet with each other's tears. They hushed each other's sobs like bairns fearful of being discovered.

'The sodger wi the poxed face, he is an angel,' Elizabeth said breathlessly. 'I had peyed the minister's man tae let me come ower wi him, tae say I was his sister, but I hadna thocht how I would get tae ye yince we landed. I had decided tae beg the captain's mercy tae let me see ye, since the boat winna return for us till the forenicht, but I was feart he wouldna like ma deceit. And when I saw the horror o the place, I kent I would hae nae mercy frae ony man that could rule here, and I jist sclimmed up the steps, thinkin somehow I would find ye. But the sodger speired did I no ken where I was gaun, and I thocht I would hae mair chance wi him, and sae I said I didna ken, but I was lookin for ma husband, and he speired wha was that, and I tellt him James Mitchel, and he looked aboot himsel and pushed me on afore him and said, dinna say that name again, he has nae freens, and syne he led me tae ye. I hae mair siller, James, and ye must gie some tae him, for it's through him we are brocht thegither.'

She had a basket, in which she had packed bread and cheese, some salted meat, tobacco and brandy. And there was a small amount of money, which she had gathered over the months since he had been brought there. The last time she had seen him had been nearly a year and a half ago, not long before he had been put to the boots.

While he tore at the bread and bit off chunks of cheese, Elizabeth removed his stocking to look at the injury. She was not hungry; she had eaten that morning at North Berwick. She did not say that she had been two days in the fishing port, waiting; not for calm weather, but for the moment when she herself was ready for crossing.

She stared in horror at his leg. There was nothing to be done for it. It was, at least, not infected, but it was wrecked. The shinbone had been splintered and had reset itself crooked; the muscles were torn and mashed beyond repair. She touched it with her fingers, which were calloused and yellow from working in the stall. As he ate, he watched her hand stroking the patchy, discoloured leg, and a different kind of pain rolled through him.

'I am sorry, Lizzie Sommervile,' he heard himself say. 'I am sorry that God's work is sae sair on us.'

They had met in 1673, at a conventicle in a house in Edinburgh, and had been married later that year by the outed minister John Welsh, in a ceremony that was illegal in the eyes of the state. Four months later Mitchel had been seized and incarcerated in the Tolbooth. In the last three years he had seen Elizabeth no more than half a dozen times. Even at Edinburgh access had frequently been denied her, and, since December 1675, when he had made an abortive attempt to escape by breaking through the roof, all visits had been refused.

'His will be done,' she said. He had never spoken to her about the shooting of Sharp, and she understood that he never would. She knew he had done it. It was a long time ago. She hoped that it was a buried thing now, that he, even if he could never admit it, was as glad as she was that he had missed.

'Aye,' he said, 'his will be done.' The Bass was a world beyond the world. It was agony for him even to think on the possibilities of her life on the mainland. She was kissing the leg now, laying her cheek against it, her breath hot over the blotched skin. It was unbearable to him to receive that tenderness.

'Lizzie,' he said, 'hae ye been faithfu tae me?'

She stopped. Her eyes filled. 'Dinna speir that unworthy question, James,' she said. 'Aw that I sell on the streets, I sell for you. Aw that I hae saved in the world, is saved for you. Dinna question ma faith.'

He was mortified. She had come to him here, at great risk. If she had taken herself off and he had never seen her again, he could not have blamed her. But the fear was still there.

'Lie wi me,' he said. 'Let me ken ye again, here in the darkness.'

She hesitated. It was the moment she had prepared herself for, the reason she had waited the extra day at North Berwick, but it had come sooner than she had expected. But then, what had she expected? His question had hurt her, but shamed her too. She had come here not for him, but for herself.

She knew her own body and its monthly changes so well that ordinarily she hardly had to think about them. But she'd been thinking hard over the last year, as it grew upon her that James might never be released. They were husband and wife, but she felt in some way she was about to betray him.

'Lizzie,' he said again. 'D'ye mind thon time at Kippen?'

He untied his breeks, feeling himself swell the way he did in dreams. She stretched out on the hard bed beside him, fumbling against him as she gathered her skirts towards her waist.

'Thon time,' she said. 'Mair than three year syne, James. There's been little else tae mind on atween us.'

After their marriage, at the suggestion of Mr Welsh, they had journeyed together north to Stirling, and from there to the west, to Cardross House by the village of Kippen. 'Come and share in the spirit of Christ's people,' Welsh told them, 'in the very heart of God's covenanted nation.' Lord Cardross was a fervent Presbyterian, who had been supporting and

152

attending illegal gatherings in the vicinity for years. The country that lay between the Fintry hills and the Trossachs, and between Strathblane and Stirling, was a hive of conventicling, where large crowds would come to out of the way places in the hills and among the bogs for the preaching.

Lizzie had never been more than a few miles from Edinburgh. To travel so far when the winter was closing in, was a revelation in itself. As far as Stirling the going was relatively easy and the towns and villages, though new to her, were not frightening for one who had grown up on the streets of the capital. But once they left Stirling behind, and she saw the great desolate mountains of the north ahead of her, and the long bleak shoulder of the Gargunnock hills closing on her left, she began to shrink and cling to Mitchel. It was not new land to him, yet even now he found something momentous about the mountains. He saw why John Welsh had encouraged them to come, why he called it the heart of Scotland, out of which both Highlands and Lowlands flowed. In such a place, where the land gathered like solid waves about them, a man and a woman would understand their place in the cosmos.

When they arrived at Kippen, news of Welsh's arrival was carried from house to house, and from farm to village. The meeting was to be held up beyond Flanders Moss, in rough wet country below the Menteith hills where the dragoons, if they appeared, could not easily ride, and from where folk could scatter and hide if necessary. It was November, and the weather was threatening rain and hail. Early on Sunday morning, before dawn, groups of men and women began to appear in the wastes, drawing together as the light slowly filled the sky. James and Elizabeth walked together along the wet paths, hand in hand, and Lizzie was smiling and James Mitchel was delirious with happiness. It was seven years since Pentland and the hanging of Hew McKail; five since he had shot at James Sharp; now he was being reborn again, with a wife to care for, a covenant to renew, and perhaps, when they returned to Edinburgh, a chance properly to fulfil the purpose God had set for him.

The people were quiet and serious but friendly. Some of the men, like James, carried swords and other weapons, but the atmosphere was peaceful. They had come from miles around. They came out from Kippen itself, from Arnprior and Balfron and Buchlyvie and Gargunnock. They came north across the hills from as far as Lennoxtown, east from Aberfoyle, south and west from Drummond and Thornhill. The country was filled with the folk of Boquhan, Kipdarroch, Cauldhame, Poldar, Arngomery, Menteith, Tamavoid, Brucehill, Ruskie, Cassafuir, Ladylands, Carden, Gartrenich, Arnfechlach, Knockinshannock, Gartentruach, Ballabeg, Gartbawn, Gartinstarry, Jennywoodston, Arngibbon, Blaircessnock, Arnbeg, Inch, Dub, Drum, Myme, Pendicles of Collymoon, Nether Easter Offerance, Claylands, Borland, Dykehead, Merkland, Shirgarton, Kepdowrie, Gartmore, Gartfarran, Offrins of Gartur. The names of their places filled the air like the numbering of Israel.

John Welsh preached with the forests and hills at his back, and sentries posted to warn of approaching soldiers. His text was from Revelation, chapter 6: *And the kings of the earth, and the great men, and the rich men, and the chief captains, and the mighty men, and every bondman, and every free man, hid themselves in the dens and in the rocks of the mountains; And said to the mountains and rocks, Fall on us, and hide us from the face of him that sitteth on the throne, and from the wrath of the Lamb: For the great day of his wrath is come; and who shall be able to stand?*

He spoke for two hours, discoursing on the wrath of temporal kings and the wrath of God, on those who hid among the rocks as they did now and those mighty men who would hide when it was their turn to be hunted; and how in that day there would be no hiding-place and no deliverance for them, and only those who had kept their tryst with God in the present times would be upheld in his terrible judgment. 'Remember,' said John Welsh, 'the dying words of Samuel Rutherford, who was summoned at the Restoration to compear before Parliament on a charge of treason: *I have got summons already before a superior Judge*, saith his servant Samuel, *and I must answer my first summons, and ere your day is at hand, I will be where few kings and great folks come.*'

There were prayers and psalms, and the grey looming sky that had seemed so heavy with rain cleared, and the sun broke on the hills and made the boggy ground gleam with many colours. Lizzie Sommervile found herself stirred with feelings that she neither recognised nor understood. She looked at James Mitchel beside her, and felt his hand clutching hers. She believed she loved him, but she did not know why. She believed he loved her but in a different way, a way through God that would always be closed to her. But she would never say this. If it was necessary to him, then she would pretend that this also was the way she loved. On a day such as this she could almost believe it.

The weather was so fine by the time the meeting broke up that, as people were leaving on the long walks back to their homes, James turned to Lizzie and said, 'Let's awa intae the hills, tae see the place frae on high.' And although she was nervous to be going in the opposite direction from everybody else, and was surprised that he should suggest a Sabbath journey that was not to worship, it was maybe like going a dauner in the company of God, so she consented. They climbed rapidly, and looked back on the brown land shining with water, and the tiny figures of the people departing, and they came to a cleft in some rocks which was thick with pine needles, and almost dry, and they spread her shawl out there and lay and watched the last worshippers disperse, and the country below become empty again.

James Mitchel undid the ties of Lizzie's dress, and put his hand to her breasts, and his lips to them. She felt the weakening warmth of the sun on her shoulders. 'I am the rose of Sharon, and the lily of the valleys,' said James. He pulled up her skirts and pushed down his own clothes and entered her, and she felt him going deep into her. He put down his head and began to thrust. Past his shoulders she saw the thick ranks of trees and the looming hills, and a tremor of fear went through her as he came. What were they doing in this desolate place, on the Sabbath, after having heard the dire warnings of the minister? This was not a walk with God but a nakedness in his garden that they should hide. But in her fear was something else, deeper, an utter *lack* of shame. And James did not feel her fear or her shame-lessness; she wondered if he felt anything of her at all. He lay on top of her, breathing heavily, his face in at her shoulder.

She fell into a dwam. She came half out of it, aware that

the sun was getting low. A cold wind was rising. She was about to shake him awake, when something moved up yonder, in the trees. A deer? A wolf, maybe? Could there be wolves here? And then the movement came again, and a figure stepped from the forest.

It was a boy. He might have been twelve, or fifteen, or maybe even older. It was hard to tell because she had never seen anyone like him. No, that was not quite true. She had seen them on the streets of Edinburgh, Highlanders, great beasts of men, cattle drovers, and others of their race who came to barter and sell and, according to most folk, to steal whatever they could. They spoke a quick, liquid language and stared at you with great curiosity and insolence. That was how the boy looked at her. He was thin and lithe, wearing a ragged peat-coloured plaid, loosely held around him by a belt and a clasp of some kind. His legs and feet were bare, which she could hardly believe out here on the hillside in this wintry season. His skin was brown as a nut, and his shaggy hair black like night. His face and arms and legs were streaked with mud and grainy with dirt. He held a long stick in one hand. There was a knife stuck in his belt.

He took a step towards her. She was about to scream, but he held a finger to his mouth and smiled. The smile stopped her. It filled his face from eyes to mouth and it was beautiful. It made her certain that he did not intend to hurt her. She almost forgot that she was lying with her skirts around her waist and a buttock-naked man on top of her. The boy took another step. He was maybe twenty feet away.

She saw his eyes flicker and she followed that brief signal and suddenly realised what it was he was after. James's sword lay a few feet away. She came to herself at once, fully awake, pushing James off her and diving to grab the sword. James jumped up, his breeks halfway down his legs, a ridiculous dishevelled sight. She had the sword by the hilt. 'Whit? Whit is it?' he was shouting. She looked around. The boy was gone.

She could say nothing. She ran a few steps towards the trees, pulling her clothes together. There was nobody there. She came back to James, who was finishing dressing himself. 'I'm sorry,' she said. 'I dreamt . . . I thocht I saw somebody there.'

'Where?' he said anxiously. She pointed. He took the sword from her. They peered into the trees together.

'It's late,' he said. 'You should hae waked me. We must get aff the hill.'

They hurried down the slope together. 'Whit's wrang?' she said. 'Whit is *wrang*?' But he did not speak until they had regained the flat land and were striding east, back to Cardross, in the last of the light.

'These Highland hills,' he told her. 'It's ma ain fault, Lizzie, I shouldna hae taen ye up there. They are cauld and evil, and the Erse folk watch frae them. They are pagans when they arena papists, and they would murder ye for a plack. Tell me whit ye saw.'

But she could not get the boy's smile out of her mind. Surely he had meant her no harm. She only said, 'I saw naethin. I thocht, for an instant, a man, but it was mair likely a beast, a deer mebbe. I was dreamin.'

He softened a little. 'Ah, Lizzie, I was dreamin also. Ma heid was brimfou wi the beauty of this day. Truly God hath brought me to the banqueting-house, and his banner over me is love.'

She recognised that. It was from the Song of Solomon. And then she understood why he had taken her up there – to make real some kind of dream that he had, to live in the Song himself. They hurried along in the dark, disorientated on the unfamiliar paths. And she felt miserable within, and jealous of the words that he worshipped.

James Mitchel clung to her on the narrow bed of the cell. She felt the wooden planks beneath her, unyielding and hard. James grunted and came into her.

Had she come to the Bass for this? she asked herself. No, she had come in the secret, vain hope that this might be her time, that by some strange deliverance God might bless them.

'When will ye come again?' he asked later, as Elizabeth was getting ready to go.

'I dinna ken,' she told him. 'It isna easy, James. Ma brither Nicol's wife has taen ower the stall these last days, but she canna afford the time and I canna afford tae pey her for it. Forby, Nicol has troubles o his ain tae thole. First he was pit oot o the clerkship o the guild o hammermen and noo he's been chairged wi disruptin their elections. He could loss the richt tae practise his craft, or be sent tae the Tolbooth himsel. But I will come again if I can.'

She knew though that she would not return, that these were just excuses. The real reason was what was between her and James: something that was nothing to do with love and everything to do with it. She could not bear the thought of repeating their act in this awful place. She could not bear seeing and smelling and touching her poor ruined husband in this dreadful pit. She was bound to him by law and by love, and yet she lived as freely as a widow, but without a widow's penury. The stall would never make her rich, but it gave her an income. And although, through James, she was firmly attached to and associated with the Presbyterian party, his past actions meant she was also set apart from many within that broad swathe of opinion; and so long as he was in prison, she need not be dragged into more trouble and danger on account of religion. The truth was – and she did not wish the Bass upon him or any man – she was better off without him.

She picked up her basket. There was one thing she had not yet given him. She had brought a book, worn, spine-cracked, its pages wavy from damp journeys. It would give him comfort, but she had swithered about bringing it at all. She had thought of it as a rival. But maybe it was more herself that was the rival.

'I had near forgot,' she said. She lifted a layer of folded linen from the bottom of the basket, and took the book out. 'Ye'll no can read muckle in this licht, but mebbe ye ken it weill enough onywey.'

She held it out and he reached for it. *Joshua Redivivus*. Mr Rutherford's damned and burnable letters.

He looked at it in amazement, pulled it into his chest. 'Ah, Lizzie,' he said. 'Lizzie, my dear love, ye could hae done nae better thing than this.'

He began to greet. She saw him there, head bowed, alone, clutching the book, and all she could think of was what she might be carrying away in secret from him, and all she felt was a terrible lack of love. She thought her heart would break. She went to him and held him again until Tammas's chap came at the door.

'Mind,' was her parting whisper. 'Gie siller tae him. The pockmarked sodger.'

As she left the cell, Lizzie almost broke into a run. She needed to get out into the open air. But in the narrow passage she felt Tammas's hand come up under her oxter and stop her. 'Wait,' he said. 'No yet.'

He was right behind her in the shadows. She could feel his breathing hard in at her back, his arm across her breast like a sack full of sand.

'How did ye pey the boatman?' Tammas said.

'Wi siller,' she whispered, 'whit else?' She tried to turn her head but his arm came up and held her more tightly. She was aware of her heart pounding against it. She thought of the siller she had given to James, who lay just a few feet away. 'My husband,' she began to say, but he clapped his other hand over her mouth. At that moment a soldier passed by the end of the passage.

'Wheesht, wheesht noo,' said Tammas. 'We maunna be seen. The boat's no in yet.'

They stood pressed together in the gloom. His hand was like leather. She could feel the coarse ridges of its skin when she moved her lips. His thigh shifted, pushing between her legs.

Edinburgh, April 1997

Jackie arrived late at Dawson's on the Monday evening. It was after eight. She'd finally got around to calling Hugh back that morning and they'd arranged to meet for another drink. 'Definitely just a couple,' she'd said. 'Monday night drinking is not a habit I want to get into.' 'Oh come on,' he'd said. 'Don't give me that Protestant work ethic thing.'

Hugh was halfway through a pint. The bar was busy and he had to wave to attract her attention. 'Sit down and guard this,' he said, 'and I'll get you a drink. What do you want?'

'I'll have a pint too. Whatever you're drinking.'

She knew as soon as she saw him again that nothing was going to happen between them. Nothing that she would instigate anyway. She couldn't have predicted this with any certainty when they talked on the phone, nor as she was getting ready to go out, nor even as she was getting off the bus and crossing the street to the pub. Only when she saw him. It just wasn't right. She'd found his boyishness appealing: now she found it annoying, a sign of immaturity and maybe selfishness. She had thought him handsome: now she saw that he would run to fat in a few years, that the line of his jaw would slacken.

He came back with her beer. There was something suspiciously like a twinkle in his eye. She hoped she wasn't going to have to fight him off.

'How's publishing?'

'All right. How's tourism?'

'Picking up, picking up. You know, people keep going on about the *Braveheart* factor, all these Yanks coming back to their homeland, but I never really believed it. But this year, I don't know, it feels good. Already I sense an influx of dollars into my trouser pocket.'

'That's excellent. You'll be able to pay decent wages.'

'I already pay decent wages. Way above the likely minimum wage.'

'Aye, you said that before. So that won't affect you if it comes in?'

Hugh smiled. 'My wage bill is what you might call an unknown quantity. Depending on what the current and future state of employment legislation is, I may or may not have more or less staff on my books than I do at present.'

'Flexible rostering taken to its logical conclusion, eh?'

'It's an up and down kind of enterprise, Jackie. Hard to predict. But basically I think I can live with a minimum wage. The thing that bothers me is this tartan tax everybody keeps banging on about. I mean, a tax on tartan would really hurt the tourist industry.'

She looked hard but even still it took her a few seconds to realise he wasn't serious.

'I'll take it you'll live with a Scottish parliament too, then, if Labour win the election?'

'Yes, if it happens. To be honest, my feeling is, why rock the boat? You know, if it ain't broke, don't fix it. Things are ticking along pretty smoothly for me just now – apart from one persistent hiccup. But if it happens, it happens. Anyway, I wouldn't bank on Labour delivering the full kit and caboodle even if they win.'

'They're going to win the election, Hugh. No question. It's just a matter of how big a majority. If they don't I'm emigrating. I don't think I could stand another five years of the Tories.'

'Well anyway,' said Hugh, 'you'd hardly know there was a general election going on in the real world. It's all done in TV studios these days. Frankly politics leaves me cold. Let's change the subject.'

'Okay. What's the persistent hiccup?'

'Guess.'

'Not Andrew Carlin. You said on the phone he was doing fine.'

'That was then. This is now. A whole new ball-game.'

'What's gone wrong?'

'Well, after I left that message, I spoke to my guide Gerry. I was a bit premature, it seems. He'd done all right the first night, but the next he didn't rendezvous with the tour at the end. Of course it wasn't a disaster, the people didn't know he was going to be there, but Gerry's patter leads up to it, and anyway the point is that's what he's paid to do. In fact, that must have been the night you went on the tour. What did you think?'

'I enjoyed it. Your guide's very good. And I thought Carlin was pretty effective too. I kind of missed him after his first appearance, but that was only because I was expecting him again, from what you'd said. The others in the group were perfectly happy.'

'Yeah, but I want them to finish on a high note. I want them spreading the word that this is the tour to go on. Anyway, I saw him yesterday and sorted it out. Turns out he came over dizzy or something, so he says, and by the time he got himself together they were too far ahead. Well, maybe. I gave him the benefit of the doubt.'

'So that's okay.'

'No, it's not. Gerry phones me this morning. Carlin did his stuff all right last night, in fact he was outstanding – Gerry said even he was nearly peeing himself. But he *diverted the tour*. For no apparent reason. Grabbed Gerry by the arm and made him go a different route. Not a word of explanation. Gerry hung around afterwards to see what the problem was but the guy had just vanished. And I still don't know where he stays so I can't contact him.'

'That's the trouble with flexible rostering. You'll need to catch him and put a rocket up his close.'

'Very funny. The trouble is, I don't want to piss him off. He's so weird. He's such a good ghost, but it's no use if he turns up some times and not others.'

'That's the trouble with ghosts. Not reliable. What are you going to do?'

'Give him another chance. Tonight. I thought maybe we could go on the tour together – if you can face it again. And we can see how he performs.'

'Tonight? Oh, I don't know, Hugh, I'm pretty tired.'

'I'd really appreciate it.'

'But we'd have to go now.'

'Fifteen minutes.'

She thought about it. It was what she'd wanted, although she'd not figured on doing the tour *with* Hugh. But she hesitated. The whole Carlin thing suddenly seemed stupid.

'Please,' Hugh said.

'Okay,' she said. 'But I'm knackered, I might not last the whole thing. If I slip off halfway along the route, don't be offended.'

'I'll be devastated,' he said. He put his hand over her wrist and grinned at her. She smiled back weakly. The tour had to be better than this. He was making her feel sick.

Carlin lit the two candles in their holders on the shelf above the fireplace. They flickered for a minute, then the flames shaped themselves and became steady. With his thumb and forefinger he traced their outlines as if he were a potter tapering them out of clay. He liked that, a light that was steady yet not still. He liked the way the glow concentrated onto his face reflected in the mirror. He stood impassively between the flames.

He'd had it again. *The horrors*. That was an expression they used in the old days, but then it meant delirium tremens. He'd read it in books. In the dictionary it also said *extreme depression*. Maybe that was what he was suffering from. Well, it was the horrors right enough. He'd get so far along the Cowgate and then he'd be hit with it. A feeling of helplessness, of events running out of control. Of having been born into the wrong life. Chance could land you on a bed of roses or a torturer's table. You had no say in the matter at all. And when you realised this, you began to break up physically. You ached, you poured sweat, you trembled like a caught rabbit. You could raise your eyes above the pain but there was nothing up there, no redemption.

The sweat had dried on him. He'd cut away from the tour again. No doubt he'd be getting his books from Hardie – not that there were any to get. He'd forced his breathing back to normal, walking across the Meadows. It was light relief that he needed. He looked at himself very steadily, an idea forming. Then the mirror started.

'Your name, please?'

'Andrew Carlin.'

'Your occupation?'

'Ghost impersonator.'

'Your chosen specialised subject?'

'The Life, Times and Sexual Deviations of Major Thomas Weir.'

'Andrew Carlin, you have two minutes on the Life, Times and Sexual Deviations of Major Thomas Weir, starting . . . now by what nickname relating to his reputation for extreme devoutness was Major Weir sometimes known?'

'Angelical Thomas.'

'Correct. In a letter to Sir Walter Scott the antiquarian Charles Kirkpatrick Sharpe hinted in some doggerel verse that in addition to mares and cows Major Weir had had sexual relations with which other animal?'

'His cat.'

'Correct. Weir had an incestuous relationship with his stepdaughter Margaret Burdoun and when she became pregnant disposed of her in what way?'

'He married her off to an English soldier.'

'Correct. When in charge of the Marquis of Montrose in the Edinburgh Tolbooth in 1650, how did Weir make himself obnoxious to his prisoner on the night before his execution?'

'He smoked tobacco in his cell.'

'Correct. In the nineteenth century Weir's house was briefly occupied by one William Patullo who awoke with his wife one night to find what apparition in their room?'

'A calf with its forefeet up on the bed?'

'Correct. In the 1650s Weir lodged in the Cowgate and became acquainted with the terrorist James Mitchel. In whose house did they both stay?'

'Grizel Whitford's.'

'Correct. A spot on the road between Kinghorn and Kirkcaldy, where Weir and his sister Jean supposedly first committed incest, was marked by what feature ever after?'

'Er . . . a cross?'

'No, it remained bare and no grass would grow there. Weir was first accused of bestiality in 1651, when a woman claimed to have seen him having sexual relations with which animal while on his way to a prayer meeting at Newmilns in Ayrshire?'

'His horse.'

'Correct. At his trial Weir was found guilty unanimously of incest and bestiality, and by a majority of two further crimes. What were they?'

'Adultery and fornication.'

'Correct. What would be an appropriate response to the suggestion that I am a ludicrous old buffoon?'

'Well ye are, but whit's that got tae dae wi Major Weir?'

'Correct. Jean Weir claimed that her mother had the ability to read people's minds. What mark on her forehead signified this power?'

'A mark like a horseshoe.'

'Correct. Weir helped to find James Mitchel work as a chaplain on at least one occasion. What is the Scots term for a clergyman who fails to find employment?'

'Stickit. A stickit minister.'

'Correct. In which of Sir Walter Scott's novels does a "great ill-favoured jackanape" called Major Weir –'

'*Redgauntlet.*'

'Correct. In which book' – BZZZZZ! – 'I've started so I'll finish, in which book by George Sinclair, Professor of Moral Philosophy at Glasgow University, were the Weirs' crimes, including their supposed sorcery, described in 1685? And you may answer.'

'*Satan's Invisible World Discovered.*'

'Correct. And at the end of that round, Mr Carlin –'

'That was never two minutes.'

BZZZZZ!

'I can assure you, Mr Carlin . . . As I was saying, at the end of that round you have scored thirteen points, and *no passes!*'

BZZ! BZZ! BZZZZZ! It was the entryphone. Carlin's entryphone hardly ever buzzed. He gave the mirror two fingers and went to the intercom by the door. He lifted the receiver and listened into it. He could hear a car passing on the street.

'Hello? Andrew, are you there? It's Jackie, Jackie Halkit. Can I come up?'

Carlin said nothing. He held the receiver away from himself for a few seconds. Then he pressed the switch that would open the door to her.

People took ages to come up his stairs. He was on the

fourth floor, and the last flight was a narrow stair that led to his flat only, in what had once been the attic space. It belonged to a man who owned one of the third-floor flats, had done a conversion years ago, and who now rented out both and lived off the income elsewhere in the city. Carlin had been there for ten years.

Jackie peched up to his door. 'Bloody hell, that'll keep you fit,' she said. He held the door open for her and she stauchered in.

'Where do I go?' she asked. But it was obvious really. The lobby was a tiny rectangle, one end filled with the bulk of a big mirrored wardrobe. There was a door with a glazed window which was the bathroom, and a doorless galley next to it which was the kitchen. She followed herself into the only other room.

It was bigger than she'd expected. There was a wide dormer window looking out over the roofs of other tenements: a row of bookshelves ran round it below the glass. There was a big armchair in the space in front of the window, with a small table beside it. Opposite, on another table, sat a television and a VCR. She noted the gas fire and the fake fire-surround, with the mirror above it and the candles burning on the shelf. There was another chair, wooden, with a straight back, and a chest of drawers. Under the sloping roof on one side of the window was a narrow bed covered with a folded tartan rug. A radio on the floor beside the bed. A few clothes lying about; a dirty coffee mug; more books. A photograph or two; some pictures on the walls. These were her immediate impressions. There was a general stour about the place, but this wasn't bad at all. She'd expected Carlin to live in a complete cowp.

She turned round. He was standing silently behind her. No doubt he was expecting an explanation.

'I'm sorry,' she said. She shrugged. 'I don't really know why I'm here. Is it all right?'

He smiled. He seemed quite relaxed, she thought. Maybe being on his own territory . . .

'Is it all right you no knowin why ye're here?'

'I mean, is it all right me having come? Just turned up? I'm sorry.'

'Is that whit ye've done? Jist turned up?'

166

He was still playing at his word games then. Although, of course, there was subtlety in it. He knew fine well she hadn't been just passing.

'You might think I'm invading your privacy.'

'Aye, I might.' She decided to treat this neutrally. One thing about Carlin, if he wanted you out he would say so. No – he wouldn't have let you in in the first place.

'You just stay here yourself then?' she asked.

Again he smiled, gave a half-nod.

Her question was superfluous. It wasn't a bad-sized room, but the more she looked at it, the more folded in on itself it seemed. The ceiling was low, and on either side of the window the coombs sloped down, making it even lower. Also, the place was more full of furniture and other objects than she'd first thought. Especially books. There seemed to be piles and cases of books everywhere, not just under the window.

'I was on the tour,' she said. 'Just to see what it was like. I thought you were very good. Realistic. No, that's daft, not realistic. You had the desired effect. Gave folk a fright, a thrill. Did you know that?' She was nervous, talking too fast and too much.

He shook his head. 'Aye, well. I don't hang around long enough tae see, but . . . I guessed. Frae the screams and that.'

'It must drive the local residents crazy,' she said. 'Every night. I mean, if there are any local residents round where you do your stuff.'

'Sometimes we go a different route. So as no tae disturb them.'

'That's good.' She was surprised, marked a wee plus for Hugh Hardie. 'That's considerate.'

'Aye.'

'So,' she said. 'How come you've not been staying the course? You're good at it. Hugh's impressed – has he told you? But he says you don't always stick around. To the end like.'

The faint smile vanished off his face. 'Is that why ye're here? Her master's voice or somethin?'

'He doesn't know I'm here. He doesn't even know where you stay.'

'No unless he's done whit you've done. Followed us hame like? That's whit ye did, eh?'

'Couldn't stop myself,' she said. 'You went one way, the tour went the other. I had to make a choice.' She wouldn't say that Hugh had been on the tour too. That he'd thought Carlin was wonderful at the first encounter. He'd not be thinking that now.

They'd been following Gerry along the Cowgate, in among the other folk, and Jackie, who'd been half-watching for something to happen, thought she saw a figure that might have been Carlin cowering away in the shadow of the bridge. She took a chance. 'I'm sorry, Hugh, I'm just shattered, I'm going to leave it here. I'll go up to Chambers Street and get a taxi.' He tried to protest – 'Oh, come on, are you sure?' – but she started to walk away, and he had to turn and catch up with the party. 'I'll phone you!' he called. She crossed the street, as if heading for Chambers Street, but then when Hugh had stopped looking she doubled back in the direction they'd just come from. A little wave of excitement ran through her: up ahead, going at a pace that made his cloak fly out behind him, was Carlin.

Now Carlin was staring at her, a kind of dull cold anger. It occurred to her that nobody knew she was there, she'd come alone, uninvited. This room was homely enough but through in the wee kitchen there could be human heads and other body parts pickling in preserving jars; saws, axes, black bin bags, buckets to catch the blood, all the paraphernalia of a bad dream.

'A choice,' he said. 'You niver made a choice. No the night onywey. Ye'd awready decided, hadn't ye?'

She sighed. 'Aye, all right. I was on the tour before. I met Hugh for a drink earlier. He said you'd not being doing things right. You know, fulfilling the terms of the contract. But I don't suppose there is a contract as such, is there?'

'There isna a piece of paper if that's whit ye mean.'

'Well, Hugh's kinda like that, I imagine. He'd rather deal in cash and keep no records. I guess what he meant was you're not sticking to the spirit of the agreement.'

'That cuts baith weys. Whit exactly was he girnin aboot? Forget it, I dinna want tae ken. D'ye want a cup o tea?'

She thought he must be joking. But he indicated the armchair, saying, 'I'll boil the kettle.'

She took off her coat and laid it on the bed. She glanced along the bookshelves below the window. A lot of Everyman classics and worn-looking Penguins, some of them the old orange-jacketed ones; she picked a couple out and saw the pencilled prices of secondhand shops on the first pages. There were guide-books to various European countries, a few years out of date: Germany, Holland, Hungary, Austria, Switzerland, Italy. Carlin had been in other places, it seemed, or at any rate liked to think about being in them.

She sat down in the chair and saw herself in the blank screen of the television. She couldn't imagine Carlin watching TV. Reading books, yes, but what would he watch? Sitcoms? Game shows? Old movies? Ah, maybe that was it. He was a movie buff. The video-player: there was probably a stack of classic movies somewhere. Or a stack of porno flicks. Come on, Jackie, she told herself, grow out of it. You're both adults now, whatever you thought of him when you were a student.

She noticed there was a video box lying on the floor beside the television table, half covered by a newspaper. She reached for it. It was empty: the tape was in the VCR.

A picture of a brick wall, with a coat or cape discarded in the wet at its foot. On the back of the box the haunted, trapped figure of Peter Lorre stared out at her. It was Fritz Lang's film *M*. She'd seen it herself years ago. She remembered bits of it: a little girl's innocence, and its destruction.

Carlin came back in with a tray: a teapot, two mugs, a carton of milk. 'I've nae sugar,' he said.

'That's okay. I didn't know you could get this on video.'

He put the tray on the table beside her. 'You can get maist things on video these days. Ye have tae look aroon but.'

'This is good,' she said.

He nodded. 'Aye.'

He poured out the tea. 'Whit d'ye think the M stands for?'

She'd thought it was obvious. 'Murderer,' she said. 'That's what the blind guy, the balloon-seller, chalks on his back – I mind that bit.'

'No,' said Carlin. 'The blind guy recognises him frae the tune he's whistlin. It's yin o the beggars that marks him wi the chalk. It's 1931, right; the heart o the Depression. The polis have been eftir this killer for years but they're useless, so the underworld decides tae hunt him doon. Mind the mob boss Schränker – "the best man between Berlin and Frisco" – he says he needs these invisible people, folk that can go anywhere, tae track the killer. And somebody else says, there's nae folk like that. Well, there is, a haill army o beggars.' He paused. 'Why d'ye think the beggar writes M on his coat?'

Jackie had never heard him say so much, nor sound so animated. 'Well, you've obviously watched it more recently than me,' she said. 'The M is to show he's the murderer.'

'Tae show he's the murderer. Aye, right enough.'

'What else?'

He took one of the mugs and waited again for a moment, as if he couldn't make up his mind.

'I think it stands for a lot o things. A lot o things that begin wi M.'

'Such as.'

'Well, I've been watchin it lately, and it makes me think o anither guy on the run, in the shadows. Here in Edinburgh. A guy called James Mitchel.'

'I don't recognise the name,' Jackie said. 'Recently?'

'Na, a long time ago. The Peter Lorre character reminds me o him.'

'Was he a child-murderer then?'

'Na, he was mair intae bishops. But he's like him somehow.'

She said, 'It's a while since I've seen it.'

'I watch it aw the time,' he said. He laughed and sat on the bed, moving her coat aside. 'Surprised I huvna worn it oot.'

He leant forward and picked up the remote control. Flicked on the TV but with the volume off, and started the tape. There was a shot of Lorre with his hands pulling down his cheeks in a mirror. There was a subtitle, part of a longer sentence: *a certain indolence, even lethargy*. Carlin fast-forwarded it a bit, his glance shifting between the screen and Jackie while he sipped at his tea. She felt self-conscious. Had he really meant what he'd just said, that he watched this all the time, or was he just playing with her?

'So what's happening?' she said.

He nodded at the screen and hit the 'play' button.

Somebody was analysing the murderer's handwriting. The subtitle read: *I'm sure that except when he has his fits he's just a harmless-looking fellow who wouldn't hurt a fly*. It reminded Jackie of something, something from another film about a different killing. Carlin fast-forwarded again, frowning.

'On the tour, I meant,' she said.

'Whit d'ye mean, whit's happening?'

'Why did you plunk it?'

'Oh. Dinna ken. Somethin's gettin tae me.'

'Like what?'

'Research. I'm researchin somethin and it's havin an effect.'

She waited, but he didn't elaborate. After a minute she tried again.

'What effect?'

He clicked the remote control. The film played at normal speed. There was a big old building of some kind, dilapidated. A disused distillery. Two ragged men were taking a struggling man up some stairs, then down some others. They had his jacket pulled up inside out over his head, blindfolding him.

'This is the trial scene. D'ye mind this?'

'What is it that's bothering you out there?' she said. But he hunched forward and began to watch.

'The crims hold an illegal court,' he said. 'Awbody's there. Look at this guy in the leather coat. That's Schränker. In a couple of years, when the Nazis come tae power, ye jist ken this guy's gaun tae be an officer in the Gestapo.'

The subtitle said, *We want to render you harmless. You'll only be harmless when you're dead.*

'Talk to me, Andrew,' said Jackie.

'Power shifts,' he said. 'First it's one gang, then it's anither. It's the same everywhere. When things are in turmoil people need a scapegoat. They need someone tae blame. An M.'

'I feel,' Jackie began. 'I wish . . . I wish I could help.'

'Help?'

'What is it . . . what is it you're looking for?'

'Drink yer tea,' he said.

She watched as the scene of Lorre's confession before the kangaroo court unfolded. The lines and shots came back to her just before they happened, pathetic, horrific. It was eerie watching the film in silence, with just the English captions appearing. She knew the mob gathered in the old distillery was baying for the killer's blood, but she could not hear them. All she saw were their mouths, and Lorre's mouth, his huge frightened eyes.

Then Lorre began to scream. In silence. He was screaming and pleading. He couldn't help what he did. What did they know? What right had they to speak? They were criminals. Maybe they were even proud of their safe-breaking, burglary, card-sharping. But they needn't do any of those things. He, on the other hand, couldn't help himself. He couldn't control what was inside him. A dreadful power drove him through the streets, following him silently. It was him, pursuing himself. It was impossible to escape. He had to go the way it chased him. He had to run through endless streets. Ghosts pursued him too. Ghosts of mothers, ghosts of children. They were always there. They would never leave him.

From time to time Jackie glanced over at Carlin. He was motionless, his attention fixed on the screen. She was drawn back to Lorre's despair and self-loathing. The crowd considered him less than a man, a mad dog that should be put down. Mothers were screaming for him to be given to them. But they had appointed him a defence lawyer from among their own number. The defence was that he was not responsible for his actions. He should be treated by doctors, not executioners. He should be in an asylum.

Schränker was dismissive. The man had condemned himself by his own words. What if he escaped? Or was released? Then if his compulsion returned there would be another manhunt, then the asylum, then release, on and on till doomsday.

The film finished on the face of a mother, a plea to take better care of the children. THE END came up abruptly, brutally, when Jackie had expected more. No credits followed. Carlin rewound the tape.

He picked her coat off the bed and handed it to her. 'I'm tired,' he said.

He obviously wasn't going to tell her anything. She couldn't argue.

She put the coat on. 'Thanks for the tea,' she said.

'Are ye seein him then?' said Carlin.

'Who?'

'Hardie.'

'Hugh?' She laughed. 'No, I'm not seeing him. I'm not seeing anyone.'

'I meant, soon. Are you going to be seeing him soon. At some point?' He spoke slowly and deliberately, as if to a foreigner.

'Oh, I see.' She was embarrassed. 'Aye, maybe. I suppose so.'

'Gaun tae tell him ye were here? Where I stey?'

'No. I don't think so.'

He stuck up his thumb half-heartedly. 'I'd appreciate that.' He seemed totally drained. It became clear that she was going to have to see herself out.

He sat down again, then lay back on the bed, eyes closed. She watched him there for a few seconds. She didn't feel angry at him. She felt sad. Then she left.

Bass Rock, June 1677/Edinburgh, April 1670

Mitchel said, 'Why are ye here?'

'Tae see you,' said Lauder.

He felt slightly sick from the crossing. It was only a short trip from North Berwick, a couple of miles at most, but the sea was choppy and Lauder hated being in boats. He still minded the journey from Dover to France when he was a student: he and a fellow passenger had fought over a bucket all night, filling it with their combined vomitings, and with every retch and boak the other man had groaned for God's mercy as if he was on the point of expiring, which had only made Lauder feel worse.

Mitchel shook his head. 'That's no guid enough, John Lauder. Yer guidfaither's Ramsay, the Provost o Edinburgh. Ye're no here tae ease ma sufferin.'

'He *was* Lord Provost,' Lauder said. Sir Andrew had written a recommendation, which the captain of the garrison had read with disdain before grudgingly allowing Lauder access to his prize prisoner. Now, left alone with him, Lauder found Mitchel equally suspicious of his family connections.

'He's a Privy Cooncillor and aw. Is it by him that ye come here? They dinna let folk see me.'

'He had a word for me, I confess. But I'm no here on his behaw nor onybody's but ma ain.'

Mitchel did not look convinced. His eyes were unblinking in the half-light.

The cell stank of dampness and squalor, and every draught of wind brought with it eye-watering wafts from the guano of thousands of seabirds. It was now the height of the solans' nesting season. It sounded like all the witches that had ever been were gathered together there in bird disguise.

Lauder tried to take shallow breaths. 'I would like tae hear somethin frae ye,' he said.

Mitchel laughed scornfully.

'Aye, awbody would like that. The Privy Cooncil would like me tae confess tae a crime so they can hing me. Is that whit ye would hear, Maister Lauder? Are ye come as a lawyer tae bargain wi me?'

'No. It's naethin o that kind. Naethin tae dae wi yer case at aw.'

'Then why else would I speak wi a lawyer?'

'I would like tae find oot . . . tae hear aboot somebody.' Lauder cleared his throat. 'I would like tae hear aboot Major Weir.'

Mitchel's brow furrowed. 'Whit's tae tell? The man was burnt for his crimes seiven year syne.'

'Ye kent him.'

'Aye. Sae did yer guidfaither. Sae did aw Edinburgh. Ye'll hae seen him aboot yersel nae doot.'

'I didna ken him tae speak tae, as you did,' said Lauder.

'Whit's this tae be, guilt by association? If ye gang doon that road, ye'll find some kenspeckle bodies claucht up in the net. It's ten year or mair since I spak wi Weir.'

'No as lang as that, James,' said Lauder carefully.

There was a long silence. Finally, Mitchel said, 'Whit dae ye mean?'

'Ye saw him in the Tolbooth, afore his execution. I ken ye did.'

'I wasna even in Scotland. I was a *rebel*, if ye mind, wi a price on ma heid for the attack on Sharp and Honyman.'

'Ye were in Scotland. Ye cam tae him in prison. I ken it.'

'Whit maks ye think that? Did ye see him in prison yersel? Did he tell ye?'

'I did see him. The mornin o his death. But it wasna him that tellt me. He was ayont speakin by then. It was his sister, Jean. She said ye'd been in tae see him, in secret.'

'Haivers,' said Mitchel. '*Weir* was ayont speakin, ye say? Jean was awa daft lang afore then. If she tellt ye I was there, she was haein a fit. How would I get intae the Tolbooth o Edinburgh in secret? Dae ye think a man wantit for a capital crime against a Croun servant would o his ain volition enter that place tae collogue wi a convicted felon in his cell? I'd as weill hae pit ma heid in a noose.'

'Jean wasna as daft as some folk think,' said Lauder. 'I believe she tellt the truth.'

175

Mitchel was silent. He lay back on his bed and stared at the roof. The movement, in the gloomy atmosphere of the cell, instantly provoked a memory in Lauder's mind. He was transported back seven years, to the visit he had made on Major Weir. Just fifteen months married, with a four-month-old son, he had been in the company of his wife's father, then Lord Provost of Edinburgh.

Wt my goodfather Sir Andrew I was at the Tolbooth Monday 11th day of April 1670, to see the monster Major Weir. We ware admitted in the fornoon, a cold day wt winter's grip not yet lowst, but the sun was shyning, which made the prison house yet mair mirk and grim when we ware within. The provest had seen him when first he confest. Believing him insane he got his ain doctors to him, but they said his faculties ware lucid and thereafter witnesses ware found that seemd to prove his crymes. I wished to see this phenomenon of wickednes, and went wt the provest and divers others, ministers &c. The crymes of his flesh ware revolting, but it was his spirituall backslyding and consorting wt the Devil (though this was not in the indytment but only drawen from his sister's testimonies) that fascinated the ministers mair. As Sir Andrew said its seldom you get a chance to look depravitie full in the face. But there was mockerie in his tone which I perceived was directed at the godlie amang us, for they ware some of them of Weir's inclinatioun, in religion at least. See the Devil ance and ye'll not misken him next tyme, says Sir Andrew, bowing at them wt a false respect, which I doubt did not fool them for an instant.

For a monster Weir was a sorry object, auld and slumpt on his bed agaynst the wall, much changed from the muckle figure of controversie I mynd as a bairn. There was no fire left in his eyn. The ministers presst him to acknowlege his sin and pray for God's mercy, but he only shook his head and moand. When by progging and shaking him as if he ware a carnival brute that would not do its tricks, they finally rowsed him to sit, he stared at them blearily with a dead look and said, Wherefor do ye trouble me wt your cruelty? They said wee do not trouble ye, Thomas, it is your soull that troubles ye. Pray with us for your soull.

He answered, What for should I pray wt ye? I care not for your prayers and I doe not hear them.

One said, Sir, I will pray for ye in spite of yr teeth and the deevil yr master too.

He said to him, Doe it at your perill.

They said, Even now, Thomas, in the day of your death, seek out the mercy of God.

He lauched and said, God, where is God? I see him not. They ware affronted and asked, Think ye there is a God? He said I know not. Then one said O man, the argument that moves me to think there is a God is thy self. For what else moved thee to informe the world of thy wicked life? He said, Then pray to him if ye will, I'll not pray wt you. All the prayers that men and angels can offer will not make a better man of me. Pray that to yr God.

They conjured him as ane brother even now to repent and ask God for his mercy.

Repent, he says, repent, whats to repent? Will repentence alter one jot of his law? Will repentence weigh in the scayles of justice? Think ye that the grovelings of one human ant will alter the plan and purpos of Gods universe? What papisticall trash is this? Get back to your bible, brothers, says he, before ye try to sell me ane indulgence.

Then when they said again, Thomas Weir we beseek ye he says, Trouble me no more wt your beseeking. My sentence is sealed on earth as it is in heaven. I am hardend within like a stone, brother. If I could win God's pardon and all the glory of Heaven wt a single wish — that I had not sinned as I have sinned, yet I could not prevail wt my self to make that wish.

Then when they said he does not ken what he is saying, and asked him did his heart not shrink at thoucht of God's eternal ire he interrupted them impatientlie, Tell me no more, torment me no more. You are not in my place and your soull is not in my soull's place. Gin ye ware, ye would see the waste and delusion of your exhortatiouns, for there is no thing within me but blacknes and darknes, brimstone and burning to the bottom of hell. Now let me alone, ye have deaved me ouer long, I'll hear no more.

He fell in a kind of stupor and though they spake at him some tyme more, there was no rousing him. Bailie Oliphant

177

that was there began to leave the room, saying, I have had my fill of beseeking, the man is to die and we should leave him to redd up his soull gin he wish. Soe led by Patrik Vanse the keeper of the prison we went back out into the licht.

The provest said to the companie, There goeth corruptioun incarnat. I am glad he's to burn outwith the citie's walls. I would na like to see his foul ashes settle on the heads of the good burgesses.

But, said the bailie, some will take a dander furth to the Gallowlee to see him consumed.

They had better wear ther hats then, said Sir Andrew, and clapt his wig wt much ostentatioun. Pollution the like of that will be a task to clean from the hair. Then to the ministers, that ware still rid and peching from their exertiouns wt the Beast, he said, Do ye think a man that was sa sure of his ain electioun as he can be sa mistaken? Is there nae possibility of him winning to heaven despite of all his wickednes? They ware very crosse at this, which was aimed at their ain holinesse, and raged at him to suggest a man can transgress God's law sae foully and yet be of the elect. It was a heresy, an antinomian heresy, and an English ane forby. Weir, they said, would be brunt on earth by four of the clock that efternoon and by five he would be burning in hell. My lord was not perturbed by them, but congratulated them on ther impressive certainty. I'll not be at the Gallowlee my self, he says, but mynd and do not forget your hats.

From his bed Mitchel asked, 'Whit did Jean say tae ye? When did ye speak wi her?'

'Eftir her brither was burnt. I gaed back tae the Tolbooth alane, the next mornin. She was tae hing that day. I felt unhappy aboot her death – I felt she was mair victim o his crimes than conspirator in them.'

'She was a witch or else she was made mad by Satan,' Mitchel said flatly.

'The jurors had rejectit the chairge o sorcery against her. If she was mad was it the madness that had made her lie wi her brither, or the incest that made her mad? If the former, she shouldna burn.'

'And if she was a witch?'

'If she was a witch . . . I felt pity for her. I was only twenty-three – I was grieved for her.'

'She'd hae easy led you intae soukin sand then. Pity is their weapon.'

Lauder did not respond. He could almost feel Mitchel struggling to resist asking the next question.

'Whit did she say – aboot me?'

'As muckle as John Vanse, the keeper's son – as muckle and mair, and less. Atween the pair o them I worked it oot. That twa days precedin, on the Sabbath, a young man that cried himsel Alexander Weir, the Major's son, had come tae the Tolbooth. That he begged John Vanse, that had chairge o the place that day, if he had ony compassion for yin that fund himsel wi sae miserable a creature for a faither, tae let him see him afore he was sent tae Hell. That John Vanse alloued him in and he sat wi his faither for an oor. And Vanse cam tae Jean and said he was there, and she speired at him tae hae her nephew Sandy stop and gie her his blessin afore he pairtit, and he cam by her cell and looked in but wouldna stop, and she kent it wasna Sandy but anither man aboot the same age. It was him that had sailed awa tae Holland eftir Pentland. James Mitchel.'

Mitchel did not speak. Lauder strained even to hear his breathing. After a minute he said, 'She didna misken ye, did she?'

Mitchel sat up. 'Ye are an advocate, sir. Ye hae a cousin John Eleis?'

'Aye.'

'I hear he pleads for aw kinds – witches, rebels, thieves, murderers. Am I richt?'

'He defends ony person he is cawed tae defend.'

'I hear he is amang the best o yer breed. Him and Sir George Lockhart. They are thorns in the flesh o the Privy Cooncil.'

'They only dae their duty as advocates. But ye're richt, they are baith excellent lawyers.'

'I want them for ma case, Maister Lauder.'

'Yer case is done, Maister Mitchel. Whit for dae ye think ye're cast on this Rock these last months? Whit for did they crush yer leg in the boot? They canna prove onythin against ye.'

'They will try, though. Sharp wants me deid. And when ma case comes again, I want thae twa men as ma coonsel. Dae this for me, siccar me their services, and I'll tell ye aboot Major Weir.'

'I canna mak such a pledge. An advocate canna jist pick and choose, nor can a panel wi nae siller elect his ain coonsel.'

'But,' said Mitchel, 'choice willna be in it on this occasion. When they bring me back – which they will, hae nae doot – nae lawyer in his senses will dare plead on ma behaw – it's an offence in itsel tae argue for a traitor. I ken ma law and ma rights – I will demand a defence. The Privy Cooncil will hae tae appoint me lawyers. Sir George and Maister John can let the Cooncil ken they'll compear for me if alloued and commanded by His Majesty's government. Sir George is Dean o the Faculty, is he no? Naebody else will contest him for the honour.'

'Ye ken yer law, indeed,' said Lauder.

'I hae plenty time tae think on it,' said Mitchel dryly. 'But ye must instruct yer cousin anent this maitter – it maunna be left tae chance. It'll be a kittle enough business, athoot findin masel in the hauns o Prestoun or some such kiss-ma-erse.'

'Prestoun? John Prestoun o Haltree?'

'Aye, him. Mention o Weir pit me in mind o him.'

It was Prestoun, the hunter of witches, who had been appointed a temporary judge for commission to try the Weirs, none of the bench being available. Lauder recalled that Prestoun had been disappointed that he had had to throw out the evidence of sorcery against Jean Weir.

'He's ower pernicketie tae pit up a fecht for a scuggie fellow like masel,' Mitchel said. 'Ma case will be won on principles, no ten-year-auld evidence, and Sir George and John Eleis are the best for statin a principle.'

'And if it's lost, in spite o them?'

'Then the testimony o ma bluid will hae mair weicht and credit. A man like me disna win tae God like a lawyer, sir, wi wishin and wordspeakin, but by the skailin o his bluid. There's nae safter place tae lie than on the altar for Christ.'

Mitchel, Lauder observed, seemed to swing violently between a worldly humanity, tinged with regret, that was almost touching, and a kind of inflamed righteousness which rose like a barrier between him and everything else. It was like watching someone half-drowning, then swimming with extraordinary power in heavy waters, then beginning to slide under again.

'Ye unnerstaun,' said Mitchel, 'I hae nae fear o death. Ma soul is in Christ whether I live or die. Death will be welcome eftir this. It will be a new and better life, an eternal life. Did ye ken, sir, they kept me in chains in the Tolbooth mair than a twalmonth? Can ye think whit like that is? The iron bands skive the skin aff ye till ye're raw tae the banes. Ye wouldna see a dug treatit sae ill. But that's by wi – they can dae naethin tae ma flesh noo that I canna thole. Aw the legal pliskies that we'll see in coort are meaningless tae me, but for ae thing – I would see James Sharp and his pack damned and defeated in this life as they surely will be hereineftir. So will ye dae it for me?'

What he was asking would not be difficult to arrange. It was merely organising the most likely chain of events should the case ever come back to trial. But why would that ever happen? Why would Sharp and Lauderdale and Rothes stir up an ancient episode by bringing Mitchel into the public eye again, for a prosecution that carried such risks. Even if Sharp was obsessed with the case, the others would have nothing to do with it. They were better off with Mitchel where he was, mouldering away in the Bass, forgotten. It would come to nothing.

'Aye,' Lauder said, 'I will – if ye tell me noo that ye saw Major Weir in the Tolbooth.'

Mitchel nodded. 'I confess it.' And for the first time Lauder saw him smile. 'Oh, Maister Lauder, ye dinna ken the tears James Sharp would greet tae hear me say thae three words.'

Mitchel had come back to Scotland when he had been a year in the continent, working for his cousin John the merchant. He came home on a ship from Amsterdam, that let him ashore at Limekilns in Fife. He flitted around in Fife a while, where he had contacts, and then returned to Edinburgh. Aye, he was there when that thing happened, the stramash when the bishops were shot at. His name was associated with the deed and he had to flee again. He was in Ulster, among the

Presbyterian planters. He went to London, that stinking bog of tolerance and vice. By now he was a travelled man, hard-footed and lean, winnowed by the weather. About the end of March, in the year 1670, he was in Lanarkshire, with old friends.

They heard a rumour from the capital that Major Weir, that used to bide in those parts, was sick or mad, or both. The story came from a Strathaven man, an honest fellow who had attended a prayer-meeting in a house in the West Bow. Weir had opened his mouth and a stream of black filth had poured out upon the lugs of the worshippers. They had tried to hush him but the flow would not be stopped. Then Jean, that was already wandered, had lowped in and what she had had to say seemed to confirm that some at least of it was true.

Mitchel was a two-day walk from Edinburgh. Weir had helped him in his youth – he felt he should go, to find out the truth of the stories. Forby he owed him money – a debt he had not repaid when he was there in '68, what with all his jouking and hiding from the authorities.

He slipped in through the west of the city one evening, a few hours too late. The Weirs had been taken by the bailies that day and were locked in the Tolbooth. He could do nothing but wait. There were places he could stay if he kept his head low.

The whole town was claiking about the Weirs – they had knocked all other news off the street. Mitchel waited, and he listened. He was appalled. He could hardly recognise, in the snatches of scandal and gossip he heard, the man he had so respected, the woman he had so pitied. The dripping tongues of Edinburgh had transformed them into grotesques.

Oh, he was aye a fearsome man, and she's a shilpit, peuchlin body.—He's no been seen sae muckle lately.—Weill, he's gettin auld.—He uised tae gang aboot the toun wi that stick o his, wi the carvit heid at its tap like the heid o a bogle.—Aye, and they say noo that he couldna pray at aw if he didna hae it in his nieve. Did ye niver see the wee deevilock face in the wuid o't, that would change frae a grin tae a girn frae ae minute tae the nixt?—Ye would hear him chappin through the toun at nicht, ye could niver misken the soun o him, and when ye saw him, there was the stick oot in front, wi a lantren hingin frae it, guidin his wey.—Aye, the stick uised tae gang his messages for him, I ken a man that's seen it himsel.—He couldna pray athoot it, that's a fact. He'd bring the words doon oot o the air wi it, the Bowheid saints thocht they were haly words but they werena, they were Satan's.

That stick has a life o its ain, they hae tae keep it apairt frae him or the Tolbooth'll no haud him.—It's a force for his sinfu desires. When he striddles it it can tak him through lockit doors and sneckit windaes. It got him intae the chaumers o mairrit weemun and daicent widdaes, and they'd be bumbazed at his appearin.—Och, but they were that uised wi him preachin and prayin in their hooses, he would owercome them wi his subtleties and explanations. They trustit him on accoont o he could reconcile a man and his wife that were cauld tae each ither – jist by touchin.—But that worked anither wey, for there wasna a wumman that he'd touch, puir or gentle, that could be mistress o hersel, but would yield tae act the harlot wi him.—He liked tae see them in their nicht claes or hauf-nakit, hard and lang was his stick in the munelicht. He would touch them in their privates and when they cried oot, they'd turn aroon and there'd be nae man there, they could niver prove he'd been in tae insult them at aw.—Ken whit it was, it was like a dream tae them, a foul and shamin dream, but it wasna a dream tae him.

And when he couldna get at them, there was his sister Jean. She's the Deil's ain though ye would niver ken it tae look at her, she's rade the winds hersel but the Deil gied her up tae him and she'd tae dae his biddin.—He's uised her maist foully for fifty year wi the pouer o his stick. He's confessed it, she's confessed it. Ye hinna heard a hundredth pairt o whit I hae done, that's whit he tellt the bailies when they cam for him.—Aye, mebbe, but she's nae innocent, she didna resist him, she's as deep in the fulyie as himsel. The ither sister Margaret fund them raw nakit thegither in their faither's hoose at Carluke, and Jean was the tapmaist, and the bed was shakin wi their sin.—And syne she sellt hersel tae a witch wumman that cam tae her when she had the schuil at Dalkeith. The wumman was frae the fairies and Jean gied her aw her siller and bocht hersel an unco skeel at spinnin. She'd spin mair in an oor than ony ither wife could spin in a day. Whiles she'd gang oot and when she cam hame there was the spinnin-wheel, birlin awa like a mad thing its lane.—But the skeel didna profit her: the yarn was ower brittle, it aye broke when ye tried tae work wi it. It was deil's yarn, it had a curse on it.

Can ye credit such wickedness? But he's the worse. Major Weir the *great sodger o Christ, that'd dip his whang intae ony flesh he could get in his hauns. His sister wasna spared, his stepdochter Meg Burdoun wasna spared, his servant Bessie Weems wasna spared.— Faith, he didna even spare the kye. A yaudswyver he is, a mutton- driver and a duglowper.—But his dippin days are ower noo; he'll get his reward in Hell. The reid-hornit deils will prick him wi their lang pikes and sodomise him for eternity.*

On Saturday 9 April the Weirs were brought before Mr William Murray and Mr John Prestoun, depute justices, and fifteen jurors, and the charges against them read out. The court was packed with the prurient and gleeful. Mitchel, stern-faced, was among the crowd. Other stunned and mortified Christians, who until lately had counted the accused among their most devout and worthy friends, were noticeably absent.

This was the indictment against Thomas: that he did commit numerous incests, adulteries, fornications and bestialities as specified in the dittay, all over a period of more than fifty years, in Lanarkshire and Edinburgh and elsewhere; and that he was conscious to himself of these abominations, yet he had the confidence or rather impudence to pretend to fear God in an eminent way and did make profession of strictness, piety and purity beyond others, and did affect and had the reputation of a pious and good man, thereby endeavouring to conceal and palliate his villainies and to amuse and impose upon the world and to mock God himself, as if the Lord's all-seeing eye could not see through the slender veil of his hypocrisy and formality.

And Jean was indicted for incest with her brother and diverse sorceries committed when she lived and kept a school at Dalkeith, and that she did take employment from a woman to speak in her behalf to the queen of fairy, meaning the Devil, and was guilty of consulting, com- muning or seeking and taking advice and help from the Devil or from witches and sorcerers, as well as of the said crime of incest.

The dittays having been read and found relevant, Major Weir was questioned anent his guilt. 'I think I may be guilty of these crimes. I cannot deny them,' was all he said. The court took note that this was not a positive declaration of guilt. Then for the prosecution the King's advocate Sir John Nisbet brought forth his witnesses. Four bailies of the town who were sent to bring the Major out of his own house, deponed that they heard him confess frequent incest with his sister Jean, and many other immoral acts, including carnal dealings with a mare and a cow. And Mr John Sinclair, minister of Ormiston, deponed that being called to the Tolbooth he heard the Major confess his sins to him – incest with his sister, adulteries and bestialities and that he had converse with the Devil in the night-time. And Margaret Weir, sister to the panel, deponed that she discovered Thomas and Jean in the act of incest when she was fourteen, when they all lived at their father's house at Wicketshaw by Carluke in Lanarkshire, and she found them in the byre, and heard Jean say to him that she thought she was with child. And other witnesses deponed that they heard him confess on Monday last and again that morning that he was guilty of incest with Jean, and with his stepdaughter Margaret, and of carnal dealings with a mare, and also with his servant Bessie Weems these last twenty-two years.

Sir John Nisbet then produced the Major's own confession, taken in the presence of himself and Mr John Prestoun, depute justice, and the bailies of Edinburgh, that he did ride his mare into the west country, and near Newmilns he did pollute himself with her, and a woman seeing him delated him to Mr John Nevay, minister at Newmilns, who had him brought to Newmilns by some soldiers but then dismissed the charge, there being no proof but the woman's word. And the woman, who was from near Lanark, was whipped through the streets of that town for raising such a calumny against so holy a man. And Mr Nevay, being in exile, could not be brought as a witness. And this was all the business against Major Weir.

Then as against Jean Weir, since she made no admission of guilt, the advocate prosecuting produced her own declaration, made at the time of arrest, whereby she acknowledged her own incest with her brother; that she knew Margaret Burdoun, her brother's stepdaughter, was with child in his house and that all believed it was the Major's; that Margaret did not deny it when she asked her; and she confessed all the sorceries in the libel; and that her brother had a mark like the Devil's mark upon his shoulder.

Then the assize bent their heads together, and soon they with one voice found the panel Major Weir to be guilty of the said horrid crimes of bestiality with a mare and cow, and of the crime of incest with his sister Jean, and by a plurality of votes of fornication and adultery. They found the panel Jean guilty of the incest also libelled against her, but they took no notice of any other points in the libels notwithstanding of the Major's confession before the court because it was not positive, and notwithstanding of the extra-judicial confessions of the two, which they chose to pass by.

This was the sentence of the court: the said Major Weir to be taken on Monday the 11th inst. to the Gallowlee betwixt Leith and Edinburgh and there betwixt two and four hours in the afternoon to be strangled at a stake till he be dead, and his body to be burnt to ashes. And his sister Jean to be hanged at the Grassmarket of Edinburgh on Tuesday, being the day thereafter.

'Aw this I ken,' said Lauder. 'I was here as weill, mind. Ye are tellin me naethin I dinna ken.'

Mitchel sneered. 'Whit is it ye would ken? How we fanatics are aw hypocrites under the skin?'

'If it was that easy, I wouldna be here. It's less trouble tae think Jean Weir mad than no. If ye believed her brither was jist a base hypocrite ye wouldna hae risked gaun in tae him.'

'I believe he was guilty o thae crimes. I believed it then. There was nae dootin it.'

'Why gang in then?'

'You hae come here. You tell me.'

'If it was me, it would be because ma ain faith had taen a dunt. Ye'd been sure o Weir, as ye were sure o yersel. He had been sure o himsel. Whit happens when such a man shatters in front o ye? Tae him, tae you? That's whit I would want tae ken.'

'I hadna seen him in three year. It's true whit ye say, I niver saw a dooncome sae sair. But ma ain faith was siccar.' He glared at Lauder. 'It aye is. It's taen waur dunts nor that.'

He clapped his ruined leg, and Lauder acknowledged the

186

gesture with a nod. But he didn't want to get diverted.

'Ye kent Alexander Weir wasna in Edinburgh, and that even if he was he wouldna gang near his faither. Sae ye gaed in his place, and young John Vanse let ye in.'

'Aye, on the Sabbath. John didna look ower hard at me. Mebbe he kent I wasna Sandy. Mebbe he didna want tae ken.'

'He left ye alane wi the Major?'

'Aye.'

'Whit like was he?'

Mitchel shook his head. 'Like naethin I iver want tae see again.'

A broken dishevelled wreck, was how Thomas Weir had appeared to Mitchel. His hair white, and matted with grease and dirt. A week's white stubble over his lined face. Several teeth lost. The bones of his chest and shoulders projecting through a filthy thin shirt. He looked like what he was: an old man of seventy who had been condemned to death the next day.

Mitchel took his hand and sat beside him on the bed. In a low voice he told him who he was. Weir stared ahead in a dwam. Mitchel told him again. 'I am James Mitchel, that ye helped in the past, that fled oot o Scotland wi yer assistance. D'ye no mind me?'

Nothing. Weir seemed unaware that there was someone in the cell with him.

'I am James Mitchel, him they say that shot at the apostate James Sharp.'

Weir turned his head, peered at him, nodded slowly. When his mouth opened it cracked with dried slavers. There was a pitcher of water by the door. Mitchel fetched it and, pouring some into his hand, wetted the old man's mouth and lips with it. A foul stench came from Weir's mouth. His whole body reeked. He tried to speak.

'Hae . . .'

His voice was barely audible. Mitchel waited.

'Hae ye brocht me ma siller?'

'Ye are past wantin siller. Whit use is siller tae ye noo?'

'Tae buy a passage. Get me tae Leith and I'll gang wi Forrester tae Holland.'

187

'He's gane. There is nae ship for ye. Ye hae further tae gang the morn than tae Holland.'

Weir groaned. His eyes dimmed and brightened like failing candles. He took more water.

'James Mitchel,' he said contemplatively. 'Ye crossed the sea as a rebel. How can I no cross the sea as a rebel?'

'I am nae rebel. The rebels are them that has broken the Covenant. But you are a rebel against God, and there's nae sea sae braid it'll keep ye frae his vengeance.'

Weir nodded. 'I ken it, I ken it. It's a dark, seik sea that's in front o me.' Then, with a hint of his former English-touched voice, he said, 'Are you come to preach at me like the others, James? I am weary of preaching and praying.'

'Na,' said Mitchel. 'I believe ye are ayont thae things.'

Weir's face lit up. 'Aye. I am ayont hope and ayont mercy. I'm glad that ye understand that, James. Ye were aye a good student.'

Nobody had ever said that to Mitchel before. It reminded him of where he was, who he was with. It was the Sabbath. He should be in a kirk, or at prayer in his own company. He should be in hiding. He moved himself a foot or so away from the other man.

'Whit has happened tae ye?'

Weir drank from the pitcher again. He began to mumble, staring at nothing.

'I fell,' he said. 'I had grace and I fell. And when I looked back I saw that I had never had grace at all.'

Mitchel shivered. The shadows in the room felt heavy, like damp earth. Weir's voice, stronger now but with a resigned flatness to it, droned on.

'We were blessed. We were blessed and chosen. I felt God in me. I was seventeen. That was when I felt the assurance that I was saved. I felt it like a wind rushing through me, a light exploding in me. God had saved me for himself. What he had done no man could undo. I was part of God. I was Christ-like. This is how it was.'

The words were right. They described what you were supposed to experience. If you were of the elect it was revealed to you in such a way. Then you moved ever closer to Christ's perfection in thought and deed and understanding. Your goodness did not save you because it could not, you were not good, you were human and sinful: only God could save you. But the knowledge of assurance filled you with righteousness. The elect were not saved by their own works, but you could tell the elect because they walked in the way of God, with a spiritual lustre and beauty that strangers to Christ did not have. All this Mitchel knew and believed. But to hear it from Weir in this place, in his condition – it was as if as the words were uttered something in his own mouth turned to dung. Weir made words hateful that should have been full of hope.

And yet, even here, Mitchel felt his feelings divide. He thought back to that conversation they had had on the High Street, outside, looking up at the wall of this very building and seeing the head of James Graham. The moment of rebirth, of revelation, that Weir spoke of, it had evaded Mitchel then and he still found himself desperate for such a memory. When Weir spoke of it, Mitchel hated him for having betrayed its beauty, and yet he envied him for having experienced it. He believed, he was sure, that he was chosen. But when he heard other men talk of *their* assurance, it made him uneasy. Why did he not have the same sense of it as they did? And now, to hear a man confess – *this* man who had been so important to him in his youth – that he had been mistaken after all, after so many years . . . Mitchel felt as if darkness were closing in upon his own mind.

Weir was still speaking, the words muttered and indistinct.

'Our nation was chosen. We were the bride of Christ. We felt this. We *both* felt this. We became as one with him. When we thought, when we prayed, when we felt, our thoughts and our prayers and our feelings were God's.'

Mitchel tried to speak. In the cell's gloom, his voice sounded as if it came from somewhere else.

'You and Jean?'

'It was his impulse that moved in us. It could not be denied. It could not be temptation because we were moved by him.'

'It was sin.'

'It wasna sin. It couldna be sin. It was God.'

Mitchel thought of what it was like. Sin. How it had felt

with the gardener's wife. That had been sin – he thanked God now for showing him what sin was. How it would feel each time. How beautiful it would be if it were not sin. He was listening to his own body. That was the flesh in conflict with the soul. The body said, why would God implant these feelings, if they were not to be acted upon?

'I was of God and God was of me,' said Weir. 'He gave me power over all things.'

Mitchel struggled to overpower his body's arguments. 'It was sin,' he said again.

'When you are of God you are beyond sin. There is nothing but the urges he puts in ye. All your urges are prayers and praises to him.'

'No,' said Mitchel.

'All of them,' Weir insisted. 'There's nae line to draw. We are damned or we are saved. What difference does our feeble conscience make to that?'

He turned suddenly and seemed surprised to see Mitchel there. He seized him by the shoulders. The foul breath poured onto Mitchel's face.

'We are all instruments in God's hands. Ye canna deny it.'

Mitchel pushed him away. He stood and took a few steps in the gloom. It was as if there was something rotting in a corner of the room, growing and shifting as it decayed.

'Your desires were unnatural!' He heard the horror in his own voice. 'How could ye think thae things were frae God? How could ye?'

'*Then from where?*' said Weir. A terrible groan rose from his throat. 'Ye needna answer. I ken. I felt the change.'

Mitchel was silent, appalled. There was nothing he could think of to say.

'It was forty years coming. I didna ken it at first. I thought it was still him. God. But God had tricked me forty years. He betrayed me. I had a feeling of him in the dark and it wasna him. Not him at all. It was a woman.'

'Jean was your *sister*,' said Mitchel.

Weir cackled. The sound turned Mitchel's stomach.

'No that auld hag, I'd nae use for her. She was a done creature. Ha! *She* still thinks she's going to Heaven. This, no, this was bonnie. A beautiful woman in the night. She used to come to me alone. *The lips like a thread of scarlet. The breasts like young roes.'*

'Dinna speak thae words,' said Mitchel. 'These are God's holy words.'

'It was *God* that came, d'ye not see? *I am black, but comely, O ye daughters of Jerusalem.* Every night. And I felt her beside me. Every part of her.'

'Sweet Jesus,' said Mitchel. He was choking on something. He wanted to leave. He wanted to call out for Vanse to let him out of the cell.

'Every night I felt down her body. Her arms, her breasts, her belly. *I put my hand in by the hole of the door.* Then her legs. Then, one night, she guided my hands with hers. She took my hands and put them to her feet.'

He drank more water. Mitchel did not call out.

'They were *hairy*. Coarse, short, thick hair. Covered wi it. I shrunk away, but I couldna. She had a grip of me. And then I felt the change. She was laughing. I kent who it was, who it had been all along. He stood up before me laughing. Huge, like a giant. I saw that I was destroyed.'

Mitchel could take no more. He went to the door and started banging on it. Weir's breath was filling the whole room with a cloud of poison. He began to shout as the old man's voice rose.

'He is with me always,' Weir said. 'I am his, not God's. I was always his. I was always chosen, but not for grace. I never had grace. I am damned.'

The door was unlocked. It was Vanse. Mitchel had paid him to be on hand. 'Let me oot,' he said. 'I canna breathe.'

Vanse nodded. 'He fouls himsel,' he said. Mitchel lurched outside and Vanse closed the door. Behind it they could still hear Weir ranting.

Mitchel sucked in great gasps of air. He thought he had seen something, a dark figure, looming up behind Weir.

'On yer wey oot,' said Vanse calmly, 'ye hae tae see Jean.'
'I canna.'

'Jist a prayer,' said Vanse. 'Ye can spare that for her surely.'

Mitchel held a coin out for Vanse. Weir's laugh still cackled in his head.

'Please,' he said, 'I canna.'

191

Vanse plucked the coin and took him by the arm. 'She is sweet compared wi him, *Maister*.'

There was something about his voice. Maybe he intended to betray him, not let him go. Mitchel realised he was entirely at his mercy.

They went down a passage barely wide enough for the two of them. Doors, each one with a nightmare behind it. There was a small room at one end of the passage. Vanse pushed him forward into it.

Jean Weir was sitting on a bench. The door was not locked because her foot was chained to a ring set in the floor. She looked up placidly.

'Sandy.'

Mitchel looked behind him. He shrugged at Vanse, pleaded again. 'I hae nae prayers left,' he said. 'Let me awa. I beg ye.'

Lauder waited for Mitchel to go on. But he seemed drained by the memories. A minute passed.

'He thocht he could dae nae wrang,' said Lauder at last.

'Aye, that was the worst thing, there was nae hypocrisy in it. His haill life he thocht he could dae nae wrang, then it was borne in upon him that he could dae naethin *but* wrang.'

Lauder shuddered. 'And aw ye can see in front o ye is eternal punishment.'

'He niver lost his faith in that sense. He niver stopped believin in the life tae come.'

'It'd been better for him if he had,' said Lauder.

'It wouldna hae saved him. He'd hae burnt in ony case. At least he walked through this world wi a kennin o the next.'

'Did ye gang tae the Gallowlee?'

'Aye. It's a solemn thing, tae see a man sent on his wey, whether it's tae Heaven or tae Hell.'

'I heard he wasna deid when they burnt him.'

Mitchel shook his head. 'Mebbe no. It was the hangman's job tae thrapple him but he couldna get the breath oot o him. It was strange – he was that seik and feeble they'd tae harl him on a sledge aw the wey frae the Tolbooth, yet when they had him bound tae the stake there seemed a byordnar strenth tae his struggles. Ye'd think the life was thrawn oot o him and then he'd lift his heid and this roarin noise would come oot.

The hangman cam back wi the tow tae try again and Weir's heid would start tae batter itsel aff the stake. They couldna get the tow on him. They said tae him tae speir for the Lord's mercy but he wouldna. He was shoutin, *I hae lived as a beast, let me die as a beast!* Sae the hangman gied up and they pit the lunt tae the fire.'

'And his staff?'

'That was flung in tae, yince the flames had gotten haud. The people wouldna let them pit it in afore for fear he would use it tae escape.'

'Aye,' said Lauder. 'I heard that. I heard folk say they thocht it was alive.'

'Mebbe it was.'

Lauder did not rise to the challenge in Mitchel's voice. There was another story he'd heard, that Weir and Satan his master had concocted a plan to foil the executioners. A mysterious man that had visited him in prison had been bewitched and substituted for the Major, who had taken on the other man's appearance. While the innocent double was being throttled and incinerated, Weir was stepping past on his way to Leith to catch a boat for Holland. It was a ludicrous idea, probably put about by the bishops, who thought all Scotsmen residing in Holland were no better than devils, but folk would believe anything if they wanted to. Lauder was thinking of this as he asked his next question.

'Vanse let ye oot, when ye'd finished in the Tolbooth?'

'Aye. He was jist a lad. I think, eftir aw, that he didna ken me.'

'Where did ye gang?'

'That's for me tae mind and you tae guess. I said I'd tell ye aboot Weir, no aboot folk that helped and bieldit me. But I didna stey lang in Edinburgh, I'll say that. It wasna safe. Ma face was ower weill-kent.'

'Ye were safe wi some. Jean didna betray ye.'

'She hardly saw me. Ye ken the licht in there.'

'She kent ye werena Sandy, though. When I visited her. I tellt ye that.'

'She was a witch and a hure. And dementit tae. I wouldna credit muckle o whit she had tae say.'

'Aye, mebbe,' said Lauder. 'Ye're mebbe richt.'

193

He was suddenly tired. He wondered what time it was. Even though the thought made him queasy, he was looking forward to being summoned for the boat back to Scotland.

He looked up at the narrow slit of the window, trying to judge the hour from the dirty light that pushed feebly in there. A smear of something colourful caught his eye. It seemed so out of place that he stood up to see what it was. He picked it off the stone ledge with his finger: cherry blossom, blown from one of the wizened trees further up the rock. Away from the outside light, against his flesh, it lost its pinkness and didn't look remarkable at all. He sniffed at it, but it had no scent. All he could smell was Mitchel's body, the dankness of the cell, and the salt of the sea all around them.

Edinburgh, April 1997

Tuesday. Carlin woke with a sore head and what felt like the start of a cold in his throat. He'd had a restless night, his dreams invaded by images of endless rows of heads and limbs on spikes. A kirkyard heaved like porridge and gave up its dead. Armies of skeletons emerged from broken tombs. Others were driving cartloads of naked people into furnaces. There were gallows and wheels and instruments of torture. A skeleton was dragging someone head first down into a cave.

He recognised some of these pictures. In the library at his school – he must have been about twelve – there had been these books of paintings, a series called something like *The Great Artists*. In one of them he'd found Pieter Brueghel's 'Triumph of Death'. It was reproduced as a whole and also in four details. The vision was grotesque, horrible. He studied it minutely. Kept going back to it. It was only years later that he finally worked out its fascination: the total absence of hope; the total lack of either God or reason. It was this that had haunted him through the night.

It was supposed to be springtime; he'd just come through a winter in which an appalling flu virus had raced around the city, cowping half the population; now it seemed, as the weather changed, he was finally coming down with it. He didn't feel like going out, but he had to. He needed to go back to the library and read more of the Lauder manuscript. And he needed to speak to MacDonald. Something wasn't making sense.

He was sweltering. He sat on the bed for five minutes, cooling down. Then he began to feel very cold indeed. He got dressed, put on his boots, found a scarf, and went downstairs into the street.

About halfway along it a wave of nausea came over him. He had to lean against a fence or else he'd have been on the ground.

There was a roaring in his head, a clanking engine-like din that got louder and louder. He gripped onto the fence. The roar faded, leaving only the clanking, which became like someone chapping a coin on a table to herald an after-dinner speech. His back ached. Painfully he got himself back upright. The chapping sound continued. He turned around to look for its source. An old man was angrily rapping at a window with his knuckles, gesticulating at the fence he was still clinging to.

Carlin launched himself off the fence, hoping he would have enough momentum to get to the chemist's and then home again.

At the end of the street there was a telephone box. He propped himself up inside it.

'Could I speak tae Mr MacDonald, please?'

'I'm not sure which . . . Which department is that?'

'Scottish. Or mebbe Edinburgh. I'm no certain.'

'Is it a general enquiry then? Can I help at all?'

'It's him I need. A specific thing.'

'Hold on a minute. I'll see if I can track him down. Who shall I say is calling?'

'Ma name's Carlin. But he'll mebbe no mind me. Tell him it's aboot the Lauder manuscript.'

'The Lauder manuscript. Hold on then.'

Carlin watched the units ticking down. He pushed another fifty pence into the box.

Some time passed but he couldn't tell how much. The digits seemed not to move, then they would change rapidly, then freeze again. Carlin blinked, trying to clear his vision. He heard a voice in his lug.

'MacDonald here.'

'Mr MacDonald. It's the guy ye were helpin last week. Aboot Major Weir?'

'Yes?'

'I've no been able tae manage in the day. Tae finish readin that Lauder thing, the *Secret Book*. Ken whit I'm talkin aboot? It was being kept aside for me.'

'If you've been consulting an item and haven't finished with it, it'll be held on reserve till you get in. You needn't have bothered to phone.'

'Aye, but it's mair than that. I've been thinkin . . . aboot somebody visitin Weir in prison.'

'Yes.' MacDonald's voice sounded flat and unhelpful.

'Ye said ye didna think James Mitchel could hae been in tae see him. Ye didna think he could hae been in Edinburgh then at all. That was when ye gied me the Lauder thing and said Lauder had visited him. But it's in *there* aboot Mitchel. In the *Secret Book*. That's where it explains how he went tae see him.'

There was a silence. Carlin's head was pounding in time with the digits which were now changing regularly on the display. Someone was howking in his spine with a serrated knife.

'Hello?' Carlin said. 'Are ye there?'

'Mr Carlin, isn't it?'

'Aye.'

'I did say that that manuscript was quite suspect. I only retrieved it for you from the stacks because of the connection with Major Weir. It's of ephemeral interest only. I thought I made that clear.'

'But ye don't doubt that Lauder saw him. And Lauder says Mitchel saw him tae. How can ye accept one an no the other?'

'Because Lauder says so elsewhere. In an authentic, genuine document. This *Secret Book*, as I explained, is of very dubious origin. It could be by Lauder but we can't prove it. It doesn't contain nearly as much legal terminology or passages in Latin as one would expect, compared with his other writings. It's interesting, but it's probably not by him.'

'Then why did ye waste ma time wi it?'

'*I've* not wasted your time. It's what you wanted, isn't it? You told me you wanted a way in. You said you weren't close enough. Isn't that what you said?'

'Aye but . . .' He dug in his pocket for more change, found only coppers. The display read 10. 'But if it's no real?'

'What's real, Mr Carlin? We say history's real. It really happened. But we can't prove it. We can't touch it. All we have is hearsay and handed down stories and a lot of paper that somebody else tells us is the genuine article.'

The display was down to 6. The roaring was back in Carlin's lugs. He had to shout to hear himself.

'Whit, ye mean like some huge conspiracy? But then everybody's involved, we're aw hooked intae it. And whit's it for then? Who's organised it?'

'Not a conspiracy. Just a set of circumstances we find ourselves in. Each one of us. Nothing about those circumstances is certain – not the present, not the future, certainly not the past. That's gone, if it ever existed. We just have to live as if it did.'

'But if we don't believe that stuff, whit can we believe? Ye've got a haill library doon there that disna mean a thing then. It's junk, useless. That's no whit ye think, is it? That's the very opposite o whit ye were sayin the other day.'

He thought he heard MacDonald laugh, a short, cynical laugh. That couldn't be right surely. Then his voice came again.

'I don't know what to think. I just do my job.'

A message was flashing: INSERT MONEY.

'I'll be in again,' Carlin shouted. 'Tae dae some mair research.'

'Everything's a search,' he thought he heard MacDonald say, and the line went dead.

'He's got a point, but.'

'How?'

'Well, like, prove tae me ye had a childhood. Prove ye existed as a wee boy. Yer mither's deid, yer faither's deid. So ye've got an auntie or two that'll back ye up. Photographs. A name and address. Disna prove a fuckin thing.'

'Memories.'

'Aye, that's aw ye've got. And they can play tricks on ye. Like, where did ye go this mornin?'

'Oot. I felt seik though. I cam hame again.'

The mirror waited.

'And?'

'I nearly fainted. An auld guy got angry at me through his windae. I could – I don't need tae but I could – go and chap his door and ask him if he'd iver seen me before.'

'Oh aye, d'ye think he'd open the door tae ye? Probably think ye were comin roon tae gie him a hammerin.

Probably thought ye were a junkie. Where else did ye go?'

'Tae the chemist's. For painkillers. And I can prove that. There's them on the table.'

'Where else?'

'Here. I crashed oot. And I phoned that guy in the library. Had a weird conversation wi him. He's keepin a book on reserve for me.'

'Is he?'

'Aye. He said so.'

'Did he?'

'Aye. Whit the fuck is this?'

'You were never oot this room aw day. Ye bought the drugs yesterday, cause ye felt somethin comin on. I've been watchin ye. Ye've been lyin in yer kip aw day like a lazy cunt. Totally incommunicado. Wiped oot. Deif and blin tae the world.'

'Fuck off.'

'I'm tellin ye. Fuckin buzzer was gaun twice. Ye niver even stirred. So don't gie me this phonin the library shite. Ye've been dreamin. Hallucinatin. Ye're ill, man.'

'That's pathetic. I was oot. Is that the best ye can dae?'

'Fuckin library. Probably disna even fuckin exist.'

'Coorse the library exists. Where d'ye think I was last week? Ye niver raised aw this existence shite then.'

'It wasna an issue last week. You're the wan talkin shite.'

'Fuck off. The library's real. MacDonald's real. I'm no weill but I'm no fuckin crazy.'

'Ye wouldna ken if ye were.'

'There's nae arguin wi you. I'm gaun tae ma bed.'

'Best place for ye,' said the mirror. 'Strap yersel in.'

Friday. Hugh Hardie phoned Jackie at her work.

'I've been meaning to call you,' he began.

'Look, Hugh . . .'

'I know, I know, and I'm not going to hassle you about not finishing the tour. But I wish you'd stayed. Something's happened. I need your help, Jackie. I really need your help.'

'What is it?'

'Carlin, of course. He's gone missing. Completely. He did a bunk on Monday – after you went home. Hasn't turned up at all these last three nights.'

'Are you worried about him?'

'I'm totally pissed off with him, since you ask.'

'Ooh, sorry. Is it my fault?'

'He was your contact.'

'I should put the phone down on you right now for that,' Jackie said. 'You bullied me for an introduction. You fucking hired him.'

'I'll fucking fire him when I catch up with him.'

'So fire him. It's not my problem. Goodbye, Hugh.'

'Wait, Jackie, I'm sorry. You're absolutely right. I apologise. I'm just keyed up about it. I can't fire him even if I wanted to because I don't know where he is. Plus he's got all my gear – the costume. You don't know where he lives, do you?'

'I already told you I didn't.'

'You've no idea? Maybe he's still wherever he was when you were students.'

'Maybe. It was six years ago. I don't know where that was.'

'Shit.' There was silence at Hugh's end of the line. Jackie knew he was hoping she would fill it for him. To her horror she found herself doing so.

'Look,' she said. 'I don't owe you this. I don't owe you anything. I want you to be clear about that.'

'Of course,' he said hopefully.

'Maybe I could try to find out for you. He used to stay in Bruntsfield somewhere. Maybe I could track him down through the uni or something.'

'God, that would be brilliant. I'm desperate, Jackie.'

'I'm not promising anything.'

'No, I know you're not.'

'Sounds to me like you should get yourself a stand-in anyway. I mean, whatever's happened to him, he's not exactly reliable.'

'That's the trouble with ghosts,' he said.

'That's my line. Listen, I can't do anything today, I'm too busy. And I've got stuff on at the weekend. So it'll be next week before I can get back to you. Do you want to wait that long?'

'If for no other reason than to find out what his problem is – yes. Even if he never works for me again. And I want my props back.'

'I'm touched by your selfless concern. Well, I'll let you know if I have any joy.'

'Okay. I'll substitute for him myself in the meantime. I really appreciate this, Jackie.'

'Folk are always telling me that,' she said.

Edinburgh, January 1676

These are the ployes used by the Archbischop of St Androis (whom the fanaticks call only James Sharp, for they never admit his title) to wring a confession out of Mitchel anent the shooting. The archbischop & others of the Council ware determind to bring him to the scaffold, this was their principall desire from the time they seized him at his shop Februar 1674, armed by their account wt a loaded pistol and a short swerd, and charged him wt the cryme.

First they approached his wife but she would not treat with them saying only, Ye have tane him from me, pruve what ye say he has done else let him come back to me. Then they socht out her brother Nicol Sommervile, & dealt wt him thus: that if Mitchel would but confesse St Androis would procure his pardon. But Nicol says, I hope ye'll not make me a snare to trap a man to his ruin. Sharp promises by the living God, that no hurt should come to Mitchel if he discovered all anent the acte and all that ware party to it. Nicol carried this word to Mitchel, and came back wt an answer that he would tell all for a solemn promise in the King's name. This was debated in the Council. Some ware against all treating wt him, but Sir Archibald Primrose, the Ld Clerk Register who has always hated Sharp and saw a means to trip him, says with some pertinence, was it the truth they wanted or vengence? If the first they must forgoe the 2d, for says he, It would be a powerfull eloquence that persuadit a man to confesse only for the reward of being hanged. Then Lauderdale on the Kings behalf allows them to promise him his lyfe.

Mitchel was taken on the 7th, this debate was on the 10th. Immediatly he is broght before my lords Rothes, Carringtoun (that is, Primrose) and Haltoun, and the King's Advocate Sir John Nisbet to be examind, whereupon he indicates a willingnes to speak. Rothes taking him a little aside and telling him of the offer he immediatly goes down on his knees and confesses. And they wrote out two confessions, ane that acknowledged his part in the Rising at Pentland, ane that acknowledged him as the man that shot at the Archbischop. And I have seen these confessions, baith subscrived by Mitchel, Rothes, Primrose, Haltoun and Nisbet, and though in themselves they do not mention of it undoubtedly they ware got by promise of his lyfe.

But when they pressed him for names of those privy to his intent, he said there was nane; then at last offered one name, but he was now dead. Sharp hearing of this flew in a tempest, for he hoped to catch uthir fanaticks by his word, but Mitchel would say no more. Howiver broght befoir the haill Council on the 12th he repeated his confession. Then some moved for cutting off his ryght hand, but uthirs said he will only lerne to practise wt his left. Cut them both off then, says Sharp. My lord Rothes says, How then sall he wipe his breech? And Primrose, who is ever for soft counsels and slowe methods, says, We have promised him lyfe, we risk it if we butcher him. And soe he was returnd to the tolbuith till they thought what could be done wt him.

It was decided they must make his confession stick by having him repeat it in a court of law. So on 2nd March he was broght befoir the Court of Justiciary. Now who is one of the judges of session but Archibald Primrose, Lord Carringtoun. He was out wt Montrose and captured at Selkirk, was lucky then not to be executed for treason when the fanatick party ruled the kingdome, and was alwayes loyal to Charles II in exile. Therefor he detested those Covenanters who turned their coates at the Restoration, and most especially Sharp. So as he passed the prisoner at the bar he said from the back of his hand, Confesse nothing unless ye be sure of yr limbs as well as yr lyfe. Mitchel apprehending from this that they planned to mutilate him in any case, denied the confession. And wt nothing else in the way of evidence the King's Advocate was obliged to desert the case.

Sharp raged like a bull but to no effect. The Council resolved only that since Mitchel retracted his confession they would retract their promise, & should any uthir evidence come to light anent the shooting they would pursue him in extremis. Now its a point of law that he not being found guilty of any crime should have walked free, but Mitchel's lawyers could not sway the Council to release him, Sharp protesting that no sooner was he loose than he would use him for a targett agane. And so he was put back in prison.

There he stayed nigh on two years till all had forgot him but his frends in Holland and his wyfe. And also James Sharp, who could nayther expunge nor, without the confession, acte upoun the hatred he had for him. Till in December 1675 Mitchel did bring him selfe ance more to the Council's attention by attempting to break out of the tolbuith. 16th Dec I find the Council appoints him to be removed to a surer room. By January it semes their patience wt him is run out. He having refused agane to make judicial confession to that which he previously confessd, they resolve to put him to the torture, to see if that will loose his tongue.

18 January 1676. About six in the evening, lying in chains in the Tolbooth, James Mitchel was surprised by the entry of warders and soldiers, who released the fetters on him and dragged him to another room in the building, where the Town Council was accustomed to meet. Mitchel was groggy and weak from immobility and bad food. He was thin, unkempt and depressed. In this state he found himself again before the committee that had received his confession two years earlier. Some of the lesser members, clearly uneasy at what was about to take place, put their elbows on the table and hid their faces from him with their hands.

Mitchel understood that he was in the presence of some of the worst persecutors of Christ's people: especially George Livingstone, Earl of Linlithgow, a sixty-year-old soldier, commander-in-chief of the King's forces in Scotland, and still fond of riding out at the head of his dragoons to break up field-gatherings; and Charles Maitland, Lord Haltoun, younger brother to Lauderdale, a sleekit, supercilious, grasping nepotist if ever there was one. Mitchel, ragged and penniless, was nothing against their power and wealth. Yet there was a weariness in Linlithgow's voice when he addressed the prisoner. Experience had taught that one should not expect straightforward answers from fanatics.

'Sir, ye are brought here before the committee, to see if ye will adhere to your former confession or not.'

'My lord,' said Mitchel, 'ye ken, and ithers here present ken, that by the Cooncil's order I was remitted tae the lords of the Justiciary, and indicted afore them by my lord Advocate, of my life and fortune, although, my lord, fortune I hae nane. But my lord Advocate deserted the diet, and therefore by the law and custom of the nation I ought tae hae been set at liberty, but I was returned tae prison and hae been kept there since. Sae on whit accoont I am brocht here this nicht, I ken not.'

'Ye are not accused here,' Linlithgow said, 'but only brought to see whether ye will adhere to your former confession.'

'I believe I hae committed nae crime,' Mitchel said. 'Therefore, I ken o nae such confession as your lordship alleges.'

There was an explosive splutter from Haltoun. 'He is one of the most arrogant rogues, cheats and liars I ever saw. We ken, sir, ye was up to your oxters in the rebellion of '66.'

'My lord,' Mitchel said calmly, 'if there was fewer folk o the kind that ye jist mentioned in this nation, I wouldna be staunin the nicht afore ye. As tae the ither thing, I never confessed onythin anent that time, as my lord Advocate weill kens.'

'If ye dinna gie us what we seek,' Linlithgow said, 'we will try another thing to make you confess.'

Mitchel held his gaze. 'I hope your lordships are Christians, not pagans.'

'You, sir, are no Christian,' Haltoun said.

'My lord,' said Mitchel derisively, 'd'ye ken the proverb o the auld wife that would niver hae thocht tae look for her dochter in the oven if she hadna been in it hersel?'

Haltoun, outraged, started up from the table, but was restrained by Linlithgow.

'Sir,' Linlithgow said, 'this is the paper with your name upon it. Do you not acknowledge it?'

'I acknowledge nae such thing.'

Linlithgow made a signal. A soldier approached and deposited the apparatus known as the boots upon the table.

'Sir, ye see what is there before ye. We shall see if it can cause ye to speak.'

'If ye torture me wi that,' Mitchel said, 'ye may cause me

tae dae mair than speak. Ye may cause me tae blaspheme God. Ye may cause me tae curse and speak amiss o your lordship. Ye may cause me tae cry masel a thief, murderer, warlock or whitiver, and think then tae hae me caught by ma ain words. But I protest before God, naethin ye extort frae me by torture shall hae ony force against me in law, or against ony person I micht name. I *am* a Christian, my lord, and if ye prove a thing against me legally, I'll no deny it. But I am a man tae, and I niver held masel obliged by law or nature tae become ma ain accuser.'

Haltoun snorted again. 'By God, he has the Devil's logic, and his sophistry. Ask him if that be his name and signature or no?'

'I acknowledge nae such thing,' Mitchel repeated.

'Bid him say yea or no,' Haltoun said.

Linlithgow pointed to the boots. 'Ye see what is before ye. Is this your signature? Say either yea or no.'

'I say no,' Mitchel said.

They returned him to his cell and put the chains back on him. Nobody spoke to him. It was as if, already, he had become special, different. He lay without company for nearly a week, praying, and reading his Bible. He thought of Jean Weir, chained in the same building, six years before. He thought of the Major. He thought of Hew McKail on the scaffold.

24 January 1676. Mitchel was brought before the Lords of Session, in the laich hall of the Parliament House. He was to be subjected to judicial torture. The executioner, masked, was present with the boots. Lord Linlithgow, in his robes of office, again acted as preses. He asked the panel once more if he would confess before being put to the torture.

Mitchel spoke. 'My lord, I will be brief. I hae been kept twa years in prison, mair than yin o them in irons, and in close and solitary confinement. I hae been kept frae ma freens and frae ma wife aw this time. Ye ken that ithers that hae been in prison less time hae made awa wi themsels, but I hae endured awthin in obedience tae God's commandments. If it be God's will I should undergo this torture, I will thole it. But again I say, whitiver ye shall extort frae me by this, I protest may not be used against me, nor ony ither, nor hae ony force in law.'

'You are wrong,' said Linlithgow. 'That is why you are here. This is a court of law, and you have brought this upon yourself. All we ask is that you confess. You understand perfectly well what we are speaking of. But whether you do so or not, under torture or not, whatever happens here is lawful.'

'Then,' said Mitchel, 'call the men ye hae appointed tae dae yer work.'

The executioner and two assistants came forward. They seated him and tied his arms to the arms of the chair. They brought down the apparatus and placed it on a box in front of him. Then they asked the judges which leg they should start on. Linlithgow and the others conferred: they had not considered this.

'It matters not,' said Linlithgow. 'Take either.'

The men lifted his left leg and laid it in the open boot. Mitchel lifted it out and looked with total scorn up at the bench.

'Since ye judges canna mak up yer minds, tak the better yin. I freely bestow it in the cause.'

He lifted his right leg and the men laid it in the boot. They closed up the boot. It was a wooden case, very tight-fitting about the leg. It held the leg absolutely rigid. The executioner fetched a number of large wooden wedges, and a mallet.

Mitchel stared at his encased leg, then at the bench. 'My lords, I dinna ken if I will escape this wi ma life. Therefore I must say tae ye, remember whit Solomon says: he who sheweth no mercy shall have judgment without mercy. And also I say, remember whit shall befall those that hath shed the blood of the saints and the prophets, in the Book of Revelation: they shall be judged by God, and his angels shall pour out a sea of blood, and they shall be drowned in it. And now I freely forgive ye, and I do entreat that God may never lay this work to the charge of any of you.'

Haltoun yawned and said loudly, 'Can we not stop this flood of cant and hypocrisy?'

Linlithgow turned to Sir John Nisbet, the King's Advocate. 'Begin.'

Nisbet approached the panel. 'Are you that Maister James Mitchel who for your crimes was excepted out of the King's grace and favour, or no?'

'I niver committed ony crime deservin me tae be excluded,' Mitchel replied. 'I upheld the Covenant. I should hae been included, protected and defended.'

'When did ye know of the rising in arms in 1666?'

'I kent o it when the rest o the citizens kent o it.'

'When was that?'

'When a messenger cam tae the Cooncil aboot it, and Dalziel marched oot at the West Port tae face that godly army.'

'Did ye not go out of the toun with one Captain Arnot? Did ye not meet with Colonel Wallace, the rebel leader? Did ye not go to Ayr, or join with the rebels there, or somewhere else?'

Haltoun interrupted. 'My lord, the fool never acknowledges these men to be rebels.'

Mitchel, eyeing Haltoun, said to Nisbet, 'My lord, I will follow Solomon's advice when he says, even a fool by haudin his wheesht will be reckoned wise.'

Haltoun fumed in silence. Mitchel saw Primrose smirk, and even over Nisbet's mouth a smile flickered before he hurried on.

'Where was ye at the time of Pentland?'

'In Edinburgh.'

'Where was ye before it?'

'In Edinburgh.'

'Where was ye after it?'

'In Edinburgh.'

Nisbet sighed, then tried again.

'Where did ye lodge before Pentland?'

'At Grizel Whitford's.'

'And where did ye stay at the time of it? Was ye still in the toun?'

'I dinna ken whit ye mean by bein still in the toun. Ye might cry it oot o the toun if I was at the Windmill, or the Potterrow, or Leith.'

'What, ye were never further abroad than these places?'

Mitchel let his breath go, to show that he was bored. 'I

canna mind noo where I was, it was ten year syne. I dinna keep a diary. I doot ony man here can mind thae kind o details eftir sae lang a time. But I ken this, it is ma duty tae gang aboot ma employment and calling as God hath commanded, and be satisfied wi that.'

Nisbet tried another tack. 'Ye left the toun about that time. Why was that?'

'I was reddin up tae sail ower tae Flanders. Tae trade.'

'Who did ye sail with?'

'Wi John Forrester, an Ostender.'

'How long after Pentland was this?'

'I canna mind.'

'Can ye not give a guess?'

'A month mebbe. Six weeks.'

'Then what was ye doing all that time?'

'Reddin up. And then there was a contrary wind.'

'All right,' said Nisbet. 'Ye went to the continent. How long did ye stay there?'

'Aboot three-quarters o a year.'

'Ye went to trade. What kept ye so long over there?'

'Only that I wasna ready tae return. And the war was on between the Dutch and the English. I thocht it would be safer tae wait a while.'

'With whom did ye come home again?'

'Wi some Dutchmen. Amsterdamers.'

'Was there no Scotsman with ye?'

'I jist tellt ye, I cam hame wi Dutchmen.'

'Who was the skipper?'

'I canna mind, but he pit in at Limekilns tae load coals frae Sir James Hacket. I mind that.'

Nisbet shook his head at this singularly useless piece of information. All his questions had been aimed at incriminating other persons for communing with Mitchel. So far he had failed miserably. He tried a more direct approach.

'Did ye know James Stirling, one of the authors of a book called *Naphtali*? Or William Fergusson, that was disaffected, that stayed in or about the Cowgate in this toun?'

'Aye. I kent them.'

Nisbet asked hopefully, 'Are they alive?'

'Na. They are baith deid. William Fergusson here, Maister

Stirling in the Indies. He was called tae be a minister in the plantations at Bombay. I hear he had a fall frae his horse there.'

'Never mind that. At the time that the Archbishop of St Andrews was shot at, did ye know one William Young?'

'Aye.'

'Did ye buy a horse from him at that time?'

'I niver bought a horse frae him.'

'Well, then, from whom did ye hae a horse, when ye went out of the toun?'

'I could hae had a horse frae onybody, tae lend or hire.'

'But from whom did ye hae a horse?'

'If I couldna get a horse, I took tae ma feet.'

Nisbet stopped. He turned to the bench and shrugged. The judges muttered among themselves. Clearly this was getting nowhere.

Linlithgow nodded to the executioner. 'Proceed.'

The executioner lifted the boot containing Mitchel's leg from off the box and lowered the foot of it to the ground. He inserted one wedge at the knee, pushing it as far into the boot as it would go. It did not go very far.

The executioner raised the mallet. He looked to the bench. Linlithgow nodded again.

The thud of iron striking wood was startling in the silent chamber. The wedge shifted, surprisingly, several inches. Mitchel screamed.

Linlithgow said, 'Do you have any more to say, sir?'

There was a gasp from Mitchel. 'No more, my lords.'

The mallet descended again. Mitchel screamed. The wedge moved further. There was a cracking sound.

'Do you wish to say anything?' said Linlithgow.

Mitchel shook his head. A word that might have been 'No' came from between his teeth.

The mallet struck again. Mitchel screamed. Something thick and bloody began to drip from the wood of the boot onto the stone floor.

That great scolar George Buchanan, that tutored King James as a bairn, in his historie of Scotland debates the efficacie of torture as an instrument of law. Punishments extreem in their crueltie, he says, doe not so much restrain the minds of the vulgar, by the fear or horrour they excite, as enrage them to acte as viciouslie or to thole any pain or torment themselves; nor are wicked men made good by beholding these things, but their terror at barbarities is reduced wt familiaritie.

Why must I dwell on thir matters? This world is a sair place and made na less sair by contemplatioun. But I cannot desist. The law floats on the blood of criminalls, and yet in punishing becomes its selfe a torturer and murtherer. Can law be above its makers? Gods laws are good according to his goodness, therefoir how can man, that fell from Gods grace, make good law? He may claim his law is derived from God, but how often doe we find that God and heaven hath been made from law.

Mitchel was tortured and judged according to the laws of uthir men. God kens I am no apologist for the fanaticks. It was their adherance to wrong headed principles that brocht baith Scotland and England to their sorry states in the time of Cromwell. But with Mitchel it was time to shew mercie to a man that no countrie should be feared of, unless it be not kinde or true to itselfe. Even now it is not too late to kiss farewell to controversie and lett him live.

When I was but nineteen or twenty in Poictiers I witnessd the hardest death I ever saw, which has hanted me since, for when the law kills it kills wt a coldnes that is awful to consider. A blacksmith there had strack dead one of his apprentices, who had speirt him for money, and fled to Lusignon, but was there made captive. He was tried and found guilty of the crime, but the tounes of France, being not royal burghs like ours, have not the power to pass sentens of hanging and beheading, and so in due time he was taken to Paris, whare his doom was decided in the king's name. He was condemnd to be broken on the wheel, a foul practise commoun on the continent, but which I think was seldom if ever used here, and certanely not in recent memorie. He was returnd to Poictiers but not tauld the trew nature of his sentens till about two hours befoir he was broken, for by concealing it till then they keip the condemned from attempting escape, or from taking his own lyfe, which many a man myght do, even to the greater peril of his soul, gif he knew he was to be killt in such a way. This smith was tauld he was only to be sent to the galleys, and the man laucht and crackt anent this. They have forgot my trade, saith he, I'll fyle the chains and be away. But at noon on the day of his death he was publickly sentencd by the hangman, who caused him to kneel while the doom was read, then put a tow about his neck wt the words, Le Roy vou salut, mon amie, to shew it was the king's will he should die.

Thousands awaited him that afternoon at the place of execution in the Marche Vieux. There was a Scots flavor to it, as I lightly thoucht at first (tho soon I was scunnerd at the jest), for on the scaffold was a Sanct Androis cross made of two beams nailed togither. The smith was strippt to his shirt and bound wt his back to this cross, each arme and leg stretcht upoun one limb of it. They gave him a little tyme to pray, trembling in his miserie upoun the cross, assisted by two monks maist sinister in their cowels and robes. Then the hangman took a great baton or bar of iron and begun to break him. He commencd wt his armes and broke them wt two strakes to each elbuck. His knees he broke next wt two strakes. The man's cries ware hideous to hear. I felt my bowels ryse and heize, tho the huge crowd seemed to like the play weel enough. The hangman continued with his work, striking next upon the thighs, then two great swings that smasht his ribs and stumack. All that was not smasht was his head, for that would kill him, and his chest, though commonlie, I was later tauld, a blow to crush the hart is given as the final deliverance. In this case there was no such tendernes shewn: I counted twenty blows befoir the hangman droppt his iron bar and yet the smith was not dead. The hangman then strangled him, but this I think was too delicat a job for the brute, for the tow snappt twice or it was accomplishd. Of all cruel deaths, this which I witnessd in my twentieth year I think was worst.

Yet its too easy to say this would not happen in our countrie. The French ware always a pleasant, curtious and civil people, though horridly addicted to the cheating of strangers. But they have a boot like ours, which I saw at Poictiers, and who can say we'll not ever throw a man upoun a wheel as they doe? All men judge things according to custom, not by a universal truth. Else why is Europe riven thir last hundred years by men who all have God upoun their side?

It was but ane month after Mitchels torture that the man he hit wt his shott, Bischop Honyman, died in his palace in Orkny.

212

If they could have proved it the Privy Council had broucht Mitchel up for murder, since they mayntaned Honyman never recovered from the wound receivd, but dwyned away by degries. But this no court would entertayn 8 yeirs after the event. And I think too it would have bene ower great a hurt to Sharp's conceit of him selfe if the fanatick had bene hangd at last for hitting Orkny and not for missing St Androis.

I know not what Mitchel felt when he hard of Honymans end, but uthirs of his persuasion made much of it as a signe of Gods displesour, the bischop being but 56 yeirs old. This is how it was: going up to his chamber one night, his wyfe hard him make a noise and din upoun the floor. She caused break open the door, for it was bolted from within, and they found him as was said lying on the floor, his hat to one place, his skullcap to ane uthir, his gown all rent in pieces. They broght him down and made a bed for him, from which he never rose againe, but onely said, Something came between me and my light. Some days later he passed away. The fanatick party, hearing of his words, shook their heads wt solemn glee and said, Oh its a dangerous thing to sin against light! John Eleis and I thoght his declyne no more the work of Gods displesour than Sir Geo. Maxwells was the work of witches, but we were carefull to keip this opinion to our selves.

Can a man like Mitchel go to heaven and not I? Or Sharp and not Mitchel? Or any of us and not these poor weemen lately condemned by Prestoun in the west country, for witches? I that must in publick keep a calme colde face finde my selfe in privat in a swarf to think on these things. God keip this book from prying eyes of kirk and state alike.

Bass Rock, July 1677

A deputation of ministers filled the cell: James Fraser, Thomas Hog, William Bell. Mitchel understood that they had not come on a social call.

It was extraordinary that they were there at all. Although the garrison had become quite slack – Mitchel could hear much coming and going between cells, as the prisoners prayed together or invited one another for little walks among the solans – he was still excluded from any easing of conditions. On recent Sabbaths common worship had been permitted – for all but himself. Even some of the soldiers had been allowed to join in, if they could bear the mockery of their fellows and officers.

Mitchel kept Rutherford's book hidden. Apart from his Bible and a few shreds of tobacco it was his only comfort, his only relief from boredom and discomfort. All his teeth were loose. His skin was flaky and constantly itchy. When he scratched he caught small moving things under his nails.

There was no letter or return visit from Elizabeth. He wondered if messages from her were being intercepted. He hoped that that was the case.

William Bell was a field-preacher of some repute. He had been arrested in September the previous year at a meeting in the Pentlands and taken to Edinburgh, then transferred a month later to the Bass. He was a poor man, like Mitchel, but he had kept his distance from him till now. He did not waste any time with formalities.

'Ye ken the sodger cried Tammas?' he said.

'Aye.' But Tammas had not been near him for weeks.

'Whit dae ye ken o him?'

'Whit is there tae ken? We hae smoked a pipe thegither.'

'Whit else?'

'Naethin else. He has been kinder than maist tae me in this place.'

214

Fraser said, 'Aye, we have heard that.'

Mitchel sat up. There was something more, he could feel it.

Hog said, 'Did ye hear about the captain's son's wager?'

'I hear naethin,' said Mitchel reproachfully.

'He wagered ten shillings that none of the garrison would dare to debauch one of our servant-women and get her with child. All the soldiers were made aware of this, a challenge to them to vex us and to reflect the deed upon us.'

'It's tae be expected,' said Mitchel.

Bell looked furious. 'Your kind Tammas has been speirin his ten shillins,' he said.

Mitchel almost laughed, but restrained himself. 'Away! The man would fleg the lassies wi his ill looks, no fleetch them.'

'There was nae enticement needed,' said Bell. 'He got a lass fou, and took her up on the Rock alane wi him. It was rape in aw but name.'

'God forgie him,' said Mitchel. He thought of Tammas's hairy pockmarked face, his brute body forcing himself on a woman, the birds rising and screeching around them. He said, 'God comfort her. Has he been punished?'

'He's been sent awa, that's aw. We protested,' said Bell, 'but they only laugh at us. They brocht the man afore his officer, though, tae question him.'

'To pay him, when our backs were turned, no doubt,' said Hog.

'The rogue said it was but business,' said Bell. 'He said it was his right tae earn whit siller he could in such a place as this.'

'He is ignorant,' said Mitchel. 'The officers pit the men up tae such ploys, we ken this.'

'He said he would hae had siller frae yersel, sir, for a service he rendered ye. But ye niver peyed him for it.'

Mitchel hesitated. It was true he had not given any of Lizzie's money to Tammas. It was too precious, and Tammas would have despised him if he had handed it over for nothing. But how much did the ministers know? Was it known that Lizzie had been with him? He thought of her in Edinburgh where she could be found and punished.

He said, 'If it was for tobacco and the like, he had only tae ask. Though he has had as muckle frae me as I frae him.'

'Tobacco!' said Bell. 'It was for a woman, sir. He procured ye a hure and got her tae ye frae the land, and noo he complains that ye owe him for her.'

'That is a lie.'

'Whit is a lie?'

'The haill o it.'

'We ken ye had a woman here.'

Mitchel felt a surge of anger. 'Ye ken naethin. Would ye believe a man like thon afore ye would believe me?'

'Sir,' said Fraser, 'we are by circumstance associated with ye, and by our principles are in some way at one with ye, and we grieve for the treatment ye have suffered at the hands of an unclean, adulterous and oppressive government, but we have not condoned your rash act against the apostate Sharp, nor can we condone your dealings with the soldier and this woman. Ye stand separate and apart from us, sir, and your own actions have brought your solitude upon ye.'

Now Mitchel did laugh. 'Then I am a solitary man for guid reasons. Ye accuse *me* of foul union wi a hure. Ye accuse *me* of dealin backhandedly wi the enemy. Ye must think ye are like Phinehas when Israel abode in Shittim. Ye must think ye act noo as he did when he saw the man that brocht a Midianitish woman intae the camp. He rose up frae amang the congregation and took a javelin and went intae the man's tent and thrust baith o them through wi it, and thus he stayed the plague frae the children of Israel. And the Lord said, Phinehas hath turned away my wrath, I give unto him my covenant of peace; and he shall have it, and his seed after him, because he was zealous for his God. Ye condemn the lawbreakers that bring desolation and sorrow upon Israel but ye shrink tae act against them. But *I* acted. *I* am Phinehas, sirs, no you! So dinna come tae lecture and preach at me aboot ma solitude. I thole it for Christ, no for ony sins ye ascribe tae me.'

'We need nae Bible lessons frae you, sir,' said Bell.

'The woman that was here was nae hure. She was ma wife.'

Mitchel had never had a text that fitted so perfectly the moment for which it was required. He had scoured the Testaments for justification of his action against Sharp – he had an arsenal of Scripture at his command – but the

Phinehas story struck both at Sharp and at these blackmouthed clatterers. He felt a rush of superiority over them. He believed that they would serve their time and survive the Bass, while he would not: he would die here, or he would be killed by Sharp. But they would survive precisely because they had not his zeal. He would die early but while they inherited the earth, he would inherit Christ.

The three ministers were speechless. They did not know what to do or say. They might not even have known about Lizzie – and their friend John Welsh was not there to confirm that he had married them. They backed out in confusion, Bell muttering that they would have to consult further among themselves.

A few days later a boat brought a new prisoner to the Rock. Robert Traill, the younger, had returned from Holland a year after Mitchel, but he had gone to England, and settled as a preacher in Kent. In May of that year he had come discreetly to Edinburgh to visit friends. There he had participated in house-conventicles. Somebody had got wind of his arrival and he had been arrested, and, being wanted in connection with the Pentland Rising, brought before the Privy Council and sent to the Bass. Traill knew all the ministers there. He was also on friendly terms with Mitchel. He confirmed to them that he was married. William Bell came grudgingly and apologised on behalf of the others. Mitchel received him coldly. He had got beyond them. He had no need for any of them, now that Traill was there.

And yet, alone in his cell, he felt a new and chill wind blowing, even in the height of summer. He kept thinking of the visitation of the ministers, and of Lizzie. Supposing he *had* been deluded? Supposing Tammas had tricked him? Tammas was long gone, transferred to the mainland. Supposing it had not been Lizzie at all, but a harlot from North Berwick? The woman had brought him siller, though, and Rutherford's book – of course it had been Lizzie. Did he not ken his own wife? But these might have been sweeteners, to confuse him. How could Lizzie have saved that amount of money? And where had she found the lost book?

Tammas's appearance – his ugliness, his half-hairy face, his scaly, unhuman skin – began to prey on his mind. Had Lizzie really come to him? He had mounted her, been inside her. It had felt like her. But it was dark in the cell, it was always dark. Could he have miskent her?

He thought of his hands on her. He tried to mind what she had been wearing on her feet. If at any time he had seen her feet.

He tried to mind if he had seen the two of them – Lizzie and Tammas – both at the same time. There had been just the one moment – when she had passed in at the door and he had gone out. He tried desperately to see that moment again, to see them as two distinct figures.

He listened in the darkness of the night and thought he could hear Tammas laughing at him.

He took some comfort from Rutherford. And he had one other message to which he could turn, a brief, crumbling note that had been smuggled into him a day or two before the transfer from Edinburgh to the Bass. It was a letter from Rotterdam, unsigned but bearing the initials J.C. and J.B. He thought of Carstairs and Brown, the men who had spoken out for him against MacWard. Whoever had sent it, the letter had taken three months to reach him. It had been written some months after his torture. *We were much refreshed to hear how the Lord helped you to be faithful in that sharp piece of trial*, it said. *Who can tell but God may be more glorified in poor Mr James Mitchel, whom many of our wise dons may look upon as half-distracted*. That was a winning thought, but it contained its own seed of doubt. Was he half-mad? He hurried on to the last few lines: *Justice you can hardly expect, but in this you are not the first, and it may be shall not be the last. I think they thirst for blood more than ever . . . The God of peace be with you.*

The letter itself was half sermon, half prayer. He began to wonder – because he had no real proof, no sense of anything shut up in this terrible place – whether it had come from Rotterdam at all.

He didn't know which was worse – the possibility of having been fooled by Satan or these insane journeys of his imagination. All he knew was that he was utterly alone. Even Robert Traill disappointed him, spending nearly all of his time with the others. They had turned him against him.

Mitchel began to think almost affectionately on James

Sharp. He longed for him to make his move. He had a picture of the Archbishop, writing by candlelight at a desk in his palace in St Andrews, signing arrest warrants and planning the further suppression of conventicles. And then the figure looked up, and it was Robert MacWard in the cold Dutch morning, writing letters under his alias Mr Long, organising, controlling, sending and receiving – safe in Utrecht.

Mitchel lay between them, waiting imprisoned in the Bass, in the grey, cold sea.

Edinburgh, April 1997

'Hih,' said the mirror. 'Where d'ye think you're aff tae? I want a word wi you.'

Carlin had tried to sneak back to bed by crawling. He was skeer-naked. He'd managed a bath eventually. His body was warm and clean again, but still aching below the flesh. All he wanted to do was strip the sheets off the bed, throw on some clean ones and get between them.

'Come here when I'm talkin tae ye.'

'I'm no in the mood.'

'Oh, excuse me. So it's awright when *I'm* no in the mood, when you come in bleezin frae the pub or wantin a mantel-piece tae greet on, ony oor o the nicht or day, I've got tae listen tae the fuckin pish comin oot o *your* mooth, but when *you're* no in the mood I can jist fuck off and hing here, is that it?'

'Aye. I'm seik. I need ma bed. At least let me pit on some claes.'

'Aye, cause look at ye. Ye're like somethin the cat decided tae leave oot. Ye're aw sticks, man. Ye're mair a draigelt deck-chair than a human being.'

Carlin went back out into the lobby. He opened the drawer at the bottom of the wardrobe and pulled out two sheets and a pillow-case. When he stood up he saw himself in the full-length mirror. There was no denying it: a painter could have used him as a model for a study of trees in winter. His bones poked at his skin as if it was a tent. His face was taut and his eyes were like pinheads. He brushed his prick and balls with the palm of his hand. There was about as much life down there as you'd find in a balloon three days after a party.

He wrapped one of the sheets around him. It felt cool and wonderful. He went back into the front room, chucked the second sheet and pillow-case on the bed, then went back to the mirror.

'Right,' he said. 'Say whit ye've got tae say.'

'That was gaun tae be ma line,' said the mirror.

'Eh?'

'I was gaun tae say, let's no beat aboot the bush ony langer. Let's get tae the root o the problem. Let's cut tae the fuckin chase, ken whit I mean?'

'Like whit?'

'Like eh, how come ye're so intae these cunts that've been deid three hunner year? How come ye're hung up on psychopaths and duglowpers and miserable wee deid junkies? How come ye canna haud doon a job? Whit is it wi you? How come ye're stuck up here in a garret wi the flu, dreamin o folk gettin tortured? Whit kinna wey is that for a grown man tae pass the time?'

Carlin stared back.

'Awright, if ye're no gaun tae say nuthin, I'll gie ye a few hints. Get ye stertit. Aw I want is a full confession. Eftir that, I'll lea ye alane. First thing is, I've noticed ye dinna touch folk. Ye ayewis seem tae avoid it. Whit's that aboot then?'

'It hurts tae touch. It's better no tae. Safer.'

'How's that?'

'Dinna ken.'

'I'd hae thought it would be nice tae touch. Ye'd think it wouldna hurt. Jist the opposite in fact. Say, if ye touched a lassie. That'd be nice.'

'No. Ye'd be wrang. Ye ken fine aboot that.'

'Like that Jackie. Be nice tae touch her.'

'I huvna even thought aboot it.'

'Awright. Leave the lassies oot o it for the time being. How aboot yersel? Ye can touch yersel surely.'

'How d'ye mean?'

'Oh come on! A magazine or two, a video. Tae get ye gaun, ken. Or jist a few nice thoughts o yer ain, use yer imagination. Then a wee feel tae yersel. Ye can dae that, can ye no?'

'Ye're a bastart. Naethin happens, ye ken that. Look at me. Naethin happens.'

'I am lookin at ye. It's a sad state o affairs, Andra. Whit are ye gaun tae dae aboot it?'

'Dinna ken.'

'Listen, I'm no meanin tae grind ye doon. I'm tryin tae help.'

'Aye, right.'

'I am. Honest tae God. Come on. Step in a wee bit closer. Pit oot yer haun. Touch me if ye canna touch onybody else.'

'Whit d'ye mean touch ye? Ye're jist glass.'

'Right, so it winna hurt. Come on, gie it a try. Ye can dae that. Ye ken ye want tae.'

He watched himself doing it. Very slowly he raised his hand. His forefinger came up, probed towards the finger coming towards it. It was weird to see them closing together. Their prints met, the pressure flattened the pads and he could see the skin turning yellowish as the blood was pushed back. He rested the tips of all four fingers and thumb on the mirror, looked into the shape that was there, a kind of upside down cradle of fingers.

'Now the rest,' said the mirror.

He felt exhausted. The fever, doubtless. He would go back to bed in a minute. He brought his face in, rested his forehead against his forehead. His eyes in the mirror were that close they looked like one eye. He stared as deep into himself as he could go.

He felt a tremble. He was breathing but he could not hear himself breathe. He wondered vaguely if he was in a dream about himself.

He stood there in the sheet, going deeper in. Like rain on a window, tears began to run down the glass.

Memories. Whit ye mind as a wean. Ye come fae nowhere. Ye gang back tae naethin. Ye had a faither that dee'd. A mither that was aye huntin things in charity shops and auction rooms. Rowp tae cowp, dust tae dust, ashes tae ashes.

She asked for him when she was deein. Whit was that, love, fear? That's wan thing, deein. Ye dae that alane. Whoever ye are, whoever ye've been.

Ye niver saw yer faither tak his haun aff yer mither's face. She niver shawed a bruise or a black eye. It was jist talkin. Ye uised tae lie there at nicht and wunner how he did it.

Ye held yer breath. If ye didna breathe oot they might no hear ye. But *you* could hear *them*. Yer ma and da. Yer ma was greetin.

Words werena supposed tae hurt ye. The only things that

could hurt ye were sticks and stanes. Skinnin yer knees on gravel. Duntin yer heid aff a tree. Awthin else was in the mind.

When she wasna greetin she was doon-moothed and silent. She did the things a mither was supposed tae dae – washed yer claes, cooked yer tea, cleaned yer hoose. But that was it. She niver tellt ye stories or sang or laughed wi ye. When yer faither was oot ye could go haill days athoot a word atween yese. It wasna till eftir he was deid that ye realised this wasna normal. Up till then ye'd managed tae fool yersel that it was him bein awa that caused the silence. But when he was awa for guid, the silence was different. It held yese apairt and ye realised it was naethin tae dae wi him. And she'd be aff buyin even mair stuff frae the junk-shops and bringin it hame. Whit was it aw for, was she tryin tae full the silence? Yer faither when he was alive would see the latest lamp or vase or hideous porcelain doll and he'd look up and coont the cracks in the ceilin.

'Whit did ye waste money on that for? Hae we no got enough vases?'

'It was only a shillin. A bargain.'

He would shake his heid at her. If you were in the room that was aw he would dae. She'd learnt tae hae the tea ready so that ye were in the kitchen wi her when he cam in and ye were a kinna insurance policy. Sometimes he wouldna even ken she'd bocht somethin. She'd stick it awa oot o sicht afore he spottit it. She'd hae a wee hidden smile in her mooth, ye could hardly see it twitchin ahint the doon-turnt lips but it was there. Like a wean soukin sweeties in a classroom.

Later, when they thocht ye were asleep, the low talkin began. Ye had tae listen through the wa, had tae. Ye could hear his voice, yer faither that niver swure in yer presence in his life, that would aye speak his mind but only wi words ye could uise in the presence o weemun and bairns. Ye could hear his low voice at yer mither as they lay in bed. *'Fuckin this . . . fuckin that . . . ye fuckin . . . ye stupid fuckin . . .'* Over and over. And eftir a while ye'd hear her sobs, and his voice again. *'Stop that . . . jist fuckin stop that . . . fuckin stop.'* And she'd be tryin tae steek hersel, ye could hear the catch in her breathin, jist the wey ye were yersel when ye skint yer knees.

Yer faither had forced the tears oot o her and then he forced her tae turn them aff. And ye niver kent why.

In the daytime, it was yer faither ye wantit tae be like. The auld sodger, the philosopher, the politician. No yer dour-faced mither that grat in the nicht. He was a hero wi German shrapnel in him. But ye heard thae low voices comin at ye, and ye realised that they lived a secret life that ye would niver ken, they had reached an accommodation o some kind, a wey o existin, that didna include ye and niver would.

Ye niver saw them touch in the daytime, let alane kiss. The only time ye thocht aboot them touchin was through the wa, when they were in their bed and you were in yours. They'd be in there and he'd be talkin at her like that – the sweirin talk. And ye imagined their bodies thegither and then ye didna want tae think aboot it ony mair.

Ye imagined haein a lassie o yer ain tae, but somehow ye were the odd yin oot afore onybody even realised it, even afore ye were fourteen. Ye were jist no richt. White as the mune, and as tall, ye shot up like ragweed in simmer, ye'd a neb like a flat-iron and sparse heathery hair and mannerisms that made folk look twice tae see if ye were haein them on. Ye learnt early no tae hing aboot, tae keep flittin, tae stey at the edge o things. Grannies clocked ye starin at them and shiddered. Lassies were feart frae ye. Ye would let a wasp settle in yer haun sooner than kill it, hustle it oot the windae wi a paper, but ye couldna get near a lassie.

Lassies yer ain age wouldna look at ye. Ye wantit a kiss or tae haud hauns or even a smile but ye would get naethin frae them. And aw the time yer body was talkin tae ye, tellin ye aboot yersel though ye didna richt ken whit it was sayin. Ye'd wake up in the nicht and think ye'd peed yersel. Ye'd hae a hauf-mindit dream in yer heid and glit aw ower yer belly. Ye worked oot whit was happenin tae ye but only by instinct, and by whit ye heard frae boys at the schuil. Ye were growin but it was aw inside ye, ye were like a pot-bund plant.

Later, when yer faither was deid, ye would think aboot the lassies. Then ye would feel yer prick comin up intae yer haun. Ye'd work awa at yersel wi a ragin urgency. But it was a bitter kinna feelin when ye came. Yer body exploded oot o itsel but yer mind was thinkin how the lassies didna like ye, how this was as close tae them as ye were iver gaun tae get.

So ye tried tae pit it oot o ye and got guid at the schuil and ye went tae the uni in Edinburgh, and yer ma helped oot wi the maintenance but she didna hae much tae pey, she fetched it oot the Post Office savings in twenty-pound notes. Ye steyed in the student halls for a couple o years, a teacher had recommended it, said ye'd meet mair folk that wey, but ye didna. They aw seemed tae be in pre-formed groups and nane o them wantit you as a member. That was awricht though, ye jist kept yersel tae yersel. Years later folk would mind o a few loners in the halls, they'd mind their faces but no their names. That's how ye'd be tae them: a vague anonymous memory. It would bother them for a minute that they couldna place ye, then they'd get on wi the rest o their lives. Ye liked the idea o that.

Ye were back and forth a wee bit the first term, and in the holidays, but it wasna lang afore ye were spendin maist o the year in Edinburgh. Ye worked in shops and bars in the simmers and steyed in digs where the only person ye had tae speak tae was the landlady, and ye didna hae tae say onythin tae her if ye kept up wi the rent, it was hame frae hame. Wan year ye got a passport and went tae France and picked grapes. The money was terrible but ye liked bein in a foreign place. If ye didna want tae speak tae folk ye could make oot ye didna hae English, or French, or whitiver it was they wantit tae speak tae ye in. It was weird: ye could uise language tae avoid communicatin. Eftir a while folk jist left ye alane.

In Scotland ye'd gang back tae yer mither's at Christmas, and phone her yince a week, but it was jist a wey for baith o yese tae ken ye werena deid. Yer final year ye had a room in a hoose in Newington. It was a huge auld villa wi a gairden, owned by a doctor and his wife. There were three rooms at the back that the faimly didna uise, so they rentit them oot tae students like yersel. It was a guid arrangement. Ye had yer ain keys, ye could come and go as ye wantit. The only rule was ye couldna hae guests steyin ower. That wasna a problem as far as ye were concerned, although anither student would sneak his girlfriend in and oot frae time tae time. It was a quiet, hidden bit o the toun. In the simmer the doctor and his wife let ye sit oot in the gairden. Ye'd take yer books oot and study for yer finals, and faw asleep in the heat wi the birds giein it laldy in the bushes.

Eftir the exams ye wunnered whit tae dae next. Ye'd a job in an office for the simmer, tedious clerical work. Ye could stey on in the hoose, save some money. Ye had guid results – ye could mebbe apply for a postgraduate coorse. Ye didna ken. Ye felt like ye'd had enough o studyin for a while.

The doctor was workin aw the time. The doctor's wife would look at ye in a weird wey sometimes. She'd a wee passion for ye mebbe. She was twenty years aulder than ye, that was yer guess. She was friendly enough, but ye could see it in her tae: that uncertain, hauf-fleggit look, as though she didna quite believe ye were real.

'And?' said the mirror.

'And whit?'

'You tell me. Whit did ye dae wi her?'

'The wife?'

'Aye. That's whit this is aboot surely.'

'I didna dae onythin wi her.'

'But ye wantit tae, didn't ye? Ye fancied her. The doctor was workin aw the time. She uised tae sunbathe at the weekends. Ye'd be readin a book and watchin her. Yer prick was hard wi thinkin aboot her. Ye didna think they had a very guid marriage. He worked too hard, she was bored. She was guid-lookin tae? Am I richt?'

'Aye.'

'They had a son and a daughter that went tae private schuils. Ye didna see much o them. The boy was in his room playin Elvis Costello records, or he'd be oot wi his mates. The girl was fifteen. She jist seemed tae slounge aboot the hoose, bored like her ma. Am I richt?'

'Aye.'

'So how did ye get it thegither wi her in the end? The doctor's wife?'

'I didna. As ye ken.'

'Then whit did ye dae?'

'I've tellt ye, naethin happened.'

'I'm really haein tae drag this oot o ye, amn't I? No wi the wife then.'

'It wasna ma fault.'

'Dinna start that again. Tell us whit happened.'

'She uised tae talk tae me. The wife. She was the first female that had iver done that. Mair than superficially like. We'd talk aboot everythin. Books, history, music. Feelins. But there was aye this skeerie thing aboot her when she looked at me. It uised tae bother me. How could she be that nice and still be feart? Whit was there tae be feart aboot?'

'Well? Whit was there?'

'I dinna ken! I've never fuckin kent.'

'Go on.'

'So we'd had this lang conversation one evenin, oot in the gairden. She was sayin I should go back and dae a PhD. I was sayin I wasna sure. She said it was too guid a chance tae miss. She was rich and she educated her kids privately but she was political, ken. The Tories had come intae power. She said if I didna take the chance then I might no get anither yin later. And then she looked at me and said, if I did the postgrad thing, I could stey on in the hoose, as lang as I wantit. She said she'd miss these conversations if I didna. She was starin intae me, ken. There was nae mistakin whit she was sayin.'

'Ye thought ye were in there. Ye thought ye'd finally made it.'

'I went tae ma bed that nicht and I lay there thinkin how it would be if the door opened and she came in. If she slipped oot her bed, left the doctor sleepin and came alang the passage tae me. I was gaun tae hae a wank jist thinkin aboot it but I didna want tae waste masel, in case it came true. So I lay there thinkin aboot it and I fell asleep.'

'And it came true?'

'I woke up and there was this flesh next tae me. Squeezin intae ma bed. I've never felt onythin like it. A woman gettin intae yer bed in the dark, athoot a word. Somethin has crossed ower between yese earlier, a message, and this is the message bein acted upon. She didna hae a stitch on. I was still wakin up when she startit tae kiss me. I pit ma hauns up tae her. She pit her haun doon and grabbed me and I was like a fuckin rock.'

'Then whit?'

'I was gaun tae speak but she pit her haun ower ma mooth.

She was straddlin me, lettin me intae her. But there was somethin no richt. Aboot the haun ower ma mooth. The fingers werena richt.'

'It was dark.'

'But no that dark. I came awake. I pushed back her hair. It wasna the wife. It was the daughter. The fuckin lassie. I was inside her. I was aboot tae fuckin come in her. I pushed her aff. I felt masel collapse as I did it. I got her haun aff me, I says *Whit the fuck are ye daein?* She didna speak. She lowped aff the bed and ran for the door. I got on ma feet but she was awa. I stood there shakin. I had this big pain in ma baws. Like there was this big knot aw tangled up. I felt I was gaun tae puke.'

'And did ye?'

'No then. I went back tae ma bed and lay there. Didna sleep aw nicht. I was thinkin aboot the doctor's wife and if I should say onythin. But I kent I couldna. I couldna say a word.'

'But somebody did. Somebody tellt somebody.'

'The next evenin, it was a Monday, the doctor was hame early. He was niver hame early. I had been oot at work. I was fucked, puggelt. I came in and he was staunin in the hall. He says, come in here. He had a kinna study. He uised tae work at hame tae. He was a big shot in the Infirmary.'

'Ye kent ye were for it.'

'I was in a dwam. He looks straight at me and says, you know I could press charges. I says, *whit?* He says, my wife has asked me not to. On condition that you leave. At once. I asked him whit he was talkin aboot. He says, oh I think we understand each other. My wife says you've been ogling her. That was the word he uised, *ogling.* She feels very uncomfortable around you. I felt masel gettin angry, I says, that's no ma problem. He says, that in itself I might forgive, though I can't condone it. My wife is a very attractive woman. Then he stops and gets even mair serious-lookin. He says, it's the other thing I can't overlook. My daughter is impressionable. She is also under the age of consent. I cannot have her at risk. When she told my wife that you had come to her room and tried to seduce her, my wife of course insisted that I speak to you, and that you must agree to leave this house. If you do, that's as far as this matter will go.

'I couldna believe whit I was hearin. I was that shocked I wasna even angry. I was staunin in front o him like a wean, and him daein this fuckin heidmaister routine, and I was aboot tae come oot and say, haud on, pal, ye've been misinformed, it's yer wife that's been giein me the eye, and as for the lassie, it was her that got intae ma bed – but I stopped and thought aboot it for a second and I realised I didna hae a chance.'

'Whit did ye dae? Ye didna let him get aff wi it?'

'There was naethin for him tae get aff wi. The idea that the doctor's womenfolk were queuin up for us was jist laughable. And this guy was power, ken? He could crush me like a slater. I couldna win. I couldna stey in that hoose whitiver happened, no eftir whit had been said aboot me. The only thing I could dae was no admit it. I turned aroon and left the room. Didna say a word tae him. There was a bathroom at the back o the hoose for us students. I went in there and that's when I puked. Then I went back tae ma ain room. I packed aw the stuff I had intae a suitcase and a few bags. I pit a note on the stuff I couldna cairry – a box o books, a few auld claes – sayin TO BE COLLECTED. I picked up the suitcase and the rest o ma gear – there wasna much – and I walked oot the hoose.'

'Ye found a room for the nicht?'

'Doon by Haymarket. I wantit tae get far away frae that place. The Festival hadna startit so it wasna impossible tae find somewhere. I booked intae this guest-hoose and I went oot for a drink.'

'Ye sat and had a few pints. Whit were ye thinkin?'

'First of aw I was thinkin, ye shouldna hae left. I was mair angry at masel than I was at the doctor and his family. But that passed. Then I began tae wunner if I'd been dreamin. Or if I was mad or somethin. Mebbe the daughter hadna come intae me at aw. Mebbe I'd fantasised it in ma sleep. Or no even in ma sleep – jist made it up and convinced masel. Cause why would she hae? I'd hardly spoken tae her. I'd got the wrang end o the stick as far as the wife was concerned so how no wi her tae? Then I thought, mebbe ma memory's re-writing stuff for me. Mebbe I'm seik. Mebbe I really did try tae get intae her room but I dinna mind it like that, I'm shiftin the guilt affae masel and ontae her.'

'Ye didna really believe that?'

'I didna ken whit tae believe. There was nae evidence either wey.'

'And then?'

'Then I calmed doon a bit. I didna need tae stey. I could get oot right then and there. The next mornin I sortit oot a few claes. I went back doon tae Princes Street and bought masel a rucksack, and took aw the money I had oot the bank. I came back tae the guest-hoose and packed the rucksack. Then I walked doon tae the bus-stop, got a bus oot tae the motorway and startit hitchin.'

'Ye went tae France.'

'France, Italy, Germany, Switzerland. I went intae Eastern Europe years before the Communists were turfed oot. I jist flitted aboot, pickin up a bit o work here and there. Usually I worked for a pittance and a roof ower ma heid. That was fine. I niver spent much so I saved a fair bit in thae years. And I'd send ma mither a postcaird once in a while, tae let her ken I wasna deid.'

'But ye came back.'

'Aye. How could I stey awa for iver, jist because o somethin that might or might no hae happened? I came back. I got the job in the bookshop. I was quite surprised tae get it, but it was a new shop, they wantit folk wi a degree. And I moved in here.'

'How fuckin convenient. So but whit happened tae yer healthy attitude? Yer ditch the baggage, go tae Europe attitude? How come ye've regressed?'

'I niver ditched the baggage. I thought I had but I was still cairryin it wi me. Ye canna ditch it.'

'Bury it.'

'Ditch it, bury it, whitiver. Ye canna. No stuff like that. It's aye there.'

Edinburgh, September 1677

That storme of witches that cousin John foretellt raged all throgh last summer, that is 1677. First there was them hangit at Paisley. Then the dumb lassie Jonet Douglass haveing regaind hir voice, it seemd she could not stop her selfe discovering more of Satan's servants. Mr Hew Smith, minister at Eastwood, no favorite of government, had some time been suffering much pain and sweats, to the changing of his shirt half a dozen times some days. Jonet Douglass took 6 men to a wuman's house in Carmonnock, where they found ane image of the minister, made by a wife in Eastwood that had carried it to hir sister in the black arts for safe keiping. It was full wt pins, which when removed ware found to have been the cause of his illness. The weemen ware execute.

Meantime Sir George Maxwell, whase life the lass Jonet had seimingly saved by discovering the plot against him, growes seik again and dies. She had offered to take a party of men to a house in East Kilbryde, where she said the mischief was, but they declyned, wt this dire result. But she did detect ane uthir effigy of a gentleman Robert Hamilton of Barnes by Dumbartoun, who was tormented wt maist grievous chist pains. The image had pins intil its chist, and a circle of 5 women was taken and throwen into prison at Dumbartoun for meaning to injure him. But they had roasted uther picturs of him, so that the discovery was made ower late, and he died while they ware waiting trial. In June a commissioun into the affair was established by order of the Privy Council, it consisted of four lairds of that countrie, who ware gyded in all their procedings by the 5t member, Mr John Prestoun.

Jonet continued in hir wark. Robert Dowglass of Barloch had lost two sons drouned in crossing a water. The dumb lassie persuaded him they perished by designe of some witches that bade near the place, 2 men and 2 weemen. They ware arrested and taken to the tolbuith at Stirling, where they ware pricked and witch-marks found upoun them. While othir evidence was being soght, 2 of them hanged them selves in prison.

About this time Jonet begins to hint that some great persons in the land also are witches. At this the Privy Council decides she has over reached her self, and orders her apprehended wheirever she should be found, and broght to Edinburgh. They put her in the Canogate tolbuith whare I saw her.

She was ane dorty sour looking body. She looked wt scorn at ony that came near her, and seemd to relish that she could enthral men and women far aulder than her selfe. She at ance informed Bailzie Charteris that his wife was witcht by 2 auld weemen in the Castle Hill. They ware imprisoned but denied any knowledge of what they ware accused. Jonet desired they be made to say the Lord's Prayer in front of the bailzie, 2 ministers, my selfe and others. This they did, I could detect nothing wrong wt it, nor could the ministers.

Ye did na tak tent, says Jonet. They did na say it rycht.

Ay they did, says I. Ane of the ministers bids me be silent. How did they say it? he asks her.

She says, They did say 'Our Father which wert in Heaven', not 'Our Father which art in Heaven'. At this baith Charteris and me protests. All had hard them. They made no such error.

The lassie fetcht me a look. They meant their maister Satan, she says, he was a fallen angel. Likewise they said, 'Thy will be done as it was in Heaven'.

The bailzie says, She is haivering. This can not be taken as evidence against thir weemen. Then the ministers askd me as a lawyer my opinion. She is an impostor, I said. That, or she is hir selfe suffering delusion. We ken nae thing about hir, nor can she tell us how she is possesst of hir wisdome. She may have the 2d sight, or words and picturs revealled in the air, I said, but this proves not a thing against ony body but hirselfe. She has caused trouble enough in the West, I said, without us importing her mischief this side.

Yet there was alarums of witches alredy in Fife and at Hadington. I was a witnesse to the latter. It was in June when I came back off the Bass from seeing Mitchel. A walthie widow Margaret Kirkwood, being suspected of witcherie, hangs hir selfe one Sunday forenoon. The storie arose that she was strangled by the devill and witches to keip her silence. The base *of it was this: hir serving woman Elisabeth Mudie was in church, she makes some moan and noise during the sermon, and is heard to number till she reaches 59, hir mistresses age, at which she cryes out, The turne is done, and fents away. This was the very instant Margaret Kirkwood is making away wt hir selfe. Moodie was examind and given over to the pricker.*

The pricker was a skunner, yellow of eye, and tummocks of hair sprowting from his lugs and neb, a jurneying man who sauld potiouns &c when not pricking witches. I thoght him a fallacious rogue, he could give me no accompt of the principles of his art, and also he was often in drink. It was a wretched thing to see, a drunk man paid to stick pins in a simple mynded wuman. He tryed in hir eye brows, hir nostrills, hir mouth, breists and privitie. When she screamd out he says he must try mair, for their are different sorts of witches mark, and the subtilest witches may easily feigne pain wheir their is none and hide it wheir it is felt. Eftir an hour or 2 of testing, using pins the lenth of ones finger, and one he thrust in to the head, the man got Lisie Moodie to delate 5 other witches in Hadington, 2 of them midwyfes and one a man. These ware examined and subject to the same. Also he kept them from sleip, a commoun practise, for to deprive of sleip makes a persoun say oniething to get it, or they become as a dremer and know not what they say.

I felt a danger in protesting but I can no longer uphald this way of battling wt Satan, since if these unhappie creatures are his servants it is by delusion, ignorance and poverty he has won them. Not I nor any thing could save them thogh once Lisie Mudie had confesst and delated them. She and they ware all deid by the months end.

Now I did fear greatly for the accused at Dumbartoun. John Eleis was their counsel but he faced Prestoun, who would doe what he could to keip the other commisionars to a firm line agaynst witchcraft. I never saw couzin John sa douncast. The effigies ware but feble childish dauds of things, wt two stumps for legs and two for arms, holes made wt the fingers for eys mouth &c. That they had a likenes to any man was a thing to be lauched at, but that was not a relevance. The case turnd on the weemen's fame, which was not good, and that Hamilton of Barnes had dyed. When the assize was met in August, half its members ware long aquent wt Hamilton, and the rest believed the weemen guilty fra their awn opinions or the commoun news of the countrie. Prestoun fed their prejudices well. All five ware condemned and brunt.

I sat many nichts in Paintons wt John and we turnd these afairs over in our heads. It seimd to us the haill kingdome was engaged in selfe destruction, like a chirurgeon that bleids him self to death beleiving him self sick, when in fact he is only a little melancholick in the mynd.

And forby the witches there was othir work afoote throgh the summer. In June Sir John Nisbet the King's Advocat gott an assistant that he never wishd for, Sir Geo Mackenzie of Rosehaugh. Sir John was ever suspected by Sharp & Rothes after his failure wt Mitchel. He or rather his wife was made great compliments of silver plait, fine silk claith, delicats of food and drink by the frends of other imprisoned fanatick gentlemen and ministers. My lords had no objectioun to bribes – how could they? – but to the source.

I never met a more ambitious man than Sir John's new apprentice Mackenzie. He knew that he was but ane step from his maister's ain seat. Soe Mackenzie spent July & August opening up all the Crown's outstanding cases to see which wt some fresh work myght be succesfullie broght before a court. This impressed the Privy Council, and Nisbet was removed and Mackenzie made King's Advocat in his place. In a week he brought forward two forgers that had been months lying in the tolbuith, presented his case, and got them hangd.

'It's a clear signal,' said John Eleis to John Lauder, on one of their sessions in Painton's. 'He is pit there for a purpose, and the purpose is tae clear oot aw Nisbet's failures. Mackenzie is a creature o Lauderdale, but Lauderdale is losin favour. He isna seen tae be hard enough on the fanatics. He will drive Mackenzie on, tae prove his ain worth tae the King and tae keep Sharp's neb oot o places where it has nae richt tae be. Twa things will happen afore this year's oot, John, mark my word. The first is that Lauderdale will come doon like a wolf on the west country, tae break up the conventicles, for he canna survive if he lets thoosans o armed fanatics gaither and defy the law wi impunity. The saicont is, he will gie in tae Sharp, and bring back James Mitchel for trial. Mackenzie will be instructit that he is tae get him tae the scaffold if he wishes tae rise ony further in the King's estimation.'

'Sax months syne,' said Lauder, 'I would hae disputed wi ye on baith points. But noo I think ye're richt. Maister Mitchel himsel was o the same opinion when I saw him in June. In fact, I find masel noo haein tae mak representation tae ye on his accoont.'

It was the first time he had mentioned Mitchel's request to anybody. Now he feared in case he had left it too late, but Eleis was easy on the subject.

'We shall hae tae get the Cooncil's dispensation, but I see nae problem wi it. In fact, I ken awready that the Dean would relish the opportunity. And I believe oor new King's Advocate would be very happy in a set-tae wi the pair o us. There is naebody he likes better tae lock horns wi than Lockhart.' Eleis clapped Lauder's arm. 'I'll see tae it, John, dinna fash.'

'It relieves me o an obligation,' Lauder said, 'and I thank ye for it. I can dae naethin mair for him.'

Eleis looked inquisitively at him. 'I'm thinkin,' he said, 'that ye must hae had somethin in exchange for the obligation. Ye wouldna want tae share that wi me?'

Lauder laughed. 'A daft notion,' he said. 'I had an idea that Mitchel would hae been able tae help me oot wi some information, that was aw. It was a delicate kinna affair.'

'And did he? Help ye oot, I mean.'

'A little.' Lauder was treading cautiously. 'John, if I kent onythin that micht help ye in Mitchel's case, I would tell ye. But I dinna. In fact, I ken a thing or twa that micht mak things worse for him.'

'Weill, dinna deave me wi them,' said Eleis. 'Cats that get oot o pokes hae a bad habit o lowpin on the legs o folk that dinna like cats. But I'm glad if ye got somethin frae him. It's mair than onybody else has got, though I canna think whit it would be.'

'He confirmed somethin for me,' said Lauder. 'No an important thing mebbe, but it sortit oot some confusion in ma heid. He confirmed for me that somebody else we baith kent, that was thocht plain daft, had a puckle mair sense nor onybody gied her credit for.'

Edinburgh, 12 April 1670

Jean woke and knew at once what day it was. Thoughts blurred and confused in her head these days, she misminded some things and plain forgot others, but nothing could have erased this knowledge. It was the day of her death. A certainty had been given to her that was given only to the judicially condemned: when the sun went down, she would not see it; before darkness fell, she would have been snuffed out like a candle.

If ever there was a day when she needed the skills of her craft, this was it. To be able to put a dwam on her jailers, shoogle the locks and open the great heavy doors of the Tolbooth. To slip on the guise of a cat, slink out, and take herself off to the shore. To sail on the seas in a sieve or an eggshell, or fly through the air on a stick, away, away from this room, this town, this country, from its malice and cruelty and brutal religion. She wanted to be in another place, another time. If she could only be transported to somewhere she could not be hurt, somewhere she could be safe, and have that feeling just for a few moments, it would make the rest easier to thole. But there was no such place. She had been born wrong in every way – wrong sex, wrong house, wrong family, wrong century – and today was the day she was going to have to pay for it.

They had taken the chain off her leg at night. John Vanse was a good lad, he felt sorry for her against his better judgment. You could see the doubt in his eyes: if he did her a kindness, would she make him regret it? If he gave her a tender look, would she seize on it as a weakness? That was what witches did. They beguiled you. It was in their nature. No wonder he felt for her: she could not help herself. But she looked in his eyes and saw something else – fear. It was the same fear that she had too, but which she kept tied up and gagged in the deepest part of her. Fear of what the world could do to you. She would not show her fear today. She was determined. She would not give them the satisfaction of seeing her afraid.

John brought her a bowl of thin porridge. She wished she had some poison to put in it, some root or sprouting thing she might have gathered from beneath the damp leaf carpet of the woods. She would like to have cheated them, to not have to go through the street to where the rope waited. She would like them to come for her and find her already gone, her body lying there empty with a smile on its face.

Yesterday some minister or other had come to her, late in the afternoon. She'd put on a good display for him. She knew what he had come for, even before he spoke. He wanted to be the first to tell her that her brother was dead.

At first she let on that she didn't understand what he was saying, even though she'd been thinking of Thomas about the time they'd be putting the lunt to his fire. She'd been imagining them thrappling him. She'd have liked to do it herself, but she didn't tell the minister this. Instead she said that she didn't believe her brother was dead. He had seen it with his own eyes, he insisted. Ah, she thought, but what did you see? Some folk are less easy killed than others.

Then after a while she asked about Thomas's staff. Where was it? All his power had been in it, all his wickedness – what had they done with it? It was burnt too, the minister said. It was consumed with him and was no more. Then Jean fell in a raging fit on the floor. She thought of all the words that would appal the minister most, especially if heard from the lips of an old woman, and she let them out in a bubbling burn of filth and blasphemy. When she thought she was running dry she pictured Thomas the first time he had let out his confession at the prayer-meeting, and spouted as much of his efforts as she could recall. The minister was suitably horrified.

She calmed down a little, and looked imploringly at him. Her face was wet with tears. 'Oh, sir, I ken he is awa noo. He is wi the divils his brithers. He lived wi them here and noo he bides in their hoose in anither place.' She haivered on with more of the same for a while, wringing her hands and eyeing the minister as he lapped it up like a glutton. Then she asked him, begged him, if he would be so good as to attend her to her own execution, and help her towards a kindly death. She could tell the man was repulsed and revolted by her. But he was a minister, he had a sense of duty and obligation. Reluctantly, he consented.

Jean was not sure if that minister had been one of the many who had crowded in to look at her in the days around her arrest and trial. She had felt like a lintie in a cage, surrounded by a cloud of crows. She had peered at them in turn and seen the glint in each eye and understood that there was no mercy to be had there. So like the lintie she began to sing to them. She sang them every tune that she thought they would want to hear: not for mercy or sorrow, but for herself. She knew they would not be able to stop themselves listening, and then repeating what they heard. They would record everything she said and she knew that though this wouldn't save her, one day it would bring their sanctimonious wisdom down to ridicule, to nothing. Meanwhile she would have gone to her safe, kind place where men like them could not hurt her again.

The first that she dragged down, further even than he had taken himself, was her own brother Thomas. She owed him that at least. For years he had owned and used her. She had been ignorant at first, she had adored him and let him into her because of the pleasure it gave him. There was a kind of holiness to it too, it was special and secret and unique to them, and Thomas was convinced that God blessed their union. He said he could feel God flowing through him when he was with her. But then their hidden life became something else, a monstrous burden. And Thomas changed, became less gentle. There must never be a child, he said, the world would take such a creature from them and sacrifice both it and them to its jealousy. He produced foul-smelling sheaths made from the bladders of pigs and used them when he drove himself into her. Or if he had none of these, he would force himself into her arse, even though it hurt her and made her bleed. She let him go on because she was feart of him; of his righteousness, of the violence of his passion, feart that he would hurt her more, feart that he would discard her.

She was tied to him because she had no one else. Their father and mother were dead, their sister Margaret and her family were not rich enough to support her. They came to Edinburgh, and there Thomas thrived. He married Mien Burdoun, the daughter of a merchant, which gave him access to the wealthier levels of society. His military career was successful if not distinguished. He was loved by the godly party: the ferocity of his faith was a thing to be wondered at. Angelical, they cried him: Angelical Thomas. And she was poor Jean, the spinster sister, that hovered in the shadow of her brother, a pathetic, faint, female version of himself. She went to Dalkeith where he would visit, coming, as she later realised, from some lonely byre or from the bed of his wife, his servant or his stepdaughter into hers. He gave her money and strengthened her sagging spirit with prayers. When Mien died she came back into Edinburgh to be his helpmate.

She knew all the things he did. At Carluke he used to talk to her of the dealings he had with the beasts. God had ordained the use of them for man, he said. The pagan Romans, when they massacred the Christians in their arenas, would set rampant dogs and donkeys upon young Christian women in heat, but that was an abomination, an inversion of nature. It was man's right to master and pacify the beasts. He would tell her this as he turned her on her face in the straw and mounted her.

She knew also that he lusted after the women of Edinburgh, the ones who doted on him and were inspired by his holiness. He would go out at night and call on them, though she never knew if he got what he wanted, for by then he did not confide in her. But when he could get no other woman, not the lush saintly wives nor the widows plump as paitricks, sometimes he would still return and skail himself into her as before.

The ministers and others in the Tolbooth listened with gaping mouths to whatever she told them. The ministers tried to prevent her from speaking of the bladder sheaths but the other men were intrigued – she could see their minds lighting up with the possibilities. She told them that Thomas was over his head in devilry. They would go together in a fiery chariot that called in the dead of night for them, and drive through the countryside to Dalkeith and Inveresk and Musselburgh and anywhere else they might wish to go. None but themselves could see this coach; sometimes they were alone in it, sometimes a dark stranger, a friend of her brother's, would accompany them. She said the staff was a gift from this friend some years ago. With the staff Thomas could do anything. She used to hide it and found that he was powerless without it. But always he would rant and curse at her, and threaten to reveal their incest to the world unless she gave it back.

She too had got powers from the Devil, and like her mother she had the mark of him on her forehead. By this mark she could discover any secret that was being kept from her. The gathered men shrank back from her, but one asked her to show them the mark. It was in the shape of a horseshoe on her forehead: she put back her mutch and frowned at them all, and the shoe appeared in her wrinkles, perfectly shaped and with dark spots like holes where the nails would go. She could hear the horror being sucked in with their breath.

When Thomas realised that he was not of the elect, he fell into a black despair. He would not even look at Jean. But he told her, speaking with his back to her, that they were both doomed: they had been fooled by God and bought by Satan and would be carried off to his kingdom when the time came. And that time might as well be now rather than later. Why hide the awful truth? Why prolong the agony and shame? He would declare their sin at the next prayer-meeting.

Jean listened and said nothing. She had been with Thomas more than sixty years: there was no point in arguing with him. But a wave of anger went through her at his selfishness: he had kept her as his accomplice all this time, and now he decided that when he threw himself to the wolves he would take her with him. For a brief moment she thought of the joy if he confessed only to his bestiality: he would be taken away and hanged, and she could live out her last feeble days alone in front of the fire. But then she saw the impossibility of that. Once Thomas got started on his confessions, nothing would stop him till he had poured himself out entirely. Seeing him there, turned away from her because she affronted him, she thought about snatching up the fire-iron and beating him to death with it, but she understood that by this she would only martyr him and make herself into something worse than what she was. Nobody would believe anything she said: she was mad Jean, he was Angelical Thomas. In that moment she saw that she was indeed doomed. The best she could do was to make the worst of things for her brother.

She knew where he kept his siller, for example, hidden away in pokes and parcels all over the house. When the bailies came to take them to prison, they asked Thomas if he had any money to secure. None, he said. Then Jean piped up, and kindly showed them all the panels and neuks where it was hidden. Even in his agony, she could see she was laying more pain on Thomas. The money was useless to him now, but still it hurt him to see it removed. She made sure that the bailies carried his staff away too, and kept it apart from him. If he should get hold of it, even for a minute, he would drive them all out of doors, she said. She looked at the broken, bowed figure of her brother and the thought of him driving anybody anywhere against their will ever again almost made her laugh out loud. So she did. If she was mad she might as well prove it: she let out a long insane cackle of laughter, and at intervals all the way to the Tolbooth she practised it until she had the guards quaking and pishing in their boots.

She did not see Thomas again until they were brought to trial. She did not speak in the court-room when spoken to by the lawyers. She knew very well what was the usual course of trials where witchcraft was alleged. If you spoke at all it was only to condemn yourself and accuse others. Whatever you said, that was how they interpreted it. They had not tortured her beforehand, but that was only because with the incest they had enough reason to kill her already. So she stayed silent. She did not look at Thomas, and he did not look at her. And she had not seen him since.

The next day, the Sabbath, the flown man had come. Him that had called in the night all those years ago, and gone away to Holland. She would like to go to Holland herself. It sounded like a dull, quiet, safe place. But there was no point in thinking on that. The young man's name was James. She could not mind his second name now. He had looked in on her, pretending to be her nephew Sandy. There would be a reason for that but she could not work it out. Was it to be a comfort to her, since she knew that Sandy would not come?

But he had not comforted her. He had glanced in and then, though she had said her nephew's name, had stepped away again, and John Vanse had let him out of the prison.

Yesterday the ministers, the provost and a number of other self-important fools had come again. They had gone to see Thomas, then they had visited her. She muttered and slavered and laughed to their confusion. When they prayed she interrupted them. 'Whit for are ye prayin for me? I am bound for Heaven the morn. Where are ye bound for yersels?' She would not show her fear to them. She knew when she was going to die, which was more than they knew.

Now it was morning. She would be dead in a little while. But before they came for her John Vanse was back. He brought a man into her cell. She was pleased to see it was James again. Mitchel, that was his name. She wouldn't speak it out loud. He had killed a bishop, she seemed to mind. That was why he was in disguise. She liked that, being somebody you weren't. A good ploy. And killing the bishop was a good ploy. She wished he would kill a few ministers as well.

'James,' she said, 'are ye back sae sune? Ye've no been tae Holland and hame again awready?'

The man said nothing. Jean smiled at him.

'Is it yersel ye are the day? Or is it Sandy Weir? I ken aw aboot ye, Sandy Weir. I ken ye wouldna come tae see yer faither. John said ye'd come on the Sabbath, ye'd begged him tae let ye in. But when I saw ye it wasna *you*. I'd kent it wouldna be and I was richt. It was Maister Mmmmm.' She closed her mouth and made a pantomime of stopping the sound coming out. 'I'll no say it. Mm-mm.' She shook her head. 'I'm dumb. I ken yer secret. I ken awbody's secrets.' She smiled at him. 'But naebody kens mine.'

'Ye can say the name,' said the visitor. 'If I wasna Sandy wha was I? I was in Holland, did ye say?'

She laughed. 'Och, ye ken ye were. I saw ye leavin. Eftir they hingit the ither laddie. Ye tellt me tae gang hame, James, back tae *him*. But he's deid noo. I'll no gang back tae him again.'

'Whit laddie was it they hingit, Jean?' said the man. She looked at him harder. How did he not ken?

'The bonnie yin, the bonnie yin. Oh, I forget him. But ye

had tae gang, ye had been oot wi the saints at Pentland – as he had. Ah, but he was bonnie. Every step he took up the ladder wi his puir broken leg was ae step nearer tae God. D'ye no mind that? Ye watched him and syne ye cam tae us and syne ye flew awa ower the sea. But ye must hae been seik for hame. Ye cam back again and ye sh –, ye sshhh!' She put her finger to her lips and wheesht him. 'I'll no say it, James, whit ye did. You hae your secret, and I hae mine.'

He looked at her knowingly.

'Whit is yer secret, Jean?' he said. 'You ken mine. I should ken yours.'

All this time he had stood just inside the door. Now he approached and sat himself on the bench that ran along one wall. He gestured to her, and she shuffled over and sat next to him.

Then she saw that it was not him at all. This was a younger man, better dressed, his face less lined and weather-beaten. The face of a richer man.

She started back, but he grabbed her wrist. 'Dinna fear,' he said. His voice had not changed. It was not a threatening voice, and although he kept hold of her wrist he relaxed his grip. There was something calming about him. She wondered if he was simply in another disguise.

'My name is John Lauder,' he said. She was impressed. He said it as if he meant it. 'I'll no hairm ye. I ken wha ye thocht I was. He was here, was he no?'

She nodded.

'Aye. We'll no mention him again. Tell me yer secret, Jean.'

They were staring into each other's eyes. He let go of her wrist and took her hand. She was old enough to be his grandmother but she felt giddy like a young lass. Could a man change his appearance so completely? It occurred to her that he had come to rescue her. To take her away. Was he an angel? She felt something like peace coming over her, a vague, hopeless happiness.

She put her other hand up to his face and touched it, as if to check that he was real. Then she brought it back and felt her own dry, runkled cheek. And the sadness rushed back into her. They were real right enough, both of them. Everything was real. The day was real. In a very short time they would make her climb to her real death.

'I amna a witch,' she said. She began to greet, then stopped as suddenly and said it again but with more deliberate emphasis. 'I *amna* a witch.'

He smiled. 'That is yer secret?'

'Aye. They say I'm a witch and they'll hing me for a witch, but I'm no yin.'

'I ken,' he said. 'But they're no hingin ye for that, Jean.'

'Aye they are. The Major dee'd for the ither things. But they want me deid for a witch, and I'm no yin. Am I no wyce?'

'But ye confessed tae the sorcery. Ye said aboot meetin the fairy queen, aboot the endless yarn ye could spin . . .'

'Aye, and aboot breengin aw ower the countryside in a muckle black cheriot that naebody could see. Whit tales I could tell! Fleein on besoms and turnin intae a hare – there's naethin a witch canna dae.' She broke off. 'Whit's yer name again, son?'

'John. John Lauder.'

'Listen, John Lauder. Ye're no daft like me, I can tell. Ye're a clever laddie, gettin yersel in here pretendin ye're Sandy. Look at me. Dae ye hear thae stories and aye believe I'm a witch? Would a witch tell such things against hersel? Na! But *they* believe me, the ministers and the lawyers and the ithers. *They* say I'm a witch, even though they canna prove it. Ye're no a minister, are ye, John?'

'No, Jean, I'm no.'

'They're gaun tae kill me the day, John. Disna maitter whit I say or think or dae, they're gaun tae kill me. So I mey as weill be a witch, then, eh?' She gave a huge grin and laughed, a triumphant, warm chuckle rising out of her.

'First ye say ye arena, then ye say ye are. Whit game are ye playin, Jean?'

'A game? Is it a game then? Ye would need tae be mad tae play in a game like that. D'ye think I'm mad, John?'

'I dinna ken.'

'Aye. Nor I. I'm auld gettin, I ken that. I'd be gaun tae God sune onywey. D'ye believe there's a God, John?'

'Aye, I believe that.'

'Aye, me and aw. And I'll be there wi him this day in

Paradise. Like the pursepick on the cross. I believe that tae.' The grin was still playing about her lips. 'Whit's yer idea o Paradise, John?' He shrugged, but she didn't wait for an answer. 'I'll tell ye mine. A place where awbody's safe, and naebody's feart. A place where there's nae witches.'

'There'll be nae witches in Heaven, Jean,' he said.

'Oh. Then hoo will *I* get there? I must no be a witch! Then whit for are they killin me? For I'm a witch! There's somethin no richt here, John.'

'Aye, Jean, there's somethin no richt.' His voice sounded old, weighted down. 'Ye arena a witch. Ye'll get tae Heaven.'

'Na, that's minister's talk, I dinna believe ye. I dinna want tae gang if I hinna tae be a witch tae get through the yett. There'll only be nae witches if witches can get in. For if there's no a witch in Heaven, somebody's sure tae find yin oot. Am I richt, John?'

But there was no answer. She found she was holding her own hands together. She found that John was John Vanse. He had changed himself again. His father was there too, Patrick, the keeper of the prison. And the minister that had promised to be with her. Oh, she was pleased to see the minister. She wanted him there on the scaffold with her, so she could look at him, despise him and keep the fear hid away.

'It's time noo, Jean,' said John Vanse.

'It's no time yet, surely,' she said.

'Ye hae been sleepin,' he said gently. And they began to make her ready.

'Oh, whit a shamefu life I hae led,' said Jean to the minister. 'Hae I no, sir, led a shamefu life?'

'Indeed, Jean, ye are a sinner ayont sinners,' he said.

She loved the cleverness with which she said next, 'Then, sir, I am resolved, I will dee wi aw the shame I can.'

'That is good policy,' said the minister. 'For in your shame lies your only hope of Christ's mercy.' And he said it so sincerely that she had to laugh again, freezing his face in a second.

Then they took her from the Tolbooth in her auld grey dress, a guard of soldiers around her and a drummer at the head, and they beat her slowly up the street and down the

West Bow to the crowds waiting for her in the Grassmarket. And Jean walked unsteadily among the soldiers, and made slow progress, and some of the people lining the route jeered at her in a half-hearted way, but most of them stood and watched her go by, daft Jean that had lain with her brother all those years, that had conjured up spells and sold herself to Satan. She looked so frail and normal, you would never have guessed the evil she had done. They would go home that night with the sight of her still before them, and the uneasy sense that something was wrong, that they wished they hadn't seen her at all.

Till she got to the scaffold where the executioner waited, and she went up onto it with the minister behind her. And there she showed herself in her true light, the limmer. For she railed at the folk for greeting and wailing at her, when they would not greet for a broken Covenant, and then as she said it she laughed uproariously, so it was evident to the angry crowd that she mocked them for being there. And then she threw off her mutch, and shook her hair free, and started to pull at her clothes, throwing open her bodice and untying her skirts, while the men around her looked on in confusion and realised that this was what she had meant back in the cell. They tried to stop her, the shame of her, and had to carry her half-undressed to the ladder, and put the rope about her neck as they hauled her up, till halfway from the top she struggled free and stuck her head through two of the rungs, so they could not budge her. Then the hangman was forced to strike her on the face, to get her back through, while she screamed and spat like a cat at him. And he got her loose, but there was no way he could fit the cloth over her face, for she would not be still, so he pushed her off the ladder with her clothes hanging off her, her head uncovered and red and cut from the blows, and with no one waiting below to pull her down and end her suffering. So she kicked and sprang there for a while, till at last her body came to rest. And the crowd dispersed, and all of them there took a spattering of Jean's shame home on their heads.

'Right, that's me away,' said Carlin. 'Aff tae that mythical place ye think disna exist.'

'Eh? Where's that?'

'The library. Mind, I was hallucinatin, you said. Like aw thae ither dreams I've been haein. Weill, that's where I'm gaun. A few loose ends tae tie up.'

'Oh. Ye're no still on aboot that auld covenanter shite, are ye? Christ. I hoped ye'd grown oot o that by noo.'

'So if it's shite, indulge me a little. There's nae hairm in it. It's jist diggin up buried stuff. And eftir aw, you were happy enough buyin in aw that shite I tellt you.'

'Whit shite? Whit are ye on aboot?'

'Aw that stuff aboot the doctor and the doctor's wife and the doctor's wee lassie. Ye fuckin loved it.'

'*Whit?* Are you tellin me, are you sayin that didna happen? Have you been fuckin lyin tae me? I thought that was wan thing we didna dae tae each ither. We might dissemble a wee bit, we might haud stuff back, we might change the subject – but we dinna fuckin lie.'

'I'm no sayin it didna happen. Like I said, there's nae proof either wey. It's ma word against theirs and an awfy lot o time's gane by since then. Water through the lade and aw that. Whit I like is the fact ye swallied aw the guff aboot *why*. *Why* I'm like I am, *why* I'm no like awbody else. I gied ye that haill story and ye accepted it – "Ah, that explains things, ah weill, it's no surprisin ye're fucked up." Eh? You, the arch fuckin cynic, that's kent me frae God kens how lang, and ye bought the doctor's faimly as an explanation for *ma* problems. I tell ye, ye're no the fuckin mirror ye used tae be.'

'Well, if it wasna that, whit the fuck was it? Why *are* ye such a weird bastart?'

'D'ye still no see? There is nae explanation. I'm jist who I am. Because I don't conform, because I'm no *normal*, because

I dinna *fit in*, folk start lookin for reasons. They want reasons why ye're different, odd, queer, weird, mad, whitiver. D'ye iver hear aboot folk lookin tae find oot why somebody's *normal?* Coorse ye dinna. But as soon as ye step oot o line, oh-ho, wait a minute, that's no on, there's got tae be a fuckin explanation for that. So ye start lookin yersel, save awbody else the bother. Ye're a loner, ye dae yer ain thing, ye dinna hae a telephone let alane ten numbers on the BT freens and fuckin faimly scheme, Christ mebbe it's aw buildin up in there, it's gaun tae burst oot o ye wan day and ye'll be anither Thomas Hamilton, anither Dennis Nilsen. When ye get doon tae it, that's whit *normal* people find disturbin aboot weirdos. They see aw these nasty possibilities and they go, there but for the grace of God go I, or some such self-righteous keech. Which is a less honest wey o sayin, mebbe that's me oot there, I jist canna admit tae it.'

'Och, is this no a wee bit . . . eh . . . self-indulgent? A wee bit like graftin yer ain hang-ups ontae the rest o the world? Is *that* no a possibility, Mr sad and lonely Carlin?'

'Aye, mebbe. Only I don't feel sad right noo. I feel angry. And as for lonely, weill, if ye ask me, loneliness is the human condition. Aw through history humans have been torn between fear o bein alane and fear o ither humans. But aw fear o bein alane is, is fear o oorsels. Which, auld pal, brings me tae somethin else. Somethin I feel I *huv* tae resolve. And I'm sorry tae say, this is gaun tae hurt you mair than it hurts me.'

'Hih! Pit that doon! *Whit the fuck d'ye think ye're daein?'*

Carlin walked from his flat to the library. It was like floating. All his limbs seemed loose, weightless, without strength. He told himself to take it slowly, walk as if he was in no hurry to get anywhere. The way an old man might walk in the evening of his days. That thought came into his head and it made him smile. Even his smile felt slow. He understood that he had been very sick.

It was a cool but dry afternoon. Edinburgh was trying to shrug off winter finally. The skyline was fresh, the grass in the Meadows green and thickening. There were not too many people about. There were posters in the windows of some of the flats, wee cardboard placards tied to the lamp-posts. It took Carlin a minute to remember that it was election day. Even so things seemed very quiet. A car with a tannoy system on its roof was turning up Marchmont Road, asking for votes, he didn't make out for which party. Everything seemed settled, there seemed a great lack of urgency in the air.

He passed the usual landmarks as if there was no rush. But in his head there was: he was anxious to get to the library and speak to MacDonald. He also wanted to finish the *Secret Book*. He'd read more than three-quarters of it, he knew from it and from the other books he'd looked at what happened to Mitchel, and he'd flicked forward to see what Lauder had to say about that. But he wanted to get right to the end.

His legs were beginning to ache when he reached the building on George IV Bridge. He went down the flights of stairs that led to the Scottish department, wondering how he was going to manage back up. At the desk was a young woman he did not recognise.

'I've got a book on reserve. Could I get it, please?'

'Aye, sure,' said the librarian. 'What's your name?'

'Carlin. A. Carlin.'

There were some shelves with a few items on them just behind the counter. She checked through them. 'Carlin, did you say?'

'Aye.'

'I don't see anything here. What was the book?'

'It was mair like a manuscript. *Ane Secret Book*. By John Lauder.'

She looked again. 'Sorry, no, nothing here. You're sure it was being held on reserve?'

'Aye, but I've been ill. I've no been in for mair than a week. But I spoke tae yer man MacDonald and he said it would be kept for me.'

The librarian's face brightened. 'Ah, well, we don't usually hold items for more than six days. Probably a misunderstanding. It'll be back on the stacks. Let me just check it for you.'

She started tapping the keys of her computer. Carlin coughed.

'I don't think it'll come up on that. I kinna got the impression it was a one-off, a rarity.'

'Oh.' She waited for the computer to confirm what he had said. 'Is it an old item? It's maybe in the card catalogue. We can try that. I just need a reference number so I can fetch it for you.'

The card catalogue was a set of wooden cabinets in the middle of the room. The drawers of these were full of index cards. The drawers had wee metallic handles on them that your index finger fitted snugly under. Pulling them out and pushing them closed again was like playing in the morgue of a dolls' hospital. But there was nothing under Lauder, nothing under Secret or, predictably, Book.

Carlin minded something. 'I'm sorry,' he said. 'I've been wastin yer time. Mr MacDonald had found it for me. I think he said it came frae the Edinburgh Room.'

The librarian smiled. He had the feeling that he had said something wrong, but that she didn't consider it important enough to correct him. 'That'll be it,' she said. 'It'll have gone back up there. Do you know where that is?' She pointed to the floor above. There was a tall, bald man leaning over the rail, looking down on them. Carlin nodded.

'Ask one of my colleagues,' said the librarian. 'They'll find it for you.'

All the staff looked different, and young. Carlin didn't recognise any of them. It was as if he had aged much more than the week he'd been away.

In the Edinburgh Room he had to go through the same process, this time with a man. Lauder's book was not held on reserve for him, nor could they find any mention of it in any of the catalogues, though they checked under both Lauder and Fountainhall.

'This is very strange,' said the librarian. 'You're sure it wasn't one of his other books?'

'Aye, I'm sure.' Carlin tried not to get irritated. It wasn't the guy's fault. 'Look,' he said, 'is Mr MacDonald around? He kens where it's kept. It was him that got it oot in the first place.'

'MacDonald? I don't think I know a Mr MacDonald. Does he work here?'

'Only aboot forty years.'

'Well, I'm quite new. I don't know everybody.'

'Ye must know him. He'll be a senior librarian or somethin. Red hair and glasses.'

The man shook his head. 'Disna ring a bell. Wait till I check.'

He disappeared through a door behind the desks where a few members of the public were poring over back-issues of newspapers and magazines. Carlin turned and looked over the rail. Below him was the room he had just been in, with more rows of desks and people reading and writing at them. He saw the bald man who had been leaning on the rail a few minutes ago, more or less where he was now, searching through a drawer of the card catalogue. He didn't remember passing him on the stairs.

He thought, this is getting out of hand. I don't know if I'm coming or going.

The librarian returned with another, older man. They were like plainclothes polis, or the last two chocolates in a box, a soft one and a hard one. 'This is the gentleman,' the first one was saying, as they approached Carlin.

'You're looking for Mr MacDonald?' said the second librarian.

'Aye. Is he no in?'

'We don't have a Mr MacDonald.'

Carlin laughed. 'Ye had yin last week.'

'Not in this library. We do have a *branch* at McDonald Road.'

'I ken which library I was in. I'm tellin ye, he had his name on a badge.'

'That's odd, you see, because most of the staff don't wear name-badges. For their security.'

'How d'ye mean?'

'You'd be surprised. There are some odd people about who might misuse such information. It's up to the staff if they volunteer their names. They don't have to display them on badges.'

'Well, he did.'

'I'm sorry. There's no librarian that I know of called MacDonald.'

'So how are we gaun tae find this book?'

'What book?'

Carlin described it. He wrote down the title, as much of it as he could remember, and explained what MacDonald had said about it.

'I really need tae see it again. Jist for an hour or two. I've still got a chunk of it left tae read.'

'I don't know how we can help,' said the younger librarian. 'I've checked all the catalogues, and nothing's coming up. Maybe if you could leave me your phone number . . .'

'I'm no on the phone.'

'Well, then, your address.'

'Could I no go in there and hae a look for it. I'd recognise it.'

The older man shook his head. 'I'm afraid that's quite impossible.'

'Then you find it for me. Or get MacDonald tae find it.'

'I've already explained to you, there is no Mr MacDonald here. It doesn't look as though this book, or manuscript or whatever it is, exists either.'

'D'ye think I'm makin aw this up? Of course it exists.'

'Do you remember what day you first requested it? We could go through the request slips and, when we find the one you would have had to fill out, check it for a reference.'

'The thing is, I didna request it. MacDonald found it for me.'

'He should have filled out a slip.'

'I've nae idea if he did or no.'

The second librarian tutted. 'That's how things get lost.'

'He was jist daein me a favour. I was readin up some stuff aboot Major Weir, and he remembered there was somethin aboot him in this document.'

'Major Weir?' the second librarian repeated.

'Witchcraft and that kind of thing,' said his colleague.

There was a moment when Carlin saw the two of them swap glances. They'd been studiously avoiding each other's eye, but when it happened he saw it. He knew then they thought he was bonkers.

'*Excuse me?*' Another voice, from one of the desks next to where they were standing.

They all turned. A tiny woman was sitting there, bent over a bound volume of newspapers. She was so old she looked as though she herself was made of paper. She was wearing a fawn-coloured coat and had a woollen hat pulled down over her hair and ears. She stared up at them angrily.

'I cannot help,' she said, 'overhearing your conversation.'

'I do apologise,' said the second librarian. 'We're trying to sort out a problem. I'm sorry to disturb you.'

'I don't care about that,' the woman said testily. She had a brittle, almost aristocratic accent. Her voice shook like a reed. 'That's not what I mean at all. I don't like to interfere, but you see this man is quite right, there *is* a Mr MacDonald in this library.'

Carlin thanked her silently. They waited for her to continue.

'Just as he said, he has red hair and glasses. I've seen him in here myself.'

'Oh,' said the second librarian. He frowned, as if that would make the old woman go away or be struck dumb.

'We canna baith be wrang,' Carlin said.

'I notice these things, you see,' the woman said. 'My eyesight's still very good.'

'There ye go,' Carlin said.

'He wears a kilt,' the woman said.

They all stared at her.

'A kilt?' the librarian echoed.

'Yes, you know, a kilt. Of the MacDonald tartan. That's why I knew his name was MacDonald. My name is MacDonald too, you see.'

'I see,' said the second librarian. 'Well, thank you very much for that information.'

'Not at all,' the woman said. She looked thoughtful. 'Unless, of course . . .'

'Yes?'

'Well, he *might* not be a MacDonald at all. How silly of me. Just because of his tartan . . .'

The librarians, in a joint manoeuvre, ushered Carlin away from her a little, out of earshot.

'Was your Mr MacDonald wearing a kilt?' the second librarian asked.

Carlin shook his head. The librarian shrugged. 'I'm sorry,' he said. 'There's really very little more we can do.'

'You're tellin me you can't track this book doon. This book that I was in here readin for two days.'

'I'm sorry.'

Carlin held the man's stare for as long as he could. As soon as he went out of the door they'd be shaking their heads at each other. Smirking. He could already hear the conversations during coffee-breaks: the weird-looking guy; the madwoman; the vanishing clansman. He sighed and went back down to the Scottish library.

He had a note-pad with him, which he hadn't yet used during his researches. He hadn't felt the need: things stayed in his head once he had read them. He tore off a sheet and wrote his address at the top.

Dear Mr MacDonald,

It is essential I speak to you. I am the man that you helped concerning Major Weir. Nobody else can find the Lauder manuscript, Ane Secret Book. *Your colleagues here do not seem to know you but you know what I'm talking about. If you receive this please contact me.*

Andrew Carlin.

He folded this in half and took it up to the desk. The same young woman was there who had sent him upstairs.

'Have ye got a wee envelope or somethin?' he asked her. 'I need tae leave a note for one of your colleagues.'

'I can pass it on if you like,' she said brightly.

'I don't think he's in just now,' he said. 'In fact, I know he's not. It might get lost. If ye had an envelope, it would be better.'

She looked in a drawer, and found a little sheaf of small brown envelopes. 'Will one of these do?'

'Perfect,' he said. He put the note in, sealed the envelope, and wrote *Mr MacDonald* on the front.

'D'ye ken him?' he asked, as he handed it over.

'No, can't say I do,' she said. A note of suspicion had crept into her voice. 'When you were asking earlier, I . . .'

'Well, if there's a place for staff messages or somethin, mebbe you could pit it there? It's jist he said tae let him know aboot somethin.'

'Right,' she said. 'I'll make sure it's put up on the board. He'll get it whenever he's in.' She laughed. 'Whoever he is!'

'Thanks,' said Carlin.

It was all he could do. He thought briefly of the telephone directories that were kept upstairs in the Reference Room, several storeys above him, beyond street-level. Just thinking of getting there was exhausting. In any case how many pages of MacDonalds would there be? He couldn't even be sure, now that he thought about it, that it wasn't Macdonald, McDonald or Mcdonald. Forby the ex-directory ones. His only hope lay in the message.

He went through the swing doors, and began the long haul back up to the street.

Edinburgh, 1 May 1997/January 1678

She'd been buzzing the door for ages. While she waited in the street she considered the possibilities: he was dead on the bed where she'd left him; he had hanged himself; he'd picked up and gone, just buggered off, with one of those out-of-date guide books in his pocket. This was the third time she'd come by in six days: she was thinking of calling the police. She kept thinking she heard the click of the receiver but when she pushed at the door it was unyielding. She gave up and turned to go.

He was walking along the pavement towards her, in coat and jeans and a big old jumper. He looked even thinner and paler than before, a tattie-bogle in his long flapping coat. She smiled.

'You're alive,' she said.

'Whit day is it?' said Carlin.

'It's Thursday,' Jackie said. 'Why?'

'I've lost track of things,' he said. 'Thursday right enough. Election day.'

'Have you voted?' she asked, surprised. It seemed a stupid question to be asking in the circumstances. And anyway, would someone like Carlin be bothered about voting?

'No yet. I was that out of it, I forgot. Whit time is it?'

'Nearly six,' she said.

'Plenty time yet then.' He got his keys out and opened the door.

'You're alive,' she said again.

'Aye,' he said. 'I am, amn't I.' The way he said it, it was with the usual flatness, but there was humour in it and she wondered if there always had been and she'd just not noticed. 'But,' he added as he let her into the stair ahead of him, 'I have been ill.'

'I thought you must have been.'

'How?'

'I had Hugh Hardie onto me, saying there was no sign of you. He asked me if I could find out where you stayed.'

'And have ye?'

'No,' she smiled. 'Like I said before, not as far as he's concerned. But I wanted to check for myself, make sure you were all right.'

'I'm better. I had the flu. Or somethin.'

'You look pretty worn out.'

'It takes it oot of ye.'

'It's okay me coming in?'

'Aye.' He drew level with her going up the stairs. 'I don't think I'm infectious.'

'I'll chance it,' she said. 'Could do with a few days off anyway.'

'No wi this,' he said. 'This was a fuckin nightmare.'

They went into the flat. 'I'll pit the kettle on,' he said. 'I've still nae sugar.'

He turned into the kitchen, while she walked on into the front room. Stopped where she was. 'Bloody hell,' she said.

'Andrew,' she called, 'you've been done over.'

He came through. She was staring at the state of the place. There were books lying everywhere. One bookcase had been overturned. The television was on its back like a beetle. The mirror above the fire hung at a crazy angle and one of the candlesticks was lying on its side. The bedclothes were halfway across the floor.

'Na,' he said, 'it wasna that.'

'What's happened then?'

'They pit him on trial,' said Carlin.

'What?'

'They finally pit him on trial. James Mitchel. Mind I tellt ye aboot him.' He indicated the devastation. 'There was a bit o a riot. Emotions were kinna high.'

'I haven't a clue what you're talking about,' said Jackie.

'No,' said Carlin. 'Neither ye have.'

She moved a jumble of books off the armchair and sat down in it. 'Going to help me out then? Give me the lowdown?'

'Tea?' he said.

'Aye. No, wait a minute.' She stood up. 'You look done in. I'll make it.'

He shrugged. 'Aye, well . . .' Then he sat down on the bed. 'I'm pretty knackert, right enough.'

When she brought the tea back through, he was leaning back, sprawled across the bed, his eyes closed. She put one mug down at his feet and went back to the chair with the other.

'So,' she said, 'are you going to go back? On the tour?'

He opened his eyes. 'Aye,' he said. 'I'll go back.'

'For how long, but?' she said. 'Hugh won't tolerate much more of this on/off stuff.'

Carlin laughed. 'Fuck him, then.'

In spite of herself she laughed too. After all, she'd never had any intention of telling him where to find Carlin. 'Fair enough,' she said.

'But I'll no leave him in the lurch,' Carlin said. 'I need tae go back wan mair time. Unfinished business.'

'Who's this James Mitchel?' she said. 'What did he do? What are you on about?'

He sat up and lifted the mug of tea. He began to tell her who James Mitchel was.

Mitchel who was at the centre of everything but central to nothing. Who was like a twig or some other debris caught in a whirlpool. For a moment he was held there and all eyes were on him, to see if he would be thrown to the edge, or sucked down out of sight forever. Carlin had watched, John Lauder had watched, three hundred years and a few yards apart.

Cousin John Eleis was right about one thing: by October 1677, the Duke of Lauderdale was acting to save his political life. The deliberations of the Privy Council were supposed to be secret, but the upper layer of Edinburgh society, with its rivalries and temporary alliances, was about as secret as a sieve: everybody knew that Lauderdale had declared to the Council that all possibility of compromise with the disaffected nonconformists was at an end; more, that he'd claimed there had never been any audience, negotiation, contact, treaty or capitulation between him and the rebels. By November he had arranged for the chiefs of Atholl and elsewhere to bring their wild clansmen down into the west country, to be quartered on the people there for the winter. The Highland Host came out of the hills and settled like locusts. Lauderdale, it seemed, was determined to break the power of the conventicles in a last effort to shore up his own.

In December Sir George Mackenzie, the King's Advocate, moved against James Mitchel. He asked the Council to bring him back from the Bass, so that he could pursue him on a charge of assassination, and for invading the persons of His Majesty's counsellors, lords, officers and ministers. The penalty for these offences was death. He asked for his old rivals Sir George Lockhart and Mr John Eleis to be appointed counsel for the defence. This was done. The Privy Council wanted a show trial, and Mackenzie understood that: it should be clear by the end that Mitchel had had the best lawyers available, and had still been found guilty.

Mitchel was brought off the Bass and held in the Tolbooth. The trial date was set for Monday, 7 January, 1678. That morning John Lauder made sure he had no other business to attend to, and made his way early to the High Court. He had snatched a few brief meetings with Eleis and knew that the trial was shaping up to be a spectacular exhibition of legal and political swordplay. Mackenzie was taking a risk in asking for Lockhart as his opponent but he could not resist the opportunity to rub his neb in the sharn. Forby that he did not believe he could lose. The jury would be packed: army officers and burgesses loyal to the Crown would make up its fifteen. He had Mitchel's confession to the assassination attempt. And he had gathered new evidence from other sources, which would be more than enough, he thought, to convince the already sympathetic jurors.

But Lockhart and Eleis had called Mackenzie's bluff. They would argue against the confession being valid, but failing that they would argue that it carried with it the promise of life, and as witnesses to this they had summoned three of the men who had been present at the confession and signed it – Lord Rothes, Lord Haltoun, and Sir Archibald Primrose. In addition they had summoned none other than the Duke of Lauderdale and the Archbishop of St Andrews, since they had authorised the terms of the confession in the Privy Council. In effect they were obliging the most powerful men in the land to come to court and tell the truth, or let a single, half-dead rebel be crushed under the weight of their bad consciences.

There was always a throng in the Parliament Close on court days, but when Lauder arrived he could hardly force his way through the crowd. Mitchel, until recently forgotten by almost everybody, was suddenly a celebrity. Lauder managed to squeeze to the front, hoping to catch the eye of one of the court officers and gain entry ahead of the rabble. Just as he was beginning to fear that he had left it too late he saw a small procession of dignitaries slipping through a side-door, his father-in-law among them. He dived after them. A worried-looking official guarding the entrance recognised him, signalled him over, and let him inside. Sir Andrew Ramsay turned as the door slammed shut, and saw Lauder catching his breath.

'John, John. I micht hae guessed ye'd be here. Come tae see yer ain chosen fanatic receive his just deserts, eh? And yer fellow advocates humbled by the King's prosecutor. Weill, ye'll hae a guid view wi us. Come alang, come alang. D'ye ken the bailies? Aye, of coorse ye dae. And Maister Hickes?'

A slight, purse-lipped man in clerical dress made a half-bow, which Lauder returned. Hickes was the Duke of Lauderdale's chaplain, a detestable scribbling Englishman who made no secret of his hatred of all things Scottish. Lauder groaned within himself. He had hoped to avoid his father-in-law, who would be bound to ruin his attention to the legal details of the case by crass interventions and asides, but he was prepared to abide him in return for a good seat. To be in the same party as the sneevilling Hickes, however, was intolerable. Sir Andrew must loathe him, but perhaps saw him as a useful conduit to Lauderdale if the latter should retain his position as Secretary of State.

The bench was being prepared for the judges. Below it, a huge table was spread about with various papers. At one end of this sat Mackenzie, the King's Advocate, running over details with an assistant. At the other end Lockhart and Eleis were doing the same. None of them looked up as the party took their seats. Some of the other places in the public gallery were already occupied, but Lauder knew that when the main doors were opened the place would be filled to capacity.

He was relieved to find himself at the end of a row, and some distance from Hickes. But Sir Andrew was next to him, his excessive size already squeezing Lauder right to the edge. The Ramsay wig had been freshly preened for the occasion, and smelt of perfume. The Ramsay breath was thick with drink.

'Noo, John, we'll be in a position tae gie each ither the benefits o oor different experiences, will we no? Ma erse was on the bench, and you hae had yours at thon muckle table where yer fanatic's proctors are tryin tae conjure a wey tae save him. So we'll keep each ither richt, eh?'

'Nae doot, my lord,' Lauder murmured. He was looking around, nodding acquaintance at the many other lawyers who had come to watch the spectacle.

'For example,' Sir Andrew went on, belching a soft, wine-rich breeze across his son-in-law's face, 'explain tae me this. Sir Erchie Primrose is cited as a witness by the defence, is he no? But he's also Lord Carringtoun, Lord Justice General, and hence should preside frae the bench. He canna be baith witness and judge in the same case, can he?'

'No, ye're richt, he canna. But there will be five ither justices. Either he'll step doon, or the counsels will agree no tae call him as a witness. The latter, I would think. The defence has ither equally impressive witnesses.'

'Aye, they hae that, the impident divils. But it's a kittle business for Mackenzie, tae ken whether Primrose is mair danger as a witness or a judge, eh? He'll mak trouble either wey.'

Primrose, a staunch Royalist who had fought with Montrose against the Covenanters, had little reason to love James Mitchel. But he had recently been removed by Lauderdale as Lord Clerk Register, a post which he had held since the Restoration, and from which a lucrative income could be made as it controlled the registration of all property transactions in Scotland. He had been appointed Lord Justice General as a sop, but who would prefer prestige to a steady flow of bribes and percentages? Worse, it was Lauderdale's queenly wife who had got him shifted, and it was certain she had not done it to expunge corruption. The post was still vacant but in these days when everyone of a certain rank was, had been or hoped to be a judge, privy counsellor or government official, when position and title were valued only because with them came the power to blackmail, fine, tax or otherwise extort and make yourself a fortune, it would not be long before it was filled. Primrose's new job was more arduous and less remunerative than his old one and he was furious about it. Sir Andrew's point was, Lauder acknowledged, a good one.

Sir Andrew, meanwhile, had swung his belly round and was expressing loudly a mixture of wind and opinion in the opposite direction. 'And as if his grace St Andrews and my lord Lauderdale didna hae enough on their plates athoot haein tae come here and swat this wretched flea Mitchel! It's an outrage, is it no, Maister Hickes?'

Before Hickes could reply the court rose as the Lords of Justiciary, bewigged and in their red robes faced with white, entered and took their seats on the bench. Primrose, ermine-draped, was at their head, preceded by the mace-bearer. Sir Andrew dunted Lauder in the ribs.

'D'ye ken aw thae venerable justices?' he asked.

'Aye, of coorse.'

'So ye ken him at the end there?'

'It's Sir Thomas Murray of Glendoick,' said Lauder shortly, wishing his father-in-law would shut up.

'And ye ken whae's cousin he is?' Sir Andrew was almost slavering, a sign, Lauder now recognised, that he was about to impart some scandalous or at least succulent information.

'Murray?' said Lauder, suddenly interested. 'Wi that name he'll be related tae maist o Perthshire.'

'Aye, but the particular connection I mean is tae Lady Lauderdale. He's *her* cousin. Nae wunner Primrose canna bear tae look at him. *He's* tae be the new Lord Register. For a share o the profits tae her ladyship, naturally.'

At that moment the court officers opened the doors and the crowd stumbled and clattered in. As soon as the place was full two soldiers brought the prisoner Mitchel in from another entrance, and seated him at the bar. Lauder looked along the row and saw Hickes writing in a pocket-book, probably a note about the undignified Scots way of doing things, the absence of due pomp and ceremony. Still digesting Sir

Andrew's titbit, Lauder turned his attention back to Mitchel.

It was seven months since he had seen him on the Bass, and those months seemed to have turned him the slate-grey colour of the sea. He was so gaunt and ill-looking, and seemed so disinterested in the proceedings of the court, that he exuded almost an air of nobility. People watching him limp in, Lauder thought, would be reminded of what had been done to him. They would be reminded of Hew McKail and others like him. They would see the ranked judges, the lords and gentry and lawyers like himself sitting in the best seats, and they would realise how the odds were stacked. Against this assemblage Mitchel would seem the man of principle, the poor man bullied and tortured by his superiors. The people would rally to him like the underdog he was. Not for the first time, John Lauder regretted that he had ended up so visibly in the company of Sir Andrew and his cronies.

Mackenzie opened by declaring that he would not be calling Sir Archibald Primrose, Lord Carringtoun, as a witness, seeing he was Lord Justice General and presiding over the court.

John Eleis returned on behalf of the panel that they accepted the Lord Justice General as a judge, notwithstanding his being cited as a witness both by pursuer and defender. A murmur of opinion went round the lawyers in the audience.

'Ye were richt,' Sir Andrew said. 'And noo I'll tell ye somethin else *I* ken. Primrose is a sleekit, snoovin snake, and nane o the pleaders had better fash him if they want tae win this case. On the contrary, I doot they'll aw be gleg tae be freens wi him.'

The ex-provost's opinion only added to Lauder's growing feeling that, like Mitchel, Primrose might, in some perverse way, represent a principle in the case. 'He's been in this world ower lang tae depend muckle on freens,' he replied.

'That'll be why he disna hae ony,' Sir Andrew said, settling back in his seat. Within a few minutes he was nodding, half-asleep.

The whole of the first day was taken up with legal arguments so rarefied that, apart from the three advocates making them, they went over the heads of almost everybody, including some of the judges. James Mitchel denied the charges against him. Thereafter he took no part in the proceedings. He would sit throughout the trial like a man on a mountain looking down on tiny men at work in a field below.

Meanwhile the lawyers thrashed things out among themselves. Eleis droned on majestically, half the time in Latin, attempting to prove the whole business a sham. Mitchel should not be at the bar at all, he said. There was no such crime in Scotland as assassination, and even if there were Mitchel could not be guilty of it since nobody was killed (the Bishop of Orkney having died, but some years later after having been able to go about his ordinary functions as a bishop, and not in any event on account of wounds sustained when shot at on the occasion alleged). As to the demembration of the said Bishop of Orkney, Eleis continued, the twenty-eighth Act of King James IV *anno* 1491 made it not a capital offence: the Bishop had sustained merely a wound to the hand, not had it cut off, and therefore could not be said to have been dismembered in any case; and the wound having been received, as stated in the libel, accidentally from a shot fired at the Archbishop of St Andrews, no malice aforethought could be attached to the act of injuring the Bishop of Orkney. Moreover, the libel seemed to be founded solely or principally on a confession, and that confession, if made at all (which the panel denied), was made extrajudicially and neither before a quorum of justices nor in presence of jurors and therefore held no legal weight and was expressly contrary to the law as contained in the ninetieth act of the seventh parliament of King James VI made for security of panels from unjust procedures against them; but, and again not admitting the confession, any such confession had, would and could only have been made in return for a promise of life; and furthermore and insofar as and notwithstanding all of the afore-mentioned . . .

The crowd, those that were standing and therefore unable to doze, grew restless. There were a large number of women among it. Neither they nor most of the men could make anything of the Latin-speckled giff-gaff of the lawyers but they tolerated it from Eleis and Lockhart, because they could see that their web of words was designed to entangle the prosecution and get Mitchel off. But whenever Mackenzie rose to speak, a noise went round the court like a rumbling cundie.

Mackenzie, in his forties and supremely confident in demeanour, appeared to take no notice of this. He was in his element as he replied to an argument of Eleis, as Lockhart duplied to him, as he returned a further argument, and so forth: the lawyers were like mechanics working expertly on an apparatus no one else understood. But the crowd had a mob's instinct for detecting the opposition's discomfort and exacerbating it, and it was to be found elsewhere than with the King's Advocate.

George Hickes had come in the long black coat of his calling. English, Episcopalian and gloating, he made too tempting a target. In the middle of one of Mackenzie's speeches, somebody launched an apple core at Hickes, which bounced off his shoulder, leaving a faint smear of juice. There was a ripple of laughter. The court officers scanned the crowd, trying to pick out the culprit, but all they could really do was stand cross-armed and glare. As soon as their attention was diverted, another missile would fly at Hickes – more fruit, a bit of cheese. If it missed him it usually hit someone else nearby. John Lauder moved to the extremity of the bench he was on, and managed to avoid the worst of it. Next to him Sir Andrew Ramsay slumped, snoring gently and unaware of an old heel of bread which was caught on the back of his wig. When his neck rolled or twitched the bread jigged in agreement and was greeted with delight by those behind him. Then somebody fired a long green gob as if out of a mortar, and it sailed like a flying slug through the air and attached itself to the collar of Hickes's coat. This was an encouragement to the bored younger men in the crowd. Over the next few minutes, Hickes's shoulders and back became spotted and streaked with slicks of varying colour and consistency. When he raised his voice in protest, one of the court officers, who could not see the cause of his complaint, hissed at him to be quiet.

John Lauder kept as much distance as he could between himself and his father-in-law, and tried to concentrate on the trial. He felt that his loyalty lay with John Eleis, and he was fascinated by the procession of arguments. He watched the aloof Mitchel, who never once looked in his direction, and thought he appeared the very model of a fanatic.

Meanwhile the lawyers battled on across the big table. By late afternoon the judges were as weary as the onlookers. They wanted more time to consider the arguments. The trial, Lord Carringtoun announced, would be held over until the Wednesday, to commence at two in the afternoon. Mitchel was taken back to the Tolbooth, and the court rose.

Lauder did not see his cousin John over the next two days. He was hard at work with Lockhart, trying to make the best of their material. Nobody really believed, however well argued their case for dismissal, that the court would throw the case out when it reconvened. There were too many reputations at stake, too much pressure being applied by the government. But in the Wednesday forenoon, Eleis called to see him, and they walked together out to Greyfriars and back again to court.

'We hae a chance,' Eleis said. 'Or I should say, Mitchel has a chance, where a witch would hae nane. It's because we're up against Mackenzie, and Mackenzie must win by law, whereas a witch is condemned by sentiment and superstition. Still, I amna ower hopeful. The opinions we and he brocht afore the bench on Monday balanced each ither, by and large, which means they cancelled each ither oot. On that basis, they'll say the indictment is competent.'

'Then whit else stands between Mitchel and the hangman?'

Eleis smiled. 'I canna tell ye,' he said. 'It's anither o thae secrets aboot Mitchel, like the yin you had. But I can say this. We hae a weapon that may be enough tae cut him free.'

'Whit kind o weapon? A deposition? A witness?'

'It's a proof,' Eleis said. 'That's aw I can say. It was pit intae oor hauns last nicht.'

'Then it's a new production. If Mackenzie hasna been advised o its existence it winna be admitted.'

'Aye it will. It comes frae a guid source.'

'Where?'

Eleis shook his head. 'Watch the bench closely this eftirnune,' he said.

Sir Archibald Primrose, Lord Justice General, opened the

proceedings. The charges in the dittay were to stand, he said. The confession made by the panel had been made before the Committee of the Council, and was therefore judicial, and could not be retracted. The confession had not been elicited by torture, since it had been made prior to same, and on a different occasion. The trial would proceed.

'However,' Primrose added, looking at Sir George Mackenzie, 'we also find the alleged promise of life and limb, made in return for the panel's confession, to be relevant.'

Mackenzie was on his feet. 'My lord, the existence of such a promise is a mere speculation. The panel does not even acknowledge the confession.'

'But my lord,' said Primrose, 'there *is* a confession. Your case depends on it. All we are saying is, ye cannot have the confession and yet not have anything that might appertain to it. That is the basis on which we continue.'

'But my lord . . .'

'That is the basis on which we continue. We spent Monday on this matter and we will not spend today on it. Our friends on the assize will decide what is speculation and what is fact from the evidence presented to them. They will now be sworn in.'

John Lauder, listening intently, detected more than the usual smugness in Primrose's voice. The judge was hinting at something, he was sure of it. He saw Eleis conferring with Lockhart. Lauder was sitting alone today: Hickes and others, in spite of the treatment they had received on the Monday, were back as well, but Sir Andrew had declared the proceedings too tedious, and gone to Fife. Lauder had not tried to dissuade him.

Mackenzie's confidence seemed to return as he watched the jurors being sworn. An apothecary, a couple of wine merchants, a tailor, a merchant or two – well, these might swing either way. But the other nine were all soldiers or gentlemen, government men. A clear majority before Mackenzie even started, and a majority was all he needed. The defence objected to several of them, but was overruled.

Mackenzie nodded curtly to Lockhart and Eleis. They nodded back. He cast a cold eye on James Mitchel, who was staring into space. Then he let his gaze pass over the public, more numerous even than they had been two days before, for today, everybody knew, the fanatic's fate would be decided. Already there was a tension in the atmosphere. The King's Advocate's survey of his audience seemed to be saying, 'I will overcome you all.'

The first witness was a bulky, dour-looking man, an advocate himself, William Paterson. John Lauder knew him – all the legal brethren knew him. He seemed, for a man habitually in courts, to be most uncomfortable. His eyes kept shifting to the defence lawyers, as if he wished to apologise for being there at all.

Mackenzie asked him if he recalled the day when the archbishop was shot at, in July 1668. He did. And did he recall being out in the town that day, in the afternoon? He did. Whereabouts? He was walking up Blackfriars Wynd. When was this, roughly? About four o'clock. And did he meet anyone? He did. Whom did he meet? He met an armed man coming down the street. How was this man armed? He had a pistol in his hand. Would this be before or after the firing of a pistol at the Archbishop? After. How did he know that? There was a commotion in the street, which he learnt was caused by the attack on the Archbishop. And did he see the man with the pistol in the court today? He did not.

Mackenzie gave him a slow, deadly look.

'Ye do not?'

'No, my lord.'

'Ye saw the man clearly?'

'Aye.'

'Yet ye do not see him here.'

'No.'

Mackenzie indicated Mitchel. 'Do ye recognise this man at all?'

'No.'

'If I put it to ye that this is the man ye saw, would ye think it possible?'

'I canna say. It's ten year syne.'

'But is it *possible*?'

'I dinna ken this man. I canna say if he was the person that shot at the Archbishop. That is the truth as I shall answer God.'

Mackenzie sat down, annoyed but not exasperated. He had better witnesses, and would not waste time because this one had balked at the fence. Lockhart and Eleis declined to question, and Paterson stepped down with evident relief.

The next witness was Patrick Vanse, keeper of the Tolbooth. He was a handsome, dark-haired man in his forties, who had taken some trouble to look his best for his day in court. He stood very upright as he was sworn in, and answered the questions put to him with an abruptness that was at first impressive, but then began to seem just a little too well rehearsed. Mackenzie took him back four years, to 1674, when Mitchel was held in the Tolbooth. Had the panel, during that time when he was in his custody, ever said anything to Vanse about the assassination attempt?

'Aye, my lord, he did.'

'When was that?'

'Twa days afore he was examined by the Cooncil, my lord.'

'And what did he say?'

'That he'd shot a pistol at the Archbishop o St Andrews, my lord.'

'He told ye that? This man that ye see here?'

'Aye.'

'What else did he say?'

'That he escaped doon Blackfriars Wynd, my lord, and gaed up the Cougate and intae Maister Fergusson's hoose, anither rebel, my lord, where he pit on a periwig, and syne he cam back oot on the street and huntit himsel.'

There were a few laughs. Lauder noticed that Mitchel was paying closer attention than he had at any time so far during the trial.

'What do ye mean, *he huntit himsel?*' Mackenzie asked.

'He pretended tae search for the man that had shot the pistol,' Vanse said. 'But it was himsel that had done it.'

Mackenzie gave way to the defence. Sir George Lockhart approached Vanse and said, in a friendly manner, 'Your evidence is most precise, sir. Ye have a excellent memory. Ye must have had dozens, hundreds of prisoners pass through your portals in the last four years. Each with their own story to tell.'

'Nane like his, sir.'

'That'll be why ye mind it so well?'

'Aye, sir.'

'And did the panel say nothing else about this violent act that he boasted of to ye?'

'No, sir.'

'How can ye be sure that this conversation occurred two days before Maister Mitchel was examined by the Council?'

Vanse shrugged. 'Weill, twa days, or a day afore. Nae mair than that.'

'Oh. So ye're not absolutely certain of the day?'

'No, sir.'

'Might it have been a day, or two days *after* he was examined by the Council?'

Vanse frowned. 'I dinna mind.'

Lockhart looked puzzled. 'A thing that is bothering me, ye see, is that, Maister Mitchel being of a particular persuasion, a particular party, what some folk call a fanatical persuasion, ye'd expect him to justify the deed in some way. Refer to a text in the Bible, or the duty of a covenanted Christian people or some such. But ye dinna mind him justifying his actions at all?'

'No, sir.'

'He told ye exactly what he did on that day when the Archbishop was fired upon, his exact movements, every particular of this criminal act, and yet he did not choose to explain why he had committed it?'

'No, sir.'

'It seems a strange omission from such a man,' Lockhart said. 'Such a man would not regard the act *as* a crime, so ye'd think he'd be at pains to explain himself. But, as I said, your memory is excellent. It must have been an oversight on his part.'

Lockhart seemed finished, but turned as he was walking back to his seat, and added, 'Except of course that ye canna mind whether this confession made to ye by Maister Mitchel was made before or after he was examined by the Council. I'm done, my lords.'

Lockhart sat down, having raised at least a doubt as to the accuracy of Vanse's story. But John Lauder observed that Mackenzie did not seem unduly concerned. When the next witness, Vanse's son John, was called, it became clear why.

'John, ye are reckoned a good man, a kindly man,' Mackenzie said. 'Ye take a care over the unhappy persons that ye are responsible for. Did ye have friendly dealings with the panel, Maister Mitchel, when he was kept in the Tolbooth four year syne?'

'Aye, my lord. We'd hae a conversation noo and again.'

'And did ye discuss with him this matter of the shooting at the Archbishop?'

'Aye, my lord.'

'And did he acknowledge the deed to ye?'

'Aye, my lord.'

'And did he ever justify this deed?'

John Vanse looked over to the panel, but Mitchel studiously avoided his eye. Lauder watched them avidly. He thought of what Mitchel had told him on the Bass. Had Vanse ever connected the prisoner of 1674 with the man who had come to visit Major Weir four years before that, claiming to be his son? If he had, or if he did now, would that make him more or less likely to hurt Mitchel? Or would it make no difference at all?

'Did he ever justify this deed to ye?' Mackenzie repeated.

Vanse was staring at Mitchel, as if a clock or some such mechanism were clicking and whirring in his brain. Then he spoke.

'I mind yince, we spak aboot evil, whit evil was, whether it was frae man or frae Satan. I'd kent aw kinds o men that had come through the Tolbooth, and it wasna clear tae me wi some o them where their badness cam frae. I mind I asked him how he could kill a man in cauld bluid. I mean, a man that hadna done him ill. I asked him how ony man could be pairty tae sae wickit an act.'

'And what was his reply?'

Vanse hesitated, looked again at Mitchel.

'He said it wasna in cauld bluid. He said the bluid o the saints was reekin at the cross o Edinburgh.'

The crowd stirred. And that, thought John Lauder, is Mackenzie's retort to Lockhart. There was Mitchel's motive, and the language Vanse said he had used was like red meat to a hungry jury. The officers and gentlemen on that jury seized it:

let a man like Mitchel away, they would be thinking, and they would be next on his list of targets. But elsewhere in the court, except where the gentry sat, there was grumbling and hissing. The popular element applauded Mitchel's rhetoric. They saw the effect it had on their social superiors. They saw a glimmer of fear. But Lauder knew that, in the jurors' eyes, it had hurt Mitchel badly.

Mackenzie pressed on. He worked on the horror of the deed, playing it up for the benefit of the jurors. He called three surgeons one after another, to describe the damage inflicted on the Bishop of Orkney. Dr Irvin testified that he saw a ball fall from the bishop's sleeve, so that he knew the wound had been caused by a shot: the bones were fractured, and the arm was permanently weakened, but they managed to cure him so that at least he could raise his hand towards his head. The Bishop had told him that he had been hit as he laid his hand on the door of the coach. Dr Jossie explained that the wound had been between the wrist and the elbow, and that several small bones had been smashed by the shot. Dr Borthwick agreed with Dr Jossie in every respect.

The Crown's case rested. It was now Lockhart's turn. He called as a witness John, the Earl of Rothes, Lord High Chancellor of Scotland.

'My lords,' Lockhart said, addressing the bench, 'I would not want ye to think there is any insolence intended in the calling of this or other witnesses. But we must discover the truth of the matter of this confession. Was it made freely and without an assurance of life, or was it no? Only these noble and honourable lords know the answer, and it is for this reason that we have called them.'

Rothes, enormous and red of face, glared at Lockhart as if he would like to eat him.

Primrose nodded affably and his robed arm made a sweeping gesture around the court. 'This is the nub of the matter,' he said. 'I cannot think for what other reason all the world is in attendance. It is fair to say, I believe, that many think there has been a promise of life given to the panel. Many have heard that there was even an Act of Council made about it. So, we must establish whether or not this is the case. Proceed, sir.'

John Lauder saw the glint in Primrose's narrow eyes. The Justice General disliked Rothes, he loathed Sharp, and he blamed Lauderdale, or at least his wife, for his removal from the office of Lord Register. He would happily see them perjure themselves. By making his remarks, he had effectively dared them to do so. But if they did, if they flatly denied that Mitchel had been promised his life, it would be Mitchel's word against theirs. How could that save him?

Primrose had been Lord Register in 1674, Lauder thought. He had been responsible not only for deeds of property, but also for all the important documents of state. He must have seen all the records of the Privy Council. He must know whether or not a document promising Mitchel's life existed. But no such document had been entered as a production in the trial. Had it been destroyed? Lauder remembered his cousin's words about a secret weapon: *It was pit intae oor hauns last nicht.* And he understood that they had something in writing, and that it had come from Primrose.

Lockhart showed Rothes the confession. Rothes acknowledged that he recognised it, and his own and Mitchel's signatures upon it. He had heard Mitchel make the confession, and he had seen him sign it.

'Did your lordship not take Maister Mitchel aside, and offer him his life, in return for this confession?'

'I did not.'

'Did ye not promise to secure his life, upon your own life, honour and reputation?'

'I did not.'

'But surely Maister Mitchel sought such an assurance from ye, before he would subscribe his name?'

'He did not.'

'And your lordship does not remember any warrant or Act of the Council to that effect?'

'No.'

'So if it were possible to produce such a warrant or Act, how would ye explain its existence?'

'I couldna explain it. I dinna comprehend whit ye're driving at.'

'Ye would say that such a paper does not exist?'

'Aye. But – '

'Aye, my lord?'

'But – but if there be ony such paper – weill, all I mean to say is, if there be ony such expression of a promise, I can only think that it must have been inserted by mistake.'

Rothes was now puce. Lockhart had backed him into a corner and at the last minute Rothes had perceived that there might be a trap, and that he had better, however clumsily, leave himself a way out. Lockhart seemed very pleased. He declined to question him further, and Rothes, barely able to contain his rage, stormed from the witness stand.

Charles Maitland of Haltoun was next. As a witness he had not been allowed in the court when Rothes was giving evidence, but his nature alone made him more circumspect than the blustery Chancellor. He had been present when Maister Mitchel made that confession, he said. He had heard him make it verbally and then had seen him sign it. When Lockhart pressed him as to whether the panel had been promised his life in return, Haltoun answered very carefully: *he* had not heard Mitchel seek, nor had he heard any other person give him, such an assurance.

'My lord,' said Lockhart, 'that is not what I asked. Was Maister Mitchel promised his life if he confessed?'

Haltoun stared icily at the advocate. '*I*,' he repeated, 'did not *hear* any person give him such an assurance.'

Lockhart let him go. The courtroom stirred again. Now came the big guns. The Duke of Lauderdale was summoned to the stand.

He was a great, ugly beast of a man, with a full set of chins and a look of dissipated exhaustion on his face. He had been riding the horse of political power for seventeen years, and it showed. When he spoke, his tongue. which was too big for his mouth, slapped around, half-in and half-out of it, like a lump of liver, spraying the air with slavers. Nevertheless, his heavy, richly decorated clothes, massive dark wig, fat ringed fingers and imperious sneer, all gave the impression of a man of immense authority, whose involvement in such a trifling affair was altogether beneath him.

He had not been present, he explained, when the confession was first made, but only when Mitchel was brought before the

Council subsequently, when he had acknowledged it to be his own and had renewed it.

'And this was done on the promise of his life?' Lockhart asked.

'I never heard that given.'

'But as the King's commissioner, my lord, ye must have discussed this business in council before. Ye must have agreed to offer him his life, else why would he have confessed?'

Lauderdale shook his head. 'It's not for me to say why the man confessed. But I never promised him anything, nor did I grant that anybody else could.'

'Of this ye are quite positive?'

Lauderdale's voice boomed. 'I could not have given such a promise. I did not have the King's authority to do so.'

A murmuring through the court indicated that nobody believed him. The gentry sat stone-faced. Lockhart seemed to toy with the idea of pressing him further, but then let him go, and, like the previous witnesses, the Duke made his way, with a brewing storm in his face, to a seat in the gallery.

'I call his grace the Archbishop of St Andrews,' Lockhart said.

Mitchel went rigid. The soldiers on either side of him studied him, as if they thought, even now, he might produce some hidden weapon and charge across the room. James Sharp crossed the floor in his black robes, and let his gaze drift as if he were watching the progress of a moth which at last alighted, with a flutter, on the head of the fanatic.

It was the fourth time they had come face to face. Ten years before, they had stared at each other across the barrel of a gun. Six years later, Sharp had recognised him selling tobacco from his booth on the street. Then Mitchel had been brought before the Council and Sharp had seen him acknowledge his confession. Now, in the High Court, Sharp was determined that this would be their last meeting, that Mitchel would go to the gallows and he could finally be rid of him.

At first Lockhart could make no headway with Sharp. He repeated what the other noble witnesses had already said: that Mitchel had made his confession freely, and that at no time had a promise of life been given. He, the Archbishop, had never personally given any such assurance, nor authorised anybody else to do so.

'But is it not true, your grace,' Lockhart said, 'that when Maister Mitchel was apprehended, ye offered that ye would use your best offices to save him, if he would only confess to the deed?'

'He didna like the offer,' Sharp said. 'He, or his wife, I canna recall which, declined it.'

'But then, your grace, ye treated with his wife's brother, Nicol Sommervile, a craftsman of this town, did ye not?'

'Aye, and with the same result.' Sharp stared with utter contempt at Mitchel. 'When he was first taken, it's true I promised that if he made a full confession, out of court, and tellt us who else was involved, and if he truly repented of the deed, then I would do what I could for him in the way of mercy. But if he didna, I would leave him to justice. And look where we are, sir. These people are beyond treating with.'

'Nicol Sommervile is also a witness, your grace. He may say different.'

Sharp said angrily, 'He may say what he likes. I pledged Nicol Sommervile nothing but my belief that the prisoner should make a full confession. It is a false and malicious calumny if he or anybody pretends that I either promised that man his life, or gave anybody else warrant to promise it.'

Lockhart smiled. 'Your grace, I thank ye for your candour. Ye could not have made your position clearer. Now I would like, my lords, to hear Nicol Sommervile on this matter.'

John Lauder almost laughed out loud with nerves. Lockhart had no fear of these men; it was as if he intended to bring the whole edifice of government down about their lugs. Cousin John, though, who had pleaded only on the first day of the case, was now busily conferring with Lockhart while Sharp left the stand. Eleis did not look like a man about to win a famous victory. In fact, he looked slightly confused – a thing Lauder had never seen before – as if Lockhart had got ahead of him, and he did not know exactly which road he was taking.

Sommervile, Lauder estimated, was in his thirties, a sturdy man with the quick, assessing eye of a silversmith. He appeared to be terrified. But when Lockhart took him through the events of four years before, he spoke out clearly and slowly even though his knees were knocking together. His grace the Archbishop *had* promised Mitchel his life if he admitted everything. He, Nicol Sommervile, had taken this word to Mitchel, who had agreed, and Sommervile had conveyed this back to the Archbishop.

'I will ask ye to be precise, Nicol,' said Lockhart. 'Ye returned to his grace the Archbishop, and ye conveyed that Maister Mitchel would confess all?'

'Aye, sir. But only if he had a solemn promise in the King's name that his life would be spared.'

'And what was the Archbishop's answer?'

'He swore, as he should answer before God, that he would grant him his life.'

There was a commotion in the gallery. Sharp was standing, pointing at Sommervile with a shaking finger. 'That is a damned lie! My lords, ye hae heard my testimony. How can ye tolerate this – this treasonable – '

Primrose half-rose from the bench. 'Ye have had your say, sir. Be seated!'

Sharp ignored him. 'Nicol Sommervile, ye're a traitorous rebel like your brother, and ye should hang like him!'

'Be seated, sir!' Primrose shouted. There was a clamour of shouts throughout the court: '*Shame, shame!*' Sommervile turned and appealed to the bench. 'My lords, I swear on my salvation that awthin I tellt ye is the truth!'

For a minute the proceedings looked like dissolving into a riot. The old bread and fruit that had been evident on the first day of the trial began to be flung about again. Boots stamped on the wooden floor, women shrilled abuse at Sharp, men spat at him. It was with difficulty that the officers restored order.

Mitchel sat in impassive isolation throughout. His face slightly tilted, his eyes half-closed, the trace of a smile on his lips, he seemed to be in a trance.

The bench conferred. Primrose dismissed Sommervile, and gestured to Lockhart to continue. After a word with Eleis, Lockhart picked up a document from the table. It was, he said, a copy of the Act of Council in which the details of this whole sorry tale were given. It corroborated everything that

Nicol Sommervile had just said and confuted everything stated by the noble witnesses. With the bench's permission, Lockhart would like to read this document out.

Sir George Mackenzie had been sitting as if clamped to his chair for the last twenty minutes. He had not cross-examined the witnesses, for fear of making things worse than they already were. He had sat tight when Sharp had had his outburst, a hand over his mouth. But now he sprang back to life.

'My lords, this cannot be allowed. This paper that my learned friend has in his hand, what is it? He says it is a copy of an Act of the Council. Why has he not produced the Act itself? If there is such an Act, and he wished it to be used in evidence, he should have used a diligence and cited the clerks of council to produce the register. He did not do this. He cannot now introduce it. It is against all procedure.'

'I would like to hear what is in this paper,' Primrose said silkily. 'Then we can see if we should proceed further with the register.' To Lockhart he added, 'You may go on, sir.'

Lockhart's reading took fully five minutes. It was so detailed, so precise in its statement of facts and naming of names, that there could be no doubt that it was an authentic copy. The crowd heard it and knew they were hearing the truth. But Mackenzie was no longer concerned with truth and falsehood. All that mattered now was what was admissible and what was not. When Lockhart had finished, the King's Advocate returned to the argument.

'My lords, this pretended paper proves nothing. It is the panel's arguments written down and given the name *an Act of Council*. Not even that – a *copy* of an Act of Council. It is worthless. I say again, my lords, the panel's counsel should have cited the clerks of council to produce the register. Instead he has read out something the panel might have written himself.'

'My lords,' Lockhart answered, 'we have no objection to the register of council being produced. In fact we crave it. Let the register be produced. Then the court will see everything that we have alleged and attested, written down in the Acts of Council and furthermore, my lords, signed by the noble witnesses who have just deponed they know nothing about it.'

'No, my lords,' Mackenzie said, 'that is a sleight of hand ye must not allow. The panel's counsel is seeking a new production after all the witnesses have been examined. And even if such a pretended Act exists, my lords, it is unwarrantable, it cannot be made use of, because we have already heard the depositions of the Chancellor, and the Thesaurer Depute, and the Secretary of State, and the Archbishop of St Andrews, that no assurance or promise of life was given. My lords, it is against all custom and process to admit this paper or to send for the register.'

'It is only up the stair, my lords,' said Lockhart. 'It would take but a minute to fetch it and see what is the truth.'

'No, my lords!' There was a note of desperation in Mackenzie's voice now. Lauder knew that everything hung on this one issue: if Primrose and the other judges decided to send for the register, the King's counsellors would be exposed as liars. And it was Primrose, of course, who had set this whole thing up.

'It would certainly clarify matters,' said Primrose reflectively. 'I think –'

There was a sound from the gallery like a bull breaking through a fence. A voice bellowed into the court, drowning out whatever it was Primrose thought.

'Enough! That is enough!'

Silence followed, punctuated only by the patter of a few spots of saliva onto the floor and, from somewhere in the crowd, a hushed blasphemy. The thunder that had been building in the Duke of Lauderdale had finally broken.

For a moment he stood there, vast and swaying, as if he had surprised even himself and did not know what to say next. But then it was apparent that he was only pausing to gather breath before he roared again.

'I did not come here – these other noble persons did not come here – we were not brought hither to be accused of perjury. We came as witnesses, to give evidence, and that is what we have done. Now there's an end to it. And *you*' – glaring at Primrose and the other judges – *'you*, my lords, are not to call for the register of council. I forbid it. The Council's Acts are the King's secrets, and may not be looked into, not by this court or anyone but his counsellors. I trust I make myself clear.'

Lauderdale's tongue slapped once more round his lips and then retreated. He sat down heavily, still with his eye on the bench, and dared them to challenge him. Even Primrose, who had been so quick to shout down Sharp, seemed cowed by the Secretary's intervention.

John Lauder heard a voice muttering, *'This isna law, this is a mockery of the law.'* And then he realised that he was talking to himself. Elsewhere he could see other advocates whispering urgently, or sitting dumbstruck. The judges were in a huddle. Even those people unsure of what was going on could see that Primrose was in a passion, arguing that the register should be sent for. He seemed to have only one doubtful ally. Murray of Glendoick was adamantly opposed – if he wished to be confirmed as the next keeper of the register, he had better heed the instructions of his patron.

Lauder thought, is this what we are come down to? To a clutch of judges torn between pishing their breeks in the cause of justice, or keeping them dry in the cause of self-advancement? Is this the state of the law that I love?

In the end, there was no contest. The judges all had more to fear and more to gain from Lauderdale and Sharp than from the Justice General.

Primrose brought the court to order. The downturn of his mouth told all. He spoke like a man who has just swallowed a glass of sour milk.

'We find that the copy of the pretended Act of Council was never urged or made use of till this afternoon, after the swearing of the assize, and that it cannot be admitted as evidence in this state of the process by the law of the kingdom and practice of this court; also we find that the validity of the narrative of the copy is cancelled by the depositions of the noble witnesses. The court is adjourned. The assize will inclose, and return their verdict tomorrow at two o'clock in the afternoon.'

Uproar broke out. Primrose, without waiting for the mace-bearer, and followed by the other judges, fled the court.

'Ye canna imagine whit like this was,' Carlin said. 'The drama o it. These were the biggest names in Scottish life. It was like calling Michael Forsyth, Malcolm Rifkind, Lord James Douglas-Hamilton and the Moderator of the Church of Scotland tae gie evidence against some mad lone nationalist who's sent a couple o letter-bombs through the post. And seein them aw lie in their teeth.'

'The verdict was a foregone conclusion, presumably,' said Jackie.

'Aye.'

Carlin had been getting more animated throughout his description of the trial. Now it seemed he could contain himself no longer, but stood up and paced across the room two or three times. Jackie wondered if he was going to start flinging things about again. There was a pent-up frustration, an anger that seemed to have ignited from deep within him, in his movements. His feet caught a couple of paperbacks and sent them spinning across the floor, but he didn't notice them. Then suddenly he stopped in front of Jackie and spoke again.

'The jury finds him guilty on aw counts. Mitchel stands up, a wee bit sklent cause o his leg, and hears Adam Auld, the dempster o the coort, read oot that he's tae be hanged in the Grassmarket in eight days' time. Mitchel disna speak. He smiles. The weemun are greetin and shoutin, folk are pushin each ither aroon and batterin the furniture. The coort room is cleared. Mitchel's taen back tae his cell.'

'You're not really trying to tell me you did this, because of a trial three hundred years ago?' Jackie made a sweeping gesture across the strewn books and cowped television.

'I was ill,' said Carlin. 'I was in and oot o bed, fallin aboot, crashin intae things. I thought I went oot a couple o times but noo I'm no sure. God kens where I went. I don't really mind whit I was dreamin and whit I was daein. I guess I jist knocked things ower.'

'With a vengeance,' said Jackie. 'It looks like a tornado passed through.'

'Aye, well.' He hesitated. 'I was ayewis a vivid dreamer. I used tae sleepwalk when I was a wean.'

'Me too,' she said. 'But I grew out of it.'

'That can take time,' he said. 'Tae grow oot o things.'

She watched him turn to the fire, pick up the candlestick.

He raised it to shoulder level and looked at himself, then set it back on the shelf in its correct position. 'Jist kiddin,' she heard him say. Then he adjusted the mirror till it was straight, stood back, and returned to sit on the bed.

'Mirrors, eh,' he said. 'Canna live wi them, canna live athoot them.'

They sat and thought about that for a while. The room had grown dark. Jackie didn't really want to move. She was thinking about Andrew Carlin from an earlier time, when they had been students together. She felt guilty. Then she decided not to do that any more. That was all there was to it.

'Somethin weird happened the day,' said Carlin.

'Uhuh? You mean weirder than this?'

'I went tae speak tae somebody. In the public library. Somebody that had been helpin me oot wi researchin aw the stuff I was jist tellin ye aboot. And it turns oot I was mistaken. They said he didna work there.'

'Staff cutbacks,' said Jackie. 'Public service isn't what it used to be. Maybe that'll change after today.'

'Na, it wasna like he'd been made redundant. They denied he existed. Said there was nae such person. And that the book he'd gien me tae read didna exist either. Only I wasna mistaken. I spoke wi him. I read the book. They were baith there. But I canna prove it. I ken I'm tellin the truth but I've nae evidence except whit's in ma heid. And I've been thinkin aboot that and wonderin whit it means.'

'It means you have to watch yourself,' she said. 'Cause if you're not careful you get wiped out, de-registered, disappeared.' Then she realised he wasn't joking. And that maybe she wasn't either.

'Well, it looks like I'm niver gaun tae finish that book,' he said. 'A shame, that. I kinna wantit it tae tie up aw the loose ends.'

'That's what books are supposed to do,' she said. 'But life's not like that.'

'Aye, right,' he said. He sounded disappointed.

'I better get going,' she said. 'It's getting late.'

'Aye,' he said. 'I better get oot and vote.'

They stood up together. 'I'm not supposed to ask this,' she said. 'Secret ballot and all that. But how are you going to vote?'

'Wi ma feet,' he said. She watched as he found the plastic bag that contained Major Weir's cloak and wig, and the rat on a string. Going out to the front door he lifted the black staff from the corner where it was leaning. She'd not noticed it there before.

'Going to work then?' she said.

'Aye,' he said. 'Ye could say that.'

They went down the stairs together and out onto the street. When they got to Bruntsfield Place she slowed down. They were approaching a bus-stop.

'Think I'll wait here,' she said. 'It's too far to walk all the way home. I'm pretty tired.'

'Right,' he said. 'Well, thanks for comin by. I'm awright, as ye can see. Better, onywey.'

'Yeah,' she said. 'Me too. Thanks for telling me all that stuff. It was uh . . . interesting. I'd kind of forgotten that about history.'

He nodded. She felt ridiculous. She couldn't bear to see him walk away from her.

'Maybe see you for a drink some time?'

'Aye,' he said. 'See you around.'

He crossed the road and disappeared into the darkness of the Links. She was left considering the flat tone of his last three words, which conveyed no wish, no hesitation, no anticipation, only a statement of fact, or of probability.

It wasn't until she was sitting on the bus that it occurred to her that, for a man who lived in Bruntsfield, he had been heading in entirely the wrong direction if he intended to get to the polling place before it closed.

Edinburgh, 10, 11 January 1678

John Lauder attended court to hear the verdict against Mitchel on the Thursday, then went home, locked himself in his study, and turned up a new page of his journal. He was limping slightly, from a bruise on his leg where he had been kicked in the struggle to get out of court the day before. The case was fascinating from a jurisprudential point of view. He would fill several pages with the arguments, the technicalities, the points scored and lost on both sides. He should write it down before he forgot the details. But as he was thinking this his enthusiasm waned. He closed the book again – he would do it later. For the time being, he had an urge to write of the other thing he had seen in the court-room: the state, a huge, bejewelled, white-bellied monster, devouring a broken and deluded man.

He pitied Mitchel. He pitied him even though he well understood that a fanatic did not ask for pity. And yet when Lauder thought of Mitchel it was not his cause, not his strength, not his faith, but the pity he inspired that dignified him. You could have all the politics and religion and philosophy and learning the world could take – and you needed these things to imagine the world and see how it was – but it was not these things that were locked up and left to rot in the Bass, or brought back from there to be hanged. It was a man. If he lost his pity for the man, Lauder thought, he would lose some essential part of himself. He would himself become less human.

He did not wish to think about the following Friday. Mitchel would glorify God in the Grassmarket. That, apparently, had been Lauderdale's bad joke when, after the court adjourned, he and his fellow Privy Councillors had retreated upstairs to the Council chamber. There they had discovered, in the register, the fact that they had promised Mitchel his life recorded in black and white. The clerks of Council were aware of it; Sir John Nisbet, who had been removed as King's Advocate to make way for Mackenzie, also knew it and was busy broadcasting it to those who wished to hear. They could tear the page out but they could not erase their perjury.

Lauderdale had set about some damage limitation already. George Hickes, his chaplain, was even now writing an account of the whole affair, to be published as a pamphlet as soon as possible. Hickes's task was to depict Mitchel in the worst possible light. Lauder had heard that he was seeking information on how close the fanatic had been to that monstrous hypocrite, Major Weir. How he would love to hear Lauder's story: well, he could whistle for it! Other rhymers and scribes were being encouraged to make up verses linking the two men, and to recite and sell them on the streets. There was a week to go before the execution, but the machinery of malice was clanking into motion already.

Would Sharp sleep any easier in his bed tonight? He had what he had wanted for so long – Mitchel's neck ready for the tow. But now that Mitchel was about to be removed from the world, might he not make room for another to take his place? If I were the Archbishop, Lauder thought, I would double-lock my doors from now on.

Jean Weir came into his mind too. There had been a daft kind of logic to her. He would need to talk to Eleis about that, once he'd sorted his thoughts out on paper, and once Eleis had come to terms with losing the Mitchel case. But he probably had already – he wasn't a man for dwelling on the past, and it had been more Lockhart's show than his. Lauder should probably seek him out, take him to Painton's for a few hours.

Eleis and Jean weren't so far apart, maybe. He was cool and calculating and rational, and she was the very opposite. But Jean had talked of a place where there were no witches, or where everyone could be a witch in safety, and Eleis saw somewhere like that ahead of him too.

Lauder knew that his cousin, though he would have to be gotten very drunk in a private place to come out and say it, didn't believe in God. Himself, he couldn't let go of the idea. He needed some greater thing outside of himself in order to be able to understand the world, and himself in it. God was a fearful presence, but Lauder worried for the world without him. Eleis, on the other hand, longed for a world rid of all gods.

There were so many wanderers in the world: deceivers and deceived, folk that planned and organised and folk that scuttered through life, the ones that seized the moment and the ones that were seized by it. He thought of Jean Weir and of Jonet Douglas, who was dumb and then did speak. The old and the young, the accused and the accusing. The Privy Council had not been able to decide how to deal with Jonet: in the end they had banished her, but then the problem of how to get her out of the country arose, for few skippers would take such an unchancy cargo on board. But there was always somebody with a price. At great expense, a ship had been found at the back-end of the year, and the lass was away now supposedly, gone to oblivion or to new tricks across the sea.

If, back in 1670, Jean Weir had been Jonet's age – if she had been capable of making a new life for herself – Lauder would have liked to have smuggled her off to that other land, wherever it was. Somewhere in everything that had happened was an answer to the riddle he had posed to his cousin. But it was too late, eight years too late, and he wondered if in fact that was how men always came to an understanding of the times in which they lived: too late. And now, even for himself, the years were beginning to pile up. He felt a growing need to sum up, to explain, to record his thoughts and his memories. He was – even in his thirties – entering his middle-age.

He reached for another, smaller book, one with its pages still blank and uninked. If he took his quill and began to write, how, where would he begin, to make sense of it all?

10th day of Januar 1678 – I am just now returned from the tryal of James Mitchel at the Criminall Court. He was pannelled for attempting the life of the Archbischop of St Androis. This tryal is the sum and end of many bad things, that I have sein and heard thir last ten years, whilk I maun putt doune tho I fear to doe it. Unsemely and stinking are the wayes emploied to

sicker this man's doom, but soe is al thats gane befoir. I am
sweert to write anent this afair in my other journal. This is ane
new and secret book.

Elizabeth Sommervile, sister of Nicol, wife to James Mitchel,
lay in her bed in a house in the Canongate, sick with the
fever. The house was quiet. The silence pressed in on her, but
at the edges of it she could hear the sounds of the city,
strangely muted. Her brother had promised to come to her as
soon as the verdict was announced. But she did not need him
to come. She knew what the verdict would be.

Nicol had still not given up all hope. If James were found
guilty, he had told her that morning, she must write a letter
to the Privy Council at once. She must explain that she was
sick, had been confined in childbirth, and could not attend
the trial, had not even been able to see her husband since he
was brought back from the Bass. She must beg for a stay of
execution, on grounds of humanity, at least until such time
as she was well enough to visit James and say her farewells.
And to show him the bairn, Nicol added, it was important for
James that he saw and blessed the bairn. Meanwhile, he
would talk to Eleis and Lockhart, to see if there was anything
else that could be done. An appeal to the King, perhaps. And
some of the ladies of the town were talking of a subscription,
to raise money for her and the bairn.

'They'll no see the seed of the righteous beggin their breid,'
said Nicol. 'That's whit they tellt me.'

'It's frae the Psalms,' Lizzie said weakly. She would take
the money if it came, she'd be mad not to, but she was
scunnered of Scripture, endlessly quoted at every opportunity.
And as for farewells, she had said her farewells. She had said
them nine months ago, in the stinking hole on a rock in the
sea where they had kept James for a year. If she were to see
him again now, she would not be able to comfort him, relieve
him from whatever pain he was in. She would want to
ask him a question, one that would only anger him or
make him sorrowful. She would ask him if it was worth
anything: the love of Christ for which he had tried to kill,
and for which he was to be killed. She would ask him if it
was worth more than the love she had once given him.

He would not be able to answer. He would only be able to stare ahead of himself and see the coming kingdom. If he took his eyes off it for one second, as she had, he might lose sight of it altogether. And all his certainty would be lost, as hers was.

She believed she was a better person for her uncertainty. She did not want his blessing on the bairn. She did not want her growing up touched by the hand of a martyr or a fanatic. Whatever these words meant, she wanted them not to mean anything for her daughter.

She did not know what she would tell the bairn about her father, or how and where she was conceived. When she grew up, who would she look like? Like her mother? Or would there be something in her face, some shadow, that would link her to that day in the Bass? She thought again of James and how he had clasped Rutherford's book to himself when she left. She thought of Tammas, holding her back, saying they must wait a minute before going down to the boat, that they must not be seen coming from Maister Mitchel's cell. She wondered if even their seed had fought in her: the seed of the righteous and the seed of whatever Tammas was. She thought how little it mattered, which one of them was the father.

She would write the letter, as Nicol suggested. She would do it because it was expected of her. The last thing that was expected of her: after that, nothing. And nothing would come of it – the men that wanted James dead would discard her letter as a concoction of sentiment and deceit. So she would wait. Then one day very soon, they would drum James down to the Grassmarket and he would make a speech and they would kill him. And all the waiting would be over.

She was going to get better. The bairn was beside the bed in a crib, sleeping. Lizzie could hear the anxious wee breaths that it made. It had come early by nearly three weeks, but like her it was fighting to stay in the world. Lizzie would get better and her daughter would survive. When they were both well enough, they would leave. With whatever siller they were given, and whatever she could scrape together, and with anything that she could sell on the way – tobacco, ribbon, cloth, anything – she and the bairn would go away from here. England, Europe, America, maybe some other part of Scotland, she did not know where, but they would set out on a journey and sooner or later they would arrive.

In the Tolbooth, James Mitchel sat writing his death speech, his last address to the Christian people of Scotland. He was not often interrupted, as he was allowed visits only from his lawyers, ministers and his immediate family. The lawyers could do nothing more for him: he dismissed them. The date of his execution would not be changed. As for ministers, any that he might have wished to see could not come near him – they were in exile or in hiding. He received a letter from a Mr Annand, the dean of Edinburgh, offering to attend upon him notwithstanding their theological differences. Mitchel wrote him a stinging reply, thanking him for his civility and affection, rejecting his offer, and hoping that God would open his eyes to his wickedness and to his insulting of an unjustly condemned dying man. He was beyond ministers of all colours. He stood alone. He had precisely seven days to perfect his final act of glory.

As for family, Nicol had come, but Lizzie was too ill. They had a daughter, Nicol told him; she too was very weak. Lizzie would bring her into him whenever she was able. They were trying to get the hanging postponed.

Mitchel shook his head. He did not want any more delay, he told Nicol. He had been kept waiting for four years. If Lizzie could not come, she could not come. He was beyond her now. He hoped, though, that she and the lassie would live and prosper in a better Scotland than the one he was about to leave.

He wrote his speech over and over, until he had it right – not so long that he would not be able to read it all, but long enough to make all the points he wanted to. He knew in any case that the government had learned the political dangers of executions. It was likely that when he began speaking the drums would be beaten to drown him out. So when he had the speech to his satisfaction he copied it out half a dozen times so that he could throw it to the crowd. Somebody, surely, would recognise its worth and have it reprinted. He kept another copy with his private papers to be returned to

Lizzie. In this way, he hoped, his testimony would be preserved for posterity.

I have been before a court set up within me of terrors and challenges, he read in Rutherford, *but my sweet Lord Jesus hath taken the mask off his face and said, 'Kiss thy fill!'; and I will not smother nor conceal the kindness of my King Jesus. He hath broken in upon the poor prisoner's soul like the swelling of Jordan. The Bridegroom's love hath run away with my heart. O love, love, love! How sweet were it to me to swim the salt sea for my new Lover, my second Husband, my first Lord . . .*

After all else, he had nothing to do but read his Bible and pray. He understood now why God had made him miss Sharp with the pistol. What had happened to him since then had been a far greater test of his faith. And his trial and death, for *not* having killed the Archbishop, did this not show God's people the true spirit of their enemies in an even harsher light? God was magnificent, incomprehensibly clever. He was about to do James Mitchel the greatest honour, and raise him up as upon a cross. It was the most a true Christian could hope for.

At night he dozed fitfully, but sleep was an irritant to him now, not a relief, an animal function that he did not want and scarcely needed. He kept awake as much as he could, concentrating on the day ahead, the blazing light that was coming for him. He did not dream, either in waking or in sleep. He was past dreaming. All he wanted was to go through death and into eternal life.

He had never been a great singer, but now he filled the cell with his voice, and it seemed to him melodious and powerful, drowning out the shouts and bangs of others in the building, who were already far distant from him. He sang the psalms of his childhood, not the newer versions that had come in in Cromwell's time, but the ones he had learned as a boy from the minister who had held him on the bridge at Linlithgow all those years ago, whose language, that of the reforming fathers of Knox's day, was sweet and unchanging and came from an age when Scotland had been smiled upon by God. In their simplicity they outstripped even the wisdom of Samuel Rutherford. He did not know what language he would speak in Heaven, but he hoped that when he finally limped in through the yett, one of Christ's good bairns, he would not have to change one word of them for all eternity.

> *The Lord is only my support,*
> *And he that doth me feed:*
> *How can I then lack any thing*
> *Whereof I stand in need.*
>
> *He doth me fold in coats most safe,*
> *The tender grass fast by:*
> *And after driv'th me to the streams,*
> *Which run most pleasantly.*
>
> *And when I feel myself near lost,*
> *Then doth he me home take:*
> *Conducting me in his right paths,*
> *Even for his own name's sake.*
>
> *And though I were even at death's door,*
> *Yet would I fear none ill:*
> *For with thy rod, and shepherd's crook,*
> *I am comforted still.*
>
> *Thou hast my table richly decked,*
> *In despite of my foe:*
> *Thou hast mine head with balm refreshed,*
> *My cup doth overflow.*
>
> *And finally, while breath doth last,*
> *Thy grace shall me defend:*
> *And in the house of God will I*
> *My life for ever spend.*

Edinburgh, 1 May 1997

There was no guarantee that he would find her. The homeless lass, Karen. It would be a week or more since he'd disturbed her sleep. She'd probably got fed up being disturbed by the tour going past her every night, and moved on. But he still thought it was worth looking.

He was early though. It was a few minutes before nine o'clock when he walked up Stevenlaw's Close – she'd hardly have gone to her bed yet, surely. There was no sign of her at the patch of concrete, not a blanket or a plastic poke in sight. He was wasting his time. She could be anywhere. Maybe she wasn't even in the city any longer. Maybe she'd headed off into the country, now that spring was here. If he was homeless, he wouldn't want to hang around in the hard, dirty streets when he could be living out in the hills or down by the sea. He had that thought, and as soon as he had it he saw what a romantic, fake version of someone else's life it was. The hills were big and splendid for a day's walk, or a winter trek in the right gear, but they were cold and brutal most of the time. The city was where there was shelter from the rain, money to be begged or borrowed, food to be cadged or bought or stolen. In the city there were others like you. Life was there. Outside it, a person could starve or freeze to death and nobody would know.

He walked up through the square and onto the High Street. Quite often there were folk hanging out behind the Tron Kirk, in Hunter Square. People like Karen that she might be among or that might know her. He laughed out loud and a couple who looked like tourists passed him with frightened stares. The way he was thinking of her. *People like Karen*. It was rich coming from him.

A wee bit up the street was where the tour started. He could see some people milling about. He didn't want to be around these parts very long. He didn't want to run into Hardie.

But there was nobody at Hunter Square. The daytime crew had gone. He sat on a bench there and wondered what to do. He could always vote: there was still an hour left; but this wasn't about a vote. It wasn't about anything much – he could just chuck the stuff away if he wanted. He didn't owe Hardie anything, and Hardie didn't owe him.

He didn't want to meet Hardie, have to explain things that the tosser wouldn't understand anyway. He didn't want to have to tell him about Weir, who he really was, and then leave the cloak, stick and rat so that Weir could become Hardie's puppet again. And behind Weir there was Mitchel. Carlin felt in some way he had set them both free and that they didn't need somebody going around play-acting on their behalf. But if somebody who knew nothing about Weir, made no pretence of knowing anything about him, could make use of his trappings, maybe that would be different. History would just go on then, run into the present unwittingly. And Carlin could walk away from it.

That was why he had thought of Karen. But how was he going to find her?

He found a biro in his pocket, settled the carrier bag on his knee, smoothed a clear white portion of it over the bulk of the cloak inside, and began to write.

Dear Karen, this stuff is for you. There's a ghost tour comes by here every night about 10. You can earn £5 every night before you go to sleep by wearing this gear and jumping out at them. Talk to the guide. His name is Gerry.

A. Carlin.

He went down Blair Street to the Cowgate and back along to where he'd found her before. He tried to picture where she'd been lying, how far in, how well concealed. He placed the carrier where it was visible but only if you were looking closely, and laid the staff beside it. The message was face up but you couldn't read it in the darkness.

He wasn't fooling himself. She might never find the stuff and even if she did she might just think it was garbage. But he would leave the things anyway. They might stay there or they might not. Karen or somebody else might recognise them or they might attach their own new story to them. It was the best Carlin could do in the circumstances.

He walked away slowly and headed for home. He wasn't carrying anything any more. That was his vote. You had to leave things behind. You had to shed the guilt and start again. You had to stop thinking everything was your fault or you'd not ever be able to go out and make mistakes again.

He went by the familiar sights and ticked them off in his head. He felt better about himself than he had done in a long long time.

Edinburgh, May 1997

This happens later. In a few days, after everything else is over. We don't really see this, it is beyond the last page, but then again, it would be a pity to miss it.

Hugh Hardie is not a happy man. He is trying to train a new ghost, and the ghost is slow to learn. It is a bright, warm afternoon, but Hugh is not impressed with the change in the weather. He just wants to get his show on the road again, by this evening if possible.

The ghost is a student, the younger brother of a guy he knows that he bumped into in a pub. The student needs some extra money. Hugh needs a ghost and he can't afford to be choosy. But he can't help thinking of Carlin as the new Major Weir trips over his cloak, walks too fast, pulls the rat too soon, keeps breaking into smiles. Carlin the natural weirdo, the born spook. Carlin the magnificently eerie. Carlin the disappearing, the unreliable. Carlin the bastard who made off with Hugh's gear, which has cost considerably more than twenty pounds to replace. Carlin whose absence for nearly two weeks has robbed the tour of its essence, its magic, and forced Hugh to reduce the ticket price by a pound.

He tries not to dwell on the past. It's over, he and Carlin are finished. It was a mistake getting him involved in the first place and Hugh should have seen the likely problems a mile off. Jackie warned him but he paid no attention. He's blown it with her too, she's not been back in touch and why should she?

A guy like Carlin was always going to be trouble – too eccentric, too resistant, too determined to question and query and not just shut up and get on with the job in hand. And yet, and yet, he had the touch. He could have been perfect, but he wasn't. He was untrustworthy, irresponsible, a time-waster. Hugh just has to forget about him.

But he can't. He watches the boy's amateur dramatics

attempts at looking ghostly and he almost despairs. Carlin didn't even try, for God's sake. He just *was*. If Hugh can only find out where he lives . . . No, there's no point, the only reason he wants to see him now is to give him abuse and get the props back. But he doesn't even need those now. One thing's for sure, this new kid's getting his first pay docked, by twenty pounds at least. Maybe thirty pounds. He looks docile enough, looks like he'll accept that that's the way it goes these days if you want cash in hand, no questions asked.

A few times in the last week or so, Hugh thinks he's seen Carlin. A sudden movement glimpsed out of the corner of one eye. He's turned quickly and there's been no one there. It might be in a crowd, or in a shop, and once it was as he was walking along Nicolson Street, and he thought he caught a glimpse of a bald, cloaked figure vanishing into a side-street. A lot of crap really, he knows. There are no such things as ghosts, not even of the Carlin variety.

He takes the boy up Stevenlaw's Close and brings him out onto Tron Square. He explains the stage that the tour has got to. 'Meanwhile,' he says, 'you'll have gone on ahead. Into one of those closes over there. Gerry will tell the party a few stories at this point, and then bring them round and along at the back of the buildings. That's when you emerge from whichever entry you're hiding in and scare the life out of them.'

There are two women sitting over from them on a bench in one corner of the square. They are watching the toff and the young lad in the funny outfit. Both of them are smoking. Occasionally one passes a comment to the other.

'And what do I do?' says the boy.

Hugh explains, grinding patience in his teeth. 'You are Major Weir, you are terrifying, Gerry has wound them up like springs, all you need to do is put on your ghastliest expression and come out at them. It'll be dark, remember. I want you to extract the maximum volume scream when you confront them.'

'Oh,' says the boy. He thinks about this for a minute. 'Like this, you mean.' He emits a hysterical shriek that ends in a parody of demoniac laughter.

'No,' says Hugh. 'I don't want *you* to scream. I want you to make *them* scream.'

'Oh, right,' says the boy. 'I thought you wanted me to extract a scream.'

'From them,' says Hugh. 'What did you say you were studying again?'

'EngLit,' says the boy.

'Right,' says Hugh. 'Well, anyway, let's try it. You go up there, and I'll walk you through it.'

One of the women gets up. She throws her fag-end on the ground and stands on it. She looks about fifty. She's wearing a cardigan over a tee-shirt and a bulging pair of leggings. She waddles over to Hugh as the Major wanders off.

'Is this you practisin then, is it?' she asks.

'Yes, it is,' says Hugh. 'I'm training him.'

'Ma daughter there,' says the woman, jerking her thumb back – the other woman gives Hugh a brief wee wave of her hand, then stands up and goes into one of the tenements – 'was jist wonderin, ken. Are you one o thae ghostie tours then, that comes by here maist nights?'

'That's right,' says Hugh.

'Aboot ten o'clock?' The woman is eyeing him steadily.

'About then, yeah. Is that a problem?'

'No for me,' she says. 'I dinna stey here. It's ma daughter that steys here. We were jist wonderin.'

'Well, then,' says Hugh. He steps past her. 'If you don't mind, I've got work to do.'

He doesn't mean to be rude, but he's aware it probably sounds that way to her. The intonation is all wrong. He tries again. 'I mean, if that's all you were wanting.' He knows he is making it worse.

'Aye, that's fine, son,' she says. 'On ye go.' She stands aside, gets out another fag and lights it.

Hugh calls up to Major Weir. 'Ready?' There is a muffled cry in response.

'All right.'

He starts to walk across the square. He feels self-conscious with the woman watching him. Then he puts her out of his mind. 'I've finished the talk,' he says loudly. 'I'm leading them up towards Assembly Close. Now I'm directing them along this path. It's dark, remember, they can't see exactly where they're going. You can hear them stumbling along towards you. Here they come. Now, any second now –'

Major Weir steps out of his hiding-place. As he does so, there is the sound of a window being opened above them. Hugh glances up. He sees a bucket held out over the window-sill, upside down, directly over his head. A bucket-shaped quantity of wetness is falling, spreading into a shimmering sheet in the sunlight. Major Weir steps smartly back under cover. Hugh Hardie is baptised in a gallon and a half of cold water.

The woman in the square marches past his dripping figure. 'That,' she says, 'is whit they uised tae dae in the aulden days. Ma daughter's had it up tae here wi yous. Every night, every bluidy night, jist as she's got her bairn aff tae sleep, you come along here and wake it up wi aw yer daft screamin. Have ye nae consideration for others? I mean, whit the hell dae ye think this is, a fairground or somethin?'

She doesn't wait for an answer. She marches on inside. A few moments later droukit Hugh and dry Weir hear a door slamming and a loud peal of female laughter.

Major Weir comes out but stands well back while Hugh shakes himself like a dog.

'That was amazing,' says the Major. 'A direct hit.' He is looking at his employer with a new awe. 'But,' he says, 'I don't suppose that happens every night. I mean, does it?'

Edinburgh, 2 May 1997

A strange figure was coming down North Bridge towards the east end of Princes Street. It was too small for itself. It was an old man's head on a young woman's body.

The woman was thin and frail-looking and was shuffling a little awkwardly, as if unused to the clothes she was wearing. The black cloak around her was too big and kept catching under her feet. She had to hoist it up and grip it in a bunch at her waist. She also had to manage the long black stick with the knuckle-ended top, which was as tall as herself and seemed to be conspiring with the cloak to make life difficult for her. And there was the baldy-heid wig that sat too loosely on her head: the brow of it was forever slipping forward, cutting her vision in half. The grey wisps of hair stuck out crazily above her ears, and from below the wrinkles of the false head her own brown hair escaped in dirty-looking straggles. It was ten past nine in the morning and the sun was shining as she made her way uncertainly past the queuing cars and buses to the junction at the foot of the bridge.

Aye, the sun was shining. The wee figure waited for the green man, then stumbled across Princes Street. Folk were going to work, in the same direction as her and in the opposite direction. Shops were opening or already open. Folk were late but few of them were running and many had smiles on their faces. The woman didn't know why they looked so pleased with themselves.

She'd been asleep, more or less, all night in a close deep in the Old Town. She'd woken and sat smoking her last roll-up in the early morning sun. When the baccy started to burn her fingers she'd nipped it and flung it away. That was her quit, she'd thought, the way she always did when she smoked her last, just to make herself feel positive about the loss. Then she'd decided, if it was going to be a fine day, to head for the shore. She couldn't quite think why but she always liked it down there in the sunshine, even though she couldn't afford to sit drinking wine or coffee at the tables outside the expensive new cafes. She'd packed her blanket and the few other items she wasn't wearing in a plastic poke, and stashed them in a recess where they were safely hidden. Then she'd considered the new rig-out she'd acquired, and decided to put it on.

She'd found it in another poke which she'd thrown away. At first she'd thought the stuff was from a theatre. Then she'd minded the guy from the ghost tour: it looked like his outfit. Funny, until she'd pulled out the wig she'd almost forgotten about him; he'd been like something out of a dream. The wig was like one of those things folk brought back from other worlds in fairy tales: proof that they must have been there. There'd been a rat in the poke too. She'd not much liked the rat, and halfway up the close she left it sitting at the bottom of a rone-pipe, to give someone a start. But the rest of the gear, she quite fancied it. It made her want to laugh. Plus it might be worth something; she wasn't going to just leave it lying around.

She picked up speed on the slope past the St James shopping centre. It was a monstrosity that place, but she didn't really notice it too much because the weather was good – the first really good day for a week or two. She did notice the big bronze Paolozzi sculptures, though – the foot with its smooth toes you could slide on if you were a wean, which just polished them smoother, the ankle like a tree-stump, the outstretched hand with the huge grasshoppers, or locusts or whatever they were, mating in its palm. She made a figure-of-eight around the sculptures because she liked their outsizeness. And she liked the fact that you could come from Leith and be called Eduardo Paolozzi; or be called Paolozzi and come from Leith. She said it aloud a few times, enjoying the sound of it: 'Eduardo, Eduardo, Eduardo.' There was a man in four overcoats lying asleep in the lea of the muckle hand.

She breenged on. When she crossed at the next set of lights, she noticed that Mr Sherlock Holmes, up on his plinth in his Inverness cape and holding his curly pipe, had had a wild night and was wearing not one but two traffic cones on his head. And here were more people smiling, as they went late to their work. Some of them looked tired, a wee bit hungover maybe. Some of them looked drunk.

The faster you went, the less the cloak tripped you, that was what she found. You could let it go and it just swirled out behind you like a steam-train's plume of smoke, only black. And the big stick, you could manage it by letting it run through your hand like a pole-vaulter's pole, plonking the end down a couple of feet in front of you, your hand going down, then up, lifting the stick and repeating the movement. It was all in the rhythm. And it made a satisfying tapping noise every few steps you took. And the bald head, you just pushed it back a bit, so that your own hair escaped and held it up. You looked a bit mad probably, but you couldn't see yourself and anyway you didn't care what people thought.

Some folk were giving her the eye but most weren't. She wasn't so weird. She crossed over the road to Elm Row because she liked to stick her head in at Valvona's and inhale the coffee and cheese smells. She passed boards outside newsagents that had terrible words on them – DISASTER, WIPE-OUT, LANDSLIDE, ANNIHILATED – and she remembered about the election. For once these were good words, they meant the news that people were smiling about. She went into a shop and read the front pages of a couple of papers, getting the gist of the night's events.

She'd not voted because she wasn't on the electoral roll, she was of no fixed abode, but it seemed the folk with homes had done something pretty amazing. About time though. It had only taken them eighteen years to decide they didn't like the Tories any more. Plenty of them had done well enough in the eighties. Ach well, she couldn't complain, maybe she'd have taken the money and run too if she'd ever been in their shoes.

A wee spring came into her step, in spite of herself. She felt pretty good. It would wear off of course, the new government would be bound to make an arse of things, it would be simpler to return to the old standby of grinding the faces of the poor, folk would go back to being disappointed, dulled out – but today was different. A wee sensation in the air. Something had changed.

Someone shouted at her, 'Hey hen, who are you, the

301

grim reaper?' And someone else shouted, 'She's too late if she is, they're aw deid. Aw the Tories.' She wondered if she'd notice the difference, and thought it unlikely.

She crossed the road again because the sun was brighter on the other side in the morning. Faster and faster she went down Leith Walk, the big wide pavement spreading out before her in Haddington Place. There was a grey polis box, like the Tardis in *Doctor Who*, all closed up and padlocked. The polis didn't use the boxes any more. You used to see bobbies brewing tea and reading the paper in them but not these days. Funny how you always thought polis boxes were like the Tardis. There must have been a time when people thought the Tardis was like a polis box. She wondered, if she could get inside that box would it open up into something much bigger? Would it take her off in time somewhere? In other parts of the city someone was buying up the polis boxes and turning them into wee coffee kiosks. One day fathers would point them out to their weans and say, 'See aw thae coffee kiosks, years ago they used tae be Tardises.'

On past the bus depot. On the hill next to it was where they used to hang the poor in the old days. Hang 'em and burn 'em. They still dealt with the poor there today, only now it was Shrubhill House, the social work department. Ha. Even her cynicism felt good this morning. She could see the blue band of sea ahead of her, and above it the coast of Fife. The sun was shining over there too, and there wasn't a trace of haar in the firth. Something was right. Someone was smiling on them all from up above.

Not that she believed in any of that. Religion. Religion was a terrible thing, it had been the cause of more trouble in the world than anything. But you almost could, on a day like this, you could almost believe in it. God's in his Heaven and all's right with the world. It was a day of possibilities.

She crossed the line which had once been the burgh boundary between Edinburgh and Leith. The pub licences were weird down here. Folk had a pint for their breakfast and went to work at ten at night. Dockers, postal workers, nightshifters of all kinds. And here were some folk stauchering out of the Walk Inn, dazzled by the brightness. They were laughing and singing. Out of their faces. Not sad, the way really drunk people usually looked to her. Happy people. She looked at them, a few men and a couple of women. They didn't look like they'd been sorting mail all night. She keeked in through the door of the pub as she floated past and saw the backs of men lined up at the bar, reading the *Record* and the *Sun*. Smoke hung in drifts between the ceiling and the men's heads. They would be there every morning, whatever had happened the day before. *They* were the workers, not these drunk folk skailing onto the street.

They must have been up all night watching the election, she thought as she met them. They must have drunk their house dry. Then they'd had to hit the pub. They'd probably been there since five or whenever it opened.

They were jubilant. Their laughter was infectious. She jouked in among them, striking the pavement with her staff, stepping out. 'Hey! Brilliant!' they said to her. 'Is it no brilliant?' They must have thought she was a show or something. A mascot.

'Brilliant!' she agreed, and she stormed on down to the Foot o the Walk. They'd be off to their beds, but not her. That was one thing about the shore, though: out beyond the restaurants, by the docks, there were old bits of wooden wharfing where you could sit and doze in the sunshine, and nobody came near you or bothered you. You could catch up on your sleep there, with just the sound of water lapping under you and the noises of men and ships somewhere a little distance away.

There was always a big cargo ship tied up, loading or unloading. And other, smaller ships, that were about to set off somewhere or that had just arrived. She liked the idea of that. She minded there was an old ship due to come into Leith any day now. Or rather, it was a new version of an old ship. Captain Cook's *Endeavour*, that had sailed to Australia in seventeen something or other. Somebody had reconstructed it, and was sailing it round the world as a kind of tribute. Or to see how Cook had done it, or maybe just to prove he'd done it. Something like that. She wanted to see the tall ship. If it wasn't in today she'd have to come back for it.

That was something to look forward to anyway. The thought of it: the tiny wooden shell that men had stepped into two hundred years ago and taken to the end of the earth. You'd feel your way along familiar coasts and then you'd be off into the unknown. You'd go blindly but you'd keep an eye out. If you kept going forward you would eventually get to a place you recognised.

Portobello, 2 May 1997

A couple of miles to the east, several hours later, Carlin stepped onto the sand at Portobello and went down towards the water. He'd gone into the city centre in the morning, and in the sunshine the walking had seemed so easy, and his mind so empty, that he had just kept going, down the Mile, past Holyrood, through the Park and out by Jock's Lodge to the sea. The lamp-posts were covered with election posters. The billboards proclaimed a new era. He went by them all, scarcely noticing. And then at some point he was walking down one of the narrow streets in Portobello that led to the promenade, and there was the firth with the light glinting on it, and the beach with a few figures walking their dogs between the breakwaters, a handful of children running, a woman pushing a buggy along the hard sand.

The coast stretched away before him. Musselburgh, Cockenzie power station, the Berwick Law; and there, away on the horizon, was a speck just detached from the land. Was that the Bass? No, surely not. He didn't recall seeing it from here before: on a map it looked like it would be off round the next corner. But the lines on a map were clear and distinct, whereas the sea and sky met in a blur, and the speck seemed too faded and far off to be real. After a while he could not focus his eyes on it properly.

Puerto Bello. Some old sea-dog had built a house here and named it after a Caribbean town he'd helped capture from the Spanish in the War of Jenkins' Ear. For fuck's sake. That had to be the stupidest fucking excuse for a war ever. A lug in a jeelie-jaur. What did anybody get out of it? Well, Edinburgh had got a seaside suburb with a name that – today anyway, in the warm sunshine – suited it.

Carlin felt a kind of dull elation. It was nothing to do with the election result. Yesterday he'd been telling Jackie Halkit about the Mitchel trial, about Lauderdale and Sharp and the others being like Forsyth and Rifkind. Today the Tories were all gone: if he told the trial again he'd have to substitute a bunch of new names. One gang for another. It wouldn't change the story one bit; wouldn't change the outcome. And yet people had voted for a change. Whatever they got, change was what they had voted for. In a way the mood, the expectation, was the most important thing about it.

But the wee surge of feeling he felt in his chest was something else: something about coming to the edge of the land. He always pictured the beach here as grey, but in fact the soft sand above the highwater mark was reddish, and the flat, streaky expanse below it shone in the sun. His steps left only slight indentations beyond the tideline. He stopped a few feet from the sea and watched it slap the beach with thin, lazy waves. It had always been doing that, would go on doing that, whether or not there was anybody there to watch. The sea did not care: it was indifferent to anything that might happen on the land which it defined. When Carlin went away, the sea would come up, thoughtless, and wipe out every trace of him.

His father was gone, his mother was gone. All that was left of them was in his head. And that would never be complete. However much he wanted to, he would never know, never understand their secret lives. However much he thought that the knowledge would help, would tie up loose ends, it never would. Jackie was right: life was all loose ends. The past was never over, the future had always begun. That was the terrifying thing: there was no end to life. Like the sea, it was utterly oblivious of you.

The only thing was to be recognised by someone else, however much of yourself you kept hidden. To touch somebody, and not be forgotten by them. And to remember them also. It might be a feeble, helpless, tiny gesture, but it was something. An acknowledgement, a sign that you had once existed.

He turned around. The sun was in his face and the figures further up the beach flickered in the light. Above them beyond the promenade the houses looked bleached and ancient. He wondered who was seeing him there against the sea. If there was anyone looking at all.

These things could make you depressed. And yet he felt good. He thought of Jackie. He would see her again, or he would not. There was nothing more to it. But he would always have her in his head, along with all the others. That was the best, the most human thing, that you could do for another person: not forget them.

There was a kind of comfort in the way he was. He saw the worlds shifting and sliding over one another. You could slip between them. You could feel them moving through you. It was an amazing, miraculous feeling, if you only had the time for it. That was what you had to have: time.

He made his way back off the sand. It was a couple of years since he'd been here, but he knew where he was going. The amusement arcade was still standing, but a bit battered looking, as though it might not last for ever. He wanted to go inside before it wasn't there any more.

It was full of machines, old and new, and a cacophony of electronic bleeps, explosions, jingles and background music. Carlin had no interest in the sparkling, jazzed up fruit-machines, the racing simulators and war games. He was drawn to the older installations, operated by coins that had almost no value any more: one-armed bandits with three reels spinning in their metallic chests, clunking up Xs, Os and bars; penny falls with great heaps of copper that seemed as though they must tumble with every forward sweep that the machines made. He went up to the cashier's booth and changed a couple of pounds for two plastic cupfuls of tuppences. They were weighty in his hands as he turned away. It seemed unlikely that he could ever get rid of them all.

He could spend hours in there, losing himself in the ebb and flow motion of the falls, in the clanking repetition of the bandits, scooping up his winnings and feeding them back in, giving himself over to the endless, broken rhythms of the place. There would be other people standing first at one machine, then at another; moving among them; passing each other as if in dreams. Carlin knew he would lose all his money but it didn't matter: that wasn't why he was there.

When he put the last coin down the last chute he would find he'd hardly spent a thing. For a while, it would be as though time had slowed to the pace it had had when he was a child. When he stepped back out into the afternoon, he would have to be grateful for that and then let it go. And outside, the people, the houses, the cars, the city and the long walk back into it, for a while at least they would be what was real.

A Historical Note and Acknowledgements

Most of the seventeenth-century characters in this novel were real people. As usual, history has recorded far more about those at the upper end of the social ladder, especially men, than about those further down, especially women. I have been unable to discover, for example, what happened to Elizabeth Mitchel after her husband's death, and indeed most of what happens to her in this book is invented.

By contrast, we know exactly what happened to James Sharp. The Archbishop's triumph over his would-be assassin did not last long. On 3 May 1679, while travelling in his coach towards St Andrews, he was overtaken by a group of nine Covenanters on Magus Muir, dragged from the vehicle and murdered in front of his daughter. Before they killed him, his attackers declared that they were acting in part to avenge the death of James Mitchel.

Sharp's murder was the final blow to the Duke of Lauderdale's crumbling authority in Scotland. The government reacted with extreme violence against all non-conformists, and several years of persecution ensued which became known in the folklore of the south-west as the Killing Times. Lauderdale was dismissed from office and died unlamented in 1682.

I have taken many liberties with the character and actions of John Lauder, some unlikely though none, I hope, that seriously misrepresents him. In researching the background to this novel I found both his *Journals* and his *Historical Notices of Scottish Affairs* immensely useful. But the reader will search in vain for a copy of his *Secret Book*.

Among the many other works which gave me insights into this period in Scotland's past were: those consulted by Andrew Carlin; Robert Wodrow's *History of the Sufferings of the Church of Scotland* and his *Analecta Scotica*; William Steven's *History of the Scottish Church, Rotterdam*; James King Hewison's

The Covenanters; James Kirkton's *Secret and True History of the Church of Scotland*; Robert Law's *Memorialls*; the *Lauderdale Papers* edited by Osmond Airy; John Howie's *Scots Worthies*; and Sir James Stewart's *Naphtali*, later editions of which contained the collected papers of James Mitchel. In these and other books there is a mass of information, disinformation, prejudice and intolerance, much of which is fascinating material. On Thomas and Jean Weir there exists more myth than fact, but David Stevenson has written seriously on them, most recently in his collection *King or Covenant?*

I owe much to Leo Hollis at Fourth Estate, for his careful and sensitive editing and in particular for his advice on how to get all this material into shape and remove the excess. If too much of the latter remains, the fault is mine.

Finally I must thank the staff of the National Library of Scotland and of the City of Edinburgh's Central Library. The staff of the Central Library's Edinburgh Room, and in particular of its Scottish Library, were unfailingly helpful and patient in dealing with my requests, which must sometimes have sent them into dark and distant places among the stacks. None of them was ever as unprofessional as the mysterious Mr MacDonald, nor as defensive as the two invented librarians who disbelieve Carlin's claims. Had they been so, I could not have written this book.

All Fourth Estate Books are available from your local bookshop, or can be ordered direct (FREE UK p&p) from:

Fourth Estate,
Book Service By Post,
PO Box 29, Douglas
I-O-M, IM99 1BQ

Credit cards accepted

Tel: 01624 836000   Fax: 01624 670923

Visit the Fourth Estate website at:
www.4thestate.co.uk

*Please state when ordering if you do **not** wish to receive further information about Fourth Estate titles.*